Celebrated Navigation

Selected Stories

Jarda Cervenka

WHISTLING SHADE
PRESS

1495 Midway Pkwy   St. Paul   MN   55108
www.whistlingshade.com

First Edition, First Printing
July 2014

The two new stories in this collection have appeared, in slightly different versions, in *Notre Dame Review*.

ISBN 978-0-9829335-3-4

Cover art by Jan Kavan
Cover design by Peter Foltera

Book design by Joel Van Valin

Printed in the United States of America

To Luca, Henry, Bohdy and Jackson,
whom I love, big time.

Contents

Preface

Navigating through the stories of Jarda Cervenka—moving from country to country, as it were—readers often find themselves in unfamiliar territory. The strangeness accumulates until, at some stage in your journey, you begin to understand that Cervenka is a different kind of author. It's not just the exotic settings, or his own foreign origins, but something deeper—that Jarda Cervenka is not really an author at all, in the strict sense of the word. He is a storyteller. His stories may not be avant-garde or literary in style, or particularly fashionable. And yet they fascinate. Perhaps this is due to the simple yet profound difference between Cervenka's fiction and the fiction of most living writers—the wide gulf that separates the author and the storyteller.

Authors create from within. Of course their fiction is often embedded with impressions from the outside world (like seashells in concrete); still, their stories are prefabrications of the mind. It's a separate world in there—the author's interior landscape. Storytellers, on the other hand, relate and retell the things of this world. They may enter the scene in a tangential way, but it's never really about them. They're simply picking up the seashell and listening to it. It's about us—about the world we live in.

A talented storyteller, like Cervenka, can craft a story so well that it often seems, on the surface, like the work of a great author. "The Drowning in Staryk Slough", for example, begins with some incidental (but interesting) remarks on the history of the sport of hockey in Prague and the narrator's friend Lars; but this is only the doorway to the real story, about a former soldier in the Tsar's imperial guard and the woman he left in Kiev. The contrast between skating over ice and fishing the deep waters of Staryk Slough is subtle and may only register subconsiously—but a reader feels it as an ominous, emotional undertow that pulls us down into the end of the story. Ernest Hemingway and Isak Dinesen, storytellers in their own way, used a similar technique.

Sadly, there are few true storytellers left these days in the West. Most confine their craft to oral renditions at the bar or dinner party, seldom venturing into the craft of writing. Cervenka's stories are not only well composed, they come to us from diverse backgrounds, from the Eskimos of Hudson Bay to the backwaters of the Amazon and the slopes of Kilimanjaro. In this respect he is an interpreter of cultures, a figure standing midway between the traditional bard and the modern writer.

Born in 1933 in (what was then) Czechoslovakia, Jarda Cervenka spent his childhood in Prague. An avid swimmer who narrowly missed an appearance in the Olympics (he is Fausto in "Fausto's Afternoon"), Cervenka went into medicine, graduating from Charles University in 1958. An interest in genetic disorders (in particular cleft lip and palate and pre-cancer diagnosis) brought him to the University of Minnesota as a visiting professor in 1965. Three years later, after the Prague Spring, he woke up to find Soviet tanks passing down his street. He and his wife Sasha hastily packed their bags and, with their young son Vojta, drove out of Czechoslovakia before the borders were closed. The family arrived in Brussels (see "Ladies of the Brussels Night") where, much to his astonishment, Cervenka learned that a position had already been procured for him back in Minnesota. Soon after the family settled in Minneapolis a daughter, Tereza, was born.

Cervenka spent most of his career as a geneticist and researcher, living in or visiting many of the countries that form the settings of his stories. He took up writing later in life (like Joseph Conrad) and (also like Conrad) mastered it in English, the language of his adopted country. His first story, "Loss of an Enemy" (1989), was based on a personal experience from his own childhood in Nazi-occupied Prague. Once he began writing, he quickly met with success, winning first place in the Many Voices Project for *Mal d'Afrique*, Japan's Blue Jacket Prize for the title story in that collection, the Richard Sullivan Prize for *Revenge of Underwater Man*, and the Franz Kafka Award and Medal.

Though Cervenka collects his stories from real events, he often switches characters and locations, "reimagining" them in different ways. Africa (he lived for short periods in both Nigeria and Kenya) seems to have been his most fertile hunting ground, while the Midwest yields very little—and reading this collection, one can understand why. Hardship, savagery, extreme forces of nature, exotic customs, curiosities—these are the wheels that move his lightly fictionalized narratives. Yet the main theme that emerges from his body of work is the expression of love—sometimes romantic love ("Hurricane", "A Matter for the Management") but more often the companionable bond between friends ("Infallible Weapon of Temptation", "Revenge of Underwater Man", "How I Came to the Feast"). His masterpiece, "The Delta", the story of a Peace Corps worker facing the emptiness of Western culture after her profound experiences in Africa, charts a middle ground between the two. The rich, Cervenka seems to be telling us, are those who love, who embrace life and value true friendship, even when living impoverished in a desperate country.

As a young man, he was impressed by *The Stranger*—in Camus' unflinching statement of the truth. This commitment to truth is mirrored in his own stories, some of which are quite dark (the existential "Possibility of Hope" might have been penned by Camus himself). If his descriptions of non-Western cultures do not sit well with our more politically correct readers in America, it is best remember that he is sharing the real experiences of a world traveler, rather than notions of an armchair idealist. And in any case, First, Second, or Third world designations are more or less irrelevant with Cervenka, who seems at home in all three.

For *Celebrated Navigation* I've selected pieces from Cervenka's three previous story collections, *Mal d'Afrique* (1995, New Rivers Press), *Revenge of Underwater Man* (2000, Notre Dame Press) and *Fausto's Afternoon* (2007, Whistling Shade Press). Two more recent stories, "Pearls of Lady Seraphim" and "Kamikaze Dream of the Butterfly Collector", have been added, to round the collection out at 30. They're waiting for departure now, so I'll just shout "Ahoy!" and let the celebrated navigation begin.

-Joel Van Valin

Drinking in Iranduba

The first thing I did when the canoe turned the corner was wash the paint off my face. Minutes earlier the wife of the chief of "my" Santere-Mowe Indians had said goodbye in Portuguese, dipped her forefinger into a seed pod of uruku and, with a pensive expression, standing on her toes, painted one vertical slash on my chin and one oblique on each of my cheeks. I wondered if she truly wanted to safeguard me from evil spirits or just intended to make good fun of the whiteface. I knew I did not want protection from the one spirit, cachaça, the sugar cane distillate I craved after behaving so well for so long, and which waited for me about eight hours downstream in Iranduba. No, less than that, since in the rainy season the Amazon goes like a shot, about six miles an hour, before she joins with the Rio Negro in Manaus.

My pilot, an untalkative *caboclo* (local mix of Indian and Caucasian) named Sergio, steered us perfectly, smoking some, humming and exuding the satisfaction of a man who is one with the river, who knows the stream's navigational secrets as if they were inscribed into his genetic code. Looking at him, I knew he could happily subsist forever on only bananas, beer and smiles, all of which we carried aplenty for the trip. He steered us with the careless abandon of a child but still missed all the sawyers and stray logs by at least an inch.

We floated in the silence of worshipers, through cathedrals of trees, with buttresses in water and crowns in clouds, past "lakes" carpeted with blooming water hyacinths like purple meadows, past waterfalls I remember from romantic paintings of Paradise, and took shortcuts through flooded forests while navigating between the tree crowns, where monkeys shrieked in panic. Giant otters approached us, curious and smiling. Unexcitable, motionless caimans wallowed by the shore, fitting well into the Jurassic landscape, and birds were everywhere in such variety as to drive an ornithologist to distraction. River dolphins in pairs, and solitary, displayed their pink sides and bellies, breathing asthmatically without the happy grin of their cousins in the sea.

Just at the moment I had decided to float down the Amazon for the rest of my life, Sergio turned into a side channel, *igarape*, which looked to me as any other of hundreds we had passed by on our way. But he knew. The *igarape* surprised me with its sudden shade, hum of insects, and bizarre philodendrons and lianas reaching at us as if alive; I could touch the exuberant bromeliads. It felt like a secret passage. Sergio widened his permanent smile, opened another can of Kaiser beer, and before finishing it, we landed between kids splashing and floating garbage, next to two sinking barcas and one large sunken one. We heard the sounds of semi-civilization, and smelled the town, the homey smoke and whiff of burned oil, home-brewed beer, and nose-stinging scent of rotting cabbage. We had arrived in Iranduba.

To find my acquaintance Renato was an easy task. Most of his evenings are spent in Zazoeira, the "club." The club was a wooden structure without architect, without furniture, and without walls—save the one behind the bar. It was air-conditioned passably by the breeze from the jungle only feet away. My attention was attracted to the floor made of dark tropical hardwood which years of stomping by the feet of sweating dancers and other natural phenomena had transformed into something like semi-gloss ebony. I imagined panelling made of this stuff for some millionaire CEO, the beauty and the price of it. The rest of this edifice was just the result of the infamous tropical carpentry.

I hugged Renato, made faces, sat down, and Renato ordered cachaça with an imperious voice and gesture one could use only mocking an old friend-waiter. A few months ago I had met Renato in Manaus. He worked there, on and off, as a tourist guide, taking people to the forest, up different *igarapes* to catch-and-release caimans by night and piranhas by day. He had spent three years in San Francisco as a teenager, and had learned English and the ways of the gringo there, which upon his return home, elevated his social standing permanently. He became an English speaking guide in demand, and ultimately, an owner of a car! To catch his breath and replant his feet on the native ground of the club Zazoeira he would return from Manaus to Iranduba as often as he could.

"How was it with the Indios? And mosquitoes?"

"Good, I learned a lot, Renato, a lot."

"You're like the German tourists, they want to know about everything."

"Is that bad?"

"No, is good. French are bad. They only want to know about dinner. And never tell you if they like anything. Know what I mean?"

"Yeah, I know. But can you ask the *moso*, your friend over there, to make me one great *caipirinha*? *Por favor.* Not *caipirissima!*"

So, in a minute I got that creation of fabulous simplicity: a double shot of cachaça, with a spoon of sugar, crushed wedges of lime (vitamin C, mind you!) and crushed ice. I thanked him profusely, knowing how pleasantly it would dissolve the mucous in my passages.

"Indians, they know much, they are not scared of the forest. Like some of the *caboclos* are here. Huh?" I suspected I might provoke my friend to more lively discourse about Indians.

"Well, people from around here, they know the forest very well, too, it's their livelihood, you know. But there are things, strange things which happen in the jungle, so some people become scared. Is true."

The palaver continued in a direction I couldn't predict.

"Like being scared of *curupira*. Right?" I suggested.

"*Curupira?*" He shook his head in a pantomime of disagreement.

"Is it true, what people say," I continued, "that he is a young and very handsome boy with red hair, that guards the forest, seduces the traveler off the path, and when one follows one gets lost, forever?" Renato still shook his head. Undeterred I continued, forcing it as is allowed to drunks. "I bet it might be true that his feet are pointing backwards—so when one follows his tracks one wanders deeper and deeper into the bush…?"

Renato glanced at me sideways and with a sarcastic grin told me he didn't believe in any *curupira*, and also, if there was one, he wouldn't have only one eye, as some folks say. One eye? Nonsense. Renato is a modern man, he has been in America. So I decided not to push it, and just have a good time and another *caipirinha*.

"But, you know," Renato said, "there are some things one cannot understand well, so one has to believe, to be on the safe side … and not to wade into any shit. I tell you what happened to me last year. And I want beer and not cachaça, one more would put me under the table."

Renato pulled the chair closer to me and lowered his voice. He had risen to my bait—or was just in a good storytelling disposition. I liked this about the people, there. I could have listened forever to their narratives about the seven-colored serpent ruling the forest, about the Indian carver, blind from birth, who carved perfect likeness of animals only from "tribal memory," about the terrible demise of a fisherman who made love with the river dolphin, about the poisonous ant conga in initiation ceremonies, and tale upon tale, depending how well their storytelling voice box was oiled with beverage. Since in all my years of living in an American suburb I could not recall hearing a single story of fantasy or of magical content I was, now, on a different planet.

It was about the same time in the season of rains a year ago, when Renato went with his father to visit an uncle who lived in a shack at the edge of the jungle about a mile up the *igarape*. When they arrived, the uncle was half drunk, already. They had brought a piece of fried pirarucu fish, good stuff, but the uncle wanted only to drink more. They were arguing with him when they heard it. It must have been close, behind the shack, the distinct call "killy klee klee … killy klee." Machinta pereira! A machinta pereira bird called from the jungle. The bird was feared by all. It has been traded about that it lures people deep into the jungle, then changes into a terrible old woman, a witch so vicious-looking, that one flees away; running and crawling and never finding the way back. "Killy klee klee, killy klee," it wailed.

"Singa! Singa! Fuck, fuck you!" Uncle screamed. "I kill you sunavabitch, fuck…!" He got up. Renato and his father had tried to hold him down but he was a strong man, unstoppable now. He lurched out, crashed through the thicket. They heard him breaking branches … then silence … and then came the scream. Renato and his dad rushed into the thicket and managed to quickly find him.

"His eyes were big like an owl's, they did not blink, and he couldn't speak," Renato continued. "We led him back, asked questions, but he just stared with those eyes, sank to the floor in the corner and did not move or even bat an eye." Renato imitated the unblinking stare. "He was a big man, strong, could wrestle caiman six feet long with his bare hands. But he just sat there silent, and even later, never told anybody what he saw…" Renato finished the beer and shook his head several times. He looked at me with his dark mestizo eyes, his crow's feet deepened, lips tight with corners down—as if asking me: What do you say to that?

I said: "I'll be damned."

People were wandering in and out of the club; some approached us and exchanged words with Renato while looking at me, and raised their hand with the thumbs-up, as is the pleasant habit here, in central Amazonia. We needed some food to go with the drinks, so Renato arranged for a plate of fried plantains and beans and murdered, blackened, pieces of beef, all sprinkled with farinha (fried manioc crumbs) and a fiery sauce of juice squeezed from grated manioc mixed with powdered hot peppers. It was a dish seasoned by flames from Hell, so we slurped and aerated wordlessly, raised our eyebrows and wiped off the tears, as if at a funeral.

"Wow, there goes a beautiful woman, amigo!" I opened my mouth in genuine admiration.

Renato smiled: "Gloria. Oh yeah, she is the best in Iranduba. Gloria Beatriz Ribeira de Nascimento, mon!"

She walked to the bar, straight like the palm for making blowguns, her helmet of hair absolutely black and glossy as if she had just emerged from *agua negra*. And with the face of an angel with some Indian blood. She couldn't be more than eighteen. In the crux of one arm she carried a baby, in the other hand she held a basket. She looked straight ahead.

"Where did she get such a beautiful face?" I asked. "And look at the baby!"

"She is *mameluca*—her mother is Indian, Santere-Mowe, and her father a white man from Manaus. He disappeared though … did not give her his name. People say he was a German who had come here to tap the rubber."

"And the baby?"

There was a long pause which made me alert, despite my difficulty to focus well, caused by the active ingredient of *caipirinha*, the cachaça.

"The baby. How about her kid?" I asked again—and again I did not hear an answer. Now I could actually smell a story.

Renato finally leaned over the table and in a low, hoarsely conspiratorial voice told me, "… *esta nene do boto cor de rosa*." He looked me into the eyes as if challenging me to challenge his statement. "*Do boto!*" He added.

"You're talking to me in Portuguese, Renato!"

"Oh, sorry, so sorry. The *bebe* … is a child of a dolphin, *bebe do boto*, we say."

"A child … fathered by the pink river dolphin?" I asked, incredulous, specifying the subspecies, to be sure.

"We believe it is true."

The beautiful woman passed by again on the way out. I looked at her baby. It was a girl, light-skinned but with the hair of her mother, she was perfectly formed, the object of desire of grandmothers all.

"Yeah, it happens." Renato looked at the high buttocks of Gloria Beatriz Ribeira de Nascimento, passing by, with concentration.

I ordered banana chips and a round of Kaiser cerveja and heard the whole story.

Once in a while there are dance parties organized in the club Zazoeira. *Caboclos* come to drink and to dance *forro*, the dance they love with passion. A year ago, at the time when the Amazon floods everything, there was a big gathering of dancers and drinkers here. All able bodies from Iranduba took to the dance floor, visitors arrived in their canoes paddling from distant *igarapes* through *igapos*, the flooded forests. Beer (Antarctica Pilsen, Brahma, and Kaiser) and cachaça for the first hour trickled like the source of a mountain creek, then later flowed in an uninterrupted stream of a great river. Acquaintances and friends greeted each other with exuberance and thumbs-up: how warming to the heart it is to be with friends! Young women seemed to arrive in estrus, exuding receptive rowdiness, the depth of their eyes enhanced by charcoal and poorly concealed desires. Men came in shoes and some even in boots, their oiled hair reflecting the flames of women's eyes.

Then a white stranger arrived.

He mingled with people but did not dance. He was a different sort. Dressed in all white, "*blanco como muvem*," Renato said, "white like a cloud." He was taller than anybody else and his white hat made him even more conspicuous. He had pushed the hat so low on his forehead nobody could see his eyes. Later, not a single person could recall making eye contact with the alien.

Soon the suave man in white gained sight of Gloria. He stalked her, moving smoothly like an anaconda on the prowl. He talked to her between dances; he whispered, his unsmiling, handsome face turned to her at all times. This was the way of seduction.

Before the end of the celebration a few people saw Gloria leaving with the stranger. He pulled her. Holding his hand, she followed him to the shore of the *igarape*. It has been well imagined by everybody in Iranduba what transpired next. How at the edge of the water the white stranger removed his hat, and while kissing her changed into the dolphin—then pulled her down into the deep.

They stayed together only one night and a day but nine months later the baby was born to beautiful Gloria. People understood—she was not the first one in the history of the village to have a child fathered by the pink river dolphin.

"You might not believe it—but you saw the baby for yourself." Renato's storytelling dried his throat. "Beer!"

"Yes, I did see her. But tell me, why did the stranger in white cover his eyes with his hat?"

"He did not cover his eyes. He covered the blow-hole on his forehead!"

"Wow," was the only commentary I considered appropriate. A while later I asked: "Will Gloria have a chance to marry here, in Iranduba? With the baby like that... you know?"

"Of course. People here understand that life can be complicated, and magic things happen. Must happen ... sometimes." Renato was thinking, and it showed as a slight pain on his face. Then he brightened up. "To think of it—she just got married a couple weeks ago. Gabito, the son of the pharmacist got her, finally."

"Gabito?"

"Yeah, you American city folks would call it a 'great love.' He was after her since they were kids. Gabriel Garcia Marino. Is a good boy."

Afterwards, I did not remember well how the evening ended, or how I got to bed, but I remembered the story.

The next day, I took a canoe down the *igarape* to the main channel. I floated in between the treetops of the flooded jungle, since I wanted tranquility, silence and to be alone. A small caiman, a jacaré, peered at me between the floating leaves, thinking he was invisible. Cute, for a reptile. A woolly monkey, strangely alone, like me, followed from branch to branch, for a while. Under one tree a hundred white fallen blossoms floated, as if to mark an underwater celebration there. I was thinking about Gloria, her gentle face, her calm confidence gained from a newly acquired status—that of a married woman, about her beauty.

Then the surface of water bulged and a dolphin emerged next to my boat. He looked at me with his large human eye, turned on the side and dove without a splash, not to emerge again. This time I got disturbed. The rosy, pink belly he flaunted seemed so unnatural, feigned—it was obscene! And he should have covered his goddamned blow-hole, too!

I turned the boat around and paddled through the fallen white blossoms again.

My sentiment surprised me. I felt a surge of emotion: it was a gratefulness for the love which the pharmacist's son affirmed for beautiful Gloria Beatriz Ribeira de Nascimento.

The Drowning in Staryk Slough

Some memories seem strange, but that is only because things often are remembered as different from what they really were.

Lars had several true friends because he was sincere. However, not many people knew that his real name was Ilja, Ilja Larson. Everybody called him Lars, even the guys from our hockey team, LTC Praha. His father was not a Swede as his last name would suggest, but rather a Russian emigré. Old Larson was Russian only in the way he was perceived. In truth he *was* of Swedish blood—born to the son of Swedish immigrants to Russia in the time of Peter the Great.

LTC Praha, which stands for Lawn Tennis Club Praha, was, in fact, the hockey club where ice hockey started in Prague long before World War II. The game was introduced by a Canadian, Johnny Buckna, who was basically a Czech, Jan Bukna, born in a small village near Nelahozeves.

My friend Lars had an uncle, who was not his real uncle, but the best friend of Lars's father, after whose death the friend moved in and became "uncle" to Lars. And in a way, to me too, but only in secret, since I wouldn't take the liberty of being so familiar with him. Everybody knew him only by the name Borodichka, which means "a little beard" in Russian. He had been clean-shaven ever since anybody could remember, and it was understood that Borodichka was not his real name. The question of his surname and family name never came up. He himself was a Russian refugee, escaping not from Russia but from Kiev in the Ukraine.

Borodichka was built slender but of a military bearing which stooped forward a little in his later years. A slim nose of a good size seemed to precede him. His lips were rather thin but without strictness to them. His eyes I remember well: they were the color of an old man's eyes (pale early morning sky), decorated by hundreds of creases fanning out from their outer corners. And his eyes radiated kindness in a way that cannot be captured merely by describing that anatomy. They remained serious even when the rest of his face smiled, but I was never sure if they were serious or sad. When talking he would never rush. His hands lay calmly and his eyes looked into your eyes calmly as well. His ears were definitely outsized.

He always wore the same cardigan over sport shirts and a selection of carefully knotted woolen ties of patterns long forgotten. Conservative, restrained, with a smile—that is how I remember him.

His own room, next to the kitchen (intended for a servant, I believe) contained the neatly arranged essentials of a bachelor fond of books. Bookshelves entirely covered two walls to the ceiling. Next to the third wall was his bed with an old-fashioned brass frame, made up impeccably, as if ready for military inspection. His desk was by the window, and, as might be expected of the desk of a Russian, both a chess set and samovar were on it. His samovar was a towering brass contraption that looked so strange and complicated that I was certain it made tea the mysteriously proper Russian way. Only later I learned that he had not made tea in it for years.

I never asked about the history of this samovar, suspecting it to be a personal object, intimate to Borodichka's past. Anyway, questions were always asked by Borodichka, in perfect Czech of somewhat archaic purity, with an accent as pleasant as it was exotic. He was interested in us youths who were aware of the general disinterest of most adults. His long ears were ready to listen at all times. He took me seriously, talked to me seriously, asked all questions with genuine involvement showing in those concentrated eyes. About hockey, about school, and, without teasing, about girlfriends.

The little I knew about Borodichka's past was told by Lars, who did not know more than he revealed.

Borodichka was a graduate of the Czar's Military Academy, then an army engineer and officer in the elite Tereshchanskij Polk of Kiev, known for its fierce loyalty to the Czar. When the Bolshevik Revolution erupted in Russia and the Ukraine he fought the Red Army of the proletariat, was decorated, and later never talked about it. When his White Army was decimated, he managed to escape through China all the way to Prague, where he met Lars's father and became his best friend. He never married and never made a serious female acquaintance in Prague. That was all I knew about his past.

There was one bit of information more. Lars overheard his father once saying that when Borodichka drinks vodka he becomes sad instead of happy. It is so because he remembers his love of the Kiev that he lost.

✳

Lars and I made the B team of LTC, dated successfully many fair hockey fans, and entered Charles University. Borodichka was kept informed about our achievements and failures and, if asked, he advised us in his restrained way. After the first year of higher learning I managed to get on a group vacation trip to the Soviet Union—to Russia and the Ukraine. Borodichka was the first one to know, of course.

"We will spend three days in Kiev," I told him. "Your city, Borodichka!"

He listened intently to my itinerary till I finished. Then without a word he got up and disappeared into his room. Soon he returned, walking quickly, leaving the door open. On the table he carefully lay an old-fashioned photographic album bound in purple velvet with brass corners and with golden letters in Cyrillic on the cover.

"This is an album of photographs taken in the city of Kiev during the time of my residence."

So somber was his voice and so formal his diction it made me apprehensive. He raised his eyes from the album, attempted an apologetic smile, brushed his hair in place, and straightened his tie as if readying himself for important rhetoric. He turned the book for me to see better and opened it to the first page.

"The Byzantine temple, Sophia Sabor, is the crown jewel of Kiev's architecture. It has survived one thousand years." He paused. "Survived wars, invasions, fires. And the revolution, which destroyed everything, as you know."

When we finished with his album, I asked Borodichka to name the one single place in the Kiev of his youth which had been dearest to his heart. I said: the dearest to your heart. He hesitated with the answer, looking away, as if he did not hear me.

"There is a place on the Dnieper River," he said finally. "An old slough, on the left shore. It is called Staryk. 'Old man' in Russian, you know. Almost the same as in Czech. It is the most beautiful place I know."

I waited through a long silence. "I used to go there with my girl." He surprised me with the sudden intimacy.

Then, briefly, with a formal smile, he wished me a good trip and safe return, as one wished a departing traveler.

✳

In the laser-bright light of the Ukrainian fall, Sophia Sabor was a vision only vaguely resembling the sepia-tinted black and white photographs on the first page of Borodichka's album of photographic memories. My eyes were hurting from the rays of early afternoon sun reflected off the golden onion topping the main steeple. Six smaller gold-plated onions seemed to accent its dominance. Most of the passersby lifted their eyes, some slowed down, some stopped as if paying respect to their own fairy tale castle, then hastened away. I was in a hurry too, looking for a bus station, so I decided to return another time.

This was the day I hoped to accomplish the most important task of the trip I had assigned myself: to photograph the Staryk Slough for Borodichka. I was going to find the slough and make a series of pictures, the best still photographs I would ever take. Daily, through the last couple of weeks, I had thought about it. I planned the lenses I would use, the exposures, composition, lighting. Some shots I wanted to take with slow shutter speed, letting the wind blur the treetops to a dreamy image. Some I wanted to make sharp against a towering cloud. I would lie down by the water and use the wide angle objective for a view such as would be seen by a frog. Some pictures would have a fallen tree for the foreground and the depth of field would vary. I would do a very careful job for my friend. That was my big project for the trip.

On Khreshchatyk, the weathered Champs-Élysées of Kiev, I boarded a bus going to the river, where I disembarked.

The river Dnieper—there it was! I repeated the name in a whisper. Wide as a lake, the vast surface still, sandy beaches and sand bars on both shores, right bank high, the opposite shore rising just a few feet and covered by trees in golden autumnal fashion. A barge with a red flag the size of a sail was pushing upstream, but no other traffic disturbed the flowing oily calmness.

In my pocket dictionary I found the word for a "ferryman": *perevozkaja*. The one I discovered nearby was an old man, looking like a gray boulder in his loose quilted pants and heavy army coat, dressed ready for a sudden blizzard, which, I guessed, would come in about two months. He took me into his wooden skiff with an outboard motor of ancient vintage, and I made it over the river with that pleasant excitement one feels crossing a body of unknown water.

Indeed, the old-timer knew about Staryk. Not far downstream from here, he assured me, the first slough cutting in from the mainstream, right across from Pitchevskaja Lavra monastery on the other side. I found it easily.

The waters of Staryk became darker but more transparent as I proceeded along its sandy shore farther inland. The banks became gradually devoid of the debris left from the spring flood, the smell of decay decreased in intensity, and frogs called louder their claim for this pleasant still water. The aspens and willows, now in their most brilliant yellow, shared their gold with the ground. Everything shone brightly, smelled clean with the leaves and water and sun of fall. It is a beautiful place, Borodichka had said in Prague.

I photographed, changing exposures, depth of field, and composition. With some shots I waited for the breeze to subside so not a leaf would shiver; others I blurred intentionally. I finished the roll of film unsure as always about the results, put the equipment in my rucksack, and walked farther upstream. There, by a little bay, near an aspen sawyer with roots in the air, sat a fisherman with a long cane rod supported by a stick forked in a V at the end. Not the bobber on the water but a book in his hands held his attention.

He answered my greeting "*priviet*" with surprise on his face. Maybe seventy years old, I guessed by his face with high cheek bones, wide mouth, bulbous nose, and narrow eyes hiding under the bush of eyebrows. A Russian *mujik's* face, I thought.

He closed the book, pushed his round wire glasses on to the tip of his Slavic proboscis, and gave me a long look, a welcoming look, I realized with some relief.

I asked him about the efficiency of fishing with a book in his hands.

"I am just giving a bath to the worm, young man," he said. "It is in no danger where it bathes now." He pointed to the bobber and put the book carefully on a stump next to him, indicating that we might converse.

"But there might be a fish passing by that will like your worm," I said.

"No, it is not possible," he smiled. "There are a few carp, *kasha*, in the middle of the slough, but they feed on the bottom. As friendly as kittens they are." He appeared to enjoy this subject. "It is true, the eel might pass by unannounced. Now in the fall it is the time for them to migrate, but they are becoming rare. Not like in the old times." He raised his hand in the gesture of futility.

Knowing the answer, I asked "Have you been fishing here before?"

"For fifty years." He nodded. "For half a century. I know every centimeter of this place like I knew my *babushka*, God save her soul." The smile did not leave his face, which seemed to me younger now, almost handsome, for a *mujik*.

"You might ask, what will happen if I cast it right next to that fallen tree down there," he said. "I'll tell you that it will tempt the catfish, the *som*, which has been lounging there for years." He stretched his arms apart in the time-honored fisherman's gesture. "The biggest fish around, the *som*, real *molodiets*!"

"Over a meter?" I asked.

"Over a meter, and some. I pulled him out a few times, so we are friends by now. You see?"

"Isn't it good to eat, the *som*?"

"Would you eat a friend?"

I liked his laugh. It came from the depth of his bowels, like the sound of the bass bombardon playing staccato.

"Heaven forbid," he continued. "You look to me like a gentleman, *kulturnyi chelovek, komilfo*. You wouldn't!"

Out of a well-worn German army backpack with a calfskin cover flap he pulled out an aluminum field flask. It had many scars and depressions, a long history. He unscrewed it and passed it to me. I sat down next to him and took a swig of it, cautiously. But it was Russian vodka, powerful but smooth, which went down like olive oil with no aftertaste, and heated the entrails instantly in a miracle of physiology. I thanked the fisherman-reader and returned the flask for his turn.

"I was taking some photographs for a friend of mine," I told him while he took a sip. He paid no attention.

"If I threw the worm to the bend over there," he pointed with the flask, "and if I pulled it in as one would pull a lure, I'd bring in a walleye, a *studak*. Pure silver with a touch of gold on the gills. That is the fish to eat, the best you have ever tasted!" He looked at me as if expecting disapproval. "So good and pretty, it is a pity for a plain fisherman like me to kill a fish like that."

He continued: "But once a week I'll cast the bait—a ball made of bread is the best. I'll cast it right in the middle where the slough narrows. *Plotva* and *yaz* are always there scrounging around. Ay-a, how good for *ukha* soup!" He licked his lips in exaggeration. "Few potatoes in it, some veggies, any you can get will do. And you must use the heads with the eyes still in them—for the consistency—and cook it very, very slow. *Kievskaja ukha*—a rare delicacy, my friend."

I was getting hungry. The sun was diving behind the aspens, making them dark against the light, and the mirror of Staryk was broken by the black shadows of trees falling on it sharply. We shared the aluminum flask and again I told him about having made some photographs for an old friend of mine, a Czarist officer living in Prague, who used to come here in the old times. I hoped to talk about those old times on Staryk.

"Of those years I remember everything, *molodiets*," he said. "The trouble is I don't remember what happened yesterday, or an hour ago. That is the truth."

I stood up but still asked a question.

"Was it different here, then—the Staryk?"

"Everything about Kiev is different now, but Staryk is the same," he said. "That's why I come here."

"And how about the officers in the old times? Did they use to come here? Before the Bolsheviks, I mean. My friend told me he used to come here with his girlfriend."

"They would rarely come. Just one. Or two. They liked to walk down the Khreshchatyk in their fancy uniforms. Oh ya."

"The Tereshchanskij Polk used to be stationed here in Kiev, I heard."

"Tereshchanskij—what a glory! But their officers, they were all killed by the Bolsheviks, or escaped abroad, who knows where. Oh, were they a sight! They had the fanciest uniforms you have ever seen, ever."

"Pretty?" I asked.

"Pretty? All the girls in Kiev, and married ones too," he chuckled, "they all dreamt to have an officer from the Tereshchanskij Polk."

We had another sip of vodka.

"One of those ladies drowned herself right past this bend over there," he pointed. "In that spring after the Bolsheviks won their Revolution. I remember that well."

I sat down again and said: "What a sad thing, such an accident. I have been told there are pretty bad floods here in the spring."

"Oh no, my friend. No accident. She took her own life, she did. People said that her officer, her lover, did not return to her. Killed by Reds, or escaped abroad, that is for sure." He stared at the water. "Besides, I know she took her life because I found her and saw her face."

"It happened right here?" I asked.

"Right here. I was the unlucky one who found her here. And—this is what I want to tell you—when I pulled her hair off the face I was amazed. It had the color of ivory and it was so beautiful. Beautiful! I can still see her if I close my eyes."

We watched the bobber floating on the water in silence for a while as if in a tribute to the fisherman's memory.

"Beautiful, you said?" I did not understand the connection of beauty to suicide.

"I have never seen a more beautiful woman, dead or alive. Does it surprise you?" He lifted the flask and shook it. It was empty, its contents sharpening his memory now and enhancing my imagination.

"A woman who takes her life must first rid herself of the fear of death, you see?" he paused. "We all would be beautiful if we had no fear of dying. Even me." He laughed. "A woman is in her greatest beauty when she chooses death, frees herself of fear just before she takes her life. It must be like that."

He picked up his book with both hands and lifted it above his head as a sacred object of worship.

"It is all stored in books like this one. Everything amazing is said in books like this, my friend."

Then he reeled in the worm, removed its miniature pale carcass from the hook, and threw it in the water.

"My buddy *som* will find it with his whiskers. He has whiskers like a Czarist general—you should see him some time. *Do svidanija!*"

He said goodbye to the dead worm, packed his book and fishing gear, and we were on our way. Soon we reached the river, where the reader-fisherman stopped. Across the Dnieper, the Pitchevskaja Lavra monastery was flooded by the setting sun, its green steeples like theatre stage props against the darkening sky, looming high above the ageless stream.

"Dnieper—our soul, you know," he said, and we stood there watching her flow.

"She is our soul, that is the truth. Heavy, you know, deep soul, as is the river. Powerful in floods, peaceful and steady on sunny days. You cannot dam it, the soul or the river. And to explore her? Oh ya, ya."

I thought how lucky I was to meet a reader, and a fisherman to top it.

"But not very cheerful, you see," he went on. "Just like some great love—it isn't much fun and it could be a tragedy. Drowning. Not like the laughable loves, affairs that cheer your heart up and, some say, keep it healthy, even." He looked at me with a wide smile. "And that is why I go to Staryk. It is a love affair of this old fisher."

I wished we had some more vodka left. To drink to this old man's health.

"You are a foreigner, so when you go home to your friends, tell them you have met people whose soul is a river." He laughed with those sounds coming from deep within him and sounding the bass bombardon playing staccato. I thanked him and promised him I would tell my friends at home about the reader-fisherman I met, about Staryk, and the big soul-river.

He shook my hand with a squeeze as powerful as I expected from him, and we said nothing more and went separate ways.

✳

Back in Prague I told Borodichka everything about my expedition to Staryk in the greatest detail. Everything, except the story about the drowning of the girl with the beautiful ivory face.

Then I gave him the photographs—eight by ten-inch black and white enlargements on semigloss Orwo paper.

He opened the envelope and pulled out the first one, the one with the fallen tree in the foreground and aspens by the bend of the slough. He held it in both hands. The leaves of the aspens started to shiver, then shook as if in the first blizzard of the Ukrainian winter.

I looked at his hands, then at his eyes, and I knew it was time to leave him alone.

A Matter for the Management

He assumed the basic stance of a hitchhiker, with a meek-to-subservient expression on his face, his thumb at the ready. Lena Casperson (Ottertail, Minnesota) gave him a pat on the shoulder and walked a few steps "downstream" against the rarefied traffic from Nairobi traveling northward to the desert territories of Kenya. It must have been a hundred degrees in the shade—if there would have been any shade for miles around. Only the desert rose and the chimneys of termite mounds threw a pitch-blue shadow on the ground.

"I'm gonna die, Sven. I'll dehydrate and shrivel like a prune in ten minutes… unless we'll get outta here." Lena's shrinkage started with a hoarse voice. But she knew that her duty as the hitchhiker's bait for truckers and other male drivers demanded that she shut up and look as sexy as possible, never mind those crumpled shorts and the T-shirt which had been washed a hundred times. So her complaints were short. Sven Ruzicka (Madison, Wisconsin) gave her a smile and a mock V for Victory. A sand devil, as tall as a house, wobbled in its solo dance on the moonlike landscape across the road, changing direction with pensive slowness, a silent mini-tornado making the sand alive in a performance meant for nobody but two hitchhiking exchange students.

The vehicle arrived with a warning: Congo "music," about half static and punctuated with explosions from the exhaust. It squealed to a stop about ten yards past them. It was a *matatu*, a gutted minivan converted to a bus, the ubiquitous killing machine and the most popular means of transport in Kenya, manned by drivers famously deranged on ganja and teenage conductors high on the hopeful vision of an evening meal.

"It'll get us outta here," Sven said with a gesture of resignation. "That's all what we want. Right?" They got in.

✳

Lena and Sven's was an incipient romance, still tentative, their emotions masked by nonchalant utterances, and occasional touches as fleeting as the proverbial brush of a butterfly wing. His urges had been concealed by juvenile horseplay mostly, at inappropriate moments. Lena's desires had been camouflaged so well that Sven oscillated between doubt and a sort of distant hope. This state of mind made him jittery and unsettled at times, but on this trip to Lake Baringo their relationship seemed to him more relaxed than when they were under siege by acquaintances and surrounded by the distractions of the city. Now, on the road, they were alone and they saw each other only against the background of the silent desert, against the horizons of the Rift Valley. They walked on the road which disappeared into the sand and then appeared again, sand devils the only "living" phenomena around. Neither one could even conceive of tomfoolery or pretense in their communications—after all, serious things could happen here; Somali shiftas were reported at this end of the World.

Lena was beautiful in the way Scandinavians from Minnesota are reputed to be—light chestnut hair (done in Nairobi into braids), an indistinct Eskimo nose and good cheekbones; substantial lips were there, too. She was tall with athletic shoulders and perfect legs, of course. When Sven met her in the corridor of their Nairobi dorm he stopped as if hitting a wall, stunned. "You are beautiful," he uttered. He had never done this before.

"Shut up," she whispered and awarded him a smile which finished him off, then walked away. That evening Sven took Lena to the Treehouse for a dinner. By dessert time he suspected he might be in love. So simple is the beginning of these affairs.

Lena sensed his affection and she did not mind. She had just parted ways with her boyfriend, by correspondence but definitely, so she was content to try this all-American boy from Madison. He pleased her that first evening by his wide-eyed earnestness when raving against the "big men" of Africa and for the cause of saving the ecology of Kenya. Yes, he looked good, too, and to Lena it felt pleasant to be scrutinized by everybody, walking with him, as he lead the way into the restaurant. He was not tall, that is true, but made up for it by his ramrod straight posture, his handsome face with the manly nose, and with his chest of a swimmer. Later, as a stunt, he carried her over the flooded street in his arms and she could thus evaluate—and approve—his musculature. Let's see what will develop, was her initial attitude.

✳

The *matatu* was packed; the usual ruinous smell of bodies steaming at one hundred degrees welcomed them. The only breathing space was the area around two desiccated Maasai morans, each one with a spear, motionless, staring nowhere. Their heads were shaved and painted with ochre. Extended perforated earlobes wrapped up around the upper rim of their ears, and one had inserted a Kodak film cartridge in the hole in his earlobe. They differed from the Kikuyu passengers by their aquiline noses, reddish skin stretched tight on the facial bones, and eyes not white but caramel, the color of their wraparounds. Was it fear, respect or repulsion which kept other passengers at a distance? All three reasons were plausible, Lena thought, and used the space near the Maasai, faking fearlessness. The warriors did not flinch.

The *matatu* got going with a few jerks. The Americans surveyed the situation.

The most interesting cargo were the "seats" of the only two passengers who did not stand: two jerry cans filled with gasoline, vapors of which leaked out and filled the air with the indescribable scent of a gasoline-sweat mix.

"Boy, if somebody were to light a cigarette—it would be *bahati mbaya*, bad luck as they say," Lena whispered. She imagined the enormous explosion, charcoaled body parts flying like projectiles; the mushroom cloud rising over the Rift Valley made a beautiful rose color by the setting sun.

"Yep, it would be painless," Sven smiled happily. He caught a glimpse of amusement in the granite face of one of the morans. Sven noticed the Maasai's nostrils widening in inhalation of the gasoline vapors and the "oh my god" movement of his eyes. Death they know well, the raiders of Serengeti.

"But I wanna die … in a fetal position, not disassembled and gross," Lena said.

"Yeah? Myself, I'd like to croak in missionary position. Smiling."

"Why do you always think about getting laid? One wonders where evolution went wrong, with you guys."

"Evolution? But worry none, babe, nobody will light a cigarette; they are too poor here to have a smoke. And we should be there soon, I bet. By the lake—Campi Samaki. The place is called I think, something like 'fishing camp' in Swahili." Sven wiped off sweat from his forehead with a forearm, lacking a sleeve. "Why are we slowing down?"

The *matatu* came to a stop with squeaking brakes. They were in the middle of arid nowhere, made Jurassically eerie by the termite mounds, which resembled fantastic castles of extraterrestrials with their multiple spires of Martian architecture. The occasional desert rose, a botanical boulder which blooms in pink, failed to brighten the landscape. There was no tree in sight, no dwelling under the chrome-yellow sky as far as one could see. Out of the vehicle jumped a small girl with a shaved head and a happy smile, in a school uniform worn out by a couple of generations. She took off her little sandals, waved merrily goodbye, and commenced to walk off the road without hesitation, not turning back. She assumed the pace of an experienced tracker, steady, loose. The direction of her journey was between the two tall termite mounds, about thirty degrees to the left of the setting sun, straight to the southwestern horizon of this primordial scrubland.

"Unbelievable!" Lena sighed. "What does this mean?"

"There must be hyenas there, wild dogs, perhaps…"

The vehicle started to move. Lena and Sven did not talk, letting the image of the girl between the termite castles embed itself in their memory.

"Did I tell you Robert finished his basement? Soundproofed it—it will be a cool studio," Sven said, after a while.

"Good for you. Hope you'll record something saleable, there."

"Well, that is the plan."

"Oh," Lena raised her eyebrows and made a smile. "When we come back to Nairobi let's go to the Carnivore. I need meat; I need *nyama!*"

"Yep. Me too. Eland steak for me, or that spicy hippo goulash!" Sven licked his parched lips and put his hand on Lena's behind.

"You know that Rita snared a new boyfriend? She is not sure, though," Lena talked more to herself than to Sven.

"I know her," Sven remarked, shaking his head.

"You think you know her. That's different from knowing her for real, Sven."

"I'd like to buy a Harley, a used Fat Boy."

"Boy, it's getting dark. Fast."

"I wonder what Dad would say," Sven said.

"I miss my sis."

"You know Pete Dancer?"

"I think we are here. That must be Campi something," Lena elongated her neck and squinted her eyes.

The *matatu* came to a stop centimeters before hitting an oil drum. Passengers fell into each others' arms with apologetic smiles, except the Maasai, and emptied the van in a few seconds, appearing panicked. Their faces expressed elation—they'd survived! The two Maasai moran descended leisurely, as if to affirm their royal superiority. One of them said goodbye in English to Lena and gave her a smile, which increased her pulse by twenty heartbeats per minute.

"Ha! The fata morgana of Campi Samaki!" Sven exclaimed and shook his head as if seeing but not believing the apparition of a ghost town. The unmistakable scent of rotting fish assured them of the authenticity of the name. They had arrived—with the cognizance of not having a return ticket, which silenced them for minutes.

A dusty plane sloped gently to the enormous Lake Baringo, its slate-colored surface without a ripple. The few fishing shacks seemed deserted except for chickens and one mangy dog. The only remarkable structure was a long table with two benches anchored to the dust and covered by a roof of corrugated iron. Next to this open dining room stood a hut from which smoke leaked between the planks and from under the roof: the kitchen, no doubt. Sven and Lena dragged their backpacks to this dwelling, since it appeared to have some authority. (A kitchen often does—nourishment comes from there.)

Not far from the kitchen, nearer to the lake, stood four metal cubicles, their sidings and roofs of crinkled sheet iron, emanating the heat they had accumulated during the day, which made the gauzy air shimmer as if the walls were alive.

"*Jumbo!*" They were greeted by the owner, cook, manager and concierge of the establishment, a sprawling lady with steatopygia, a hundred kilos of rippling haunches and a hundred-dollar smile.

"*Hodi, hodi. Habari gani,*" she welcomed them, expressing her joy at gaining paying customers, and led them to cubicle number two. "Dinner will be served after the definite sundown. Then you will sleep well … and tomorrow the sun will shine again. Kesho jua tashona!" She added that she sold homemade cassava liquor, *kindingi*, and banana wine, *kasiks*. "*Kasik* is fresh, *mzungu*, very delicious … and nutritious!"

And a helluva laxative, too, Sven thought, and thanked her for her kindness in more refined Swahili: "*Asante sana, kweli!*"

Abbreviated comments ("whoa," "gee") were all the travelers mustered upon entering the assigned shelter: two army cots with straw-filled bags for a mattress, pillows made of USAID flower sacks and army blankets folded with military precision stood by opposite walls on a swept mud floor. Above the rough-hewn bedside table was the only window, screened with mosquito netting, which let them view the western sky suffused with a rosy glow. "It looks like a beautiful painting on the wall," Lena approved.

"And there are no holes in the netting!" Sven cheered the most important observation. One learns a new set of values and rules in Africa: first, always check for holes in mosquito nets; second, relieve oneself at any and every opportunity. Sven and Lena found the outhouse functional; it stood adjacent to an actual shower screened by two walls of sticks. They used both of these luxuries and felt elated, settled, and ready for a feast.

✳

Two hurricane lamps gave enough light to illuminate the pink eye infection of the taller of the two white women—more new arrivals. Her companion, besides the hungry look and hollowed cheeks, showed no major pathology except, dermatologically speaking, the borderless lesion on the bridge of her nose which screamed for a biopsy. They appeared to have been in Africa longer than was good for their health. These travelers took a seat at the opposite end of the table from Lena and Sven. The Americans greeted them with smiles and air handshakes, but received only a fleeting glimpse and a short good evening. The two women looked away and talked between themselves only in short utterances in low voices. From what could be heard they were English, middle class, public school. Somehow, they looked very far from home.

The reserve was abolished by the chatter of the big woman, who brought dishes of smoking *nyama*, a variety of goulash from an undetermined species of an antelope, perhaps, and a plastic washbasin full of spears of fried cassava. The consistency of the meat resembled chopped fallopian tubes, but the sauce was delicious and "Kenya fries" (cassava) would beat French fries hands down, painstaking research by McDonald's notwithstanding. The cold beer, *bieru barindi* of the romantic Tusker brand, which followed, tasted like the nectar of the gods to the dried up travelers. Two tall and wide men, truckers, passed by carrying four bottles of Tusker each, greeting everybody boisterously. They were so black that only their amused eyes could be seen in the darkness. The dinner ended when the proprietor took away the lamps with apologies, to save on fuel.

Back in the metal sleeping box Lena read for a while, by a candle, Graham Greene's *Journey Without Maps*. When the wick collapsed into the puddle of wax, the day was definitely over.

"Our neighbors are those English snobs, Lena," Sven whispered. Sounds between the huts carried unhampered by the metal walls. The women could be heard getting into their squeaking cots. But soon just distant voices of the two truckers drinking their beer and the music of cicadas mitigated the silence of the night, providing a measure of romance to the romantically inclined.

"*Lala salama*," Lena whispered. Good night. "I feel beat."

"*Lala salama*," Sven said. "I'm full."

✳

It must have been about midnight, judging from the position of the Southern Cross in the sky, when Sven woke up. The source of the pleasant tintinnabulation was difficult to qualify, but it was near, as if next to his ear. Then an English woman's voice penetrated the walls.

"I would greatly appreciate it if you would not urinate on the wall of our cabin."

A brief silence followed.

"Mama, if you don't like it … take the matter to the management!" The trucker's voice seemed to acquire a cultured intonation. Sounds of his steps were heard as he trudged away.

Sven covered his mouth to mute his laughter. All of a sudden he felt a warm flood of happiness. It was a surprising, unexpected feeling without any apparent cause, which filled his chest. He half raised in his cot and through the window caught sight of the sky covered with a million stars set dreamily out of focus by the mosquito net. He did not search for the origin of his beautiful emotion; he looked at Lena. In the darkness of the hut she was invisible—only her white undies shined brightly as on a stage of the Black Theatre.

He rolled down off his bed onto the floor and on all fours crossed the short distance to Lena's bed.

"Woof, woof," he barked in a whisper. Lena moved to make space for him. "Hi," she whispered and he felt the smile in her voice.

The cicadas were still at it.

African midnight.

Ladies of the Brussels Night

On dévient moral des qu'on est malheureux.
(As soon as one is unhappy one becomes moral.)
Marcel Proust

As soon as one becomes moral one becomes a moralist.
(Tak se z n?j stal moralista, nabub?elej, v?c to jistá.)
Jára ?ervenk?

Mixing colors makes, sometimes, unexpected hues; a few drops of black paint in the white brightens the white whiter. A bucket of black night over the beige haze of city lights made the sky above the horizon glow the color of an old-fashioned dusty rose. The stretched noodle of the autobahn, thinned in the distance into a hair by the rules of perspective, led directly into the center of the rosy horizon. Their SKODA, the asthmatic four-cylinder "FAVORITE," did the best that Czech engineering allowed, in the right lane. They had been driving all day, and finally, the sky in front of them announced the city of their destination, Brussels.

The glow brought a memory from what seemed to be prehistoric times. When Tara was little she used to spend a couple of weeks in grandmother's house in Kladno every summer. That city has been known for the largest steel plant and smelters in Czechoslovakia. And everybody knew it was the ugliest town in the country, urban refuse by any standards except those of a little girl with ponytails at Granny's house. Tara used to love everything about Kladno, including the unpaved, muddy streets where one could scrape the butter-smooth ochre clay from the deepest rut, and the skeleton-like acacias that were dwarfed nicely by acid rains to climbable size, and under them the prematurely ancient men and women wilted into incredible bends, who either smiled at you or threatened to tell Grandma; and the rowdy packs of kids with their homemade carts, and slingshots, and dolls with heads made of old stockings with sewed-on buttons for eyes.

If pure accidents, such as the fight with Kaja Blaha from Krocehlavy or perhaps a broken window, or a fence climbed, or an exclamation in foul language, had not been reported to Grandma by the end of the day, and if Tara had already washed her hands and neck without being reminded a hundred times, she could be sure of a special reward. After darkness fell and the cuckoo clock in the kitchen announced bedtime, Grandma would take her hand and lead her to the bedroom, switch off the lights, push back the drapes, and put a stool under the window. Tara would climb on it, press her nose on the windowpane, and wait. Always, they waited in silence, as if even a whisper could prevent the magic from happening. Tara would peer into the darkness, trying to make out the concentration of flickering dots of light outlining the steel plant and smelters in the far distance.

Then the magic would happen, without warning: a volcanic eruption on a South Seas island on a tropical midnight! A faintly pink halo appeared over the plant, grew bigger and brighter, and all the horizon and all the sky would turn rosy, then change to crimson crinoline covering the city, without a sound. It lasted and lasted, then contracted, died, gave way to foggy darkness again. In the steel plant they had opened the smelting tower and let the man-made lava flow out. But Tara did not want to know that. She witnessed a volcano erupting, raging forest fires, hell, battlefields—depending on the daydream. That had been three decades ago.

"Tara, you are crossing the line again," her husband, Pepa, sighed from the passenger seat. "And you're going too fast!"

"Yeah." Their SKODA was braving the maximum RPMs she could muster and still machines with Belgian and German license plates passed them as if they were parked. The car was tired, and they were tired. The rosy sky over the horizon brought back Tara's memories but did not generate nostalgia or dreams of romance. The only dream she had was a vision of a shower and a bed. It was a realistic hope, finally.

"It must be Brussels under that sky. It better be," Tara said.

"Yes, you might be right. It's almost midnight." Pepa's throat felt like a drainage pipe.

"How's ma baby doing?"

Pepa leaned by her side and looked at the back seat. His face returned with a smile. "Sleeping. Can see just his hair from under the blanket. He doesn't mind nothing. And we are on the way for about ... let me see ... sixteen hours. Sixteen!" He stretched. "Do you want coffee, Tara? There might be some left in the thermos."

"No, thanks, we should be there soon. Maybe an hour?" She felt her back aching, neck stiffened, beat. "I was thinking," she said while another Mercedes jetted by, doing well over a hundred miles an hour.

"Did you see that?" Pepa interjected with an admiring accent on "that."

"I was thinking. We just can't knock on Lejeunes' door in the middle of the night, drag them out of bed. What do you say?" Tara said.

"Crossed my mind too."

"So?"

"So, we'll try to find a place to shack in," Pepa said. "There must be some small hotels around the Grand Place. I remember, vaguely."

They had crossed all of Germany, stopping just for minutes at a time, and were nearing their limit of endurance. That is how their vacations abroad had always started, always, Tara thought. This time the plan was to stay for a few days in Brussels with their friends, the Lejeunes, and then, together with them, go to Westende, to the beach, cooking mussels, fishing on the Lejeunes' boat, doing nothing, talking about everything, a lot.

Tara tilted the mirror to see the blond tuft of hair on the back seat. *His coloring takes after mine,* she thought. *At his five years it radiates like platinum, even in the twilight. And his eyes are Scandinavian blue, to match the hair.* She wondered if they would turn khaki with age, like hers. In those five years he had grown like a bamboo shoot. Amazing, from a zygote to such a precious kid! She wished he wouldn't change so fast, though, lose his sunny disposition, the smile that didn't leave him even in sleep, the eagerness and abandon in anything he did. *He has been a good traveler too. He had to be.* She tilted the mirror back. They were past the suburbs, now, in the city, still on the throughway.

"Tara, I would take the first exit, and then we might ask somebody." It had been two years since they last visited here. The Lejeunes took them around the town, this Eurocapital. They visited the sites, the old theater quarter, Petit rue des Bouchers where every house is a restaurant, and Grand Place, the fairy-tale square. In the Royal Museum they marveled at the imagination of home-boy Magritte, the magician of realistic surreal; they drove through the red-lighted street of sins; they took part in the photographing orgy at the tourists' favorite—Manneken Pis, the eternally pissing statue of an angelic youngster. Not to speak of churches.

Maybe I can get a position-reading, direction, at some of the "orientation points," she thought, *maybe the pissing kid statue, or something.* "We are lost, Pepa. I don't have a clue where we are now." Then the sprawling Gare du Nord appeared in front of them, lighted like an amusement park.

"Hey, I remember this train station! We are not far from the Centre." Pepa woke up from his dormancy. "There are always a few hotels near a station."

She turned into the first side street, drove up, turned the corner, entered another street—but nothing. No hotel sign, nobody on the street, deserted. The watch said one-forty. When she spotted a man sauntering with uncertain gait in a winding track, she stopped the car.

"Pepa," she said, and pointed to the walker. From the backseat Alex mumbled something about pulling the fish in, his sleep disturbed by the sudden absence of the engine's rumble.

Pepa stumbled out of the car, crossed the street, and surprised the lonely walker. Thick vapors engulfed him: Stella Artois, the most popular of local brews, Pepa was certain. "*Bon soir.* I am wondering if you might know, by chance, about a hotel around here, nearby?"

The man steadied himself on a lamppost: "Huh?" Pepa repeated his query in three simple words. The man scratched his eyebrow and put on a frown of seriousness: "Yeah, you are in luck. That way." He detached himself from the lamp, wavered in the night wind drafting down the street, and pointed out a general direction in a sweep. "Just turn the corner over there. You'll see many hotels. Many." His benumbed tongue articulated with an effort. Then he shuffled backwards, emitting strange sounds, watching Pepa crossing the street back to the car.

There were many hotels in the street behind the corner, many. One next to another, small hotels announced their hospitality in bright red neon signs. There was nobody walking the street at this late hour to enjoy the celebratory lighting, which contrasted so pleasantly with the grimness of the streets they had just left. A shower and a sprawling bed appeared imminent, to Tara and Pepa, and they stopped in front of the first hotel on the right.

The door was locked. Pepa rang, waited, rang again. His resignation to fatigue changed to a furious determination to break in. Then a key rattled in the lock, the door moved, and in the fissure a man appeared. His waxy face did not beam with joy under the disheveled remnants of colorless hair; his expression, wordlessly, accused them of dragging him from a pleasant dream.

Pepa apologized and begged him for a room: "*Nous voudrions une chambre,*" adding the "*S'il vous plaît*" with as much humility as he could manage. The old man appeared not to understand. "We have been driving eighteen hours," (he exaggerated by two) "across all of Germany. What shall we do?"

"You've got an accent," the man said after a while, his face showing signs of involvement, which Pepa translated as "hope."

"Yes, we are Czechs, from Prague."

The man lighted up in an instant, opened the door, and motioned Pepa in. He actually smiled. "Karlsbad, Karlovy Vary!" He raised his arm as if lifting an object on his open palm. "I have spent half of my life shuttling between here and Karlsbad. *Jak se mas? Nazdar, kamarade!*"

Pepa knew they'd found shelter. With Tara in the car, surely anxious to know what was happening, he listened to this kind man with his impatience concealed. It was an abbreviated, ten-minute story, how the man used to be a porcelain salesman, buying china in Czechoslovakia and importing it to Belgium and Holland, and how he had one mistress and one serious girlfriend in Karlsbad for all those years, both wonderful and, in spite of them, how he still saved money to buy this place for retirement.

In the time-honored Gallic gesture the man puckered his lips, inflated one cheek, blew out the air while shaking his hand from the wrist as if it was burnt. "Sorry, sorry, taking your time like that! You must be fatigued." He gave a key to Pepa and pointed to a circular staircase. "Number two. You'll find it quiet. And clean." Then he descended down to somewhere.

Tara dragged the army-surplus duffel bag and Pepa carried Alex, still asleep, upstairs. Entering their room, Tara dropped the bag and Pepa tightened his hold on Alex, speechless. They surveyed the chamber: blood-red flutter-drapes covered one wall from the ceiling to the floor. A mirrored dresser was decorated by a vase with artificial flowers in colors never seen in nature, not even on the shore of the Amazon. Two cardinal-red plastic chairs stood near a gold and red painted imitation-antique almirah, and the floor was covered with an obviously fake Isfahan, its crimson mercifully worn down. The most prominent structure, which took up a quarter of the floor space, was an airport of a four-poster bed. "Wow!" they said, shaking their heads.

After a symbolic wash-up in a porcelain washbasin they took off the red bedspread, speedily, and collapsed onto the fluffy heaven without much comment, laying Alex between them. "Good night."

"Night."

But the last word heard in the red chamber was "Unbelievable!" Tara pointed above their communal bed. Pepa looked up to see all three of them in a large mirror attached on the ceiling above the bed. Then the Sandman blurred the mirror with a puff of sand, bringing dreams to the weary travelers.

✳

After six hours of blissful unconsciousness, Tara's hand touched only a vacant space between her and Pepa. She opened her eyes. The narrow sheet of light penetrating between the gory drapes confirmed that Alex was missing. She sat up and scanned the room. He was gone. It took a hurried minute to put on jeans, a sweater over her naked torso, and shoes sans socks. She shook Pepa: "Alex's gone! I am running to check outside." Pepa's eyes opened wide but remained dead, absent, his stupor still deep.

Tara ran down the stairs holding onto the banister with one hand, combing her hair with the fingers of the other. At the bottom of the stair-case there was a short, dark corridor lighted by a naked bulb of low voltage. The corridor led to a room flooded with golden light, the light one feels one can almost touch, like in Vermeer's paintings or Sudek's photographs. "*Belich tung ist alles,*" she would agree with the German photographer. It was an illumination that makes common things glow as if coated with wildflower honey. It poured in from a large window, set from the floor almost to the ceiling, facing the street full of the morning sun. There, Alex took part in a scene which halted Tara's steps. "Alex," she said quietly.

"Hi ma!" He turned his head, donated a smile, and turned away again. It took a second. At least half of the room was taken up by a bar. Behind the bar was the usual wall of shelves with liquors and distillates. One of the barstools was occupied by an impressive specimen of a female.

Tara noticed her crossed legs of athletic build which the leopard-patterned leotard hugged tightly, to be admired in their entirety. The second thing she noticed was the ease and comfort of her son sitting on the woman's lap, pushed slightly to one side by her chest, the size of which would be difficult to describe believably. It was revealed to the maximum possible extent. The lady was holding Alex around his tiny shoulders with one hand; her second hand was lifting a glass of what looked like orange juice to Alex's mouth.

A second girl was coming from behind the bar carrying a tray of pastry. She gave Tara a surprised look but, in an instant, concentrated on arranging the sweets in front of Alex. She wore a metallic microskirt, black net stockings on swift runner's legs, and a top made of a small piece of leather constructed to enhance her abyss-deep cleavage. The most remarkable feature was her strawberry hair, ripe strawberry, forming a tower of luxuriant curls. She petted Alex's scalp of platinum and in hushed, machine-gun French promoted her pastries. Both girls chuckled when the kid told them, in Czech, that he would eat it all.

"He said, he likes everything," Tara translated and stepped farther into the room. Two steps.

"Is your boy?" the leopard-leotarded lady asked in a stark voice.

"Yes, he is. We have to leave soon." The amusement disappeared from the girls' faces.

"I don't wanna, Mom." He did not turn around; his voice was muted by the Belgian pastry. Both girls nodded in his support, understanding the meaning without knowing his foreign words.

Tara noticed the third girl, who sat, motionless, on a chair by the window. She had round eyes which gave her face an expression of wonder because the eyelids did not cover even a part of the iris: the eyes of a kid looking at a lighted Christmas tree. They did not leave Alex for a second. The head of that girl was completely shaved. Tara nodded at her, but remained unseen.

Tara looked out the window across the street. The houses were narrow, none wider than three lengths of a car. In each house there was a large picture window, elevated just a few feet above the sidewalk. In each of the windows there was a chair or two, and on the chairs sat living females, like mannequins, in scant clothing of pastel or fluorescent hues.

She knew this street! Two years ago, Lucien Lejeune had driven Pepa and her around the town, showed them the tourists' sites and included this street because it was "*tres intéressant. N'est-çe pas?*" She remembered her reaction of disgust as well: yes, it was *tres intéressant,* as *intéressant* as a liquidation sale. She recalled Pepa's remarks, too. Embarrassing. He wanted to drive slower and babbled something about the oldest, honorable profession in the world, giggling like an idiot. She was sure she remembered this place.

The girl with the shaved head and the eyes watched the miracle of Alex intently, as he spilled the juice, which the strawberry-haired girl gently, carefully wiped off his chin.

"We really have to go, Alex. Alex, dear!" The leopard-leotarded lady put him down on the floor as one would lower an alabaster statue of great value. Alex extended his arm and touched the black net stocking of the strawberry lady. She smiled at him. She bent down, holding her breasts in place with one hand, smoothing Alex's hair with the other.

"You have slept here?" The Leopard turned to Tara. "In this house?"

"*Oui*, we did. My husband waits upstairs," Tara said. The girls looked at her, as if not understanding. Only the one with the shaved head still did not take her eyes off Alex. He wandered to her, to the window.

"May I ask something?" Tara took courage. There was no response, just questioning stares. "I was wondering, why did the lady by the window shave her hair? It is quite unusual, isn't it?"

Strawberry said: "Her best friend lost her hair after chemo. Chemotherapy, you know? So she shaved, too. Sympathy."

"I understand. How unhappy she must have been, about her friend."

"Oh no, she wasn't. That's how life is," Strawberry said, with a hardened expression. "But she cried a lot; she cried."

"Most of the customers want her just to hold them now. Just that, you know?" Leopard came to life, a little, turned to her strawberry friend. "The older ones."

"They want me to do the same," Strawberry told her. "Some of the older guys, married mecs, they want just to be held. Has nothing to do with hair. And you know it."

"Yeah, they need that, *ç'est vrai.* Has nothing to do with the haircut." Leopard turned to Tara. "You married, aren't you?"

Tara nodded.

"No fucky-fucky pas, just to be held they want. *Vous comprenez? Pige?*" She giggled.

Tara felt uneasy, tight in her chest. *This conversation is not very good,* she thought. She did not know what to say, if anything.

"But you have a very handsome boy. Nice *bebe*," said Strawberry, the smile melting her painted face.

"*Merci bien, merci.* You took good care of him," Tara said, grateful for the change of topic. She forced a short laugh: "You would spoil him rotten. With those sweets, I mean," she added very quickly. "But we must be on the way now." She took the sticky hand of Alex. "Thanks, again. So kind of you."

The room became very silent then. Alex followed Tara with his head turned back, waving at the girls in a child's way, just with his fingers.

✳

In their room Pepa was dressed, ready to go. "Where was he? Is he all right?" he asked about Alex. Tara looked at her husband. He was shaved, had combed his hair and packed their things, even tidied the bed, sort of. He looked good. For his age he looked very good. She should hug him, hold him, she should. Just hold him. She looked at the bed, with the mirror above it. She took a deep breath. She had a strange thought. How about not just holding him. Wouldn't it be something? The enormous bed, the mirror and all? But what to do with Alex? She took another deep breath and swallowed. She felt heat in her cheeks.

"You have slept in a whorehouse, Pepa." She tried to sound matter-of-fact. Pepa put down the bag, stiffened, and spread his arms, staring at Tara without words, his forehead in a wrinkled frown.

"Where did you get this idea? I don't want to talk about anything like that, now. I mean—let's go, let's get going, Tara!" Pepa stuttered and moved to the door.

That despicable lowlife; he certainly has been in a whorehouse, somewhere. I know it. Look at him! She wanted to kiss him for how worried he looked. He had been good to her and to Alex, always, a good friend, too, that lowlife. She really loved the guy—later, she'd hug him, later.

"Pepa, I am telling you, this place is a bordello, brothel, house of ill repute, whatever. Look around!"

Pepa sighed as if relieved and looked around, obediently. "I'll be damned," he said. "I'll be damned." He managed a smile. His relief showed plainly.

Tara told him about Alex and the ladies downstairs, about the window to the street. "Do you remember? Two years ago we drove through here with Lucien?"

Pepa laughed. Alex looked at him and laughed, too. They went downstairs and Pepa paid the ex-porcelain-salesman a price obviously discounted (since no special services were rendered and the bed provided had been uninhabited). They got into their car parked in front of the house. It started after a series of coughs.

Alex knelt on the back seat, peering out of the car. "Bye, bye. Bye," he was shouting. All three girls stood behind the large picture window, waving; even the motionless one without hair raised her hand. The window blurred their images, took off their colors, the window's tempered thickness giving it strength exceeding the strength of prison iron bars and seven locks, making it impenetrable.

They drove the length of the street. Alex was waving at all the large windows with beautiful ladies. Then they turned the corner. The displays in the large windows changed with an abruptness which surprised them both and prevented any comment. Ladies were replaced by grilled quails, cheeses the size of a wheel, miniature castles of chocolate, marinated octopi. The rows of *charcuteries*, *brasseries*, *boulangeries*, and *patisseries* announced the domain of *citoyen moral*, whose chief permissible celebration of life was a pleasurable way of feeding.

"We should get something small to eat. Or at least a coffee, and milk for the boy," Pepa said, slowing down, looking for a cafe or brasserie.

"That house, the 'hotel' where we slept tonight, was number three, I think. Wasn't it?" Tara said. "Did you notice the name of that street?"

Pepa looked at her for a long time, considering he was driving in traffic. "Tara! Don't even think about that! Tara, I know you."

"What do you mean?"

"What do I mean? I mean: don't even think about taking Alex back to that house, to those girls, there! Jesus Christ, Tara."

"Ma, can you take me back to those girls? Please," Alex whined from the back seat. Pepa held back a smile with an effort. Always, he had admired her "compassion for the sediment"—that's what he called it. Compassion for those lacking good fortune. That's what he admired about her.

They drove in silence. It looked like an optimistic day in the making; the sun was high already. Pepa placed his fingertips on Tara's cheek, then laid his hand on her thigh and squeezed gently. He shook his head with a small smile on his face, looking straight ahead.

Tara seemed to watch the road, too. Her thoughts were too crowded, louder than the morning traffic rushing by, louder than the roar of the moral city around them. She thought about Strawberry and Leopard and the Shaved One, about the world she had always imagined as being carnival or carnivore, but glimpsing into it she had found it might not be either. About the world she had left just minutes ago, the world which would not leave her.

The second day of their stay with the Lejeunes, Tara and Alex said they were going shopping. They returned very late for lunch. They'd got lost in town, she explained, trying to look believable. They couldn't find a taxi, she said. Pepa didn't ask anything. She looked happy, radiant. She smiled at him, and he smiled at her, silently, knowing.

The Calm Sea

When Nayak was born, his grandmother decided that he must not be nursed and should be left outside the hut to die. The gods had told her that this is how it should be. He had been born with a deep groove encircling one of his legs above his ankle, the foot tiny and twisted. These were the signs the gods had sent to his grandmother, and she understood. But it was the gods' will, too, that the second day after Nayak's birth, his grandmother would not wake up from her sleep.

Nayak's mother had started breast-feeding her firstborn, because she knew what had really happened, what was the true cause of the strangulated foot. She remembered well the time of her pregnancy, a night when a group of armed Chinese had landed near her village on the shores of the Malay Peninsula. It had happened on a night when all the young men had gone fishing with the big communal net, far offshore. She remembered every sound of the raid. Every scream she had heard from her hiding place under the roof. When morning came and she recognized only familiar voices, she had climbed down to join the other women in front of the village chief's house. There, his legs tied tightly above the ankles by a rope, his arms spread and nailed to the wall, the old chief was dying. She watched for a moment, horrified.

When Nayak was born, many months after the incident, she remembered well seeing the tied legs of the chief. She knew that that was the true cause of her baby's deformed foot. Everyone in the village understood this, too, but still Nayak was treated differently from other children. Next to the particular Malayan insanity of *amok*, physical malformations were the most feared and despised by the villagers.

Thus, growing up, Nayak had often looked for a hidden place along the shore to be alone. And when he went diving for fish, he dove without a companion, against the custom of his people. In his teens, he became darker in complexion; nobody knew why. For that, they called him Tamil, after the immigrants from South India. When he reached the age of twenty, his mother died and his uncle took over the house and let Nayak know that he could stay there if he really had to. With that, Nayak decided it was time to leave this village of strangers, his home.

There was a chance to make a good living on Pulau Tioman, an island in the South China Sea. The island had a hotel for tourists. Nayak had learned this from his cousin, who lived there, when this relative had visited the village wearing bell-bottomed pants and a colorful T-shirt and carrying a portable radio. He had been admired by everyone, as a successful man should be, and his words were important. Cousin told Nayak that he liked his foot in a way—it reminded him of the flipper of a sea turtle, he said, and he liked sea turtles best of all creatures. He had given Nayak a present, a plastic snorkel for diving. In his admired bell-bottoms and carrying his radio, he often walked on the beach with Nayak where everyone could see them together. Nayak was very proud of Cousin's friendship, and so he made his decision.

In two days they landed together on Pulau Tioman. That same evening they sat on a soft mat in his cousin's hut, listened to the cicadas, talked, and drank warm beer. The hill behind the hut was covered with dense forest and was so steep that the night-music of the jungle seemed to come from the sky. From the hut, they could see the sea between the coconut palms, shining back in the full moon. The beer was good—so good that Nayak wanted to hug his cousin and all of Pulau Tioman Island.

A smile was still on Nayak's face when he saw the morning mist over the calm water from his bamboo cot. Quietly, he gathered his net-bag with things for diving, broke a couple of bananas from a cluster hanging under the roof, and slithered down the ladder to the sand. His cousin was still sleeping; all was quiet. Nayak thought, "If I do not get rid of that grin on my face it will soon hurt."

He started walking briskly along the sandy shore toward the rocky cape in the distance. He remembered the instructions for reaching the hotel. There, straight in front of the hotel, about a kilometer from the hotel beach, he would see a small island. His cousin had explained everything to him the day before. Around the island he would find a fringing coral reef, and on the outer side of the reef—coral rubble.

Cousin had said, patting him on the shoulder, "There, Nayak, there you'll find tridacna shells. Some are so big that two men can't lift them." He had stretched his arms wide apart, exaggerating the size. "You'll find some good ones on the windward side of the island, in about fifteen meters of water. When you bring them to the hotel, just ask for the gardener. He is my friend, and he will take care of you. You'll make good money, Nayak. Tourists will pay good money at the hotel shop. You'll buy a radio with two speakers. You could even buy me a couple of beers." They had both laughed.

Nayak remembered his cousin's every word and wondered about his new life, his lucky future. "I am a good diver, Cousin," he had answered the day before. "I'll bring up the biggest tridacna shell. You see my flipper here?" He had pointed at his malformed foot. "My flipper will work like the fin of a giant green turtle." They had both looked at his foot, knowing well that it was useless for diving.

But it worked quite well for walking, and Nayak quickened his stride. He left the sandy shore and went through the coconut palm grove, to bypass the rocks. There he trod carefully, watching his way, to avoid the dried palm fronds on the ground. Cobras gathered there, looking for rats that feed on fallen coconuts. The narrow path wound back to the shore through a small forest of black mangroves, some caped with vines. The sun was rising above the horizon now, warming the air, making it pleasant to walk in the shade. Nayak slowed down for a while to watch a gigantic long-horned beetle cross the path. Almost the size of a hand, the copper wings reflected light with a beautiful metallic luster. He rested on a boulder—this time to enjoy the view of an orchid in bloom, its emerald-green blossoms arranged in a single row on the stem like minimal roosters, still glistening with morning dew.

His eyes narrowed against the sun as he descended onto an almost white beach of coral sand. A short distance ahead was the hotel. He had never imagined such a large and strange building, such an order to the landscape. The hotel was surrounded by tall trees and royal palms, planted in a pattern. Clumps of hibiscus and bougainvillea, flaming with color, formed a wall separating the hotel from the forest in back.

Very few tourists visited remote Pulau Tioman, and it was still early in the day. He could not see any people on the grounds, just somebody on the beach. Cousin had told him that there would be a few skiffs with native men who waited to give tourists a ride, and one of them would take him to the island. But there were no boats yet.

Off shore, over there, was the island. Small, it appeared far away, but Nayak could distinguish silhouettes of trees. If he swam slowly he could reach it. There were no waves on the sea, and it seemed there was no current in the strait. He reminded himself that there were tridacna shells around that island, and for shells he would be paid money. He did not question what to do. He limped to the edge of the water and sat upon the sand.

He noticed two people on the beach now. One was a boy who came running toward him. He was naked and light yellow, just slightly darker than the sand and, despite his child's face, his body was bulky. His hair had no color, Nayak thought, and his big round eyes were strangely pale.

The child stopped nearby and watched Nayak with an expression of wonder. A very tall white woman followed and talked to the boy in sounds without melody. She had no dress on—only a small piece of cloth on her hips. Shyly, Nayak looked at her breasts, which were white and very large. He would have liked to watch the breasts longer but was ashamed.

He must think now about his task. Trying to concentrate, he carefully attached the wooden fin to his good foot with bands made from an inner tube. Then he put on the goggles, with a frame he had carved from soft wood and glass lenses glued in with resin from a euphorbia tree. He rinsed the lenses once in the water and spat on them to prevent fogging. Then he closed his lips over the mouthpiece of the snorkel—the present from his cousin. This would allow him to swim near the surface, breathing with his face always submerged.

After tying the netbag to his rope belt, he entered the water slowly, without a splash. The woman and her boy watched him, motionless. The sea was very calm. Nayak began swimming rapidly but soon reminded himself that he must control his excitement. It was a long way to the island. He settled into steady, fluid strokes, feeling the water gently, not thrashing through it, his good leg with the fin moving up and down in a dolphin-like way, barely making a single bubble or turbulence on the surface. His bad foot moved only slightly, not so much to propel as to avoid creating resistance. It was the deliberate, efficient swim of an experienced diver.

The great visibility surprised him. He could see the bottom gradually slope down, far ahead. Underneath him, clean sand formed familiar rows and shallow trenches, over which the shades of ripples on the surface drew changing patterns, making the bottom seem alive. A school of silvery fish passed under him, now and then rapidly changing direction for no apparent reason. A solitary sea cucumber lay shapelessly on the sand, where it did not belong. This was the sea Nayak knew, the environment where he felt safe and good about himself.

The bottom was rapidly sinking now, and the sand acquired a gray hue. At home, divers rarely swam over such depths, since there was no need for it. The spearing of fish was done in the shallows, between the rocks or coral heads, where both fish and diver could conceal themselves.

When the bottom disappeared, all became silently blue in every direction. This was an unknown world to Nayak. He could easily believe that no bottom existed at all, even beyond the depth he could perceive. For just a moment he imagined himself falling down, which was an unpleasant and confusing feeling.

He stopped swimming to raise his head above the water. The island was still so far, the beach closer, and he could still recognize the woman and her boy. He submerged his face again, breathing now through the snorkel with a little more effort, and resumed the swim toward the island. The water underneath changed into to a dark blue. Beams of light of different thicknesses descended, changing position, converging nowhere, enhancing the feeling of bottomless space. Nayak felt supported by the columns of light one moment; the next he felt as if he were falling between pillars of light, down into the abyss. But he continued swimming.

Then a solitary Venus lantern appeared close to Nayak, a small, transparent, jelly-creature with tiny fluorescent dots along its gossamer frame. He touched it, and the turbulence made by his hand caused the Venus lantern to somersault. "As helpless as me, now, that lantern in the darkness," Nayak thought, and had to smile. Feeling better, he increased the power of his strokes. Maybe he should think less, and avoid looking around—just to reach the island, reach it soon.

Nayak was finally approaching the island when the first shark appeared. It was a great hammerhead, coming upward from the deep, slowly, not directly toward Nayak, looking like a gigantic gray cylinder streamlined to perfect efficiency, emanating power. The hammerhead's head was out of any imaginable proportion, not resembling a mallet—more like a shelf hiding its jaws. Without an enemy in the seas, it was a threat to all those less powerful. With a barely visible movement of its tail fin, it propelled itself away, then disappeared. Nayak had seen the shark with a surge of surprise and a sudden sadness more than fear. But everything inside him tightened. He checked his distance from the island—it was still too far for a sprinting swim, and Nayak knew that he must avoid causing any commotion in the water.

The hammerhead appeared again on the other side. Now it was obvious that the shark was circling, that it might not go away. Movements of its tail were sparse and fluid; the bizarre head never moved even slightly. Nayak looked into the shark's eyes, which stared nowhere, also motionless. There was a remora fish attached to the shark's belly, hoping for leftovers from the hammerhead's feasts. Nayak wished for a companion of his own, too.

He stopped swimming when the shark abruptly changed direction and passed so close to Nayak that he could almost touch it. The shark accelerated and sharply turned around. Its back arched and its head raised up to encounter Nayak's fist—which sent the shark aside. But it returned so fast that Nayak could not maneuver to face it. The feeling was not of a sharp pain. It felt more like being hit with a flat board over his bad leg. His flipper-foot disappeared into the rows of teeth framed in bared white gums. There was no blood at all.

The fish started to thrash from side to side, descending deeper and deeper, effortlessly dragging Nayak behind. The wooden fin came off the good foot. Then the hammerhead detached itself with nodding jerks of its head. Nayak saw that his flipper-foot was gone. Strangely, there was still no blood escaping from the stump.

Now submerged deep under the surface, he felt the high pressure and the coldness of the water. It was quite dark. With astonishment, Nayak became aware of the peace and stillness around him and of no need for breathing, no urge for air. A blacktip shark from the reefs joined them now, passing high above Nayak. The hammerhead came again, from behind.

Nayak's body arched and shattered—arched violently, as if being hit at the waist by an enormous dull fist. His goggles still in place, he perceived himself to be slowly surrounded by a purple cloud, quite beautiful, changing shape, expanding in pulsating rhythms, engulfing his torso like smoke, heavy, yet rising upwards, more and more of it, streaming from his body, as if being fed by a dying fire. Only the remora fish disturbed the purple cloud, gulping at it wildly. Then the blacktip shark's head cut through the cloud baring its teeth.

The woman on the beach, shading her eyes with her hand, observed the silver surface of the water. There was no sign of the strange diver. She took her boy by the hand. The sun was hot now. It was time for a late breakfast—"brunch," as they called it, she was quite sure.

A dark papilio butterfly approached the island in flight from across the straight. Almost like a bird, effortlessly, without fluttering, it glided over the still sea, suspended in silence.

The Best Time in Life

It felt almost like slow dancing with an unexplored high school date. That good. I was walking again through the West African jungle, in the morning, moving lightly in my shorts and thin shirt, not a drop of sweat on me but soaking in everything around me. The freedom was tangible. After the night rainfall, the humid air took the scent of orchids and sweet jasmine well. The bamboos sounded music powered by the light breeze. The golden shafts of light between the canopy of trees and palms changed patterns, making everything around me appear in motion, alive. I sensed the biology in every blade of grass and fern edging the path, even in the pebbles strewn on the red laterite ground. It would take an hour or so, Joseph had said. No sweat. So I stopped often, looked around, listened, smelled.

Near the creek, a foot-long millipede crossed my path like a shiny brown train, and the rainbow-colored agama lizard greeted me with vigorous pushups meant to impress. It was a male, of course. A display of shining jewelry glided above my head—iridescent morpho butterflies, glossy wasps, even a rare-sized buprestis, the jewel beetle, buzzed up in a straight line above. I noticed a group of fruit bats, hanging like wet pouches on the branch of a slender afara. They have been passing over my house in Nunugu every evening, making inimitable sounds, but nothing like barking—despite their resemblance to miniature Dobermans. They are my friends.

Strange shrieks from the shadowy undergrowth and the increasing staccato of an unknown bird halted my steps. Then silence again. You want to either sing or think in the holy green stillness after a night rainfall, so I rested by the mute creek that spread over the path into a shallow ford, compelled to think about big things, Nature, the Creation. But I had to go.

It was a rainy season Sunday morning and my destination was the village of my acquaintance Joseph, where he lives with his wife Amadiume. Joseph is a technician in pathology at the Nunugu Hospital. We talk often because he likes to practice his English and I like to learn more about him. Like most of his tribe, his manners appear gentle and his speech is always measured and quiet. Unlike many of his countrymen he looks directly at your eyes when speaking and his smile is always at the ready. Recently, he gave me a nice bowl made by Amadiume of the fruit of the cannonball tree. I will give him my Bowie knife before I leave. I looked forward to meeting him in his own environment, in the place of his forefathers, and I suspected it would be a significant occasion for both of us.

Approaching the village I passed the burial site, recognizable from the scattered clay pots for sacrificial offerings. I was curious to inspect them, but I was in a hurry. A young couple crossed the path in front of me, holding hands by their pinky fingers only, according to local custom. A woman approached with a bundle of firewood balanced effortlessly on her head, the tightly-packed baby on her back swinging its head impossibly back and forth in a peaceful sleep. Then the first hut appeared, surrounded by orderly rows of yams and cocoyams.

It was my first visit here, so I was unsure about what kind of welcome to expect. But my hesitation disappeared when a crowd of naked children with umbilical hernias swarmed around me, their eyes wide open in amazement at my paleness. Joseph must have been alerted by that mysterious African telegraph, since he appeared within moments of my arrival to save me from this crowd of little people. In a flowing toga (not unlike my grandmother's nightgown) and embroidered skull cap, he looked more distinguished and taller than he did at the hospital. He shook my hand without squeezing it, released it with a ceremonial swing, gave me a friendly smile of welcome, and led me to the square.

The important elders had already gathered in the men's house. They greeted me with the customary limp handshakes and somber sentences I did not understand—with stateliness, without deference. The frailest of the sages motioned me to sit down on a clay ledge worn smooth. It was the place of honor. Then the men talked quietly among themselves, paying no attention to me, since only women and children show uninhibited curiosity toward strangers. I watched the faces around me with interest. Each one was sculptured differently, in varying hues of brown, none disfigured by deposits of fat, the skin taut over their cheekbones, the whites of their eyes red, the creases and wrinkles in various configurations of seriousness. None of them carried a necklace of the dried navels of their enemies. Perhaps they had left them home for my visit. None wore a goat's heart on his neck (the heart of a virgin had been forbidden by the colonial administration a long time before), so there was no way to recognize the chief.

I lit a cigarette without asking permission, since a small display of arrogance is expected from a white man (and, frankly, I craved a puff), and when followed by friendliness, it helps to establish a mutual respect—not unlike in the boardroom of an American business. And the "board members" in front of me were not much different either, except for two phenomena: the mean weight averaged fifty pounds lower and the posture of dignity was maintained with a natural ease.

I smiled politely when an old woman brought a gourd with palm wine. Joseph explained in his amiable accent that the palms had been tapped yesterday at sunset and the village tapper had collected the juices this morning before sunrise. This way there would be less quantity but the wine would be fresh and cool. The tapper is an experienced man. With some apprehension I asked if the wine had been diluted with water—as is usually done—and learned that it had not. That pleased me to no end. I could avoid this dilemma: either I could drink and get sick like a dog or not drink and offend everybody in the men's house. Palm wine is an almost sterile fluid, self-fermented by its natural yeast only. But when water is added, it comes from a creek or pond, thick with such a variety of bacteria, amoebas, and other pathogenic organisms (responsible for the fifty percent child mortality here) that an unaccustomed visitor, drinking watered wine, unfailingly ended up with diarrhea or an even more serious ailment. Having seen, in autopsies, bags of yellow mash in place of livers as a result of amoeboid infection, I took the news of undiluted wine with barely disguised pleasure and thought of the customs of this village with respect. And the wine was pleasantly cool, with the taste of bread and the scent of Urquell beer from Pilsen. It made the morning committee of biblical sages smile and talk with increased vehemence.

Joseph translated the few formal questions of the *ozos*—the elders—about my occupation, country of origin, domicile, and state of health. Then I distributed my spare pack of Benson and Hedges. With solemn bows and handshakes Joseph excused us and we left to visit his house.

Our way was circuitous so that we covered much of the village. Joseph delighted in soliciting the admiring looks of his peers. Young ladies giggled. Their erect elegance and brown beauty has never ceased to stir my post-pubescent fantasies, and I wondered if it could be confirmed that they put the biting boatman bugs on their breasts to swell and enlarge them. An old woman approached us and Joseph translated what she said. She asked me to stay with them in the village permanently. If I didn't agree, she would steal me. She roared with laughter. Her pitch-black face and negroid appearance aside, she bore a striking resemblance to one of my old aunts. I wondered how that could be possible.

An emaciated woman, stark naked, ran across our path with arms above her head, and, farther on, an older man, grimacing wildly, forced me to accept a palmful of coins. These were insane people, victims of a cerebral form of malignant malaria known to readers of romantic colonial novels as "blackwater fever." I assured an embarrassed Joseph that all was well, that I understood they were ill—because only the insane would display bodies no longer beautiful and only the insane would give money to a white man. Joseph and I understood one another perfectly.

Joseph's house did not have a thatched roof but distinguished itself by corrugated sheet iron. This "progress" is the price a successful man with a job in town has to pay for his eminence. An iron roof, in contrast to the "barbaric" palm-thatched one, creates heat in the house which is often difficult to bear. The mud walls of his house were nicely hand-polished with only a few cracks, and the half door was made of the traditional, simply carved iroko wood. Bending our heads we entered with greetings.

Inside, the beam of light from one of the two windows flooded his wife Amadiume as she sat on a metal cot. She startled me with her beautiful face, peaceful smile and shy eyes. Her hair was done in tiny braids that met in a complicated pattern at the top of her head. Her complexion was a warm brown in shade, lighter than Joseph's, and smooth, without a wrinkle. My thought was to wonder why Joseph would plan to take a second wife, as he had confided to me in town. On the wall above her head hung a framed picture of Christ.

Amadiume was very pregnant with a girl to be born in just two days and to be named Ifuome. My mental photograph of this scene is titled "Waiting for Ifuome," and I can still recall it clearly in every detail, any time.

She got up with graceful effort, greeted us in her language, and brought cola nuts on a saucer advertising Cinzano. It is an honorable custom to offer a cola nut to a guest. We dipped the nut segments into a very hot paste—a variation unknown to me before. Then Amadiume said something to Joseph and he explained that she would have to leave us to visit her younger brother who was recovering from a bad scorpion bite. Judging from the way Joseph looked at her wobbling away, I knew he would be a good father to Ifuome. Amadiume parted with a smile so warm I wished she would stay.

I looked around the room. "You have a nice place here, Joseph," I said as I sat down on the "kitchen" stool. The mud floor was swept clean and the clay walls were polished smooth. A wooden stand had a saucer and a few cups neatly arranged on it, and a pole spanned a corner on which hung European clothes and a couple of sparkling clean shirts. In poverty cleanliness is the highest virtue, and neatness is a sign of good upbringing. Both are signs of a long pedigree.

"We try, Prof. There is not much money, you know."

"Your wife is expecting. It is good you have the job in the hospital," I said. "And the war is over."

It had been two years since the end of the Biafra-Nigeria war, and the country was slowly getting back on track.

"It's good to have the job. I only wish it paid more."

"Did you have a job during the war, too?"

"Now I have a few coconut palms and the yam field, with my father," he said.

It appeared that Joseph didn't want to talk about the war. So we exchanged several polite phrases and talked about farming for a while. I did not want to make him uncomfortable, but I needed to know.

"At least we have peace now," I said. "And the war is long over."

"Ya, peace. It is good to have peace now."

"In that war, you were a young fighter then, Joseph, weren't you? On the Biafra side?"

"For two years," Joseph said, shaking his head. "A long time and much hardship, Prof, much hardship."

"Were you fighting around here near Nunugu, or down south?" I asked. "I've heard it was more difficult down around Port Harcourt, in the Niger delta. Lowland forest, lots of disease, malaria, and such."

"I fought around here, but at the end we retreated to the delta. That's where I was stuck when it all ended."

It was a vile war. Villages and towns were wiped out, thousands of women and children were massacred, and thousands died of starvation. Atrocities were committed on a mass scale and were so barbaric one can not bear to think about them. It was typical, sadly, for the sub-Saharan part of the continent. It solved nothing and helped nobody except for a handful of "big men," and it was soon forgotten. I had heard some about it and read much, too, but had never talked with a fighter before. I did not want to appear too eager, though.

"Wars go on all over the world," I said. "I just hope it was the last one here. Forever."

"I don't know, Prof—not even the elders have much hope."

"What was your function in the army, Joseph—artillery, tanks, or what?"

"We did not have any tanks, had no airplanes, nothing like that. Nigerians, they had all that. They had everything from the British, you know. We were fighting with rifles. I got me a repeating revolver, too." He looked around the room, as if somebody might be spying on us. I believe he almost told me he still had it hidden there.

We chewed on a piece of cola nut. It showed its stimulating effect pleasantly. His eyes seemed brighter and he helped his English with his hands, pulled at his robe often.

He continued. "Maybe you would say reconnaissance—that's what I did a lot, because I grew up here in the forest. We would slip through enemy lines, spy on their positions and numbers. Took prisoners sometimes, too." I nodded and Joseph continued. "It was dangerous, but me and my friends, we knew the forest. Not like those Hausa or Fulani from the north. We could move like forest spirits."

"I can imagine," I said, "like juju spirits, invisible."

But Joseph did not like me to use the word "juju." His face showed it and he stopped talking. I offered him a cigarette.

"We had cigarettes and plenty to eat at the beginning of the fighting. We got cans from Sweden, with meat and fish in tins. Very good. The cigarettes—when they got wet we did not dry them, just threw them away. Just like that." He smiled and paused.

"You were a big man, Joseph."

"I was a big man."

"Like the chiefs are now?"

"Oh bigger, Prof. I could do anything I wanted. Anything, when we came to an enemy's village, anything, Prof."

"Powerful weapons?"

"The best U.S., best Italian. You know Bereta? Very good and beautiful."

"You were a big man, you were," I said, pushing it too much, maybe. "You had some good times, too."

"Oh, ya, Prof, good times." A smile crossed the still youthful face of my friend. "But bad times, too, mind you," he added hastily. "Very bad war."

We sat quietly for a while, looking in different directions. Some children peered through the door and Joseph shooed them away, almost angrily.

"Like once, down in the delta, west of Port Harcourt, we made camp on a creek, with a lot of catfish in it. We did not have much to eat by then, but we would not eat the fish. Dead bodies up the creek, women, they had bellies cut open, you know. Fish was no good to eat." He asked me for a smoke and continued. "As I said, it was in the delta, a bad place even in peace. In the evening, the men returned from patrol. And they told me about my cousin, Okonkwo. He was named after his father." He paused, staring at the floor. "You see, Prof, we were more than brothers. We were always together. Best friends, like donkey's teats, always together. They told me Okonkwo was dead. He got lost and when they found him, his soul was gone. His head was gone, too." Joseph took a deep breath and looked at me while turning his head from side to side.

I turned my head, too, and we became silent again.

"Just as they were telling me about my cousin, the other group of soldiers came from the forest. They had prisoners with them. I don't know how many. Some were just kids, spy kids, you know. Naked and smeared with palm oil so that when you caught them they could slip away." I gave

Joseph my last cigarette and lit it for him. "I became so sad, Prof, so sad about my cousin. He was like my brother, I told you."

"Yes, I can imagine, Joseph."

"I was so sad I grabbed a zap gun and mowed them down. Those prisoners. All of them."

It was getting late and I knew I should not wait for the dusk, since it would not be wise to return through the forest in the darkness. I wanted to thank Joseph and get going, but slowly. We finished the last cola nut with that hot relish. Joseph was sitting on the bed with Christ above it. But he was now staring at the opposite wall, his mind somewhere south of here, in the past, I guessed.

"The war," he said quietly as the smoke came from his mouth. "That was the best time in my life. Ya, the best time, Prof."

"I know."

We shook hands limply, as is the custom here.

The Killing of He-Who-Is-Without-Shadow

From high in the air the village of Eskimo Point resembles a spilled load of cardboard boxes on the deserted shore of the bay. Just mirrors of small lakes decorate the bleak expanse of the surrounding tundra, as far as the horizon. In the blank ink of Hudson Bay, quite far off the shore, pods of beluga whales move slowly in synchrony. The Inuit people would wish them closer to the coast at this season of the year, since there is an urgency in gathering enough stocks of meat and blubber for winter. And winter is in the air; one can smell it in the evening.

There is no word to describe the smell of winter in the language of *kablunak*, the white man, or in Inuit. But there are many Inuit names for polar bears, who follow the shore through the village to their southern denning grounds. They come at this time of year. Perhaps, they too smell winter in the air.

The southwestern sky played colors with the orange target suspended above the horizon of Hudson Bay. But still snow geese could be spied in the distance, despite the hour, late by *kablunak's* watch. Most children dreamt already; some huddled under a blanket from the Hudson Bay Company store, some were heaped under a caribou skin, hugging each other for warmth. The older youngsters, still unmarried, rejoiced in the game of doused lights and other copulation schemes in Young People House. That would seem to be the usual summer evening in Eskimo Point.

But tonight the women intensified their visiting to discuss the eagerly anticipated drawing by the men. This was the most important event of the late summer. Everybody knew that. Women paced from one house to another, crossing their paths at different points between houses, like lemmings, in unpredictable patterns. They shuffled pigeon-toed, wobbling from side to side in the Inuit women's gait; some carried babies in an *amaut*, a pouch under the hood of their caribou parka.

When Akyak met Aklavik, she bent and jerked forward, and the head of little Oolulik popped out at her shoulder, his surprised faced surrounded by a halo of wolf's fur lining. Aklavik laughed with approval: "Mmm, mmm, how handsome. Good baby *namakto*. Eh!"

When women went visiting, their tongues were with them, so Akyak and Aklavik talked some before separating to walk to different houses to talk more. Oh, Akyak almost forgot to mention that the wife of Sorquaq (Sorquaq and his wife were Padlermiut, "caribou people," from the far-away tundra of Padlei. These people knew nothing of seals and beluga. So strange.)—that she, the wife of Sorquaq, had lain overnight with young Napartuk. That made Napartuk the fourth one, just this summer. How interesting, the women thought.

"Well, her good reputation might spread, and her husband's honor increase. *Uvang okrartunga*; I have spoken." Akyak tried to look serious, in vain.

"Eh, eh, my mother said it is good for a woman to collect memories," Aklavik said. "That later in life a woman will look backward, but not forward, for the thrills of life, she told me, my mother." Both women nodded, and their eyes took on a distant expression, as if looking backward.

"She pinches her cheeks to take a good color, often, often," Akyak giggled.

"Eh, she might not let her hair loose to show she has the period, it is said," Aklavik added, and the women laughed, putting their noses so close they touched. What a pleasure! The wife of Sorquaq laughs with many men. Maybe, this is the way of Padlermiut, it has been deduced.

"Some words are spoken to the air."

"Somebody is thinking of meat."

The women started to walk backwards, still smiling at each other, before turning to their destinations. The wind from the bay raised swirls of dust from the disturbed ground between houses, and women sped up their crossings and pulled hoods over their heads to keep their progeny buried deep in the parkas' *amaut*. When the sun dove into the bay, all the women of Eskimo Point had already made several pleasurable offerings to the great Spirit of Visiting, with the exception of Tutiak and Ayorsalik.

Ayorsalik had been in trouble; she was shamed by a loss of face. Up until recently, her marriage to two men had worked to the satisfaction of all three involved. She could take care of the soapstone lamps so they never sooted; she dried the *kamiks* well for both husbands; she scraped skins with the *ulu* knife without a single nick; she set and tended many fox traps to get enough skins for cash to buy tobacco; with narwhale sinew she could make stitches so small that seams on her sealskin *kamiks* and covers were invisible. She was an Eskimo woman, Inuk, to be sure.

She had been rented out to laugh with men of the village by her two husbands, now and then, and that caused much felicity to many, because she was cheerful and quite beautiful. Looking at her face from the side, one could not see her nose at all, so small was it (not protruding like a narwhale horn), and her hare-skin panties were filled very well, without stuffing moss in them. So all men desired her, and some women envied her. A deal had been made, a deal honorable and fair as judged by the villagers and all involved: the income from Ayorsalik's excursions to the igloos of men who rented her would be split into three equal parts for her and for each of her husbands. Since Ayorsalik was no *sequajuq*, lazy-bones, the income was good, and all three members of the family could smoke enough and buy corn flakes from the H.B.C. store.

However, it became common knowledge, recently, that some of the gains Ayorsalik did not divide by threes but only by two. The older of her husbands had been the shorted one, and the only one of the whole village who did not know, as is often the case. This is how Ayorsalik lost face and was dishonored in such a way that she was ashamed to show her face tonight.

The other of the two women who did not participate in visiting was Tutiaq, the coveted one. She had become a woman of great consequence, since in her house men were gathering to draw who would shoot *nanuk*, the polar bear. She was their host, and it will be remembered.

✳

The Canadian Government rations one polar bear (*Ursus maritimus*) per year to be shot by a man of Eskimo Point Village. If it is wounded and escapes, no attempt to shoot another bear can be made that year. The proceeds from the skin, skull, and claws, many thousands of dollars, are to be shared by all the families of the village. Sometimes it is agreed that the front third of the skin, *nanurak*, can be kept by the shooter, to be made into outer pants.

✳

The last few hunters were still arriving in Tutiaq and Minik's house. Ayagutaq entered. "*Igloo namakto unaktoalu,*" he commented on the warmness of the house and smiled his peculiar smile which everybody admired. His upper lip was split all the way to the nostril due to a congenital harelip which had not been repaired. He sat down near the pot boiling on the gas stove, rolled a cigarette with one hand, lighted it, and blew the blue smoke through his cleft lip in a way which children often requested to observe. The smoke made a sheet that folded into several whirls rising up, which was very beautiful. A renowned storyteller he was, but tonight was no occasion for a story, not even a true one.

"Aiya! Pollak pak tunga." I am visiting, said Ungarpaluq, swaying his parka when he entered, as if to shake off imaginary snow. He was a famed hunter, reputed to have spent two days and one night motionless above *allu*, the breathing hole a seal makes through the ice, before harpooning the seal and taking it out with one pull, in the way of *nanuk*, the polar bear. When he sat down his movements were slow, as if harnessing his might. He stretched his legs and remained calm, as always.

Last came Quapagnuq. (It is certain he had killed two Dene Indians while hunting caribou near the Churchill river last year.) "Somebody comes visiting, as it happens." They shook hands with Minik, raising them eyes-high and bending their heads. Quapagnuq sat down, lifted his parka, and scratched his belly. Last fall he had shot a polar bear. With one bullet.

They were all here, now, all twelve hunters of the village confident enough to face the mightiest predator in the world, the only one known to attack a man without hesitation. *Nanuk*, the eternal wanderer, would meet one of these men, and the man would not show fear and would even deny that a word for retreat can be found in his Inuit language. Even in the secret abyss of his mind a seed of doubt about that had not been allowed to sprout.

In that prefabricated house, shipped in by the government from Churchill, the hunters sat in a circle on the floor of wooden planks. The house had been made Eskimo-cozy by the odor of men, by hanging skins, fur clothing, and fox traps on the walls, and by the steam rising from a large pot. The smell of boiling caribou meat, *tuktuk*, and seal blubber, *muktuk*, added to the well-controlled excitement which showed only in the eyes of the men, not on their weathered, powerful faces. Theirs were the faces of men who have not known chiefs, headmen, or almighty gods. The pieces of *muktuk* curled, and the hostess, Tutiaq, assessed their tenderness by piercing them through with a stick. Her rosy cheeks and permanent smile revealed her happiness at being able to host this occasion by offering the best to the best.

Then Minik, her husband, rose up and talked with gravity, the way a host and hunter of his great reputation is supposed to talk. "One wishes you can lower yourself to taste the poor carcass this *Inuk*—*koak*, old man—can offer you." He hung his head down, letting his long hair fall over his face. Not one hair was gray. "It is inedible," he continued, "and you would show me kindness if you'll leave me now with my shame and my useless woman. *Uvanga okrartunga*, I have spoken."

Upon this invitation the men started to eat. The chunk of steaming meat was passed around. Each man bit into it, cut it with a knife in front of his lips, and passed the meat to his neighbor. They smacked their lips and praised this incomparable delicacy. When the succulent *muktuk* made the rounds, they farted politely and belched, to show they were digesting with appreciation.

"*Umm! Mammaraii?*" Delicious; what makes it so good? mumbled Kaviuk, the simple man, his strange face serious, his eyes mere slits, his mouth open. "Ace, ace," he said, as was his habit of saying on many occasions, not only when playing cards, his passion. He could not talk well; "ace" he would say when things were good. And times were good for him often, because the diminished powers of his mind did not allow him to comprehend well the causes of adversities in life. He was not laughed at because he showed abilities to survive the harshness of the arctic, because he understood the hunt, and dogs, and friendship.

Dogs were "aces." While he made dogs with a whip, he made friends with kindness and helping hands, not with wit or speaking, in both of which he possessed only the rudiments. He understood stealth in the hunt and the value of a bullet. So he survived, did Kaviuk. "Umm, umm," he said, and licked his lips and wiped the grease off his fingers in his hair.

Nobody else talked; their thoughts were ahead of them, on the drawing for *nanuk*. When the last piece of meat—of *tuktuk* and of succulent *muktuk*—had disappeared, nobody dozed off, as is the custom sometimes. No story was offered. Tutiaq moved to the corner, trimmed the lamp, and lighted herself that which banishes weariness—a pipe. Then Minik, with calculated carelessness, tossed a can from Dunhill tobacco into the middle of the circle of men. Twelve small bones of equal size from the flippers of a seal rattled in the can, announcing the draw. The men looked at the can, not at each other, wondering, perhaps, about their chances.

Great Ungarpaluq picked up the can: "It will not be just if such a lame half-blind man would draw the black bone. *Nanuk* would be safe, and the village sad. So one will draw." He opened the lid and, looking away, he pulled out a white bone. He put the lid on and passed the can to Totterat, clockwise, the direction stories are always told. The hopeful dream came to an end; his face showed no emotion, of course.

Totterat briefly commented on his lack of hunting skills (mostly true), drew a white one too, and passed the can further. And so it went around, all the men drawing white bones, none commenting on his misfortune. One-but-last was Kaviuk. He understood the meaning of this lottery and showed excitement by wheezing and inhaling deeply after each hunter pulled the bone out of the can. He could not manage a speech when opening the can, as others before him had done. He tilted his head far back, staring at the ceiling with an open mouth, while his hand reached into the can and pulled out the seal bone stained black with a mixture of oil and lamp soot.

It lay on his palm while he looked at it. His fingers closed into a tight fist over the bone, so tight his knuckles became white. A strange sound came from him; then he looked at the other men. "Ace," he whispered.

The men nodded their heads. "*Namakto*," very good, Minik said after a while and pointed to Kaviuk with an outstretched arm. All the men said "Eh, eh, eh," then, and did not reveal their thoughts.

✳

Kaviuk stayed awake that night. He sat on a pile of discarded skins in his shelter, which was not the Government's prefabricated house but a toolshed left in Eskimo Point by a group of astronomers who had come to observe an eclipse of the sun there years ago. He held his 30/30 carbine in one hand; the other still clutched tightly over the black seal bone. It was still predawn, the eastern horizon tinted faintly green above the pink outline of the distant vastness of the tundra, when Kaviuk emerged from his shed in the only caribou parka he owned, sealskin shoes, and *kamiks*, to step noiselessly over ground hardened by the morning freeze. His carbine was slung on his back horizontally with the rope strap over his chest in the Eskimo way.

His steps were certain, his direction clear, toward a small hill about a mile from the village. He bypassed carefully two large circles of stones, reminders from ancient times when they had weighted down the skin tents of his forefathers. Near the summit of the hillock he stopped, turned around, and scanned the landscape around the village and along the shore. The flat and barren ground could not conceal the whiteness of a polar bear for miles; there was no snow, yet. The light was sufficient; no *nanuk* in sight.

There were two graves just under the summit of the hill, a favorite place for Kaviuk to sit on summer evenings. Villagers thought he came there to ask for wisdom from his ancestors to improve his feeble mind. Through the stones and broken driftwood he could observe a skull, bones, a deck of cards, the rusted head of an axe, and the shaft of a harpoon. He bent down, looked at the hollow eyes of the skull, and smiled as if meeting a friend. This time he did not sit down but continued to climb the few yards to the top of the hill. The other side of the hill gently sloped down to a small lake. It was covered with a rubble of boulders, dwarf willows not higher than a foot, berry bushes now heavy with fruit, and pillows of moss.

They saw each other at the same instant, and the polar bear, without a moment of hesitation, started toward Kaviuk at a rapid pace. The hunter stood erect and calm. He took his rifle off and cocked it. That was the only moment his eyes left the animal. At fifteen yards the man called: "*Audlar mat!*" One has arrived! The bear raised his might up on his hind-paws, walking like a man, showing his enormity, two thousand pounds of power at an awesome height and wrath. *Tara i tualak*: he-who-is-without-shadow. *Tara i tulak.*

60

Kaviuk aimed his carbine, then, and shot him through the heart. He had been told many times that cartridges are expensive, that he must aim calmly. He did not reload, did not move; his weapon remained pointed at the bear. The bear dropped on all fours and charged forward. It collapsed with a moan at the feet of the motionless man, the true Inuk.

That is how the villagers found them. Great Ungarpaluq took the rifle from Kaviuk's hands and put it on the ground carefully. Then he slapped Kaviuk's back: "*Namakto, namakto!*" Children came. They romped around, yelling, pointing imaginary guns at the carcass.

Women came. They talked and laughed in groups. Their faces were very happy. They were deciding, perhaps, which of them would visit the shed tonight. The toolshed left by *quabluna* astronomers.

Then the men of the village came. Some slapped their thighs; some checked the fur and teeth of the *nanuk*. They all slapped Kaviuk's back, one by one. All of them.

Loss of an Enemy

Life is made of stories, not atoms
—Muriel Rukeyser

Life was very good. There were smiles, and happiness was on the faces of everyone in the classroom. The air-raid siren sounded like sweet music to them, because it was "preparation" and because it was afternoon. And "preparation"—the long, uninterrupted howl of the siren when it sounded after the noon hour meant that they would all go home and not need to return that day for classes. No more torturing math, no more history or Czech grammar, so incomprehensible to natives and occupiers alike.

Maybe the "acute" would follow: a series of short, undulating wails of the siren, announcing that American planes were actually high above the city, silvery beautiful birds from a faraway unimaginable world, on their way to Germany for a bombing raid. Creeping home from school, the students would be showered with Christmas decorations falling like snow over the alleys and the grim streets and the roofs of ancient buildings, glistening on the grass and linden trees of nearby parks. And free for the taking. Those thin strips of aluminum foil released from the planes were supposed to confuse the radar, but also, Peter was quite sure, were intended to be saved for Christmas—to adorn the spruce, to be scattered over its branches decorated with real candles, candies, and magic glass balls. Even the wire star at the top could be improved by American aluminum.

Today the explosions of anti-aircraft artillery boomed from the distance, and that was good news, too. The artillery had never harmed the aircraft anyway. Twelve-year-old Peter could see clearly the puffs of explosions, well below the planes. But exploding shrapnel was made of handsome material—shining bronze fragments fell back on the city, still hot. Sometimes, with luck, nice pieces could be found, with letters or numbers on the shiny surface. Such a find was of real value. With careful bargaining, it could be exchanged for marbles, even for the yellow ones (but almost never for the glass ones with colored stripes inside).

Peter was not lucky today. On the way home from school there were no fragments of shrapnel and only one small bunch of aluminum strips, which he stuck in the pocket of his short pants. He found the bunch near his apartment house in Marinenstrasse, a peaceful street of unchanging moods and changing but not peaceful names. Before the occupation, it had been known as Vedun Street, after the Battle of Vedun in France. During the occupation, it was named after Marinen—the German Navy.

For Peter it never changed. He knew every single pavement stone there—the few missing ones were in his room. They contained precious fossils such as orthoceras, graptolites, and even part of a real trilobite (extracted from the sidewalk across the street from his apartment). He knew every acacia tree there, having climbed almost all of them for the blossoms, which tasted like honey and were "good for the lungs," as Grandma had taught him. He often wondered how different the trees were from pictures he knew of acacias under Kilimanjaro, shading the olive-colored baboons from the scorching sun of East Africa. The sun was a rare visitor to Marinenstrasse, so the crowns of acacias there were ragged with leaves more gray than green.

He entered the apartment house, closed the main door, and looked around to be sure nobody could see him doing a task he thought to be pretty humiliating. He had to change his clothes fast before being seen by his mother. The hated brown, thigh-high stockings were rolled under his knees and held there with a red rubber band originally intended to be used under the lids of glass containers for canning marmalades and compotes. Now the rubber band went into his pocket, and his stockings were rolled back up under his short pants, where they were attached to the passionately hated garter. Those indescribable rubber devices for attaching stockings were broken, so the smallest of coins, one heller, had to be used in joining the stockings to the garter. Then he removed his cotton V-necked sweater and pulled it back over his head again, only this time backwards, on purpose.

Breathing heavily after this secret operation, Peter decided to have one more look at the street before going up the stairs to the apartment. And there he was—Hans—just in front of the house next door. Peter's reaction was swift. In a second, the stone was airborne in the direction of the unsuspecting German. He missed him by quite a bit, almost two feet. Since many stone projectiles had left Peter's practiced hand in the past, and since stone-throwing was considered to be one of the very basic, almost primitive skills in the Bubenec section of Prague, the miss by two feet must have been intentional.

"Czechishe Schweinhunde!" screamed Hans, surprised, as his eye caught the parabola of a stone flying by. "Czechishe Schweinhunde!" Czech pig-dog. Swine-dog. What a nonsensical animal, Peter thought. To be called swine would be pretty offensive, so much that revenge, or better a swift attack, would be required, to maintain some degree of honor—especially if a third person were around. But swine-dog? What to do about the "Czech" part? The "Czech" part made it so much less personal. It made this offensive call just a sort of political, all-encompassing statement, and therefore of lesser impact on a pragmatic twelve-year-old's mind.

Hans began his approach. It was a strange attack. The beginning was indecisive, and a careful observer would have noticed hesitancy in Hans's steps. And Peter was a careful observer. He recognized that Hans's attack was a ritualistic response, and thus he responded in a ritualistic withdrawal to the door. The exaggerated and faked expression of fear on his face changed in seconds to an aggressive sneer as pronounced and perfected as only a Kabuki actor could perform. With the sneer, just in front of the door, Peter turned to face the approaching Hans. "So come on, chicken, come on, you shitty coward."

Hans stopped on the spot. He expected to be stopped anyway, his face vainly trying to contort into hate. There they stood, a few feet apart, under a gray sky deserted by the migrating bombers. In the echo of the last howl of the siren, their aggression somehow abated.

The scene did not resemble a Diane Arbus photograph. One might think more of a painting in Norman Rockwell's style, but in a rather grim mood. Their hair had no color, just sort of brownish, washed only once a week, on Saturdays. Their faces had no trace of tan—spring had not yet descended into the depths of Marinenstrasse. Their stomachs longed for a better future—better than dry bread dipped in chicory coffee for a smoother trip through the esophagus, better than daily dinners of mashed potatoes, with chopped onions fried in lard and poured over them for some taste. Two hearts, beating fast now, ready for acceleration. Two brains, seats of two pretty gentle souls, laboring hard on the decision for action, since action must follow this stand-off, and soon.

Many times before, Peter and Hans had performed this routine. By now the rules were well established and were followed with only small deviations. They both knew how "real" enemies should behave. Peter, with the threatening mask still on his face, initiated a mock counterattack; Hans performed a short retreat. And that was enough for today.

In the evening, supposedly doing his homework assignment for school, Peter allowed himself a few pleasant daydreams. He liked the one about the handgun the most. Peter had found a revolver in the bushes of Stomovka Park. Wrapped in oiled cloth, in perfect condition, its white, opaque mother-of-pearl handle and blue steel barrel gave him a feeling of great power and excitement. On the way home, that luckiest of days, Peter had met Hans again in Marinenstrasse.

Hans must have sensed that things were different that day. He had

retreated right away to the entrance to his apartment house, with surprise on his face, watching carefully every move of his adversary. Peter's
steps were springy. He felt a thrilling feebleness in his knees, though, and
could barely suppress the urge to sing from happiness.

He had also forgotten, for the first time, about the rituals, about all
the apprehensions and pleasant fears of Hans. Just when he had passed
Hans, at a safe distance, as was the custom, he made a decision. As he
walked away from him, he pulled the gun from his pocket, looked at it
with admiration, turned around, and slowly—as slowly as his control
would allow—pointed the gun at Hans, right at Hans's face. Perhaps only
a master painter could recreate the expression on that boy's face: not only
fear but admiration for the winner, the conqueror—Peter the Great.

Life is so nice, Peter thought, and decided to replay this "movie" in
his mind each night before falling asleep—with new variations.

In the following weeks Peter and Hans, the enemies, continued their
rites without ever touching each other, repeated their endless offenses
without ever feeling offended. They never talked, but they became an
important part of each other's daily lives. Peter had to assure himself,
often with an effort, that he hated the miserable Kraut. Sometimes he
even felt he had succeeded in hating Hans but wished to be more sure
about it.

Then came the end of the war and with it a revolution erupted in the
country. While Russian tanks roared over the border, crushing the feeble
resistance of the Germans, people rose up with an unparalleled excitement.

Barricades dammed the streets, weapons hidden for five years
appeared in the hands of clerks, bakers, grandfathers. Smoke filled the air
and gunshots and explosions reverberated from the gothic arches of
churches, rattling the ancient stained glass windows, killing Germans and
Czechs, puzzling children, thrilling teenagers, saddening mothers. Remnants of SS troops cut breasts off women in the Vrsovice quarter, exe-
cuted hundreds in front of their wives and children in Pankrac, burned
the ancient city hall in Stare Mesto. The Czech revolutionary guards shot
to death whole families of German civilians forced to swim over
Smetana's Moldau, near the suburb of Podbaba.

Peter listened to the news with fear and a child's astonishment. He
guarded Marinenstrasse from the window of his apartment, all those
days. One afternoon an unknown youngster was crossing the street.
Peter saw two soldiers kneel down, and when the echo of gunshots sub-
sided the boy was dead, strangely curled, with one arm reaching in
Peter's direction. That evening Peter saw his father being led home by
German soldiers with guns on his back, his arms high above his head.
Peter's father was an admirable man, strong-willed. He would never bow

to Germans. He would never raise his arms about his head. And yet, here he was, surrendering.

During those four days of the uprising, the Russians reached Prague. At that time in history, they were cheered and welcomed with flowers and joy. They rode in on giant tanks—primitive machines with wood mallets to shift gears. The suntanned faces of the Russians, wide with victory smiles, were admired by Peter and all his friends. The soldiers ate butter, real butter, from one hand and tore pieces of white bread from the other. They drank any alcohol they could get, and when drunk enough, drank gasoline and died. They stole watches, and many wore several on their forearms. In Marinenstrasse, a Russian soldier stole a bicycle from an old woman and was shot to death by his officer.

Another Russian visited Peter's home, to everybody's great excitement. He had the expression and the tired, kind manner of Peter's favorite teacher. He showed Peter the worn, tinted photograph of his twin daughters—in pigtails—he hoped to find still at home. Peter liked him because he was a plain soldier and not one of the officers who set a court in the yard of Peter's old primary school. The court was just a long row of classroom benches. There the officers sat, facing the German soldiers brought in front of them. After sentence was pronounced, the German was walked to the back of the yard and shot. Gunfire from the barricades was not heard in the streets and squares any more, only from the elementary school. They were single shots, at regular intervals.

Peter got a piece of real chocolate from his dad's friend. It was dark brown, with an exotic sweetness and the aroma of a tropical paradise. Father and Mother were happy most of the time now, and Peter liked to watch them smile. They enjoyed listening to the radio, which played dance music all day. The acacias on Marinenstrasse bloomed more profusely than ever, and the war was over.

"All Germans must be relocated. All must be sent back to Germany," announced the radio and the newspapers. War is no more; peace will come in the future, people thought. And they moved the Germans through the streets of the ancient city in long processions: bent women, children and old men with eyes turned down, sad suitcases, uncertain steps. Their presence alone disturbed the celebrations. A few infuriated passersby yelled hateful things at them.

Peter knew it was all true about the many unspeakable things done by the husbands of those women and the fathers of those children. So they had to be marched out of the city. Yes, they had to go and never return, to go where they belonged. And he was determined to be clear about this, despite their sad faces and worn suitcases. No, he must not feel confused—not even sad, God forbid.

On May 14, it drizzled all day. It was not windy, but the humid cold made one pull up his collar and warm his hands in his pockets. Blossoms on the acacias hung sadly wet. People were rushing home with thoughts of a warm stove and hot soup. At five o'clock Peter was coming home from Ural Park and wondering where all his friends were. School was out, and there was nobody in the park, just a few insignificant little kids. Near home, in Marinenstrasse, he lingered awhile, hoping that somebody might pass by to be coerced into a game of marbles or into planning an expedition to big Stromovka Park. It was still too early to go upstairs.

From around the corner, a procession appeared. Peter knew who they were—he had seen German civilians marching to detention and repatriation centers before. Today, again, they were accompanied by a couple of young Revolutionary Guards with rifles on their shoulders. This time it was a big group, a few hundred people.

They walked slowly, dragging their suitcases and rucksacks, not looking up. They seemed to concentrate on the road just in front of their feet. Their faces stressed the unreality of this situation, this event without precedent in this middle class, orderly, and pleasantly unexciting neighborhood. Peter decided to go inside the apartment house. He was alone in the street and did not feel enough courage to watch alone.

As the grim procession approached, he changed his mind. At the far end of the formation, something was happening. An older man was gesticulating and shouting. He was not one of the Germans. It was clear he had survived many beers that day, and he was stumbling around, kicking the suitcase of an elderly woman who was barely keeping pace with the others. Peter opened the door of his apartment house and stood there, waiting to go upstairs yet at the same time compelled to watch.

The end of the procession approached, with the drunkard shouting and the old woman still barely holding onto her possessions. Next to the woman walked Hans—shabby jacket too small to fit him, a shawl around his neck, and a cap, a worker's cap Peter had never seen on him before. His head was bent down, staring in front of him, his little boy's body bent to one side to keep his vulcanite suitcase off the pavement.

A light drizzle was still falling on the city. It was getting dark. People were coming home from work now. They did not seem to pay attention to anything. They walked by quietly.

All Peter saw now was the small figure of Hans, framed in the misery of the street, slowly fading away as the procession disappeared. Climbing the stairs he felt a heaviness and an unknown pain in his chest. In his room his scream was muted by the pillow; then it changed to sobs and, finally, the relief of sleep.

It is known that Peter woke up the next morning but that one part of him did not. That part did not die but rather remained alive in his dreams. Nothing is known about the dreams of his enemy.

Infallible Weapon of Temptation

To avoid plunging down through the clouds God must wear snowshoes, even in Summer.
- St. Jardace "Pragensis"

The routines of Vance Pepper had to be reformed. He had to interrupt the fifteen years of grant applications, committee meetings, and the sweet safety of tenured existence at the University of Minnesota. And Africa could do it, reliably, by its beauty, horrors and the induction of awe. Tonight it would be the awe.

He carried the mug of white coffee and a pack of real American cigarettes onto the balcony; the ashtray of bamboo joint half-filled with sand was already there. His Polish neighbors had made it for him.

"We'll have a rain-party, my acro-bats!" He screamed at the bats, then howled like a wolf, knowing that nobody but bats could hear him, since the downpour reverberated with such a deafening roar. Vance loved the tropical rain. It painted a spastic smile on his face, increased his heart rate, and always induced in him a sort of frenzied yearning for a party. It is a desire of the white intellectual alone in West Africa, left unfulfilled, usually. Lonely alone, most of the waking time.

At his forty years he was in reasonably good shape, trained and ready for his African year. In spite of two club feet which sentenced him to life in orthopedic shoes, he could wobble a mile. He moved slowly but without a cane or crutches on his malformed feet, using quite efficiently his insufficient calves to shuffle wherever it was necessary. When people learned about his professorship in Minnesota they wondered how he could get around in five feet of snow. He invited them over to see— and to experience—life in civilization. In his social intercourse his wavering locomotion would be fast forgotten because of the velocity and sharpness of the workings of his mind and sheer mass of his intellect. His wit was of the easy sophomoric kind, his smile and laughter unguarded and profuse.

Ladies' man? It was almost profane how he demonstrated to women the power of brain over the power of biceps, glutei magni and pectorals. Women of all ages looked at his smile, those angelic brown curls (graying at the temples) and listened with fascination to his pronouncements, rarely lowering their sight to his orthopedic shoes. Women of all different subspecies liked him; even castrating American businesswomen loved him. Somehow they knew his disorder had not adversely affected his anatomy above the knees, at the least. Ladies' man? Feminist!

Vance had been in Ile-Ife for six months on his sabbatical to the local University, teaching genetics and mathematical methods to medical students. He liked the students for their devotion to studies and their lack of cynicism; they were against cannibalism and most of them opposed human sacrifice, too. However, he could not understand their intolerance of people with inborn defects of sexual development, their regarding the bonobo and chimpanzee as only bush-meat, their belief that gorillas "rape our women." So while developing some sympathy for many, Vance could not develop a truly close rapport with them; they seemed, sometimes, to be of a different planet. He could touch only their surface, the surface warm to touch and made of smiles. Still, they were the richest crème de la crème of the jungle-towns of West Africa; they learned the science. And they admired their Professor Pepper.

While his students and the Department's staff were friendly and outgoing, his best friends became fruit bats, the Poles next door and Anezi Ukwu, the school's carpenter.

In Ile-Ife, bats were his friends from the beginning. Fruit bats in thousands gathered in the rookery, or "bat-tery", on three enormous dogon-yaru trees in front of his balcony. For hours he observed their upside-down social life, nursing their babies upside down, wrapping themselves in the cloak of their membranous wings against the daily rains—rows of organic pouches on the branch, emitting squeaks in high frequencies, some higher than castrati, with meanings hidden but making the dogon-yarus alive. In vain he warned them of approaching youngsters who would shoot them down with slingshots, since his friends were edible. Those who suffered perforations of their wings by stony projectiles died the saddest death. "Flying foxes" some called them, despite their faces which resembled Doberman Pinschers, not foxes, and despite their diet which was strictly vegetarian. Vance was spying, hoping to see a bat albino, an anyale, born because then, it had been rumored, the local "big man" would die. So far no luck, and the bad "big man" of Ile-Ife still had people sacrificed, drove his fleet of Mercedes through begging lepers, built himself more mansions in the forest, and bought parking ramps in London, all of it with the USAID greenbacks. Vance wished to be the "Batman of Ile-Ife."

Then there were the Poles. Four of them, friendly, living in Vance's guest house. They all taught in the University, each one an expert in a different discipline but all masters of repair. They salvaged and repaired

University equipment thrown away because of malfunction— computers that had crashed, non-transmitting telephones, generators which did not start, air conditioners which blew hot air, furniture which tilted and swayed. They liked their American, Vance, as women adore men who need their help. "Vance, you have both hands left," they said, and built him a shelf in front of the vent of the air conditioner for vegetables to keep cool. They brought him a fixed laboratory hot plate so he could make his instant coffee, and got him a bicycle assembled from parts salvaged from the dump—with Polish-made bamboo handle bars. It was a trial for Vance to relearn to ride—even with the modified peddles to fit his large triangular orthopedic shoes, worthy of Frankenstein.

"Shut up and try it! Don't be a pussy! Move your ass! You can do it!" They held his seat and ran next to him, until he made it and managed to ride the bike alone few yards. When he made a turn and stopped without falling they screamed some incomprehensible Polish and laughed; one slapped his back, another shook his hand seriously. Peter hugged him and Jacek hugged him, too. At such a time the African life became less of a problem and more of a pleasure. The Poles were important.

And Anezi Ukwu.

Anezi the carpenter was an Igbo in Yoruba-land, a stranger here, an interloper in a way. He understood the properties of different tropical woods, and was a master of his craft, carpentry—a natural. He felt good among the Yoruba since nobody in Ile-Ife knew about his secret, his origin, a son of two slaves back in Enugu. He cultivated a semblance of friendship with Vance for the distinction of being the pal of a white man, but soon, he started to like the *onya acha* ("pale eyes"), and before long sensed the sympathy was mutual. Vance understood him well, being an outsider himself. And thus their friendship developed easily, became saprophytic, even conspiratorial, at times. He was a kind person, too, Anezi Ukwu—and nothing more needed to be said about the man.

The rainy season drew to an end; the Harmattan wind from Sahara brought microscopic red dust to cover everything, nights became bearable without air conditioning, bats started to deliver their babies upside down, and an overgrowth of several species of molds and fungi appeared on Vance's orthopedic shoes. Some seams started to separate, and softened leather began to stretch out of shape, threatening a disaster. Without his special shoes his mobility would cease and his African academic adventure would be over. Also over would be the incipient affair with that physical wonder, Ngozi Amadiume (facilitated by faithful Anezi). Who would watch and warn the bats, the most graceful of flyers, and instruct his students, the most grateful of disciples?

The Poles couldn't help—their multiple talents did not include either orthopedics or cobbling. Physicians of the Medical School also had no clue. But Anezi Ukwu knew everything.

"Prof, you might have new shoes made by the monk. He is a miracle maker, everybody says."

"Monk who, Anezi? I need special shoes!"

"Up the river, give or take a day's navigation. With an outboard. The mission has been there—like forever."

"They don't make shoes, those missionaries, they make sort-of Christians. Don't they?"

"You funny, prof. But this one monk, he great man. He makes artificial legs and new feet of wood and leather, and hands and arms, too, he can! He uses iroko wood, I know." Carpenter Anezi smiled, imagining iroko hardwood. "People say he might be a saint. A saint!"

"Do you think, Anezi, he might help a white man, not a poor man, you know....?"

"I am sure of it, Prof. Saints have been helping the white man always, more than the black man. Even kids know that." Anezi laughed, self-amused, and shook Vance's hand, to soften the truth which seemed hard to him, maybe. He produced his widest smile displaying the orthodontist's dreams, and moved away on feet which would elate the orthopedic specialist.

Vance inquired further and in a few days he was on his way up the river. He left at dawn when the bats returned from their feeding grounds to the home trees.

"Take your malaria pills, man, you don't want to pee the black piss! And come back soon," Jacek the Pole said, helping him, with Anezi Ukwu, into the narrow dugout with a Johnson outboard fastened to the stern transom with wires. Ukwu threw a packet of roasted groundnuts into the boat. Vance waved back and the boat cut through the tepid, tea-like water, the color of cinnamon bark. A few kites, the flying scissors, looped on the lead sky, raptors as seemingly carefree as the few fishermen who propelled their vessels with splashless, deliberate strokes of heart-shaped paddles. Vance wondered about the meaning of the hearts stabbing the river: a good omen, perhaps.

"I like the paddles of the fishers," he said to Chukwuemeka, his captain and navigator, whose blue face was happy to be off firm land. "Will we get there today?"

"Yes, Massa," Chukwuemeka retorted. "About four hours. We'll be there in four hours ... if Johnson good."

Vance, knowing the natives' disregard for matters of chronometry, doubled the estimate and, indeed, in about eight hours, a scattering of lights larger than fireflies and the fluorescent thoraces of tropical click beetles appeared from the deep darkness of the jungle, on starboard. The mission, no doubt. It took a while for Chukwuemeka to find the landing, where they disembarked. Vance wobbled and staggered up a slight incline to a low stucco building. The noise of the insects astonished and excited him—the forest around the mission roared. Vance was surprised by a flood of feeling; he was an adventurer, an African explorer! He whistled thinly, to his rhythmless waggly steps. His shoes, the demise of which had brought him to this outpost, held together still fairly well.

In a stark room with a table, an old typewriter, a pile of papers on it, two chairs, and electric light which worked, Vance was welcomed by an old white man in a nondescript off-white habit. The first sentences the monk pronounced seemed to be in Italian, apparently his native tongue; then came German, and finally Spanish. When Vance interrupted with his native tongue, the monk smiled nicely and with a British accent told him he knew about his visit but not his origins. His sleeping quarters were ready. They shook hands.

Chukwuemeka followed with Vance's duffel bag into a cell with a bed under a good-looking mosquito net, a washbasin, and a stool. "Good night, Massa," he said with head bent as if apologizing, and vanished.

It was a cool night with an orchestra of jungle tunes unknown to any city. His head was full of thoughts which prevented sleep, and the stars shone dream-like through the mesh of the mosquito net, until the dream took over.

✳

Next morning, Vance was seated at the table, admiring the two pretty kitchen girls more than the mush of unknown grains he had been given as breakfast, when the monk appeared, his habit apparently unchanged.

"Doctor Pepper, I presume." The monk smiled, amused by his pun, remembering Livingstone. "I am Father Fabricius. We'll speak English?" His slender but sinewy hand reached out for a firm handshake.

"Vance Pepper is my name, very nice to meet you, sir… Father…Fabricius."

Only briefly did the men look into each others' eyes, because the monk lowered his professional gaze to Vance's feet. He saw the problem, raised his eyes, and a smile crossed his leathery face. It was difficult to judge his age, since malaria, hepatitis and different parasitemias had left their indelible marks in the parchment-like pallor of his cheeks and hollowed them, too. Around sixty years—with some optimism.

Vance pointed at his shoes: "Charcot-Marie-Tooth syndrome Type I, Father, the autosomal dominant variant with clavovarus and hallux clava caused by peripheral demyelination." He raised his shoulders in apologetic gesture.

"Two club feet, is all," the monk nodded, and motioned Vance to follow. "Old shoes need much wax, they say in Sweden. But wax will not help you, good doctor, you'll need more than a wax."

In a little cubicle, which might have been the "office" of Father Fabricius, they sat down.

"I got your message, Dr. Pepper. I was expecting you and your shoes. I can see they are falling apart."

"It's the humidity, Father. The leather seemed to become … like tissue culture media, for all these fungi and molds…"

"I know all about that."

"Well, as you might have guessed I came to ask for help." Vance studied the face of the monk, which revealed nothing. He sensed that the old man did not appreciate small talk, to which Vance had a tendency. "I came to ask you to make new shoes for me."

The monk did not react. Both men looked out of the small window. Somebody was singing in a distance; simple four tone repetitions, four tone repetitions, four tones… but in the room—silence, but for the feeble buzz of a fly.

"I see, you are a thinking man," the monk said quietly, "and so I propose to you to make your own shoes. It's possible." He nodded, agreeing with himself. "You must have heard that God helps those who help themselves!" A sarcastic grin appeared on his face. Here in the jungle, helping kids with chopped-off hands and arms, and blown-away legs, he must have learned that his God's wisdom was not infinite but finite and His intentions, often, suspect. Vance started to feel at ease, hoping that the monk might be a man of reason. He was ready to accept the old man's wisdom.

"To make the shoes myself? Sir… Father? All I can make is instant coffee. And tea!"

"I would teach you the basics in fourteen days… but on the condition that you obey."

The men let the silence rule. The monk talked first: "Between saying and doing many a pair of shoes is often worn out. Italians say that. But we will not wear out a pair of shoes, since you will have to decide now. If you agree, we'll start immediately." The monk looked victorious, knowing the wisdom of his reasoning.

In life one has to consider two dangers when making a decision: the danger of deciding swiftly, in a blink of an eye, and the danger of failing to do so and missing the boat. Vance decided. The boat with Chukwuemeka would return to Ile-Ife without its passenger. Vance started sharpening knives.

"The knives must be sharp enough to cut loosely hanging hair. Sharp as a razor blade, not a kitchen knife." The monk expressed disapproval by this announcement at the end of the first day. "Tomorrow you'll continue sharpening. I'll show you how to sharpen the bent-handle shears, too."

So two days of sharpening until the hair, hanging loosely from the grip of forefinger and thumb, was cut in front of the victorious, though tired, smile of the disciple. Then came the waxing of the threads, since "glazed" threads and cotton-wrapped polyester were either too expensive or unobtainable in the forest.

"They must slip through the hide with minimum friction, Professor, since the wedge-point needle, or this one, the sailmaker's glover, will make the hole small and neat enough. For a perfect job we wouldn't use the awl or stiletto, would we? Right?"

"Right," Vance said, feeling like an ultimate yes-man, a slave-like sharpener and waxer, waiting for praise like a dog—and surprised that he somewhat liked this feeling, which he had never experienced in his life. He wanted to please badly, to be praised, and at the end of his third day he got it. The approving smile on the leathery face he would always remember.

The dinner that third evening was better to be forgotten (bush-meat of unknown provenance), but what followed was pure pleasure. To the tune of a jungle concerto of night insects, reading *The Stranger* by Albert Camus evoked the memories of some thirty years ago, when juvenile Vance read the tome for the first time and was fascinated. He remembered his impression clearly—but had forgotten why he was so excited, then. So when he discovered the yellowed book in the mission's library he did not hesitate. He found out why he had been excited decades ago: Camus, the Nobel laureate, dared to write as close to the truth as possible and still be published. Vance wanted to discuss it, to marvel aloud, to be with another reader—but there was only a silent, honey-colored cockroach watching him from the corner like a hypnotist.

Vance yearned for music other than the one supplied by the rain forest: Hayden, Janacek, the Beatles. What first? "Let's start with the McCartneys' 'Uncle Albert'," he ordered aloud. But the beetles of the jungle did not oblige. To calm down, Vance talked to himself quietly and soon he was whispering… He counted the antelope … and fell asleep, despite the forte of the jungle's molto agitato.

On the fourth day he stepped barefoot into clay, and the plaster casts of his feet were made by Sebastian, an apprentice.

Vance worked without being aware of time, from unvarying meal to meager meal, without complaint. He had to steel himself to endure; no brooding, even when the small failures accumulated. Sebastian, a half-naked, one-legged teenager with a protruding umbilical hernia, was always at hand and handy; he even slept at the workshop on his cot in the corner, under a poster of Cassius Clay. His prosthetic leg was made of crimson tropical wood with a beautiful, vertical grain, resembling the ocean's waves painted by Hiroshige. Often, Sebastian oiled and polished his "leg" to the semi-gloss sheen of a red clarinet. The foot-ending of the prosthesis was fashioned of a rubber toilet plunger. In the morning, when the night humidity precipitated on the concrete floor, the lipstick-red plunger made sucking sounds like smacking kisses. The romance of Sebastian!

But the apprentice did not speak a word of any European languages, so his communication with Vance became a matter of hands rather than tongues. They developed their own gestures and signs, some primitive and common, such as hands in the air and eyes on the ceiling signifying failure. Their daily pantomimes lacked audience and applause, amusing only the mimes themselves.

The fifth day was the day of carving the "models," forms of his feet from a soft wood. He helped Sebastian, feeling like a sculptor.

The sixth day he started to create the upper from an elephant's belly skin, with the help of Father Fabricius himself. That was the most demanding and complex labor yet. Vance marveled at his master's hands working with maniacal perfection, with millimetric control of his moves. "When I see you working, Father, I remember Rubinstein playing piano," Vance said.

"'More than a hood and sad face is necessary to make a monk.' Albanian proverb, you know." The monk turned the corners of his pale lips down, making a mock sad face, followed by a smile. Was it a smile?

For all the blasphemer he was, on the seventh day Vance rested. During the next week, he progressed to making the sole, lining and "orthotic," and hemming the upper, which he found to be a surprisingly delicate phase of the construction and for which he received praise from the master. He learned about skins and hides, the theory of their tanning, dying, padding and curing. How delightfully distant he found himself from the theories of mutation rates, the founder effect, and the Smirnoff-Kolmogorov non-parametric test for small numbers! He touched and felt the obscene smoothness of the leather, smelled the hot cobbler's glue like a lover smells a tulip, with eyes closed.

"An item of footwear is a creation of aspiration and imagination. With practice, Professor, you would progress and you could cover your feet with art. Yours should not—and will not—be impudent shoes." The monk imagined himself on the pulpit. "They might not be the mukluks of Eskimos, with stitching as fine as invisible, or the getas of Japanese geishas with designs to be marveled at—or the ancient Egyptians' sandals of sparkling silver. But they will be your own creation. My Professor, your own!"

"I discovered part of myself I did not know… due to you, Father Fabricius. To my great pleasure, I have to add." He observed the cavernous face of the demigod of shoemaking with reverential awe.

"Well, shoes have more than one function. Your interest in the female staff of our kitchen, here in the mission, was not well concealed. I noticed." The monk closed his eyes as if avoiding a sinful view. He was celibate and so, because of his position in the mission, he was denied 'missionary positions' and other pleasurable feasts of love. He continued: "So, dear Professor, remember that perfect shoes can seduce, too. Italians don't call shoes 'the infallible weapon of temptation' for nothing." He raised his eyelids.

Both men laughed a forced laugh, knowing about the limitations of orthopedic shoes. Ortho-pedic.

It was time to leave; Chukwuemeka arrived for his passenger with only a day's delay, just before dawn. On the landing, in his new shoes, Vance offered money to the mission; it was a difficult moment.

"Worry none, my Professor. We are here to help."

When the monk heard that shoes like those they made would come to fourteen hundred dollars, his eyes widened in incomprehension: "Too distant a world for us … your world … but if you'd insist we'll take … twenty." He lowered his eyes to observe the red laterite ground.

Vance modified the sum upwards and gave it to the monk in a sealed envelope. He promised to return to report on the progress of his shoe-making. He thanked simply.

"Jews, the wise people, they say that if you stay at home, you won't wear out your shoes," the monk said with some sadness in his voice. "Come back!" he hollered and waved when the boat was taken away by the cinnamon current.

Vance felt a surge of long-forgotten happiness when the dugout turned behind a bend. The rising sun peeked above the canopy of the jungle, dividing the river sharply in black and silver streams. First the greetings of invisible birds, in different scales, sounded from the bush. The river smelled of the mist of dawn and the secret life in the deep.

Chukwuemeka smiled, with a chew-stick in his mouth, looking at the Johnson outboard for which the downstream going was easy. He smiled like happy people smile and inhaled deeply, in the morning cool of the jungle stream.

The white man looked at his boots. "An explosion of the creative genius of Vance Pepper, the Great Shoemaker," he whispered in self-admiration. "Beautiful as a triple rainbow over Fujiyama. Perhaps."

✳

At home in Ile-Ife, while Vance greeted his bats, Jacek knocked on the door. He brought a surprise: a boot rack made by his Polish friends. It was built of shiny green bamboo culms. In weeks yellow stripes would appear on them, get wider in time, and later fuse. The rack would turn sparkling yellow gold.

Promptly, Vance dispatched Anezi Ukwu around the town on his *okada* (motorized bike) in search of unusual and exotic skins. Soon, Ukwu, the shmoozer par excellence, with the aid of his multiple lovers, gathered glossy black spitting cobra skin, lightweight ostrich skin, and the most precious elephant ear with tiny indentations, the shoemaker's delight. The knives were made for Vance from a car spring by the ironman in the market. The work could start in making shoes of the rarest skins, putting the art in orthopedics. Vance Pepper remembered the "infallible weapon of temptation," shaking his head.

In the meantime, the Poles organized a welcoming party—the sign "Welcome Back Shoeman Showman" already hung over the entrance of the cafeteria in their guest house. The party started at the fall of dusk, at the time bats departed for their own parties at cashew plantations and mangosteen orchards, shitting happily, their wings whirring like a rush of susurrous whispers.

At the party, the main objects of admiration were two: Vance's new shoes and the newly invented drink, "Cobbler's Sunset." It consisted of distilled palm wine, a dash of passion fruit juice and a squeezed lime. It had to be drunk with lunatic velocity according to the Polish habit "do dna," which means "bottoms up," and results in general insobriety. All toasted to "shoemaker of miracles" and, later, "na zdrovie" and even later "to bats!"

Those Polacks, being in-your-face multiculturally sensitive, had invited several young ladies, distinct by their physical beauty and easy virtues. The young ladies did not drink or eat the "coconut candies for dandies" but asked for real food, like fu-fu of gari and pounded yams, pleading "*Aguru na gu mu!*" Hungry we are, hungry! The lovelies danced with uncommon fluidity, and clam-like happiness ruled until the small hours.

Vance, the celebrant, left arm around the shoulder of Jacek and right arm around the waist of one graceful Onuaku girl, calculated using chi-square that the probability was of the highest order of significance that the party in honor of a shoemaker and his new hoofs was the most exuberant and just the most goddamn wonderful blowout in all of the Yoruba-lands of West Africa, and beyond.

Collector of Light Bulbs

From an aerial view the chain of islands called the Florida Keys looks like a string of emeralds in the azure plain of the Caribbean—jewels with inclusions of settlements and the bridges connecting them. In the middle of May, the Royal Poinciana trees bloom incredibly red, as if their crowns were perpetually on fire, and Jamaica dogwoods (still leafless after the dry winter heat) cover themselves with light gray blossoms resembling styrofoam and never move in the wind. Then, after the first rain of the coming wet season, the thatch palms shoot new spikes of leaves skyward, and the glossy bark of Gumbo-limbo trees shines, brick-red, to justify the local name of "tourist trees" (since they remind some of the sunburnt skin of visitors from Minnesota).

It had been almost twenty years since the tourist had spent a vacation in the Keys, and he remembered it well, as if it had happened yesterday. He remembered the places where he had been diving, fishing from the bridge ... and the food, too: the key lime pie, the turtle soup, conch chowder, and fried grouper (his favorite).

This May he wandered again through Hemingway's house in Key West and withstood a Papa Double with two jiggers of rum in it at Sloppy Joe's Bar, rubbing elbows and shoulders with other tourists. Later that evening he found a cozy-looking bar well off Duval Street, with only a few visitors in bright T-shirts with colorful pictures of coral reef fish. "Development, AIDS, and drugs, my friend," his companion at the bar told him in a conspiratorial whisper, "coming from all over the Caribbean."

He ordered another couple of Coors for both of them. His companion waited for the bartender to move away, then stretched his arms like a fisherman describing his catch, and whispered, "Bales of *ganja* like this." He then ordered a shot of dark Bacardi and turned it into his beer mug. "Every night, man," and took a gulp with obvious satisfaction. "Things are dangerous on the Keys. Everything is changing for the worse." The old Conch was getting more pessimistic with each new round of Coors enriched with the dark Bacardi. Slowly his head bent lower until it rested, motionless, on the bar.

The next morning, the tourist left the crowded southernmost settlement of the U.S. for a scenic drive north. He planned to snorkel on the Gulf side, somewhere near one of the many bridges, then spend the night on Grassy Key. But first, he had to stop on the beach on the Atlantic side of Big Coppitt Key. He was looking forward to visiting the place where he had spent a few nights camping, years ago, where he used to look for washed-in mahogany boards.

It was difficult to find that place. There was a new road across Big Coppitt, but finally he located the remnants of Old Barbara's shack, which he remembered was near the beach. Old Barbara used to sell bait, Coke, chips, and candy bars there. Even here, off the main road, there were now houses with pink plastic siding, and developers were scraping the land to bare coral caprock, for still more building lots. He recognized the beach. There was the white sand strip. Parallel to it stretched the narrow but dense belt of red mangroves, and behind them the salt pond, full of water in high tide and half empty when it was low.

The beach had changed, too. It used to be clean, just some seaweed and clumps of turtle grass washed on it, and pieces of driftwood and a broken lobster trap or two. He used to find a few mahogany boards there, always wondering about whether they fell from a ship or were carried here by winds and sea currents, all the way from Honduras. Now there was plastic everywhere on the sandy beach—plastic bags, pieces of polyurethane foam, plastic bottles of all kinds, tangled pieces of nylon rope, a solitary condom here and there, odd rubber thongs. The look of it pained the tourist's heart. But at least he was finally alone. There was nobody around, as far as he could see—just a beat-up Datsun truck with a topper parked at the beginning of the beach.

It was a curious vehicle. The back gate was opened, windows down. Inside, one could see a pile of blankets, containers of different shapes, beer cans, and pieces of clothing. And in the front, there was barely space for a driver to squeeze in. On the roof of the topper a big doghouse was attached with a chicken wire door agape. When the tourist approached, he understood why the owner could have left the open pickup unattended. Tied on a long rope (fortunately), a German Shepherd charged, baring its teeth without a sound.

Giving the dog the widest berth, he passed it, walking down the deserted beach, stepping over debris, trying to avoid the occasional blobs of asphalt. It was high tide now. He inspected every board washed up on the beach, cutting into some with his knife to see the color and grain characteristic of mahogany. It was a beautiful knife with a rosewood handle and he kept it razor sharp and cradled in a handsomely worn leather sheath. But none of the boards showed the deep red, close-grained structure of the prized wood which, when polished well and soaked with linseed oil, would appear almost iridescent and feel like velvet to the touch.

Just before the beach ended, a man suddenly stood up from behind a Sea Lavender bush. He was naked, which was not obvious at first, since he was suntanned evenly, his shoulders the same dark hue as his buttocks. The tourist overcame his hesitation and continued walking, trying to look preoccupied with the junk on the beach. When he got closer to the man, they greeted each other and exchanged a few meaningless phrases.

The man looked at the tourist intently, never averting his eyes during their conversation. His rusty full mustache matched the color of his hair, which was quite long but not all the way to his shoulders, and was smoothly combed backwards. His liking for the sun was obvious, not only from his deep tan but also from the complicated map of wrinkles and creases on his face. Because of this, it was difficult to judge his age—maybe fifty or even sixty. His voice was youthful and clear, and he talked quietly, without any accent. The tourist complained about the litter on the beach, expecting to strike an accord with the man. But he did not seem to be of the same opinion.

"Yes, there are a lot of things on the sand. I find many bulbs here, mostly after a storm," he said, turning to the beach.

"You find bulbs?"

"Electric bulbs, light bulbs, *mi amigo*," the main explained. This "*mi amigo*" puzzled the tourist for a moment, but he was more curious about the bulbs. The collector of light bulbs seemed to be interested in the conversation, since he continued without further questioning. "I collect them—light bulbs, you see. From all over the world. You can find them on the beaches everywhere in the Keys." He paused. "And this is a good place, here." He looked at the tourist, apparently curious to see his reaction. The tourist obliged with an expression of wonder. He was intrigued, indeed.

"This is very interesting. You are a collector of light bulbs, then!"

The man moved a few steps away and, from behind the Sea Lavender bush, he brought up a light bulb. His physique was quite impressive for his age. There was no fat on his flat belly, his buttocks were firm as an athlete's, and he moved with surprising fluidity and ease. He was not circumcised, and his pubic hair was the same rusty color as his mustache and the hair on his head. He handed a bulb to the tourist. "Read this," he pointed to the faint inscription.

"Osram?"

"Yup, Osram. From Germany, all the way from Europe," the man said, stressing "Europe." "I have them from all over. Some must be thrown out of ships, like the Asian ones."

"Oh, really?" the tourist encouraged him.

"From Japan, Korea, and Singapore. You see, those from Asia have inscriptions in red. They are a rare find, they are," he continued. "I got bulbs from Poland and Mexico, too, and Canada. Yup, from Poland, too." He seemed quite impressed by the Polish specimen.

They talked more. The man explained that, on some light bulbs, the identification had been smudged off by the sand and that he had discovered a way to read it well, under a fluorescent light. "I take those to the library in Key West and read them there. They have fluorescent lights in the library, you see."

Like prehistoric pterodactyls, a flock of brown pelicans hurried by, on the way to their night perches, their wings almost touching the calm water. And the first night-biting mosquitoes announced themselves. The shadows of the two men elongated to the edge of the water as the setting sun touched the twisted tops of the mangroves behind them. The bulb collector pointed to the sun with a gentle but slightly theatrical movement of his arm. He smiled a pleasant smile, and the tourist recognized the hour as late. He left, feeling a sympathy for this quiet man. He wished him the best of luck in his hunt for more exotic light bulbs.

After walking for a while, he turned around to wave. He was surprised to see the collector watching him with what appeared to be powerful binoculars. After he had carefully bypassed the parked pickup truck and the watchful dog, he turned around once more. He could still recognize the reflection of binoculars pointed at him from the distance.

✳

In his motel on Grassy Key, the tourist discovered that his knife with the rosewood handle was missing. He was sure it must have slipped out of its sheath when he was bending down to pick up a board on the beach at Big Coppitt Key. The moon was almost full. There was plenty of light on the shore, so he left without hesitation, hoping to find his knife. On the way back to the beach, he was thinking about the strange bulb collector.

To his surprise the truck with the doghouse on its roof was still on the beach when he arrived. After locking up his car at a safe distance from the truck, he started to walk, feeling some wariness. To avoid the German Shepherd, which he suspected would be on guard with even more vigilance at night, he entered the bush of red mangroves which separated the beach from the salt pond. After stumbling long enough to bypass the truck, unseen, he ventured back to the beach … and instantly crouched down. Somebody was there and not far from him. A man in a black shirt and dark pants stood motionless, watching the sea.

Soon he recognized a small boat with two men pushing it silently through the shallow water to the beach. He felt the bites of mosquitoes and no-see-ums but did not dare shift even slightly. Anxiety made it difficult for him to breathe. He regretted intensely leaving the safety of his motel room. The boat approached the beach.

"*Aqui, aqui! Rapido!*" the dark man on the beach exclaimed. There was no hush in a voice used to giving orders. It was a command, not an instruction. The dark-clad man still did not move, but the boaters hurried. One jumped into the knee-high water, while the other handed him down a cube-like parcel which reflected the moonlight on its plastic wrap. For its size, it did not appear to be heavy, since the boater waded with ease with it to the shore. He placed it at the feet of the dark man who apparently supervised the action.

The boater hurried for another load while the tourist watched with increasing anguish from his hiding place. He remembered, now, the bearded customer in the bar in Key West. "Every night they bring the *ganja*. Bales like this," the bearded Conch had said to him the day before, stretching his arms. A dense cloud of mosquitoes buzzed around the tourist's ears, and tiny no-see-ums penetrated his T-shirt and pants. He felt his face swelling with bites, but somehow he stopped registering the pain of the stings. They were still bringing more parcels to the beach. Only the splashing of water by hurried men disturbed the silence of the moonlit shore. It was low tide now.

The tourist breathed in a mosquito. He could feel it, deep in his throat, which constricted violently. It felt like being grabbed. He could not inhale. He tried to remain motionless despite the shattering sensation. He felt increasing dizziness, and the spastic pain in his throat did not subside. He covered his mouth with his hand and tried to breathe out. Then his lungs exploded in a single, gurgling bark.

The boatman with a bale in his arms froze. The dark man remained standing, without movement, still facing the sea. Silence ruled again. Then the dark man turned around with lightning speed and dropped to the ground. The tourist could see him creeping rapidly in his direction, in the fluid motions of a predator.

Without thought, the tourist sprang up and ran. He sprinted, full speed, straight into the narrow belt of mangroves. He crashed through the tangle of roots and low branches wildly, stumbling but still keeping his balance, feeling no pain. When he emerged on the muddy shore of the pond, he turned sharply to the right, dashing into the soft mud along the mangroves. He ran hard in the wet silt, which reached above his ankles. He felt like he was flying, briefly hopeful, amazed by his speed. He turned his head—and only saw his tracks in the mud, glistening in the moonlight, and nobody behind. He did not decrease his pace when he reached the shallow channel running from the salt pond to the beach through the swath in the mangrove belt.

Then the dark man emerged from the mangroves. The collector of

light bulbs, breathing heavily, stopped his pursuit and watched the running tourist. Then he turned around and retreated into the mangroves.
He knew that the running man, in about ten paces, would reach the area
of quicksand.

83

Panoptikum

Walking with my grandfather down Creek Street to the river was an impressive experience for the twelve-year-old me. Unlike strolling with my father in Prague, a city of strangers, here in Baba everybody seemed to know Grandfather. Some greeted him, taking off their hats, others touched the rim of their hat with two fingers, or bowed slightly; a few raised a hand and one reached up for an imaginary air-hand shake. Grandfather was well known and highly regarded in the community. He had been the mayor, founded "The Echoes of Strings" orchestra, was one of the founders of the patriotic and sporting organization Sokol, was a local star in bowling, and was the owner of the largest cherry orchard on the river.

I held his hand and did not smile. I tried to keep in step with him and still keep ramrod straight. I was proud to belong to him and to have the same last name.

Grandmother never walked with us—in those times it wasn't done. She ruled in the house, so she would not have left her kingdom, anyway. She was strict with Grandpa but kind to me and my cousins, always having something sweet for us hidden in the pantry, where we were forbidden to enter. Only much later, in my adult years, did I learn she was so strict with Grandpa because he, still into his late seventies, had a girlfriend right in their town, in Baba, as well as one in nearby Sedlec. I treasure the old sepia-tinted daguerreotype of the matriarch when she was young. She was uncommonly beautiful, with slightly Asian eyes and her upper lip as full as the lower one, in a half-hidden smile. When she became old her eyelids tilted down to an anti-mongoloid slant and her upper lip crumbled. It was Grandfather's upper eyelids, not his upper lip, which crumbled and collapsed over his eyes, his nose becoming pitted, his teeth elongated. Only his carefully waxed mustache (it was a copy of the hirsute hallmark of Kaiser Franz Josef, the Emperor) looked victorious till his end. I loved both my grandparents, but each one in a different way.

"Panoptikum's coming to town," Grandpa said, and puffed from his "virzinko," a cigar with a straw running through it, taking a sip of his black hole-black Turkish coffee, the consistency of molasses. "We'll go to see!"

"Panoptikum?"

"Yes, ma boy, Panoptikum. It is like a circus, but there are no exotic animals there, only exotic people. You might see very strange things, unnatural phenomena, things beyond the comprehension of even an adult mind."

"Will they let a kid … with a kid's mind … in? Like me?"

"Certainly. It should be an exceptional educational experience. You'll be astonished, perhaps."

It was a non-Egyptian pyramid of gray canvas put up on a public meadow near St. Matthew Church, where people congregated like ants, greeting us with the usual reverence. Grandpa walked erect, his black felt hat at a slightly frivolous angle, his mustache motionless as if carved of ivory, his black jacket open to reveal the heavy golden chain looping on his vest to hold the watch hidden in the watch pocket. Inside the tent we found a good place, two rows from the elevated platform of the stage.

A row of drums was played by two little people with very high foreheads and noses with depressed bridges. Then the "Principal," in a glossy double-breasted suit and polka-dot scarf, welcomed the "honorable and distinguished" guests and announced the program: the viewing of "…the strangest wonders of the natural world will be followed by an unbelievable performance by the renowned Doctor Honoris Causa, Leroy Chiraque, the world famous hypnotist."

"Notice the faces of the dwarfs, the midgets with drums," Grandfather whispered. "Still, their intelligence is not affected." He raised his index finger in didactic gesture.

The first wonder of the natural world appeared. She was announced by the Principal as the "Alligator Woman." In a two piece swimming suit of the old-fashioned cut, the slightly obese lady's skin was covered with scales, stained green-gray. A sad mannequin, she performed a few steps resembling a sequence from the Bohemian Beseda folk dance, and then walked around the stage with uncertain gait. Her eyes teared, so she wiped off the tears often. People in the audience did not know if the applause was called for or if silence was appropriate.

The Alligator Woman bowed and was followed by "Big Foot," a middle aged fellow who hobbled in on enormous feet in enormous socks, which seemed to be cut from a sailcloth. He raised his underformed arms in a threatening gesture one would expect from the dangerous yeti of the Himalayas. His pointed fur hat slipped over his eyes; some idiots laughed.

The "Lobster Man" who followed was amazing in his defective development. His hands, indeed, were split into two halves, which could move like the claws of a Maine lobster. He was dressed in a bright orange jumpsuit, of course, being a lobster. He bared his gums, which were toothless and glossy, and performed clawing with his claws.

The "Smallest Woman of the World" was a disappointment to me because she was so small, I could not see her while sitting too close to the elevated stage. Then came the intermission, time to catch one's breath, held for so long.

"You see, even Nature makes mistakes," Grandpa said. "But the worst mistake is when the brain, not arms or legs, doesn't work right. Often, this is invisible from the outside." Grandfather shook his head in wonder, not believing the cruelty of Nature himself. He knew so much, my Grandpa!

Uncle Tonda waved at us from the first row, and my cousin Pepa, next to my uncle, made claws at me like the Lobster Man. I thought that Nature made a mistake developing my cousin's brain, not visible from the outside. Then the drums of the little people announced the end of intermission and the beginning of the evening's highlights. The Principal in a shimmering outfit floated onto the stage and announced Monsieur Docteur Chiraque, "...the greatest hypnotist of Central Europe. The power of his mind is beyond belief, ladies and gentlemen. He can steal your soul and turn you into anything he wants!" He suggested that those with nervous conditions consider leaving.

Riveted, hundreds of eyes were fixed on a short man in a creased business suit, and a white shirt with a collar too large for his slender neck. Two hedgerows of discolored hair bordered the bold cranium with pigmented spots. He bowed to three sides like a boxer winning a bout. He turned around and talked briefly to the Principal. Then events followed with a hurried pace.

The lights dimmed.

The Principal announced that Monsieur Chiraque needed a volunteer.

Nobody volunteered.

The hypnotist stepped forward and pointed at Grandpa with an apologetic smile.

Grandpa looked around, to the left, to the right. He kissed his teeth.

Friends and acquaintances encouraged him with gestures, and some with calls.

"Don't go any place," Grandpa said to me, as if I would or could. I was astonished, because he stood up and walked onto the stage in his proud way, and did not pay any attention to either the hypnotist or the Principal. He gazed at the audience with an amused smile, so confident and arrogant it remains clear in my memory. He was in control.

Meanwhile, the two midgets brought a chair. An ordinary kitchen chair. The hypnotist approached Grandpa and motioned him to take a seat. Grandpa sat down with the same dismissive smile.

The hypnotist stepped back, and looking into the eyes of the man in the chair, he raised his right arm to eye level and pointed at him with stretched fingers. The hypnotist repeated a mantra in a calm monotonous voice, which I could barely hear and did not understand.

A tense silence ruled the audience.

Grandfather's eyes closed and, it seemed, his whole face sank an inch. Unbelievably, he was asleep. One of his arms hung straight down as if dead. For me he was gone, out of the tent, replaced by a zombie, by a phantasm. The Principal approached the edge of the stage and said, in the muted voice, the obvious: "Deep sleep."

Hypnotist Chiraque, his expression unchanging and uninteresting by the lack of any distinguishing feature, approached his subject and talked to him briefly. Then he stepped back.

Grandpa opened his eyes. They seemed dead to me. He got up, slowly, turned around to face the chair and then, laboriously, sank to his knees.

I saw Uncle Tonda stand up in the first row with a fist in the air. People around him pulled him down, struggling. It was hard for me to breathe. I felt an urge to stand up with my fist in the air too, but I did not know why.

Grandfather reached under the seat of the chair with one hand and then with the other. His fists were opening and closing, alternatively, one after the other, in a deliberate, slow rhythm, right under the seat of the chair. I could see his face in profile now: he gazed nowhere. He was milking the chair.

I cannot recall many details of what happened after. I remember that one person, in the back of the tent, laughed shortly; all others were quiet and motionless. The hypnotist bowed deeply to the audience and then clapped his small hands three times and said something to Grandpa in a hushed voice. Grandpa stopped milking the chair and surveyed his surroundings, got up slowly and wiped imaginary dust off his knees. The Principal took his elbow carefully and directed him off the stage, as if leading a child.

That evening Uncle Tonda stopped by Grandfather's house. Since Grandpa was still out in the garden, he narrated the event from the Panoptikum to Grandmother. "Mother, mother," he said, "it was just horrible, very difficult to watch. I thought I would … I don't know…"

Grandma started to smile; her smile was radiating happiness … then she laughed and laughed louder, so much she had to leave the room. I had never seen Grandmother laughing before, only smile, at times, so I was confused, but Uncle Tonda seemed to understand better than me. He nodded his head.

*

Some memories are hidden deep in the darkness, so they will never fade. Even after so many years, when I unbury such a memory, the memory of my grandfather milking the chair, at that moment my liking of him becomes love.

Possibility of Hope

One would not guess that 63 was a rarely privileged man, envied by most of the inmates working in the uranium mine of the Ministry of Correction and Justice. Slumped forward and gazing down, he was dragging his feet in the mud in front of the elevators to the mine. Those who did not know—new inmates, perhaps—would be surprised to see him enter the women's shaft elevator, where any access by a male inmate was forbidden under penalty of severe punishment. Women prisoners had been assigned to clean the old rubble and debris from the abandoned shaft. Since there was less and less high-grade uranium ore to be found, the old shaft was to be extended deeper, and new tunnels were to be dug out. The official reason for 63's descent to the mine was to take care of fungi. He was a specialist: the fungus-destroyer. He was thus allowed to work in the women's shaft.

The cage of the elevator fell rapidly into the darkness of the abyss, screeching and rattling at increasing speed. When the brakes were applied, 63 almost fell to his knees. He was not paying enough attention. He lifted the wire door of the cage and stumbled into the side tunnel. A few steps away, in the light of his headlamp, he saw the fungus. It grew from a wooden beam, in the same spot where he remembered destroying it, just a week ago.

This one was of a pale yellow hue, pitted, with dark spots near its attachment to the beam. These yellow mutants grew even faster than the red ones. It hung like a bag, at least two feet across. The sweated-out mucus had collected in droplets at the bottom of the growth.

Number 63 had been very careful with the yellow ones, but this time he worked without his usual concentration. He sprayed the fungus with a colorless fluid (of his invention), waited a few minutes, and switched on the ultraviolet lamp. Rapidly, the fungus started to change under the blue beam. Dissolving in some parts, crumbling and shrinking at the bottom, the growth seemed to tremble as it broke and fell in runny, jelly-like pieces onto the plastic sheet that 63 had spread underneath. The toughest part of the fungus, its sort of skeleton, had to be cut off the wooden beam, and the stalk had to be carefully scraped away from the wood.

Strange things, these mutant fungi. Number 63 had seen abandoned side-tunnels completely filled with them. And he would swear that some of them, the red and multi-colored ones, actually moved when he approached close enough. He did not tell anybody about that, since inmates were horrified of them anyway. Some believed they caused the dreaded "cauliflowers."

✻

Still distracted, tripping frequently, 63 stumbled over the railway ties leading inside the tunnel. He had suspected something was wrong with her. Last time he was here looking for her, he was sure she hid from him. And none of her mates wanted to answer his questions. He could hear the voices of the women's crew, working behind the bend ahead. Bumping painfully into the wooden scaffold brought him back out of his thoughts. He leaned on the beam to rest, avoiding two new fungi starting to grow on its side. They were still colorless, as all the young ones were. He pulled out his breast pocket—and lit—an inch-long butt of a cigarette he had saved from yesterday.

He remembered the first time he had seen the "cauliflower." It was growing from inside the lips of old Number 105, the "Professor," out of a corner of his mouth. It was of whitish color, the size of a pea, barely visible at first. Number 105 had been able to hide it for a week or so, pulling his lips over it in a way that gave him the expression of one trying to make a funny face.

But no one was amused, not even the new inmates. The rule was known to all, already by then: inmates with a growth, a "cauliflower," must be "recorded" immediately. "Recorded" was an official term for being taken away. Anybody "recorded" never returned, and their families never saw them again. How they were disposed of, and where, nobody knew, not even the guards. The cancerous growth resembling a cauliflower was discussed only in whispers. It was feared, more than one feared death in the mine.

The first woman appeared in the tunnel, dragging the water hose, measuring her steps slowly. She approached 63, giving him no sign of recognition. She was one of the oldest inmates, but it was impossible to judge her age by her face. She had developed the common features of all inmates, which made them look like sisters, like siblings of a doomed family, which they were. Almost like clones, they had all acquired large eyes peering out of deep hollows, and narrow lips retracted over the teeth and tightened as in a denial of speaking. Their complexion did not vary from an ashen grayness. Their eyes were so prominent in their grimace that everybody knew the colors of the irises of their friends' eyes, and people were remembered by that—the most important color in their lives.

Now 63 saw the laboring women. He looked for her, for Lena. She separated herself from the group disassembling rusty rails, and approached him slowly. Lena's eyes were the pale blue of a spring morning sky. Her number was 36. When 63 met her, several weeks before, he had amused himself by manipulating their numbers, finding that subtracting hers from his gave exactly her age—an age which, by now, nobody could guess.

Number 36 touched his arm, and he looked at her face, just for a few seconds. Rapidly he averted his eyes, wavered, and leaned on the wall to support himself so as not to sink to the ground. He recovered and motioned her to sit down on the fallen beam. They sat there, shoulders and arms touching. Other inmates passing by sped up their steps, looking away.

When the cold had permeated her, she trembled, and he helped her to stand, holding her hand briefly. It was cold and wet—still clawless; he knew now she would never have a chance to grow claws. Her eyes peered at him, expressionless and as big as the eyes of a night animal. She was so pale now that her face seemed to glow in the semi-darkness of the tunnel. There was no visible sorrow about her lips. But from one of her nostrils, a creamy-colored "cauliflower" drooped, clearly visible today and to be even more obvious at tomorrow's compulsory inspection.

They both tried to distort their lips into a smile. And then they parted. He ascended the mine and walked very slowly to his barracks. Halfway, he looked up at the sky. He seemed to straighten up and increase his speed.

✳

In the story "Immortality", Kundera ponders shame: "Shame means that we resist what we desire and feel ashamed that we desire what we resist." Number 63 had succeeded in resisting his desire to cry, but felt ashamed of succeeding. Sometimes he became deadly tired of manipulating his own mind. Number 63 knew well that by now he was capable of achieving pleasurable feelings by refining the art of survival. He had trained himself in it, just as a marathon runner trains, using mental discipline.

He had cultivated subtle skills for forgetting a disturbing event, dwelling on an achievement (however minor), categorizing pain into the realm of mere inconvenience, sometimes even elevating pain into a feeling of pleasure. He had managed, consciously, to put his mind into a frame of hope. Occasionally, he was aware, these efforts blurred the distinctions between reality and the imagination, but he assured himself that the means justified the end, which was simply survival. He did not know of Zen nor other religious philosophies of the East; his was an empirical experience. In that, he did not differ much from the simple sailor who survives weeks on a raft in the middle of an ocean. The only difference between them was that he had arrived at the state of required single-mindedness by a deliberate mental process. Like an acrobat, he performed his "satisfactions," and like an acrobat, he sometimes stumbled and failed. On this sad day it was too risky to fail, so he clutched the high trapeze of hope, with all his concentration.

✳

Daniel Rosecky, number 63, in his fourth year of detention, sat on his bunk and took off his cap. From under the lining he pulled out a matchbox from which he removed a needle and some black thread, carefully rolled around a rectangular piece of cardboard. With even stitches he repaired a small tear in the sleeve of his cotton jacket. He put the cap back on his head again, to prevent any more loss of heat from his body—he must be careful about that. Then the boots went, and the square pieces of cloth used as socks were hung above the bunk to dry. He wrapped his feet in the blanket and sat with a straight back, leaning on the wall at the head of his bed, with his eyes closed.

Today, for fifteen minutes, he would imagine the town square with the inn, The Green Frog—his friends drinking beer, the barman Kadlecik explaining the winning strategy of their soccer team, waitress Klara in a miniskirt, play-acting revulsion at his friends' jokes. Then he would try to recall every detail of the stone fountain in the middle of the town square. When he could not visualize the face of the saint in the fountain, he finished dreaming. He rechecked the half-slice of bread in its hiding place under the loose wallboard, and walked to the window.

It was about time for the airplane. The plane, one of those from a great foreign airline, was on time, as usual. It appeared on the northwest and crept slowly across the vast blue screen towards its wonderful international destination. It left behind four white streaks, the possibility of hope, and a mirthless smile around the large eyes of Daniel Rosecky.

And Then There Were None

The animal was dying. They both knew it, and knew better than to talk about it. Olaf had gotten the monkey in the bazaar in Nairobi, the one by the mosque. He had gone there for a new frying pan and instead bought the baby black-faced vervet. It was compressed into a bird cage so small that the tiny monkey had to crouch like a neolithic mummy with her head bent forward and knees under her chin. Olaf had bargained, but only halfheartedly; so, finally, he had paid almost half the asking price. A Lua boy, the seller, who must have known that the monkey was sick, did not even try to conceal his exuberance at this victory over a *mzungu*, white man.

Like a tender bundle of breathing matter, she lay limply on a blanket that Olaf and Derek arranged as a nest in a corner of the main room. She did not touch the bananas and refused warmed milk with the passivity of a sick child. Her teary, questioning eyes became even sadder than the eyes of a healthy monkey. Olaf told Derek about saving her from the market, about his trip home in a *matatu*, where he almost got into a fight with some idiot who tried to poke her through the cage.

He made Turkish coffee for the both of them, and they sat on the floor watching the animal watching them with those eyes that rarely blinked, revealing little and making one wonder about the sadness of evolution. Sudden sounds and movements frightened her into jerky motions, so they tiptoed to their bedrooms and said good night in whispers. A few minutes later they surprised each other sneaking into the main room at the same moment. "Just checking."

Olaf was a Peace Corps volunteer assigned to teach English and biology in Kenya for two years. Many of his peers envied his assignment in Thika. It was a short agony-ride by bus or torture-ride by *matatu* from downtown Nairobi—but still it was out in the country, past the suburbs. Thompson gazelles could be seen near the town at any time and stories abounded of encounters with more exciting wildlife in backyards. It was an East African countryside of surprising exotic sounds, smells and weather.

Most fortunate was the deal with housing. Olaf's house (not a shack—it had electricity) was a simple structure right at the edge of the school's exercise field or playground. It came with a garden plot made tropically exciting by clumps of banana plants, some cassava, bitter leaf and a few sugar canes. For shade and for an oversupply of delicious fruit, a dark mango tree leaned on the short wall of the house. It also sheltered a lot of wild creatures: birds, lizards, and also insects for night music. The only disadvantage was that the stones and sticks thrown at the ripe mangoes by local kids and rowdies would fall on the roof and drive Olaf to distraction.

Olaf planted two rows of tomatoes. The poor soil and rich sun in collaboration created a delicacy of a taste unknown in the produce departments of the shopping centers of America. He had also built a bench of stone-hard *mbutu* wood by the back wall of the house, so he could sit there in the evening and watch the sun setting behind his own banana grove. In the dry season the dust in the air, brought by the Saharan Harmattan, made the sun grow to enormous dimensions before it descended into the Rift Valley to sleep.

Sometimes Timothy stopped by and they would share the bench, a few Tusker beers, and memories of the day, until the night-biting mosquitoes threatened them with blackwater fever and chased them inside. Timothy, a local Kikuyu, was also a teacher, always in good cheer with a supply of opinions and stories that were sometimes interesting, and frequently repeated with variations on the ending. He was a good friend, who came by unannounced and often, as all good friends everywhere must do.

Olaf had met Derek in Nairobi in the Thorn Tree cafe in front of the New Stanley Hotel. The place was popular mostly with college-aged travelers, who came singly or in pairs, in cotton shirts made in India, and jeans or shorts, the girls with hair braided the Kenyan way (it hurts like hell for days), some with toes and palms painted with henna, and always in sandals, counting shillings carefully before ordering a cheap and barely edible sandwich. One rarely encountered tourists there, in their "white hunter" safari outfits with video cameras over their shoulders, snake-proof boots, and the determined look of Ernest (Hemingway) or Beryl (Markham, of course). With their self-delusions of alluring Africa, the tourists kept to cafes in the Hilton or the Serena, or better yet the Norfolk Hotel.

People would come to the Thorn Tree (pretending thirst, hunger, or such) to see who was passing through town. Guys would check out their chances of meeting a lonely female traveler looking for "advice" or housing. They all read the messages on the bulletin board, nailed right onto the famous thorn tree in the middle of the cafeteria. Some of the messages seemed to have been written by an altogether too happy but shaky hand influenced by the potency of cannabis from Machakos. (Ganja from Mombasa would not have allowed a smoker to write a message at all.)

Olaf had read, "Larry is looking for Sandra, or Sally, McCulough or McCalla, who might be coming from Malindi or Lamu. I love you!!! Call: 23564." Olaf had laughed.

"What's so funny?" Derek had asked, and introduced himself. Olaf had ordered a can of Tusker beer, and passion fruit juice for Derek, and they had talked: some football, some baseball, some Kenya. Then they had gone to the Trattoria at the corner of Kuanda Street, had eaten Italian, and at the closing hour Olaf had rented his spare bedroom to Derek for six hundred shillings per month, which was worth about forty bucks and satisfied them both. Derek had moved in the next morning and praised the setup; he liked everything about it.

Olaf's house had one major room. To call it a living room would be inaccurate, since most of the living was done in the bedroom or in the garden. On opposite sides of it were bedrooms, with one window each. The "kitchen" was outside the house under a sheet of corrugated iron supported by four posts, and its equipment was positively native. The outhouse was a sad story for the feeble-hearted, which will remain untold. Next to the kitchen was a showerhead attached to the wall of the house in a bamboo enclosure built by Olaf himself—his proud achievement.

Bamboo is a romantic material. Olaf had delighted in watching the color of it change over time from shiny green to green with thin yellow streaks, then to yellow with green streaks, then to solid old gold. He had photographed the same segment of the bamboo enclosure every two weeks, for the record, sprinkling it with water for a glossy effect. He grew to honor the abode as his home.

Derek had moved two Samsonite suitcases into the vacant bedroom and started to camp there. He was a traveling man who lived out of suitcases, literally, so he had opened the luggage and kept it open by the wall. It never crossed his mind to build or buy a stool or shelves or anything which couldn't be carried out and around. He wouldn't even venerate his cot with a sheet and pillow, but slept on it in his lightweight sleeping bag or, during the hot nights of the dry season, on the sleeping bag. When he would leave on trips, his room looked barren and virginally cold, even in the passionate tropical heat.

✳

The monkey was never given a name because it faded away too fast. To name her would have made the inevitable only more difficult to bear. The little thing diminished day by day and then, one morning, they found her in the blanket nest, rigid, with one hand over her forehead, eyes closed. Olaf took care of her, digging a tiny grave in the corner of the garden and burying her in a shoebox too big for her body, which had been shrinking since he brought her home.

Derek did not have to go to Nairobi that day and secluded himself in his room until noon. When he came out, he did not talk, and averted his eyes when Olaf talked to him. He refused lunch and looked downcast. There seemed to be an agitation in his gloom. Perhaps he had loved that tiny monkey. She shouldn't have done it to him.

The Second Monkey

Derek was a strange bird, Olaf thought. Actually, the image of a shark (as unlikely as it may sound) came to Olaf when he'd first met him in the Thorn Tree. It was his teeth, a full mouth of them, that had invoked the likeness of the predator. Derek used to grind his teeth while sleeping, and so it happened that he had worn them down so deeply that all of the teeth had to be capped. The prosthodontist, obviously, had chosen the sizes of his crowns with an unusual megalomania. While this oversized dentition harmonized with Derek's hollow cheeks and with his drawn expression, his eyes were mild, without harshness, and one wondered whether they revealed sadness or kindness.

Besides his physiognomy, his psychology appeared also to be peculiar. He believed in many things. He believed in the National Rifle Association, in the existence of gods, specifically the Christian one, and in abstinences of all kinds. He believed that when a spermatozoon penetrates the zona pellucida of an egg, the resulting cell is a human being. He believed that all men are created equal, with the exception of some of his Kikuyu advisees. He simply believed a lot, by Olaf's standards. He also regarded smokers as despicable, so Olaf had to sneak his occasional joint of cannabis out to the garden and hide with it behind the bananas—"hide in my own goddamn garden!"

Derek would never talk about girls and dating, except once when he described the rendezvous resulting from an ad he'd placed in the newspaper. His date had a nose of such dimensions and curvature that when he saw her waiting for him, he'd actually run away, at least a mile before he felt safe.

"Did you get another date from that ad?"

"Yeah, I got one more. But I did not like her much. I went out with her for a year."

"You did not like her … for a year ?" Olaf asked.

"Didn't. She always wanted to talk. And to pretend things."

"Pretend things?"

"You know—things." Derek looked to the ground. "Forget it! She was a pain. For Christmas I bought her suppositories for hemorrhoids." Derek gave a humorless laugh.

"What?!"

"Anyway, at the end I sort of started to like her, you know." He revealed his shark dentition. "Then—so you know—she left me. Just like that." Derek looked victorious, I-told-you-so. "Just like that." He snapped his fingers.

Nothing could be said safely, Olaf thought, but the silence embarrassed him after a while. "How about friends, Derek? Do you have some friends at home?"

"I had a friend once, ya. In elementary school I used to have one. Chuck."

Olaf would have liked to talk about friendship but knew that Derek would not comply, because he could not. Neither as a contributor nor as a listener. They had agreed, silently, not to have any more confessional discussions, and Olaf thought it healthier that way.

Derek did not read; he liked to sleep or daydream. But he volunteered to do dishes and cooking once in a while: spaghetti with Olaf's tomatoes, garlic, olive oil, and Parmesan, when that was available in the Indian *duka* near Jaimia Mosque, which they liked for its owner, the turbaned Sikh of eternal and loud pessimism. Somehow, this basic meal could be eaten often, like a bread, and that is what they did.

Derek also took special pleasure in cleaning his double-barreled shotgun (kept illegally, which worried Olaf, his landlord). Weekly, Derek took it apart, oiled it, and aimed it at various objects in the room. His nervous hands would suddenly steady, the finger pulling the trigger in deliberately slow motion. He was proud of the gun, claiming it had historical value; it must have been used by colonial Brits in the good old times during the Mau Mau uprising in romantic Kenya. Olaf did not like the gun and did not like Derek's reasons for liking it. Derek had bought it in Busia, a town near the Ugandan border where he had supervised a "development project" funded by the Rockefeller Foundation, a building demonstration of houses made solely from materials available locally, i.e. mud. "Damn it, you wouldn't believe the waste of money. Just waste," was the sum total of what he would tender about his project, which he called "their project."

As time went by, safe topics for discussions between Derek and Olaf became exhausted, and while tension had been avoided in their mostly mute cohabitation, they had failed to develop what could be called a stimulating relationship. That changed with the arrival of the second monkey. She was a female vervet, again, and Olaf named her Lika. It rhymed with

Thika and she did lick her lips before and after a treat, like a kid. She was the equivalent of a human teenager in both her relative age and her nuttiness; her great hobby was people. For the first few days Derek either avoided her or tried to show indifference to her friendly overtures.

"Derek, she likes you. Lika!" Olaf attempted to help when she sneaked behind Derek and tried to touch his hair.

"So get her away!"

And so it went. After a week, Olaf decided to have a talk about the situation. Derek admitted (with some evasiveness and torturous verbalizing) that he had a problem —because of the first monkey's death. He had liked her a lot, and when she died he resolved not to get attached again to another pet. He switched to simple words with a frankness which surprised Olaf.

"How about if I grow to like this stupid Lika, you know? Like really like her... And then she would die." Pain showed on his young-old face so clearly that Olaf felt sudden embarrassment for him, got up, and brought couple of Tuskers.

"*Barindi. Kuna mzungu!*" He offered it "cold, to a white man," in Swahili, but the front Derek had put up did not relax.

"I don't want to go through that again. It has always been like that with me, you know. You love somebody—and then ... oh fuck it." He reached for the beer, looking away from Olaf. "Well, thanks for the beer, anyway." They did not talk about the monkey any more.

Later that evening Timothy stopped by and, for Olaf, seeing the permanent smile on his wide Kikuyu face felt like sunshine after a cold spell. They took Lika outside and sat on the bench, using the hurricane lamp instead of the moon. Bats were in full acrobatic action, fireflies blinked madly among the bananas, and a cooling breeze began its descent from the Ngong Hills. Derek let Lika creep up and settle on his shoulder for the first time. Timothy mused about the likeness between Derek and the monkey, and then talked about the old times, about the uprising and who in the town was on which side. Olaf played Springsteen on the tape deck and served beer.

When enough had been consumed, he recited for them his "small" poem he called "Just A Little Piece Of Shit To Remember Nights Like This:"

Southern Cross sky
equator walking distance.
Bruce Springsteen on my tape:
"Born in the USA"

Ngong Hills dressed in moonlit gowns,

my frangipani-scented night.
Beware of lions roaming near:
"Born Free"

When Timothy had left, under stars so bright they lighted his way even without their lunar companion, when Olaf had said good night and disappeared into his bedroom for a secret joint of Machakos grass, Derek sat with Lika, alone. He looked into her eyes, for a long time, to the shrill of cicadas from their mango tree.

✳

In the following weeks Derek took over the care of Lika, feeding her, cleaning up after her; he even bought a brush to groom her. They both enjoyed that, she with almost a smile on her face. He always brought her treats from his trips and explained to her where they came from: star fruit from Naivasha, guanabana from Nakuru market, passion fruit from Mombasa. When Olaf was not around, Derek talked to her, mostly about himself. When they were together with Lika his intensity vanished, and his face acquired an appearance of kindness, so skillfully concealed, otherwise. And Lika adored him, in her boisterous, simian way.

Lika was confined to the house most of the time. She was allowed into the garden only under the guarding eye of Derek or Olaf. From the window, Lika loved to watch the students playing. She was fascinated by children; perhaps she couldn't decide if they were monkeys too, because of their size and behavior.

On Friday, Olaf's classes finished early. He was working in the garden when Timothy rushed in, all excited, with Lika in his arms.

"She must have got away, the little devil. It could have been her end!" He talked fast, his eyes bulging. "I came to the playground just in time. The stupid kids were throwing stones at her; they tried to encircle her."

"Timothy! Jesus! Is she hurt?"

They inspected her—couldn't find a scratch. She looked frightened, that was all. They would not tell Derek. They had not noticed that the lower right corner of the mosquito screen on the living room window was detached and could be pushed out.

✳

She escaped a second time while Derek was writing letters in his bedroom and Olaf was at school. She approached a crowd of children running around the field with a ball. This time the boys were alert and managed to encircle her. They closed the circle tightly. She screamed and wailed. The boys showed off to the girls how fast they were, how precisely they could aim their stony projectiles and how tough were their hearts.

They aimed as well as the banker who brings to his wife, for praise (she must), a string of golden pheasants tied by their beautiful necks. They were no less brave than a physician who calls his wife to the garage to admire (she must) a doe with long eyelashes above her beautiful eyes, opaque in death. They were as macho as the two hundred pounds of red-neck American in pursuit of a slender coyote. The boys were no softies, and they could take aim, as all the girls and a few sissies who stood apart could see. Then she stopped screaming.

The Third Monkey

When Derek heard, he disappeared, leaving one open suitcase behind in his bedroom. Nobody knew where to find him or if he would be back, ever. After two months he walked into the house, and Olaf told him that he could stay if he wanted to. Derek's face was drawn, but he could still contort it into a smile.

"Thank you," he said. "I'd like to. I brought some goat meat. I can bake it if you'd like." He peeled off the newspaper from the pale shank and took it outside under the tap. He was home.

From day one he tried, he tried his best, and Olaf appreciated it, because the effort was sincere, as was his occasional gloom. Derek had come with a few new habits: he had stopped going to church on Sundays, and would accept a few shots of home-made distillate, courtesy of one of the innumerable cousins of Timothy. They had a few evenings together, those evenings that make your heart sing and make life so hopeful because one is with friends. They talked politics, movies, poaching in the parks, the corruption of dictator Moi, their plans. They never discussed the past—only once, after a bottle of some suspicious toddy from the market. "You always lose what you love. I do. Always." Derek never mentioned Lika by name.

Short rains came. It cooled down, and then the first long rain arrived on March 25th. It was as miraculous as only those who wait for rain can know. The baked ground soaked up the life-bearing water in gulps and in exchange exuded that special odor that cannot be smelled any other time but when long rains come. Red eyes turned white again, the cracks in heels healed, and when one would squeeze nostrils between a thumb and a forefinger and let go, the nostrils would unstick instantly. Thompson gazelles, lacquered shiny by the rain, stood by the road motionless—only their ears moved. Reebok, those deliberate antelopes, could be seen prancing by the lake, jumping up with all fours in the air, for reasons everybody understood. Girls, laughing loudly, paraded in the rain in front of Thika truckstop as if in a wet T-shirt contest, and the tough truckers watching them became suddenly quiet, with a strange expression on their faces.

Olaf conspired in complicated schemes to bring home, overnight, the newly arrived schoolteacher—she was an elegant immigrant from Ethiopia. (He did not want Derek to know.) Derek traveled less, and spent hours watching the grass grow under the rain, from his window. Timothy acquired a second mistress and, long rains or not, she proved to be a complicator of his life, so he stopped by for a consult, often.

On "fool's day" in April, Olaf took his students to the playground. It was a cool morning. A soot-black cloud divided the sky in half, with its sharp purple edge preceded by a steady wind. The five knuckles of the Ngong Hills disappeared, but in the south the air was purified to such a clarity that even Kilimanjaro could be spied from a hill near Thika. Olaf was trying to gather the kids and get them inside before the downpour when he saw Timothy leaving their house. It was strange, he thought, since Timothy knew Olaf was in school that morning and that Derek would still be asleep at this hour. Timothy waved at him and walked briskly across the playground, not answering the greetings of the students. All along his way the wide smile did not leave his face.

"*Habari gani*, Olaf!"

"What's going on?" Olaf answered the greeting. "Did you win a lottery, or what?"

"Olaf, sit down, because I have a big, big surprise for you. Actually it is for Derek."

Olaf did not believe in premonitions, but this time there was something that prevented him from answering Timothy's grin with a smile. "Monkey! Got a monkey!" Timothy exclaimed. "I got her from my cousin here in town. And free, man." He looked at Olaf's unsmiling face and saw it changing.

"Olaf, buddy, What is it? Can you imagine Derek? Finding her in the living room? He was still sleeping, I think, when I brought her in."

"You left the animal in there?" Olaf managed to recapture his powers of speech. "Is she in there?" He pointed at the house. Then, without waiting for an answer, he started running across the field. After a few paces he stopped, covering his mouth with his hand. An explosion had reverberated from the house—the roar of a shotgun.

The door of the house opened, and Derek appeared, barefoot and without a shirt. He did not look around, stumbling away. He walked in a straight line to the fields nearby and soon disappeared between the tall stalks of cassava, lush from the long rains.

Thallium Apple Pie

I have been taught by experts that there are many attributes to good beer, that smoothly complex fluid. The temperature must be the constant 8° C of a mountain stream. The beer must not see the light of day or be exposed to the oxidating effects of smoke in a tavern, until the very moment of its journey up from the cellar. And the tap must be pulled just as the skipper of a ship leaving a good harbor pulls the lever of the engine-telegraph from "Dead Slow Ahead" to "Full Sea Speed" with one uninterrupted move.

"It's the smoothness of the pull and the slight tilt and vibration at the top of the spigot at the very end of the move," my friend Joseph from Minnesota explained. "Cello players know that technique, too." We were in the Silver Tiger, the beer hall where the best beer in Prague is said to flow. Mr. Hulanek, the unquestioned admiral of the bar, gently put another half-liter in front of me. Gently! The bubbles in the beer, those perfectly spherical spaces filled with carbon dioxide, must be treated with respect.

"You see, this beer, as everything else, has its own essence. And if you want the best—the essence must be brought out, cleaned of all the bullshit." We were swaying a little, like reeds in a breeze, not stormy gusts, yet. Joseph peered closely into my eyes, judging whether I was still capable of comprehension.

"Take rum drinks. Rum cocktails must," he raised his index finger, "must, always, taste like rum. So—the rum is the essence of rum drinks. Or take goat cheese," he went on. "Out of the 800 kinds of cheese, the French claim that there might be more than 50 they make from goat's milk. Fifty refined creations of different textures, strengths and scents. But, my friend, you have to sail to the edge of Asia, to the open market in Turkish Cannakale on the Hellespont (Byron breast-stroked across there, you know) to find the true essence of goat cheese." Joseph licked his lips, and with the back of his hand he removed a bit of beer foam from the tip of his nose. "There, like a carcass, mi amigo, like a carcass in full sun, lies a goat skin with the hair still on it and remnants of fat, I think. This raw skin bag is filled with a half-melted substance, white cheese it is, and you can get a scoop of it for next to nothing, and when you spread it on a piece of bread you know the essence of goat cheese. You feel like growing horns, too, and you'll never forget it."

Joseph half-closed his eyes, possibly shaken by his memory of "the substance." He seemed to be in a good rhetorical frame of mind. When we went to take a leak together, the floor seemed to tilt and sway like the deck of a ship, from starboard to port and back. What wonderful sailing, through this Prague, I thought.

Back in our chairs, my friend continued: "Take apple pie, compadre." He sucked in some air. "The flag, motherhood, and apple pie—the American way, right? But what's the essence, the true essence of apple pie?"

My blank stare forced him to take another sip. "Apples?" I said.

"Of course not! Cinnamon, amigo. Cin-na-mon! True, there should be some nutmeg and mace in the pie; cloves are a must, too. But cinnamon makes or breaks it. The question is, which kind, since there are so many different varieties."

"Different cinnamons? Never heard that before."

"Sure. Chinese cassia is the sharpest, Korintje of Sumatra the smoothest—and Ceylon's old-fashioned cinnamon is the most complex, an almost citrus-flavored kind."

Joseph seemed satisfied with my enlightenment. Then he paused and uttered, "Not thallium, mind you." He grinned, looking sideways at my chin, which I dropped, uncomprehending. "Ever heard about thallium apple pie?"

"Thallium?" And that is how I came to hear the story, as American as apple pie, motherhood, or greed for money.

✳

Before she married Steve Sandine, she was known as "Merry in the Crotch" Betty Lou Stone. After Steve's premature demise, of some weird disease without a diagnosis, she became Stone again. "So, Miss Stone. Congratulations." Limply the lawyer shook her hand, sweaty from expectation, and handed her the final settlement with its attached documents.

By Maysville standards she was loaded, rich, now. From her platinum beehive hairdo, to her D-cups in a pushup bra, to those long legs in ostrich-hide boots—all of her, Betty Lou. Stinking rich, as she had always dreamed of since her descent from those dreamy blue, nightmarish hills of southern Kentucky.

"Yup," she said, "Prudential ain't no pebble; that's the real rock, as they say. Yes sir." She lowered her artificial eyelashes and raised her real eyebrows. "Rock with veins of real gold through it, if you get my drift, ma friend." The lawyer nodded with a smirk and left.

Betty Lou made herself a stiff one on the rocks (moonshine from her brother), pulled off her boots, unhooked the bra (thus changing her silhouette), put on a tape with a selection of Nashville greats and, embraced by the sounds of "Harper Valley PTA", contemplated her future. First, she would push Sandine out of her mind. It was a miserable death but hey, who says life and death are a walk on the beach? One thing was certain: she would cut down her job in the hospital to part-time, and not throw money around too much to be conspicuous.

Second sure thing: she would not change her looks, no sir. She wanted another body in the house, and yessir, men go for weird platinum hairdos, for D-cups and ostrich boots, too. She might look and sound like a ding-a-ling—so be it. She wanted a man in the house.

She knew what to do. She was smart, was Betty Lou. On the Gaussian curve for intelligence, she rated well to the right from the mean. On the scale of conservatism, she stood far to the right, too. So it was obvious she needed a man, and soon.

Betty Lou's monetary situation was good, but she wanted more. She established a business: a 900 telephone number. When dialed, callers would hear a message recorded by Leonard Burton himself, a professional preacher-man with a child molester's character, but the voice of an excited and trusted grandfather. He would explain the route to Heaven with many a shortcut, and green lights all the way.

Then Betty Lou placed an over-sized billboard announcing "CALL 1-900-901-2243 FOR SALVATION" by Interstate 75 between Beirut and Smyrna. It was situated strategically, following the sequence of billboards that advertised a strip joint down the road: "We have 24-karat girls," then "We dare to bare," followed by "We bare it all," then "Couples welcome." She made good money without moving a finger, which reveals a thing or two about the bad consciences of Bible Belt sinners. A Southern Bell employee, Dorian Bolkenstein, had helped her with the paperwork for the 900 number, and told her how he liked her hairdo, while looking at her mighty chest.

After a few months of copulation, she ordered him to the altar of Saint Barnabas in Maysville and took his name. Only then, a few days later, did she learn about his two secret passions. While her first spouse, Sandine, had made a killing by drying and curing tobacco leaves, Bolkenstein smoked them in cigarettes, incessantly. His second passion was his beetles. She was the last one to learn about it. Everybody in Maysville had known and was puzzled by his hobby of collecting jewel-beetles of the Buprestidae family. Locals felt sorry for him, and wondered why their god, in his unbelievable kindness, had let it happen to somebody still quite young.

For starters, our heroine let the beetles be, but took decisive action against the smoking, with an oration worthy of Demosthenes. Because Dorian Bolkenstein's snoring (a side-effect of his smoking) closely resembled a lion's call, she forced him to sleep with a pot tied to his body by a complex tangle of straps, to prevent him from turning on his back. Once, when caught smoking in bed while inspecting his metallic Buprestidae, his nightly joy, she slapped him across the lip, hard, then moved him to the basement. There he had to sleep covered by an asbestos fireproof tarp.

Dorian started to live the life of a secret agent, traveling in his pickup in a zipped-up rain poncho that prevented the tobacco smoke from infiltrating his clothes. His cigarettes were hidden in a series of secret drops and hideaways. He had to cover his smoky tracks at all times. His wife was not fooled. "You sonovabitch, you think you can smoke anytime, anywhere, like some goddamned European anarchist?" Betty Lou had never lost a battle in her adult life, and decided not to make an exception this time.

Soon, Dorian started to feel a strange restlessness. His muscles twitched uncontrollably at unexpected moments. His belly ached, and he vomited for no reason. Then he decided that they were after him, the CIA and contra-espionage agents that were hiding everywhere, watching and waiting … all in clever disguises. Things were getting worse and worse, and Maysville's own Doc Killian just shook his silvery mane and talked in Latin. Then Dorian Bolkenstein died.

✳

"That's life, ma boy." Joseph lifted his mug and almost finished it, leaving an inch. I counted the pencil-slashes on the piece of paper that recorded our recent drinking history. The row of them looked like marks made by a rake. I was one beer behind.

The time had advanced, approaching closing-hour, and all the guests were gesticulating with wider expressions, talking louder. The original uniform hum became a volcanic roar that filled the entire space between the heavy oak tables and vaulted ceiling. I had to raise my voice a few decibels to achieve audibility.

"But Joseph, what about the titanium?"

"Oh, not titanium: thallium. Thallium! It is an element, atomic number 81 I think, a white metallic stuff, very poisonous."

✳

Joseph had heard the story from a fellow he met in Captain Tony's in Key West (which was Hemingway's original watering-hole, not Sloppy

Joe's, as they advertise). The guy was a pathologist from near Maysville, who worked at the county morgue. He became curious when reviewing the autopsy report for Dorian Bolkenstein, which described degenerative changes of the brain, dead brain cells, dead ganglion cells, and other damage that clearly did not fit the age of the deceased. But it was the description of the nails that rang a bell, loudly. They were pigmented brown with pure white stripes across. The pathologist jogged to the library, and there it was, in the reference volume on toxicology: Thallium! A chronic, slow poisoning that is deadly after causing long and specific suffering that leaves tracks readable by an expert, such as striped brown nails and signs of brain-deterioration resembling schizophrenia.

The police were on the case without delay, interrogating people in Maysville. Acquaintances of Bolkenstein described behavior that confirmed the various signs of thallium poisoning, of the twitching muscles, the impotence, and Bolkenstein's slow descent into mental purgatory, his raving paranoia. "Somebody ... THEY ... have planted a motor inside me, a motor called 'riot'! You see, they switch it on at noon by radioradar rays from Washington, D.C. They do it every day at the same time, on the minute. It hurts too." This is what the deceased confided to a Mr. Angelopoulos around the time he was asked to take a leave of absence from Southern Bell.

Then Angelopoulos told investigators that he had known Betty Lou's first husband, too. "Yeah, Steve. Steve Sandine. He was her first hubby. He had the same problems before he died. It was so strange. We used to go coon huntin' and deer huntin' in the fall. But it became impossible, with his jerkin' and twitchin'. Just like Dorian, think of it. Just like Bolkenstein."

So the police brought in Betty Lou. They charged her with two counts of first-degree murder after they exhumed the cadavers of both her darlings, and in the few hairs, teeth, and nails found so much thallium sulfate you could kill rats just by letting the nails lie around. She laughed at the interrogators, so they became physical, in the good old Southern police tradition. She broke down fast and told them about her thallium apple pies.

Her ma in the hills taught her to bake them. She made a good crust with brown sugar, some cloves, and plenty of cinnamon—and a sprinkling of thallium powder too. Betty Lou made pie a Sunday breakfast ritual, and sometimes in the middle of the week. Her spouses smacked their lips, smiled gratefully, and slapped her ass amorously—first Sandine, and later the other one, Bolkenstein.

✳

"So that's the story of the thallium apple pies, my friend," Joseph sighed. "Teaches you that one should not add much to the essence of things."

"Or you'll get 25 to life?"

"Yup, she got life for them pies."

"She was a bad girl."

"You're right. Badness was the essence of Betty Lou. So—cheers," he said, and we banged our mugs together, empty now.

Joseph got up. Shaking his head from side to side, he pointed to the framed instructions on the wall above our table: "DO NOT SPIT UNDER THE TABLE. FRIENDS ARE THERE!"

We left the carbonated atmosphere of the Silver Tiger behind, meandering awhile with the occasional help of lamp posts, until we flagged down a taxi between the Rudolphinum and the Old Jewish Cemetery.

Celebrated Navigation

Street Person Ivanek was also called "homeless" because he lacked a home. He did not mind, but the lack of socks was killing him now. He was shivering; he felt frozen everywhere, except his soles, which burned as if they had been roasted over cinders. He had found Nike running shoes in a garbage can in Lidojedy yesterday—a great find, despite the hole in one. He got so excited that he forgot his socks in the old Hush Puppies he tossed away. You can't march fifteen rainy kilometers in wet sneakers without socks and feel good.

When he reached the village Krky he'd had just about enough and knew he had to find a shelter of some kind soon. It was still drizzling when he crossed the square with the duck pond deserted by ducks, and a chapel, which was always locked. He tried the door.

Ivanek was a sight. His long black and white mane and three-colored beard flew freely on his head, held mostly high. He sported a checkered woolen sport jacket (with a minor tear) from a garbage can in Strc, which fit him perfectly and showed quality in details—hand sewn construction, grosgrain ribbon at the lapel and functioning buttonholes, of course.

His jeans, from a certain refuse bin in Prst, were of the traditional fit and were fashionably bleached by natural elements, not manufactured. About his T-shirt, nothing more will be said, other than it was found on a clothes-line. The Nikes complemented his attire nicely. Representing the Garbage Can Collection, rather than Armani or Gianni Campagna, Ivanek looked *tres chic*, slick for a vagrant, and nobody would guess his fifty years.

Ivanek has been living with street people for several years; he was not sure for how long. He had become a street man after his wife left him for a local politician and took their daughter Milus away. The pain from the loss of Milus was not compensated even by the departure of his wife. It was so hard to bear he became unreasonable, left his upholstering business, sold everything, put the money in Milus' savings account and swallowed many pills at once. When he woke up in the hospital he was less sad. A beautiful angel, Doctor Tree, explained that his brain had been deprived of oxygen for too long a time. She held his hand and had glossy eyes when she told him that in the future he would still be able to feel happiness.

He liked it best being with other homeless panhandlers, knowing there was no possibility of failure with them. Because he was a kind man, shared things, kept fairly devoid of odors and talked only rarely, he was well-liked and even called a "friend" by some. As a badge of his social status, and for other reasons, he let his beard and hair grow long, which gave him the appearance of a protester, which was a false image, since he protested nothing and agreed with everybody, most of the time. He did not touch hard alcohol, so he remained the same.

Ivanek has been spending winters in the main railroad station in Prague, Wilson Station. It is not a homey place; it looks like a railroad station, but many people there are nice and happy. People are always happy when departing to the mountains for skiing and making love; they are always upbeat when returning from visits to friends, still with mud in their eye, and fragrance of beer and slivovice. And cheerful are the international students arriving on Europasses, all wearing tennis shoes and speaking English. Leaving the country, they empty their pockets of aluminum currency into the waiting hats of Ivanek and Co.

Summers he spent hiking and drifting through the country, like a nomadic gatherer from one step back in evolution. But the more evolved hominids in the villages and fields he had to cross had not been as nice as the folks in Wilson Station. Behind their fences they would turn their scornful faces at him and shout things; when in front of their fences they would turn away so as not to look at his face. They had big dogs and big bellies, made taut by beer and potatoes. But there was so much beauty in the Czech landscape, as if painted by a romantic painter on absinthe and in a romantic mood, to boot. Picturesque red and white villages every few miles, a brewery every few kilometers. So Ivanek liked his summers in the country.

Nobody paid attention to Ivanek in the square of the village Krky. People were pacing with agitation, rushing from place to place like ants scrutinized by an anteater, some raising their arms, some raising their voices: "Flood," "River," "Evacuation," "Jesusmariajoseph" and "Aach jo!" Nobody told Ivanek to get lost, to beat it, to make himself scarce, to take a hike. No fat children screamed "bug off, weirdo, scram, scum!" And Ivanek understood what the villagers worried about. This morning, when he passed through Prdy he saw the river Vltava flooding houses up to their roofs, so that Prdy looked like a strange city of red tents. The stream rushed over the bridge which looked like a spillway; whole trees, barrels, boards floated downstream, and he saw a skiff half filled with water, a roof floating without the house.

When Ivanek approached Ruzicka's Butcher Shop on the square he stopped as if hitting a concrete wall, struck like lightning by a sight of beauty. The sticks of salamis and handsome sausages hung in a row behind the shop window, arranged by their size like organ pipes in a house of God, capable of heavenly music, no doubt. Underneath, the cuts of ham, bacon, liver pâté, blood sausage, roast beef and head cheese were arranged in a row of hillocks of equal elevation, in hues from ebony to earthly browns, warm ochres to shamelessly blood red. The sudden revolt of Ivanek's stomach propelled him into the store without a plan of action. There he stood, assaulted by the scents of cold cuts and the fragrance of smoked pigs' feet, his smile making a wide semi-lunar opening in the hedgehog's coat of his beard.

"What are you doing here!" It was not a question, it was the unhesitant greeting by Mrs. Ruzicka, herself. Ivanek nodded as if in agreement and widened his grin.

"Hungry," he stated, "and I can work, I can help… mother," he said quietly, his arms along his hips as if in attention, his eyes firmly on several salamis on the counter in front of him.

"Get out of here!" the shopkeeper instructed the vagrant in a lower voice, ashamed of her strictness, perhaps. Then she warned the unwelcome customer that she would call her husband, who could deal with the likes of Ivanek.

"Pepo! Come here, Tato!" She turned around into the open back door of the store.

With astonishment Ivanek observed his hand, on its own, independent of the homeless mind, shooting forward and to removing a stick of salami from the counter. It disappeared under the checkered woolen jacket.

When Mrs. Ruzicka turned back to face the visitor he was on the way out of the store, slowly, shuffling away as if disappointed by the unenthusiastic welcome. Safely out of the store, he increased his pace. He lifted his knees high, felt spring in his calf, felt streams of adrenaline in his veins and capillaries, his gait resembling the march of an Arabian dictator's guards on parade. The pain in his soles was forgotten—until he found himself past the last house of the village Krky.

He stood on an asphalt county road lined by pear trees. In the distance the road dove into the forest of dark spruces straight as candles, packed tightly. They did not promise a cozy shelter for the night in their undergrowth. Ivanek tucked the salami under his belt like a gunslinger would his Colt repeater and surveyed the situation. On his right there were wheat and sugar beet fields as far as the hills. On the left a pasture, or a field put to rest for a season, sloped down to a vast lake. But the lake was not a lake. It was flowing. It was the river Vltava, in a flood whose might had not been seen for centuries, moving through the Bohemian landscape quietly. It did not roar, it rushed, destroying the land and dwellings with the silence of a mute killer. Ivanek shook his head in wonder but his mind did not linger; he had to find a shelter for the night. It was drizzling, still.

It is said that misfortunes come in threes. For Ivanek the good fortunes were coming in threes, too. After the salami fortune he saw another turn of luck in the pasture, a deserted hay storage shack, with three walls and a good shingle roof. It was not far, just half way to the edge of the flood. The dream of all hoboes, warm, fragrant hay, beckoned to the tired man.

By the time the traveler had made himself a soft, aromatic nest of hay on the platform under the roof, it was getting dark. First he took off the sodden Nike running shoes and rubbed his feet with the dry hay. There was still light enough to read the label on his salami. It was made in Szeged, Hungary, by the survivors of the famous Jewish Pick family. In disbelief he shook his head: he would dine on the best salami, the pride of Hungary, the favorite of culinary experts around the world, the salami fabled by its secret spices and undisclosed proportion of donkey meat. He used his Opinel knife to cut a couple of five millimeter thick slices and laid them on a piece of the great Czech bread Sumavan, which he carried in the breast pocket of his jacket, wrapped in a polyethylene cling-wrap. He felt entirely happy in his heart, stomach, and other internal organs.

But as always, Ivanek's happiness was of a very short duration. He had this problem with happiness: whenever he saw something beautiful, felt goodness, appreciation, good luck— she always visited his mind, an image, emerging from the hippocampus, from memory. And because he loved her—his happiness became sadness. She was Milus, his lovely red-headed daughter, who left him, with her mother, Ivanek's ex-wife. When joy is shared it usually doubles but when it is not shared it shouldn't disappear or turn to sadness. But that was the sad and strange case of Ivanek.

To abolish the pain he had trained himself in different ways of distraction. This time he used the distraction of sleep. He might have heard the river coming but he was trying to direct his brain waves to the dream world. The night of the Big Flood was without stars.

✳

Ivanek dreamt of a swim in the tiny pool in the public bath, Karlovy Lazne. Suddenly, the water became too cold and it woke him up. First, he thought he'd entered another, nightmarish dream, but it took only seconds to recognize the dream for a dream and reality for ... a disaster. The water reached up and covered his platform under the roof of the shack. He did not know that early that morning State Meteorologist Marticka

Kotrmelcova changed her forecast from "the 100-Year Flood" to "the 300-Year Flood."

He made sure the salami was firmly under his belt and then, without much hesitation, slid into the deep water and swam out of the shack to the dim light of the early morn. When he emerged from the building the strength of the current took him by surprise—in few seconds his night shelter was far away. Of the village Krky he glimpsed only roof tops and the steeple of the chapel. The nearest shore could be imagined some-where under the tops of trees. The opposite shore was not visible to the eyes at the water level, so it seemed the river had only one shore left. The river smelled of mud. On moderate waves the debris of leaves, branches, and boards revealed the great velocity of the torrent—which rushed on in collision course with Prague.

Ivanek realized he was in trouble. His strokes in the direction of the nearest shore lacked the determination to move him forward. The water-logged jacket and jeans seemed to pull him down. The thought of death did not yet enter his mind because he was overwhelmed by the wonder about his situation, its seeming unreality. The effort to keep his face above water kept him from desperate thoughts. When a large floating platform appeared nearby he exerted his best effort and mightily breast-stroked the few yards to salvation. He managed to climb up, then lay motionless for some time to recover. He sat up and concluded he was floating on the intact floor of some cabin, a nice hardwood, waxed just recently. It was no Noah's job but it did not sink under his meager weight and swayed only a little when he changed position.

Street children, the gamines of Bogota and Rio, and homeless people everywhere seem to develop survival strategies similar to those of ani-mals living in the extreme environments. They preserve energy in many ways, and find satisfaction, even happiness, in relatively small achieve-ments. So Ivanek showed his incisors in the wide smile of a happy man, and hollered over the waters, "Ship Ahoy!" It came out as a squeak—he repeated again in mightier voice: "Ship Ahoooy!"

"Now, we have to get dry, a little," he announced in a businesslike tone to a brown snake curled on a wooden cabinet floating nearby, stiff with cold and with eyes covered by membrana nictitans, giving him the look of blindness. *He is in worse shape than me*, Ivanek thought, taking off the waterlogged jacket saved from the garbage can in Strc, and wringing out the water from it. His T-shirt he left on; the water in it was warmed by his body heat. The Nikes from the garbage can in Lidojedy were gone, drowned in the flooded hay-storage shack. How unhuman his big toes looked destroyed by the fungus, he wondered, at the moment uncon-cerned about the disastrous flooding situation in Central Europe. He stood up erect and stretched his arms for balance, making a cross above the deluge.

When a wicker chair arrived alongside his raft, Ivanek managed to retrieve it. It had a rattan palm frame and armrests, and was in mint sitting condition. He placed the easy chair in the exact center of his float and slumped into it. From then on he navigated not floating debris but a "ship," his own vessel, sailing helm-less on automatic pilot downstream, final destination somewhat unknown.

The ship passed the half-flooded Zkrz and then the fully submerged Prcice. When he recognized the mouth of the Berounka river by the color change of the flood from black mud to brown mud, Ivanek knew that the capital of Bohemia, Praha, would appear soon, announced by the Fortress Vysehrad on the starboard, high above the river, unreachable by any flood water, save the biblical one. He cut himself a slice of the pride of Hungary and chewed it slowly with narrowed eyes. It stopped raining and a flock of swans flew over in V formation, copying the geese.

If only she could see him now, Milus, his love, his daughter. Would she be worried about his fate, would she call for help? Maybe she would be proud of him, admire him a little. And if they saved him, would she hug her old man? She had hugged him only once in her life. It was when she wrecked their first car, a Fiat 800, dark blue, bought used. She had hit a lamp post at midnight in Dejvice, Prague-6. She called home crying and Ivanek rushed to her by taxi, found her desperate and confused, but unharmed. He told her not to worry about anything. Milus cried, bit a streak of her red hair, and threw her arms around him. He held her tight, for a long time, and did not move. He just repeated, "It's nothing, it's nothing."

A loud voice woke him up from his daydream. It came from a loudspeaker, from a man in yellow oilskins, wearing a cap with big letters on it. The rescuers were approaching in a fast moving boat. Then the boat's motor stopped. Ivanek watched the agitation of rescue men, their failed attempts to revive the engine by kicking it. Their obscenities about the motor's mother were so loud they carried over the water to Ivanek, unaltered.

His voyage continued past the steep rock of Vysehrad. Crowds of onlookers gathered on the stretch of the road not flooded yet. Some waved at Ivanek, some covered mouths with hands in astonishment, some held their heads in both hands in worry for the poor man's life. Fathers pointed to the sailor, instructing their children on bravery. One mother slapped her boy's face because he did not want to look. Cell phones covered many an ear.

Ivanek rose from the wicker chair, buttoned up his jacket to enhance his wet elegance, and bowed to the crowd. He did not wave, since captains do not wave, but half-raised his hands in modest surrender—a little bow, a little smile. Then he sat down facing forward, his face expressing profound concentration of a man drowning in applause.

Some sailors, on their passage to Europe, are said to suffer short delusions and visions at about the mid-Atlantic. Ivanek developed a vision at about the level of Podskali. It was a vision of Milus seeing him, recognizing him, exclaiming to the crowd around her, "This is my dad, the brave sailor there, he is MY dad!"

Because of the enormity of the flood and approaching spillways and Prague bridges barricaded by debris, Ivanek's chance of survival had been decreasing progressively with time. So his vision became, in a way, his last wish. His subconscious knew. He mumbled aloud: "Ivanek's last wish—Milus. Ivanek's last meal—Hungarian salami." He shook his head, disbelieving his destiny.

Farther downstream he enjoyed the magnificent architecture of art nouveau apartment houses and rare cubist villas on the starboard side. In open windows, the inhabitants, in a state of excitement, pointed at him, some with their small silver cameras, some bearded men with binoculars. And several beautiful women made gestures of invitation and leaned over to exhibit the snow-white contents of their décolletage. Ivanek acknowledged their kind attention by a nod of his head and by raising his hand in a gesture of greeting used by Roman legionnaires, while leisurely leaning back in his wicker chair, suggesting a calm enjoyment of the cruise. Handel's "Water Music" might have been appropriate at this moment. The news of his arrival had spread through the city.

When Ivanek approached the National Theater there were already a thousand people waiting. Police and fire-rescue crews were prepared to exert their full effort to save the life of the celebrated navigator. Everyone in the city, except the hobo himself, knew with certainty that if the rescuers failed to extract him from the torrent at this moment he would die. Not more than a kilometer farther down, the Charles Bridge was almost submerged, and the debris, uprooted trees and splintered construction material created a tangle and violent whirlpools where Ivanek's "ship" would be broken and he would drown, most likely first dismembered alive. But the innocent sailor enjoyed his ride still, elated by the adoration of the multitudes.

Just a hundred meters downstream from the Theater, in front of Cafe Slavia, there gathered a lineup of video cameras on heavy tripods for the television news. One could recognize CS TV2 and Television NOVA. Even a BBC crew was present. Reporters in leather jackets from CS Radio and Radio VLTAVA talked into their tape recorders, modulating their voices in unnatural ways, then eliciting comments from stuttering bystanders. Ludek Plecity, the Mayor of Prague, arrived with his entourage, alerted to this excellent opportunity to use the occasion for media exposure and pre-election publicity. (He knew one or two things about that.)

Ivanek, the drifter, again rose from his chair, brushed his hair backwards with fingers, turned the collar of his jacket up—and bowed. A whole class of nursing students, just arrived, cheered him wildly, and since they were liberated females they used obscene gestures to appeal to the navigator. Encouraged, and being a somewhat typical variety of Czech (Homo sapiens Bohemicus, var. musicalis) he started to sing a Bohemian folk song, one of the national cultural treasures:

"My peachy cute Marushko,
you know it's May—
I wonder if I may
lay you in the hay
and spread your alabaster knees..."

He did not finish the story, this hounding melody of piercing beauty, in his pretty good baritone. He was interrupted when four steely hands lifted him into the air and deposited him onto a large rubber Zodiak with a roaring outboard four-cycle Yamaha motor. In just seconds the rescue team landed by the railing of the embankment and those steely, Schwarzeneggerish hands lifted Ivanek over the banister onto the sidewalk. One of the professional rescuers said in a low voice: "Welcome to the living, weirdo," and gave a smile to Ivanek, who wavered on firm land with uncertain sailor's legs, feet bare.

Uniformed policemen held the crowds back; cameramen were allowed to approach to about three meters away and to take extreme close-ups with their teleobjectives. Reporters were shouting questions and arguing with the men of the law. Then more space was claimed by the uniformed men for the mayor of the city and his people. Somebody pushed Ivanek forward and hissed that Mr. Mayor would like to speak with him.

"Mayor himself! Do you understand?"

Ivanek nodded, rechecked the salami, his fly, curled his big toes inward and straightened up. The tension of the media folks increased.

"His Excellency!" Ivanek exclaimed loudly. His hand shot up for a brisk military salute.

"Oh no, my friend," the physically diminutive executive retorted with a kind smile for the objective lens of the TV NOVA camera. "Call me ... just ... Mr. Mayor, please." He stepped forward further and extended his hand. At the same time Ludovik Vaculavik, the writer well known for his courageous stand against communists and for his less than mediocre writing ability, tried to position himself in an advantageous angle to the cameras. His face was strained by the effort to come up with a witty and important sentence with which to insert himself into the situation. Two of the mayor's body guards (with two indisposable and indispensable tools of their trade—walkie-talkie and sunglasses), squared their shoulders and turned the corners of their mouth downward. Idiots in the mob behind the officials made faces and gestures hoping to be seen on the TV screens.

The Mayor's extended hand, which remained suspended in space, would appear, later, on a photograph on the web site www.ceskenoviny.cz with the text disputing why the hand was not taken by the now famous survivor.

The Mayor's hand was not taken and shaken because Ivanek was stunned into a stupor, catatonia, suddenly. He saw her forehead with bangs the color of freshly minted copper. Her red hair was plaited into a single old-fashioned braid she had laid in front of her shoulder. Her face was pale and very beautiful, her eyes on him, intently. Ivanek took hold of himself and tried to step toward her—but his legs refused to obey.

"Milus," he whispered. "Milus?" He asked louder. She gazed at him calmly, her face expressionless. Then a reporter stepped in front of her. When he moved away she was gone. Not even her vacant space remained. She disappeared with the disappearing crowd. People started to run away, pushing and shouting, pointing at their feet, stepping high. The hungry, wild river spilled over the sidewalk. The flood arrived onto the street and everybody was on the move. At that moment the Old Town became the edge of a swimming pool for feces, rats and butts.

Ivanek found himself alone, his bare feet ankle high in the flowing dirt. A pair of soaked unused cigarettes floated by his feet, one lonely used condom, this ever-present whitefish of Vltava, following behind. Because he still saw her copper hair and her face, he could comprehend only a little of what was happening around him. It took some time before he turned around to survey the river, but he did not worry. He had arrived with the flood. While stooping in dejection at this moment he was not a hopeless homeless, no, not Ivanek, the man with friends.

✳

A young man ran to Ivanek, splashing. "Wanna a ride, somewhere?" he shouted. He had to repeat his offer: "I'll give you ride!"

"That will be nice, very nice," Ivanek whispered. He seemed to wake up. In contrast to everybody else's panic, they walked to the parked Skoda deliberately. The car started well and soon they reached the dry pavement of Narodni Boulevard heading to Vaclavske Square.

"So, where should I drop you off, mister… mister…?"

"Sorry, Ivanek is my name. I'd like to go to the railroad station. To Wilson Station, please."

"No problem with that, Mr. Ivanek. I'm going in that general direction, anyway." The young man introduced himself as Ivan Ketner. "Where are you traveling?" he asked.

"Oh, home." Ivanek nodded with a quizzical expression on his face.

"And where is your home, if I may ask?"

"The Wilson Station."

The young man, Ivan Ketner, shook his head and smiled in incomprehension, politely. Ivanek started to shiver so Ketner switched on the heating. He wanted to say something nice to his passenger, so he said: "It was a great voyage, sir. Such a dangerous flood. Yours will become a celebrated navigation, sir."

Ivanek's face lighted up just a little. He nodded. He thought so, too.

"Is somebody waiting for you?" The driver asked.

"They always are!" Ivanek's smile widened. "A few will be bumming around the countryside, mind you, till the fall, but Mita will be waiting for me. He's got one leg, so he stays. You should hear him play his ukulele; like Russians he plays, so good." Ivanek looked at the driver to see if he believed.

"And Pretty Boy Joseph might be there waiting for me. He is the one who believes in supernatural beings and God, like Americans and Arabs. But he is a nice man, anyway. They say he hides from two very rich wives, I don't know.

"I think, Vladimir might be back from the country, by now. He is an alcoholic and big time smoker, so the country air is too thin for him, that's what he says, but everybody likes him. He always agrees and smiles; Jura smiles too, he stays on the bench near the ticket counters. He is Slovak, you know, but thinks Slovaks are nationalists with an inferiority complex, that's what he says. So he loves Prague, where people feel superior, as you know yourself, sir. Jura goes panhandling to Lesser Town and then shares with all of us Wilson people." Ivanek looked out of the window. "We'll be there soon, there is the opera! We'll be there in a minute!"

"You've got many friends, Mr. Ivanek. Rare thing for a man nowadays!" Ivan Ketner remarked with a grimace of appreciation.

"Reckon I do. Yes, sir, I have ... and I forgot Violetta. They call her 'bag lady' but she ain't no bag ... and carries none, that's the truth. You would like her, yes sir. Mostly, she stays on the benches by the toilets, always dressed like for a carnival. Man ... so nice and colorful!"

Ivanek showed the excitement of a kid bragging about a new bike. The car stopped in front of the station's main entrance and Ivanek continued still: "And you just wouldn't believe her dog Luna. She is the smartest mutt you ever saw, walks on her hind legs like a man and—listen to this—she speaks. She, Luna I mean, barks 'good night' in English ... like an Englishman! Unbelievable, I know, but I've heard it myself. Good night, that's what she says, my friend!"

Then Ivanek waved till the car disappeared in the traffic. Being from the railroad station he knew everything about waving. Waving is a must—and must be done with smooth, wavy movements. But it was time to go in now, friends might be waiting.

People's Delights

Cover public housing with soot, surround it with a row of dirt-storing warehouses, break windows here and there, crack the asphalt on the roads and uproot few hydrants, too. And don't forget to add a bar on each street, a bar where drinks are sold that can add rainbow colors to the drabness of a day that resembles yesterday, tomorrow's twin, and on and on. And over this valley at the edge of the city build a bridge so immensely high that to the people gathering below it would seem to be a sliver of heaven.

✳

They were carrying chairs out of the beer joint onto the sidewalk. "Hurry up, you guys, hurry up!" the skinny one with the weasel's face urged them, his eyes highly glossed over with eagerness, darting somewhere high up and back again to the entrance of the bar. The big one, with a ruddy, pitted nose on which the tangle of purple veins wrote the story of a breakfast alcoholic, carried two chairs, easily. There still were some muscles under his hippopotamic wrap of blubber. He might have been a trucker, from the claim on his cap: "No F-----g, No Trucking."

There was an old man with a wrinkled gray face in a wrinkled black suit, gesticulating spastically, pointing at spots for the chairs. "Put them in a row, facing that way, idiots!" He was bent sideways and forward, but the curvature of his back was not of hunchback severity, yet. Nobody paid attention to him and he seemed not to expect any. He championed his decrepitude with an occasional coughing spell.

The woman (it seemed to be a female), in her thirties or sixties, also advised. From time to time she would abandon her agitation and with her fists buried in where her waist used to be, elbows high, she would tilt her head backward and stare up. A smile would come to her face, failing to improve it.

"Let's put out the long table, too," one beer-bellied authority ordered from the bar's doorway. "Move your ass, it could happen any minute!" He sported a sailor's cap, pushed back to provide, perhaps, a carefree image. His shirt sleeves were rolled up, and one knew the ropes of muscles in his

119

forearm did not acquire their bulk by only lifting beer mugs. The skin fold flapping from his chin to the bottom of his red neck enhanced his weighty authority, as it does in a male iguana. The table was carried out in an instant. Then the toughie brought out six mugs, three in each hand, spilling the foam only. Some pickled herring and pickled sausages with onion were placed onto the table; the bread, sliced thick on wooden plate, was on the house.

A few more customers brought out chairs to the sidewalk, while not neglecting their beer. One held a shot glass with a clear fluid. When they drank from their mugs, tilting backwards, their heads remained tilted back while their mugs went down on the table. The upturned eyes of all customers seemed fervent. Some narrowed them in a smile; most appeared eager, in anticipation. The mood was becoming festive with the clinking of beer glasses, contented chatter, the mumble and mutter of tongues made sluggish by drink. The ageless woman pointed up above her again, chuckling. "Takes her time," she said. "She takes her goddamn time."

The sun, seeing enough for today, hurried to hide behind the roof of the tallest warehouse. The air was dead. It was hot and steamy, a climate of violence for some, of lethargy for others and, possibly, of suffering which became unbearable, for one.

She was not alone on the bridge. An ambulance blocked the traffic in one lane; patrol cars rotated their blue electronic fireflies. A police psychologist talked to her with trained calmness, from a few steps away. She balanced on the railing holding onto a steel cable.

How old was she? Was she pretty? Was she smart? Had she lost a family or a lover? Was her despair unrepairable? Or was her body diseased? We do not know and if we knew, it would be another long story, because every human story must be long, if told in truth, and a story of self-destruction should be contained in a thousand pages.

She had a loose black frock which would stretch in flight like monstrous raven's wings. The wind blew her long hair over her face, but in the fall the hair would follow like a comet's tail. If she took the lethal plunge, would she make a sound, other than the swishing pitch of the wind? Or would she fall as silently as the owl flies across the moon? But are we sure that she devised the free fall of her own free will? To free herself, would she descend into oblivion now? Why was she waiting? The sun had fallen already.

✳

The only thing certain was that the people deep down on the street were ready. The beer flowed still but the supply of pale, pickled sausages with onion had been exhausted by those sitting in delightful anticipation.

On Brainwaves of Memory

What beastly incidents our memories insist on cherishing.
Eugene O'Neill

Most roofers do it. When they finish a copper roof, they pee on it to start the chemical reaction. The persimmon gloss is speed-aged to the green-gray malachite of baroque bronze. To generate a sufficient volume of urine, the roofer drinks a gallon of beer and gets very happy and uncertain in his balance. (A case is known of a plastered roofing specialist who lost his footing on the steep roof of the St. Ludmila Cathedral and slid in the direction of the two-hundred-foot drop, only to be arrested in his fall by the statue of a watchful gargoyle. Lying in the gutter, he fell asleep instantly, complicating his rescue by a special unit of mountain climbers.)

Old sandstone and marble buildings of historical significance can be aged nicely, too, not by urine but by acid rain, noxious fumes, and deposits of dust. But a building of no historical significance, like the high school in Prague-6, would not weather well, because it was a contemporary structure. At least we thought of it as modern, since the proportion of glass to stucco on its façade favored glass. Dust and grime from the traffic below has deposited a makeup of dejection and fatigue on its face, saddest on a sunny day. It seemed to match the expression of students leaving the open sky and their partial liberty for its torture chambers of dead languages and calculus.

I remember, in Shakespeare's words, "creeping like snail unwillingly to school," then slowing down to a standstill in front of that building. There, I used to hope to sight a friend who would help me through the glass door of the entrance. Anyone of our Group, as we called ourselves, would do. Pepik Pycha might shuffle up the street from Hanspaulka.

Pepik had gained notoriety for his inimitable laugh, which roared with well-separated syllables, "ha - ha," often in the middle of a teacher's monologue, and always propping up his jokes. He knew hundreds of disgusting jokes without ever writing any down—such was the memory of Pepik Pycha. His grades were far less than mediocre, because of his feeble memory (he said). After three years of compulsory Russian language, when everybody was reading Russian classics, Pepik still confused the capital letters of the Cyrillic alphabet.

Lubos Hanzlik might approach from up the hill too. We admired the many pockets of his U.S. Army jacket, the army cap, and the Camels he offered to anyone in the Group but to nobody else. He boasted a C in Morals and Behavior, for his disturbances and cheekiness. His flunking of Art was admired as a unique achievement. It was hard to understand because his creations resembled so closely the paintings of "primitives" much valued by galleries in those times of socialist realism. Lubos was a big guy but not a pretty boy. These physical attributes of fierceness had not made him less popular, because they helped him to emanate confidence. He had grown to a great height in spite of efforts by his mother, who used to give him cigarettes in his preadolescence in an attempt to stunt his growth.

I could wait a few minutes for the next tram No. 24, carrying Kaja Fot. He was the handsome one of the Group, whose unprovable stories of his amorous adventures we wished to believe, because they gave us hope. His carefully staged arrogance endeared him to some of his peers but failed to impress any teacher. This contributed to his abysmal grades.

Latin class started with the same ritual, always, without variation. When that relic of Austrian monarchy, the bearded Professor Kramar, entered the classroom following his own beer belly, everybody stood up, and in one voice we had to greet him in Latin: *"Salve domine professor!"* Without giving us a glance, Kramar marched to his desk. He turned to the class—*"Salvete discipuli!"*—and then motioned us to sit down with a gesture which might have been confused with the signal for an execution.

"Fot!" Professor then exclaimed, and Kaja Fot stood up. Kramar asked him the meaning of a Latin word, which Kaja, unfailingly, did not know. "F!" roared the old man, and recorded the failing grade in his class book. And then class began. Every day this mini-drama started our Latin education, and it soon elevated Fot to the respectable status of somebody notorious and remarkable, of an admirably strong will. So he became one of the Group, where these were the most appreciated attributes of a man in his teen years of burrowing acne and perpetual longing for a lay.

The power of scholastic failure was valued, then. It was an expression of dissent, of revolt against the authority and Communistic idiocy of the spineless, and against the political chameleonization of our poor teachers. But what mattered to us the most was that these demonstrative failures increased one's stature in many a misty eye of a well-endowed female schoolmate.

✳

Kaja Fot emerged from tram No. 24 just before I entered the building. I waited for him, and we greeted each other mutely, just with our eyes. "Again!" he said, and elongated his face.

"Shit," I said, and we entered.

"Today, I'll walk Jana Volavkova home from school," Kaja remarked, waiting for my comment.

"I don't know, man. Remember last week? When she gave you a fat lip after you praised the bulges in her sweater?"

"Yeah. It hurt. She plays tennis, man. She's some piece of work."

"That movie, yesterday. Incredible!" I changed the topic. Yesterday we'd had to attend a Russian movie about "heroes of socialist work," coal miners, who had fulfilled their Five Year plan in four. Attendance was compulsory, and headcounts had been made by teachers who watched vigilantly for anybody who might laugh. Any loud sighs of admiration were recorded, too, as provocations.

"Torture, bore!" Kaja tilted his head backward and howled, not unlike a wolf. People around us paid attention; some stopped. Just in time we entered the classroom, where we survived till noon, each hovering over our private dreamscapes.

During the noon break we had to "circulate," walk the school's corridors without stopping. Our Group of four was together, as usual, talking in short utterances about yesterday's movie, enjoying the felicities of the crudest possible expressions. Jana Volavkova passed by us during the circulation, in her new pink sweater. It might have been the view of what the sweater tried to conceal that impressed Kaja Fot again. He dropped to his knees by the wall of the hallway and, using an imaginary pick, he started to imitate the digging of a Russian miner, the hero of socialist work, from yesterday's flick. Within seconds Pepik Pycha, Lubos Hanzlik, and I, the Group, were on our knees toiling in the mine shaft with dramatic gestures and faces distorted by fatigue, barely bearable.

Suddenly, the crowd around us dispersed. There, in the vacant space, stood Professor Konecna, Party Member and terrorist, feared by everybody in the school with the exception of the janitor-doorman Pudlak, who was an informer for the Czech KGB. Like an overweight angel of death, she loomed over us, recording our names. Then she disappeared, evaporated without comment. We knew that the trouble ahead would be of the serious kind.

In a couple of days each one of us "miners" was informed by a letter of stark sentences that we would spend one month "shockworking," harvesting the famous red Semsch hops. It was dirty slavery that included sleeping in sex-segregated barns, eating tripe soup, and being harassed by moronic villagers with sadistic inclinations. The verdict was final and did not allow for any exceptions—save illness. This exception had to be discussed.

After the last lecture that day, the convicts in the Group did not leave the classroom. We sat in a circle on the desks, heads together. Of the other students, only Josh Osten stayed, writing something, in the front row. Osten was a good fellow who could be trusted, for he too was prone to rebellion and rowdiness. His extreme intelligence and sarcastic wit commanded respect from all of us but at the same time prevented him from acquiring bad grades, which were a sort of prerequisite for inclusion in the Group.

✳

The clear memory of that day lives deep in my hippocampus, the black part of my brain. The darkness of it has not come from some fetal night, but from the events of that afternoon.

✳

"Gentlemen, to the Clinic you have to present yourselves with a fever," I started the discussion. "The increase in temperature has to be stressed in the doctor's letter to the school. Only that could save you from the shit of harvesting hops." Lubos stared with an open mouth. Pepik nibbled on a pimple. Kaja picked his nose, in concentration.

"How to induce the fever, losers like you might wonder," I continued. "There is a sure and little known procedure: sterilize a sewing needle over a burning match. Thread it with a thread about five inches long. Soak the thread in gasoline. Then an intimate friend should pinch and lift the soft skin of your underarm, and you penetrate the skin-fold with the needle and lead the gasoline-soaked thread through the tissue. Very slowly!" I could see that my description of the procedure had made an impression. Lubos Hanzlik put an unlit cigarette in his mouth, where it remained hanging, glued to the lower lip.

"The fever will appear in approximately twenty minutes and will last long enough for a visit to a physician. It will subside before you can reach the sanctuary of *Na Kulatem Namesti* beerhall on the way home. End of lecture, my fellow morons." Kaja and Pepik nodded with appreciation. That's how it has always been: we nodded in agreement on all the important matters. We understood each other; we were friends, loyal to each other, loyal as losers must be at all times. I could never detect any insecurity (the major curse of mankind) which would have driven a man to any achievement. I liked them all, their faces adorned by a sneer even in revelry.

"And how about the hot potato method, *vole?*" Lubos Hanzlik remarked. "You know, you heat a potato, put it in your pocket, and when they give you the thermometer in the clinic, and when nobody is looking, you stick it into the hot potato, *vole*. How about that, *vole?*" There was no response. "Or how about smoking a cigarette soaked in vinegar and dried—you'll get real sick, *vole*. I've heard about a guy who died like that, smoking three, he wanted to…"

"Lubos, shut up! Stupid stuff," Pepik Pycha ordered, and raised a hand to command attention. He got it. "Picric acid method—it has been well tested by army recruits. You know well about their desperation, you guys! One teaspoon of the powdered picric acid in a cup of milk, down it—and the next day the white of your eyes ain't white no more. The doctor will see nicely yellowed eyes, *icterus* they call it, jaundice. And you know what that could mean? Infectious hepatitis!"

Pepik made a gesture with his hand, cutting his throat. "Show me a doc who would risk not writing you a nice letter for the school: rest in bed in peace, and fluids. No fucking hops. Amen." Pepik Pycha rested, nodding in approval of himself.

Kaja Fot imitated a vomiting sound, asking for attention. That was his way. The curls of his strangely orange hair (long before punkism) still showed, on his temples, a little of the blue tint caused by a shampoo stolen from a friend of his mother's who visited their house. Too late he had recognized that it contained a blue dyeing component. The corners of his handsome lips were turned downward to suggest that his contribution would be serious, no pun.

"Gentlemen, *volove*! The sewing with gasoline thread and the picric acid cocktail are interesting proposals, indeed. But listen to the ultimate in medical deception!" He put the palms of his hands together as if in prayer. "Pay attention, screwballs, since you are in great need of guidance." He turned his head from side to side with an expression of resignation, then he laughed briefly and continued.

"All you need is garlic and band-aids. Yes, garlic. Mash a clove with a pinch of salt. Apply a small amount—about lentil size—to the skin on the belly and cover with the band-aid. Place a few more on your decrepit trunk. Maybe one on your ass, Lubos! Go to sleep, alone—Pycha, you would have no problem with that. When you wake up, take the garlic off. And *voila*! There would glitter a sparkling clear blister under each band-aid."

Kaja spread his arms, asking for appreciation. "This is what we call an ingenious deceit, in the business, yo-yos. The doctor would never, ever fathom the nature of your mysterious affliction. No fever, tongue pale, eyes bloodshot normally, balls shriveled as usual. But all those suspicious lesions?" Kaja turned around, looking out the window to demonstrate disinterest in our reaction.

"That's good, *vole*," said Lubos Hanzlik.

"Wow!" Said Pepik Pycha, his mouth remaining agape.

"Very cool," I might have said. "But let's ask somebody else. Let's ask Osten, there, what he would think about that. He's got the brains!" I turned around and motioned with my hand to Josh Osten, who was still scribbling something in the front row. The guys nodded. "Yeah," somebody agreed.

I remember the voice of Lubos Hanzlik clearly. It had a curious pitch that did not fit well his six-foot-three bulk. He turned around and called: "Hey, Jew Osten! Hey Jewboy!"

There was a long silence. Nobody said anything. None of us did anything then. None of us.

That was five decades ago, almost a lifetime. Not only my brain but also my heart remembers clearly. The memory is unkindly lucid, untouched by time, which has elapsed in haste without helping me to understand.

※

After that day our Group disintegrated, because we felt uneasy looking into each others' eyes. Kaja and I became friends with Josh Osten, who did not know bitterness. He had an aunt who was the director of the Jewish Museum in Prague and sometimes, somehow, Osten could get the keys from the building. We would sneak in there at night, and with all those wonderful ancient things around us we would play records of Tchaikovsky with vodka, and of West Side Story with rum. The young ladies we used to take with us were amazed by our sophistication and, therefore, were kind to us. The images of their kind deeds were encoded into the sunny part of my brain with great clarity. Still, today, they radiate like beautiful wild flowers on the confused landscape of my senility.

These are the brainwaves of memory I choose to surf into my sunset, leaving the "man in the grey suit" of dark thoughts deep down in the deep.

The Strange Restoration of J.A. Splinter

Until the arrival of Jan Andrew Splinter, the most memorable events in the life of the village would have been the typhoon with its eye right overhead, and one earthquake that measured 7.8 on the Richter scale. His coming was as unexpected as the volcanic quake. He fell out of an old U.S. Army surplus jeep in front of the Chief's hut, stretched, then helped the diminutive driver to unload an enormous red duffel bag with "Eddie Bauer" embossed on it. So Eddie, people thought—those few who got the courage to approach, with a smile. The tall pale stranger smiled too and then shook the left hand of old Manolo, whose right hand was saving his falling pants.

"Eddie! Señor Eddie," Manolo beamed, and people nodded.

"Buenos tardes, padre." Jan widened his grin, actually bowed and then climbed the stairs to the Chief's veranda. At the top of stairs he turned around, descended and asked Manolo to keep an eye on his Eddie Bauer bag. You never know. When he climbed up the stairs again the Chief (who had been watching between the planks of his hut) stood there with a serious mask, in red T-shirt saying "Vegetarians Taste Better." They proceeded to greet each other with some formality while more villagers arrived to form a welcoming crowd. People gesticulated; some raised eyebrows, some opened eyes widely, some opened mouths widely, some shook their heads from side to side, and others nodded. They all exuded the excitement of bashful insecurity. The American had arrived.

✳

Splinter's elegant spiral of DNA, his genetic endowment, was solely responsible for his sinewy build, his sandy noncompliant hair and impressive height—the traits ran in the family on his mother's side. Ma towered over her husband by half a foot, like most Scandinavian females would tower over most non-Scandinavian males. She was Norwegian, and Jan's father was of Bohemian extraction. He'd changed his Slavic name by simply translating it to English. It was better that way in northern Minnesota, he surmised. But Mother towered over her hubby in her intellect, too—Father was no rocketry expert—and as he was a proud enough male, the family relations suffered. This caused Jan to search for a college geographically distant from his home town.

Jan enrolled in a medium-sized school in the northwestern corner of Washington and double majored in agriculture and botany. It was a solid and respectable achievement, of which he was justly proud. Cool. So he left the school with good feelings despite a couple of regrets: no love story and no real friend. He was wise and observant enough to understand that if he had not found a true friend in college he would have opportunity to find only acquaintances in the future.

It was his nature that served him so well in studies but not so well when among pals passing a joint at a beer party. Too serious, they said about him; a stickler for details bordering on spasticity. Keen on particulars, those printed in small type on a page, and in life, too. He looked for the perfection where perfection was not the goal. And he knew it and tried to change, and when he tried it came out so phony that everything inside him screamed bullshit, and he ran to the study or the library, alone.

That said, he had been accepted well enough, because he was a good man. He was helpful, sincere; not a trace of a mean streak in him. Good kid, that Splinter boy. Peace Corps material? Sure thing.

Jan did see the past as a mirage of placid days filled with study, but did not suffer from lack of dreams. So he decided that before committing himself to a career in the Corporate World of sterility, he would join the Peace Corps and spend a year or two in the Third World of uncertainty, saving those meager three grand a year and doing more for Mankind than if he were at Monsanto. Because agriculture is the specialty most in demand among the Peace Corps, he was accepted on the first shy try, despite some doubts by the elders on the admission committee about his ability to adjust to cultures remote from ours. Privately he was warned by an old hand to avoid any excesses "*in venere et baccho.*" Yeah, even the ancient Latins knew these dangers to *homo ludens* and *homo explorans*, the wise man said. Jan could get really screwed in the Third World, man, and even more in the Fourth, fooling around and not paying attention.

Before he had time to really take in this sudden sea change in his life he was in the air, flying to the remote region in the Philippines, there to show the natives a better way to live. He was installed in a neat thatch hut that did not leak too much when it rained. No electricity, no phone numbers, no stop signs. For the first time in his life Jan Andrew Splinter began to feel at home.

✳

Those unblessed ones who have fallen in love with village beauties would recognize in her some common and uncommon traits and attributes. Her facial components were in symmetric harmony and balance. There was no dominant nose, flaring auricles or pronounced oriental epicanthi. However, one would notice her lips were exceptionally full. Facing her, one would vividly imagine them nesting a kiss, entrapping it in their wet snare, and one would go on imagining and dreaming about it regardless of the conversation topic or the importance of matters of the moment.

Her hair was simply the hair of her people: a mane of straight, plentiful wires, charcoal black, with the gloss of a black panther emerging from a jungle stream. She was of slender build but her rump and breasts, the duo of anatomical parts desired commonly by males, were clearly present and could be envisaged to be of unaccustomed cartillagenous firmness, their caramel-hued and caramel-sweet surfaces silky smooth. They were always concealed by a sarong-like wraparound, the heritage of fanatical missionaries, those masters of shame and guilt induction.

Her hands were interesting in their deception: the long, gracefully slender fingers were upper class, high society, but the view from the palmar side revealed four horny calluses each the size of a penny, the badges of callous labor. Her feet were just the regular, beaten up rural tootsies which have never ventured to explore inside the darkness of a shoe. The big toes were spread widely apart, as in the hominid apes, and Jan marveled at what he'd got into, looking at them. They would never fit in a shoe, with the exception of Eskimo *kamiks* or *illigamaks*. Pumps? Ha!

Often, he would catch a glimpse of her in the village hurrying around with a wide basket on her head, erect, like an amanita mushroom on the go, or lumbering under a load of firewood, a beast of burden—till she looked up. Never would a strain show up on her sweatless face and never would the load affect her graceful gait. So he thought about her, evenings, and allowed her to enter his dreams, where she dispersed images from his past like a barracuda hitting a school of fat, content pinfish.

His first inspection of her at close range occurred a couple of months into his stay. He was working on his project, planting a thousand seedlings of mahogany up on Kunde Hill. He had half-fulfilled his work plan for the day, planting the perfect twelfth row with even spacing. Villagers had helped him to clear part of the jungle on the hill next to a creek, which would provide water for the seedlings.

A flock of women lumbered down Kunde with their loads of firewood and stopped to watch the American, while pretending to drink from the stream. Jan approached her with some trepidation and asked, in their native Tagalog, if the water was good to drink. Just a request of information, no smiles, and some would say that their following verbal encounter lacked sophistication.

"Is good, Señor Eddie."

"I am Jan, not Eddie, you know?"

"Ia'n Eddie!" She smiled so that his stomach constricted and his heart fluttered in dangerous fibrillations...

"Well...." He said. "And what is your name?"

"Carmencita my name."

"Carmencita is a very pretty name," he said, grateful that he could say "pretty" to her. They exchanged two, three simple sentences and Jan, aware of the close scrutiny of the other women, went back to his mahoganies, humming and smiling, while hiding their roots into the rusty laterite sprinkled with his sweat in 95% relative humidity at 95 degrees of Fahrenheit. When he stretched he cheered the violin bird displaying its plumes on the *Ravenea musicalis* palm, and marveled at the resplendent iridescence of the Morpho butterfly homing at his neck, seduced by the scent of his sweat. He smelled, with exaltation, the sweet vanilla perfume from a spray of blossoms of the Brassavola orchid swaying in the breeze like a roost of white minimal roosters, and took in with all his senses this botanical Eden.

She was gone, he was alone—so at the green wall of the jungle he hollered: "Ain't bad, kid!" He flicked a drop of sweat from the tip of his nose. "Not bad at all!"

＊

Jan Andrew Splinter was getting used to everything which comes with the tropics: tedious food, often more like bait than a meal; rough climate; diarrhea and skin fungus and, frequently, the overwhelming kindness of the natives. He rejoiced in discovering his fellow villagers, their patient resourcefulness, their ability to do much with what little was available. Lozio had glued together the twenty shards of glass of a shattered hurricane lamp cylinder. Roberto had fixed the tiny clasp on Jan's camera by multiple feather-gentle touches of two pounds sheet-metal hammer on an iron nail. Jan marveled at the many uses of super-glue (Jan's present) when mixed with fine sand, and more. Villagers took to technical imports with ingenuity and relish, but the cultural inventions of the outer world they rejected in confusion and, often, with a resentment of mysterious origin. This had been demonstrated to Jan most dramatically in the Affair Carmencita.

After the rainy season ended Jan decided to chance it. One afternoon he waited for her at the end of the beach where he knew she would go at low tide to collect crustaceans and anything else that moved on the exposed reef. The creatures of the tidal pools were an important source of nutrition, since all the fish had been dynamited out. The beach, a ribbon of subdued gun-gray, was narrow, despite the low tide. It was bordered by a belt of salt loving vegetation which made a wall hiding the village. From this Bogota-emerald belt the coconut palms shot up to the sky, then curved above the water in gracefully audacious arches and bends. The tidal current made the water murky along the shore—only at the deepest part of the lagoon, by the barrier of coral reef, did the water clear to greens and blues reflecting the moods of the sky. He used to come here, sometimes, to watch the kildeers, the sandpipers in their hunt for sand lice, the brown pelicans like archeopteryx skipping inches above the lagoon, and the magnificent frigate-birds, the perfect birds, high above it all. Sometimes he dreamt of home.

When she waded onto the shore he asked her to come see him in his hut that night. He would cook for her a delicacy of his own invention: freshwater prawns from the creek near his mahoganies, steamed in banana beer. He would have breadfruit baked in platano leaves—she would certainly like it. He smacked his lips and generated a smile he thought to be irresistibly seductive, despite his cracked lower lip. She looked down at the ground, then walked away whispering something like a chant. Or a promise?

That evening Jan waited in a newly washed Minnesota Twins T-shirt, went to urinate three times, repeatedly combed his unruly hair and rechecked the breadfruit in the open fire pit in his outdoor "kitchen." Then, all of a sudden, she appeared next to him, like an apparition of the kind which when touched would disappear. He shook her hand several times and was moved to see that she wore a necklace of white cowry shells that he had never seen on her before and that she had painted her lips with a reddish dye. He was astounded by the difference this meager tool of diluvial cosmetics made.

He rushed the prawns on a steamer of his own design and soon they were eating in silence, sitting not on the floor but by his hand-hewn table, facing each other. She looked apprehensive and did not respond to his simplistic small talk. At one moment she looked as if on the verge of tears; he did not know why and was afraid to ask, not knowing why he was afraid. But the shrimp were great, anyway, goddamn it, he thought.

She left him after eating the prawns and the last tiny crumb of the breadfruit, saying "Buenas noches, Eddie, it was muy rico." She tried to smile and then touched his forearm with the tips of her piano player digits, moving her fingers down his arm as lightly as a dermatologist would pet a puppy. *What the hell?* he thought, because a lump in his throat prevented him from talking. *What the hell?* he thought, because she had disappeared.

The next day he looked for her in all the places and niches she might be found, but without success. By evening he'd noticed that the neighbors seemed to avoid meeting his eyes. Even old Manolo, his cheerful friend, would alter the direction of his stroll seeing Jan in his path, and the widow Margarita "Mirabal" averted her eyes faster than when meeting the gaze of a spitting cobra. Only the dogs looked him straight in the eye. Some even wiggled their tails; to them he was known as the "the one who does not kick." After several days of nervous gloom on the Island of Zombies, with no explanation forthcoming, Jan decided to see the Chief and ask what was his disease. Was it contagious as ebola? Repulsive as lepromatous leprosy?

✳

The evening before the planned visit of the Big Man, two young men walked into Jan's hut without the customary calling of greetings outside. They stood by the door motionless and did not seem to notice Jan's welcoming gesture offering them a seat. Jan knew one of them—he was the oldest of Carmencita's seven brothers. The other, in his late twenties perhaps, was certainly a stranger in the village. He wore a sneer of disgust on his face, which might not actually have been disgust as it was the result of a scar pulling one corner of his mouth downwards. He wore a baseball cap with the visor backwards, common sandals of tire treads, black jeans and a faded flower pattern shirt with the collar turned up. Carmencita's brother talked to this man in their native Tagalog, while the stranger translated to fairly good English, not Spanish.

"Eddie, we came to tell you this," the tough fellow started without the customary polite hesitation. "Know Carmencita? …. It is sad. You maybe disgraced her, maybe you did not." His grin remained unchanged, his eyes looked at Jan calmly, but there was no steel, no snake hypnosis in them; there might be an amusement in those coal beads. Jan's hand began to tremble so he folded them on his chest, then unfolded them to motion the visitors to sit down, again. They did not pay attention.

The brother said few words to his companion in Tagalog which he interpreted.

"It has been decided here, in this village, that you shall marry her." Toughie paused and contorted his lips. It was a smile, no doubt. Again the brother talked.

"You must marry her before the new moon. Come tomorrow to talk to her father and grandfather! That's what her brother here said."

There was a long silence. Maybe, all was said. Jan wiped sweat from his eyes and turned his head watching a brown moth fluttering across the room, hitting the wall. The moth was trapped, he thought. His nose started to run.

Carmencita's brother raised his voice, in anger, it seemed, talking now in Tagalog full of wildness directly to Jan. He ended—then opened widely his mouth revealing two rows of perfect brown teeth and stuffed his fist in the mouth, extruding his eyeballs in a frightening enraged grimace. Jan stepped backwards, almost fell, tripping over the kitchen stool. The brother turned around abruptly and marched away, leaving the stranger behind to translate. Jan tried to control his tremor.

"He said, that if you'd try to leave, to escape, you know, before marrying, you'll be caught. That is certain. Then your balls, las bollas, amigo, will be cut off. Then your balls will be stuffed to your mouth and you will suffocate. That is what will happen!" The stranger turned, shuffled to the door but stopped and returned with a scowl resembling an acceptable smile on the left side of his lips but a sneer scar-side.

"You see, that will be my job! Ha, Eddie? So you don't worry about … suffocation. You die before that …. suffocation, mi amigo." The man seemed to be in a pleasant disposition, now. "You'll die of…" he could not come up with a word, bent his head down, thinking, shaking his forearm up and down. "Yeah, yeah, Eddie. You'd die first of terror, yes … t e r r o r !"

✳

So, there was a joyous wedding in the village of the Peace Corps volunteer Jan Andrew Splinter and his Carmencita, lovely, and virginal to boot. Marriage rites happened two nights before the new moon and, to the day, on the anniversary of Jan's arrival with Eddie Bauer duffel bag. During the wedding the groom oscillated from a bout of depressive stupor lasting several minutes to exaggerated exuberance of equally short duration, when he would scream songs with locals, his fist flying high up in the rejection of threatening gloom, accompanied by a bellow of some college profanity.

In a solitary, quiet moment, when everybody lay plastered, he leaned back on a tree, looked at his bride surrounded by old women and by the envious eyes of the young ones, mumbled "unbelievable" and remembered reaching this place a year ago with the thought that he was entering Tropical Cultures 101. He howled quietly, being certain, now, he was not in the classroom.

"My shitting days are over, my shitting days are over," he repeated without much linguistic imagination. He did not know, exactly, how he felt—but it was not the pukka sahib satisfaction, for that the stomach was too giddy and the throat too constricted. He cheered up a little when a disorganized squadron of flying foxes, fruit bats, passed above crapping on the guests and squealing at Jan: "Go, Eddie, go!" he was sure. It was a blue-bright night, hopeful for them, too.

During the ceremony and the festivities it was impressed on Jan that he had become one of them. "Now, Eddie, you are one of us," some told him cheerfully and a few told him gravely.

Then the *tuba*, the palm wine, cut him down, too. When he recovered he would walk his bride, hand in hand, to his hut, despite the rule that she should walk steps behind. "Fuck the rule," he told her with the sweetest smile he could muster at that late hour, stumbled a few times and to himself mumbled "this is god-damned exciting" before collapsing on the four-poster bed of his own construction, only to wake up at light with a *tuba*-headache to find his wife (Wow! Wife?) lying on the split bamboo floor next to his bed like a vagrant on the subway grid. He lay down next to her.

※

Carmencita grew up in a village which lacked philosophers, scholars of high learning, and social scientists. So she, as everybody else, knew that there are only three things essential in life: intake of fluids, sex, and food. Without one of them life and life's renewal will cease. With scarcity of one of them life will not be normal and the soul and body will be diseased. This was passed down by generations and well proven by cruel experiments of nature. That was what she knew.

However, she had been instructed by her mother in coitus solely for procreation. Jan, of course, was determined to become her tutor in sex solely for non-procreation and on the way, maybe, learn a thing or two himself.

Since the behavior of lovers must be so refined as to result in the greatest mutual joy and laughter known to man, it cannot be hurried—or, gods forbidding, coerced. This was the first lesson.

Fortunately, Carmencita lacked deleterious bashfulness and soon it became obvious that in her genetic makeup she carried the gene encoding for natural gregariousness in matters of intimacy, and also for plain love of fun. And Jan was a good boy, too, so the gods decided to reward them with friendship and intense liking of each other, which is rarer than love and therefore considered by some as more precious. Not long into their relationship Jan and Carmencita graduated from speaking from the brain to speaking from the heart. It was a new and astonishing experience for both of them.

Food was another matter to be explored. Carmencita smacked her generous lips over the "mashed potatoes" Jan made not by mashing potatoes but mashing pounded yams with hot goat's milk. She liked Jan's bread made of flourized manioc with the yeast from fermented palm wine, baked in a pit with hot stones. Of course, the freshwater prawns steamed over banana beer were the hands-down all-time favorite. While Carmencita's cooking was mostly directed to replenish calories, in time

Jan learned from her the sophistication of simplicity—hen cooked in coconut milk and hot peppers was on the top of the list.

Drinks, as we know them, were a problem. But our Peace Corps worker had developed an ingenious method of mixing several-day-old *tuba* wine with a little sweet guanabana juice and a dash of coconut milk, leaving it to referment overnight. A quart of this bubbly would do very nicely, after they had bolted the door. Carmencita would catch the gigantic click beetles that have two fluorescent spots on their thorax of such an intensity that they lit their room in psychedelic patterns, and when seduced to land on her naked body, illuminated her beauteous curves from angles which cannot be imagined, and when seen, would not be forgotten. Ever.

About two weeks into their domestic bliss an episode, seemingly insignificant, marked the beginning of the period of their life that resembled the excursion of a tight rope walker on a windy night.

✳

Canuto "Bárbarito", the one with one milky opaque eye, ambled into Jan's hut just as the rain stopped. He was in a tense disposition which could be judged from the deep color of his facial hemangioma—the large birth mark which changed the intensity of its red hue according to old Canuto's mood. Jan had always marveled at his habit of sitting in front of his hut with a clove of garlic in each nostril watching the pelvic gyrations of the women pounding cassava with the total concentration of a scientist studying the behavior of an ant. Canuto was slightly "different."

"Regalo, Eddie," he said. He would not accept the stool, and waited with a nervous smile, the present in his outstretched hand. Carmencita busied herself, keeping a distance short enough to allow her to hear every word said. Canuto "Bárbarito" unwrapped the banana leaf and showed a foot-long pale sausage, which looked like a subject from a dissecting room of Pathology. He explained to the stranger, who knew so little about the ways of his people: a rare delicacy, this piece of dog's gut, the intestine of a dog who was fed only boiled rice for a week, every day just sweet white rice, then killed and the gut washed on the outside and boiled shortly. To be eaten slowly, slowly, this delicacy.

Jan thanked, nodding slowly. Carmencita licked her lips in secret. On the way out Canuto "Bárbarito" stopped and with both the good eye and the milky eye on the floor, added: "Señor Eddie, if it would be possible I'd like to sit behind the driver of the airplane. I would like to watch him to steer the aeroplane."

"Which … airplane, Bárbarito?"

"Oh, oh," sounded the old man, amused. He hacked, clearing his throat, percolating there the mucus generated by smoking since he was five years of age. But it could have been laughter.

"Krch, krch ...when you take us with you to America, that plane, señor Eddie. The aeroplane we all will fly with you!"

Poor guy, loosing his marbles in a bad way, concluded Jan.

A few days after Canuto's visit Margarita "Mirabal", the widow, sauntered in. Jan liked this woman and was undeterred by her laugh, the laugh of a hyena—with her hindquarters low to match. "Mirabal", besides all the chores of a woman, had learned to cast the throw-net into the surf like a man, and better. And she could pee standing, too. Atta lady! Jan thought.

The widow was followed by Maja Dog, her constant companion, the mutt with the face of a Tasmanian devil and the loving disposition of a boxer, who would never be eaten. The collapsible Maja Dog folded herself down on the floor when Margarita "Mirabal" displayed a half a dozen eggs in a basket. She swore that they were about ready to hatch, in a day or two at the most, so the fetuses would be just right, when boiled. When eating them, the tongue should just recognize the heart, by taste the liver, and brain through the crunchy skull. Oh—so good!

And, by the way, she would like to take with her a couple of her best hens. So please, could Eddie reserve a place for the hens on the American plane? So that she, the poor widow, could keep an eye on them. And, of course, another matter, she could not leave Maja Dog behind, alone in the deserted village. Please?

✳

They would come bringing things, offering to repair the roof, the stairs. All sincere, kind people, believing every word Jan said, because Jan did not say many.

Would he give a seat to Paeng, next to Juanita, since she was afraid of flying in the sky so high that one may see stars too close and, maybe, see the dangerous secrets of the Moon? Jan could not sleep well any more. He spent more time in his nursery, made love only twice a week, and walked through the village fast, his gaze straight ahead. Now there was no reason for denying the obvious. Jan sent Carmencita on a mission to verify. Wide-eyed she confirmed that, yes, Eddie was one of us, he would take us all with him. How great would be the future of all the villagers in America, while there was no future here, under Kunde Hill, after the villagers dynamited all the fish and the coral reef to smithereens. Oh, America!

In the southern sky the stars were very bright, strewn across the holes between the clouds as they rushed behind the hill from the west, predicting rain. The breeze danced with the tall coconuts, but ignored the clump of rugged oil palms near Jan's shelter. By the ground the air was still and the hardened laterite clay returned back the heat it had received during the day, with a wisp of earthy scent added. Jan evacuated the flying zone of night-biting mosquitoes on his porch and joined Carmencita inside.

Old Manolo eased himself in, shook hands with Jan several times and nodded his head with a happy face. He was Jan's favorite storyteller, this elder who had welcomed him to the village a year ago. On the hand-hewn table Manolo put an object of Carmencita's admiration. "Wonderful. So, so tasty!" She sighed and sat in the corner. It was a pig's stomach filled with coagulated blood, chopped pig's snout, and a fistful of boiled rice and spices—mostly crushed leaves from the renako tree, the tree without bark.

Manolo wondered how Jan would remember the seat assignments for all the villagers. He worried that his window seat reservation might be forgotten. Jan and the visitor remained silent for a long time.

"Why do you want to go so much?" Jan asked, finally.

"Everything is so plentiful in America. Everything. Even things we cannot imagine!"

"And how do you know that, Manolo?"

"G.I. Joe told me, in a bar in the capital after the war. He was tall like you, Eddie." Manolo smiled at his memory, since old people often smile remembering the past and rarely smile foreseeing the future. "Unimaginable things he told me, G.I. Joe." The soldier told Manolo that there, petrol flows underground everywhere, so that pumps cover the land like a strange forest as far as one can see, and pump day and night as if the iron forest sways in the wind. "G.I. Joe told me," Manolo remembered, "that they had so many mummies from Africa they use them for stoking fires in the locomotives, their iron horses. Imagine that land!"

Jan tried to imagine the land—but failed. He shook the hand with the visitor several times knowing he could not disappoint Manolo, his surrogate uncle and almost friend. He had to get to work.

In a dry place under the pandana leaf roof, Jan kept three little treasures: one-year-old issues of National Geographic, Geo and the magazine of Northwest Orient Airlines. He pulled out the airline publication. There it was. The Boeing 747 can take 418 passengers, the DC-10 290. But the right capacity seemed to be the Boeing 757, with seating for 194 passengers, three seats on each side, a range 2875 miles at cruising speed 530 miles per hour at thirty thousand feet. And Northwest owned forty-eight of these beauties.

Jan reached behind one of the rafters carefully (scorpions hid there). That was where he kept a few small bags of native medicine (all useless, he suspected by now) and, also, pieces of chalk to paint one's face for celebrations and festivals. With the chalk he drew the cabin of a Boeing 757 on the planks of the wall of his hut, as big across as the wall, with three seats on each side of the plane, all economy class, and the aisle between.

"Yeah, sure," Jan snickered, after reading in the magazine that "Our refurbished interiors, coupled with the outstanding technical expertise and genuine commitment to customer service, will give you an exceptional experience." He shook his head. "Yeah, my people need an exceptional experience!" He said it to Carmencita, who had just walked in and gazed at the white outline of the aircraft and the names of Canuto, Paeng next to Juanita, Margarita, Manolo on the window seat, and others. She did not say a word, but sat down next to Jan on the bed, and they huddled together. Jan put his arm around her waist, his bare foot stepping lightly on her foot, both gestures as unknown in the village as their destiny was unknown to them. Would their fate be common to both? That was the question they contemplated, without asking it aloud. They knew that once words escape the mouth, they cannot be called back.

✳

Rodolfo was the oldest man in the village and it was believed he would have had 105 grandchildren if half of them had not perished, as had all of his wives and most of his friends. So he lived in poverty greater than was common. He brought one egg, put it on the table and slowly, carefully sank down on the stool, his elephantine swollen legs spread apart. He looked at the seating plan on the wall silently. He could not read but still he could comprehend that there were only a few places left unoccupied, by now. Jan thanked him for coming and for the egg.

"I like Americans, amigo Eddie." It was a proclamation of clear meaning from a mouth without teeth and with gums which had atrophied decades ago. His speech was slurred but understandable, as were his intentions.

"I know," Jan helped his visitor, smiling at this "present," this gift the old man had brought. "And where have you known ... Americans, don Rodolfo?"

"Right after the war ended they arrived at the town near the capital. I was there shooting Japanese, too." Rodofo's teary eyes wandered somewhere to the corner of the roof, acquiring a look of absentmindedness. He looked back in time through the roof. "They were so tall, we were babies next to them. They liked us. They gave us tins of meat—but we did not know how to open them." Rodolfo turned his head from side to side. Jan offered the old man a banana, but he did not want to use his toothless gums in front of Jan.

"Once, they drove through the town on their trucks as big as houses waving at us, and the people were happy, amazed. We loved them much."

A smile lit the ancient face, nicely rearranging the deep wrinkles and grooves. "They threw condoms at us! Ha ... we chewed them then because we thought they were chiclets, chewing gum. We didn't know nothin'."

"A long time ago, don Rodolfo. You remember well."

"Many years. We learned much since then, we did. Later we knew how to put the rubbers on. They prevent disease, they do! But I remember, how the American soldiers laughed, like our children. They leaned their heads back and showed their big white teeth."

"Why did they laugh?"

"Oh, when we told them we take the rubbers off when we are with the woman. So much they laughed, we laughed with them."

Jan put the name Rodolfo on the seat C, 24th row, next to the aisle. He helped the visitor to get up. The *viejo* bowed and shuffled out, thanking him.

When Carmencita returned with firewood Jan told her that the aisle seat would be good for the old-timer because of his bad legs. He could get in and out of the seat easier, but there was no window seat available, anyway, none left at all, even if he wanted, but still... She stopped Jan's stream of words; the logorrhea was painful to hear.

"What does it matter? Look at me! Look at me, Jan. What is it with you? You must know it is just a game the villagers play and Jan plays. Game, Jan!"

He paced from one wall to another, raised his arms and let them down, again.

"We will be landing in San Francisco ... there is a beautiful view, the bay, the bridge, beautiful. I would want Rodolfo to see it, he would be amazed. He loves Americans, you see!" Jan sat down, jumped up again and paced across the room, raising his voice, raving, now.

"It all got fucked up by the Chief. He has to have the whole of the first row just for himself, all six god-damned seats for himself, he demands! The Chief, the Big Man. But they will teach him in the States, he'll see. But what can I do here? Nothing, nothing." Sweat dripped from his brows. Breathing hard, he turned to Carmencita, who watched her man, first, with incomprehension in her eyes and then with plain fear——fear of the unknown.

A sudden sadness seemed to calm Jan down. He sat on the stool, hanging his head down. "The bay, Golden Gate bridge, windsurfers like ... like splendid butterflies." He shook his head and let silence rule a while. Then he started whispering——but there was a melody to his raspy mutter:

"All those who fly to San Francisco,
Be sure to wear seashells in your hair..."

The tune was beautiful. The whispered melody became quieter, until it ceased. Jan looked up with eyes filled with tears. "I wanna go home." Like a baby. "Home!"

"It will be okay, Jan, everything." She knelt in front of him, trying to look up into his face. "I'll make you the soup you like, with bitter leaves, dried fish, and I have bamboo shoots, too." She straightened his hair and held it in place with her hand for quite a long time. When she started the fire in the firepit, tears fell on the embers and hissed. In a woman's life there seemed to be many tears. Mother had told her there were never enough tears to extinguish the fire completely. But often they doused the bright flame enough to leave it just smoldering.

Carmencita shed more tears in the coming weeks, because Jan became a different man from the one who took her to his hut holding her hand, saying "fuck it" to the old customs.

When uncle Yasis caught a big dorada behind the reef she was invited with Jan, and most of the family on loan to him, for the feast. Jan praised the fish—wow, a thirty pounder mahi mahi bull, what a treat! Then he spoke less and less. While sitting down he gazed at one corner of the hut. All the people were happy and Jan sat there staring into that corner, silent in an aberrant way.

Later, one evening, he brought home dried fish and did not want to say where he'd got it. He stole a hoe and a shovel and hid them under his bed, stopped watering his mahoganies and sat at home for hours watching the plane plan, oblivious to the gecko lizard dashing up the aisle in pursuit of a honey-colored cucaracha on the pilot's seat. When he complained that at night, secretly, somebody was sneaking into their hut and switching the seating assignments, Carmencita went to see her mother.

✳

On March fifteenth in Mangayas, north of the archipelago, the Muslim guerrillas kidnapped Peace Corps volunteer Jim Presley from Prospect Park, Minnesota. His parents and younger sister who had just arrived for a visit were also taken. It appeared to be a well planned action, occurring at night, silently, with no evidence of violence, no witnesses, no tracks. A written statement, in both English and Spanish, was left on the table weighed down by a freshly cut monkey's head with a cigarette butt in its clenched teeth. The monkey still retained an expression of horror and the statement was signed "Cobras for Freedom," the most ruthless faction of the independence movement, the true believers.

The wording of the note was not made public, but a brief summary delivered to the media after a two-day delay stated that unless the conditions of the kidnappers were met within a specified time (not announced in the press release) the lips of each and all of the hostages would be delivered to an undetermined location. If there was further delay in the meeting of the demands, the heads of Americans would be delivered. *Independencia Total o Muerte*!

Intensive overnight communication between the American Embassy, the State Department and the Peace Corps Headquarters in Washington, D.C. resulted in an unequivocal decision: the activities and presence of the Peace Corps organization in the country would cease without delay, and all the volunteers would be recalled from their posts immediately. All, including the staff, would be transported to the United States by a chartered plane of a commercial airline. Local army and police pledged total collaboration with the U.S. Embassy.

✳

A covered army truck lumbered through the muddy path into the village where a naked boy, holding his little genitals with one hand, pulled out his index finger from his nostril and pointed with it to Jan's hut. The truck stopped there and several soldiers with submachine guns spilled from the back. They were joined by one man in civilian clothes who slid down from the driver's cabin. In silence, and without hesitation they surrounded the hut as if on a well-rehearsed mission.

Two military men and the civilian disappeared into Jan's cabin. It took just a short time before they reemerged with Jan between them. One of the soldiers dragged the red Eddie Bauer duffel bag. They had to carry Jan up to the bed of the truck, as he seemed to have no power to walk, much less to climb up. His face was expressionless. He tried to look back, tried to turn his head backwards.

People gathered. Mute, they huddled together as if against a cold wind. The truck departed in a hurry and the people remained standing where they were, hesitant to move. There ruled a dead silence that even the birds seemed to heed; only the palms rustled like dried bones. From Jan's hut a despairing wolf-like howl cut through that still air, then a muted wailing which made all people hide in their shelters and only whisper.

After a torturous journey through the jungle the truck came to a stop in a small town with a fishing harbor where a Navy launch awaited them. Jan was assisted down the truck's bed, stumbling, wide-eyed, unprotesting. He was allowed to go to the bathroom in the dinky harbor bar Tetas de Ramona. A soldier just waved his hand and smiled at the pale *catedrático*. The troopers were in a good mood—somebody had had the presence of mind to bring a couple of six-packs of Tsing Tao. Their task in this dangerous territory was almost completed. Marines from the gunboat were ready to transfer the American, and they seemed eager to go.

The powerful twin inboard diesels were started, the throttle checked.

"*Singa!*" a soldier exclaimed, running out of the Tetas de Ramona, his tiny fist hitting his forehead above his bulging eyeballs. "*Coño maricon!*" Then another soldier of misfortune appeared: "*Me cago en Dios! Hijo de puta!*" Then "fuck it, *singa, singa*," in a dissonant chorus.

There was no American!

Even the most inventive obscenities were no help. Bedlam, pandemonium, panic and alarm of the local police—all to no avail. Jan A. Splinter had vanished, faded into the thin, hot air.

✳

In the coming days, many sightings were rumored, many rumors were reported. An announcement was made that a tall white man was seen crossing Tuluan Bay on the outrigger holding a trident—but another sighting on exactly the same day would put him on the opposite side of the island, where a white man of enormous height was seen coming down the Merunga volcano with a blowgun in his hand.

The only officially corroborated report received by the authorities was of Carmencita Splinter. She disappeared, without a trace, on the night of the half moon, together with the steamer for freshwater prawns and the shaving kit Jan had forgotten in his hut. This last news, when it reached the Embassy of United States of America, caused additional confusion, since there was no record of Splinter's marriage, not even an application for the appropriate marriage documents.

After years of keeping the case open, it was, finally, filed as "inactive." For the record it was stated that J.A.Splinter was missing permanently, and the search would be resumed if any new leads appeared, and that Splinter's last recorded words were: "I need to take a crap. Badly." No further mention was made, and no last words recalled of the native Carmencita.

✳

In the village everybody knew that Carmencita and Jan were far away, free and safe. Everybody was certain they would come back. Jan would complete his mission.

As time passed, first years then generations, things became even clearer and better understood. In each village hut there was an uncluttered bamboo stand on which a small supply of food was kept for the journey to America. Dried copra, lychee fruit, water coconut, perhaps. It would be replenished every week or so, and arranged nicely around two statuettes carved of soft balsa wood. One was the image of a woman with exaggerated buttocks and long hair painted black with a mixture of soot and coconut oil. The fetish of the man was much taller, with a bushy beard and waist-long hair painted with a mixture of chalk and oil in the hue of the rare orchid found only on the ancient sacred mahoganies which grow in perfect rows on Kunde Hill.

The coming of Eddie was unquestioned. Old men, around the evening fire, would explain that Eddie would arrive on a tall white ship on the night when the moon was brightest and the ebb tide reached the palms. He would tower over the roofs, an ancient man with white flowing hair, and with him Carmencita, young and beautiful, in a sarong of pure silk, her almond eyes illuminating the night a thousand times brighter than fluorescing click beetles.

Eddie and Carmencita would give American presents to every woman, man and child in a joyous festivity. And then Eddie would ask everybody if they were ready.

"Are you ready to fly with me?" he would ask in a big thundering voice, his white hair like rays of moonlight, his big round eyes as blue as the sea behind the reef. "Are you ready to see the clouds underneath you, not above?" And he would laugh, because everybody would crouch down, terrified of the big, big voice. Then all of them would start to laugh with Eddie, too, and then would begin the time of great happiness and joy, happiness so excellent that they could not imagine it even in dreams.

✳

So two new demi-gods were added to the multiculturally and politically correct gallery of deities and supernatural beings, between the ju-ju gods of African forest and the soccer team of Hindu deities, among the bearded padres of Christians, Jews and Muslims. For enlightening us in this matter, credit is due to famed anthropologists Mathias Spudich, Horse Przewalski, and Josh "Bubele" Shapira who, in their collaborative study, demonstrated the expansion of the Eddie Bauer Cult into all coastal villages of the archipelago, and the rejection of the Cult in the more conservative and animistic interior. Also, they presented a learned discussion on the bizarre but understandable popularity of this Cult in far away Slovakia.

But it was Hanelore Wolavka, of the University of Vienna, in her painstakingly wissenschaftlich treatise: *"Neure Erfahrungen, Untersuchungen, Beitrage und Bemerkungen uber der frohliche Eddie Bauer Kult des Sud China See,"* who was able to isolate the defining characteristics of the Cult's fetishes and thus elucidate one of the most intriguing mysteries of modern social anthropology. She postulated that the obvious youth and exaggerated buttocks of the female figure (steatopygia) characterizes rapturous joy. The loss of pigment in capital and facial hair of the male fetish (Eddie, himself) represent wisdom and senility and his hypertrophied penis extending to the knees represents favorable exuberance and hope (well, you know Hanelore). The widely stretched lips (a smile?) carved on all the fetishes in almost gruesome detail also suggest hopeful expectations—the defining attribute of the Eddie Bauer Cult.

Revenge of Underwater Man

We had arranged to meet at the center of the Malá Strana district, at that well-worn corner where Karmelitska Street meets the square. My friends did not trust my sense of orientation yet, and they knew that one can get easily lost in the old quarters of Prague. I had been told that a few visitors get lost there every year, forever, and after only a fortnight in this city I already felt the danger of wanting to get lost, too, not to come back out to a world less magical. I felt the temptation most urgently on early mornings when the chestnut tree on the bank of the Vltava River (*Moldau fluvius*) was only a suggestion through a veil of mist, and underneath it the swans extended their wings like a schoolboy stretching in the morning, holding onto his dream of skipping school and getting lost.

I felt the urge to become forgotten here as I watched the silhouette of Hradčany Castle etched high on the hill across the river, all lit up against the blackness of the night, unreal as if copied from an old etching. I had a view of the castle, now an office of employment for the legendary Havel, from my rented apartment, so that even behind closed doors I was harassed by romantic feelings when the castle was framed by a black storm, or by curtains of rain, or was bathed in sunshine so optimistic only a tourist pamphlet could convey it. Yesterday I saw it smudged in the gun-metal gloom of an overcast sky—just to remind me, perhaps, of the gray history of this town. And to force me down from my cloud, if only briefly. However, the subsequent sunset melted my schmaltzy, soft-boiled soul and put a smile on my face which remained there for hours.

I looked forward to meeting my friends, Peter and Ivan. Petr (he spells it Peter in the U.S.) is an immigrant to Minnesota, emigrant from Prague, which he is visiting now. He has spent half his life here and half there. Ivan is a native of Prague who has remained a Prager and will be buried in the city.

"Ahoy!"

"Ahoy!"

"Ahoy!" We greeted each other. Ahoy is "Hi" for Czechs (for people who never sailed a ship and don't own even a rowboat).

"Will we eat in Velkoprerovsky Mlyn?" Ivan asked. "Okay then," he answered his own question. "The restaurant opens at seven, so we have some time to waste."

"Let's walk around Kampa Park," Peter suggested. I contributed "Okay," and we wandered past the Dutch Embassy (known more for classical concerts than politics), then past the French Embassy (known less for politics than for standing across from the John Lennon Peace Wall with its graffiti portrait of Lennon). We crossed Certovka Creek, known for kayak races in recent times and for a history dating from far before the exploits of Christopher Columbus (since even creeks have a written history here). It was still light.

"Prague would wear my legs through to under my knees," Peter whined, using a literary translation of a Czech idiom. "Let's sit down somewhere!"

We found a bench with a good view of passing lovers and behind them the river and behind the river the quay with the shining Bedrich Smetana House and behind it the props of baroque domes and Gothic spires and steeples and behind them more of the ancient architecture making a skyline. The evening light supplied shades of gold to the Old Town, removing all reality. I knew this city was built of stones, not of gold.

"Wow!" I said.

An old lady passed by us, pulled by a boxer who smiled at us, then a couple of young people who stumbled because their emotions directed them to look into each other's eyes. They would barter all the town's baroque treasures for one night in an apartment of their own. That is what Ivan said, knowingly, and stretched his legs.

"What is this building over there, upstream?" I entered the conversation. "Looks in a sorry shape."

"But what a location!" Peter remarked.

"That's Sovuv Mill, an old mill. And you are right about the location. Big bucks, enormous investments at steak." Ivan suggested support of a large object with his hands. "Can you imagine making that into a first-class hotel? Right on the river and with those views?"

"Is that why it's in such rotten shape? Because it is in such a great place?" Peter smiled.

"Exactly! Government, foreign companies, pre-communist owners—they are all boxing each other for it. So while everything historical around here is getting fixed and spruced up, the mill is rotting—because it is ancient and sits on such a knock-out location." Ivan nodded contentedly, liking the absurdity, as all his compatriots do.

And looking for more of the absurd, he added, after a while: "And those two lovers, over there?" He pointed at the couple walking away. "The fellow will not make love skillfully to her tonight." I must have looked puzzled, since Ivan turned to me with an explanation. "You saw his face, didn't you? Too much in love with her."

Now Peter joined in with a short lecture: "And also, because the grass is wet tonight." I resisted revealing my puzzlement. Still, Peter explained with mock patience, the lovers will walk 'round and 'round the park waiting for the descent of darkness, since darkness will be their roof, and the lawn their bed, and the bushes their walls, and the blossoms on the bushes pictures on the walls.

"They wouldn't be able to switch off the moon, so they hope for a cloudy night, romance or not. Police, you know," Ivan added, looking at the sky. He laughed at my lack of understanding of the world of Prague around me. Even Peter knew everything, despite having lived on another planet, Minnesota, for a quarter of a century. Both my friends lit cigarettes and exchanged a few sentences in that horrible language of theirs.

"Sorry." Ivan looked at me and switched to his accented but quite precise English. "Sovuv Mill? Did you ask about its history? I don't know much about it, but I am certain about one thing—there used to be a Vodnik living right under the mill; that has been passed on since the old times."

"V o d n i k?" I tried the pronunciation.

"Right, Vodnik," Peter agreed with Ivan. "Ivan, tell him. They call it the 'Land of Ten Thousand Lakes,' where he and I are living in the States. He should know."

And that is how I came to know about the underwater man.

Vodnik

"Mythical fellow, fairy tale character, that Vodnik," Ivan started without hesitation. "Sometimes he has been called Hastrman. A great diver. Underwaterman, you could say."

Ivan seemed to have graduated with distinction from grandmother's school of fairy tales. In detail, he knew the dress code of this Vodnik: always in a green tailcoat, a red cap and, on special occasions, a green top hat, with red boots. He has punk-green, long hair, webbed toes, and fingers like a newt. He favors whiskers, catfish-style. On the rare instances when he has talked to people, he seemed to have a speech defect, a nasality combined with lisping.

He inhabits an underwater shelter, of course, usually in the deep under a mill or in the deepest part of a lake or forest pond. He savors his leisure time. At night, when the moon is full, he climbs up a willow tree growing on the bank, lights his pipe, and mends his boots. Water drips from the left tail of his coat. It is always the left tail. So many people have seen him in this position on the willow that there remain no doubts about his appearance. Those who have seen him have been mostly peasants returning home from the tavern of a neighboring village at night, which might raise questions about the reliability of their perceptions—but they have all sworn it was true, nothing but the truth, their own living eyes saw him there.

The lovers passed by on their rounds around the park again, and the man still radiated a confusion of love from his eyes. Somewhere on their circle he had managed to unbutton the upper part of her blouse.

"Do you want to hear more about Czech mythology or not?" Ivan saw my interest in the progress of the lovers.

"Oh yeah, Ivan. Be my grandma, please!" I asked him then, if he, Vodnik, could be considered a good guy, a moral, positive example to youth.

"Well, *entre nous*, Vodnik drowns people, you know?" Ivan continued in a portentous voice, with relish. "Sometimes. He pulls them underwater, tangles them into the shoots of a pond lily, and doesn't release the body for three days. Three! And—this is important—he keeps their souls. Forever. I think the human soul looks like the air bladder of a carp, about the same size, too. He puts that soul into a clay jar which he covers with a heavy lid. All Vodniks are very proud of their collection of souls."

"So, he is a pretty lily-livered evil spirit, isn't he?"

"There is a problem here." Ivan put on a victorious expression. Absurdity again? "We just cannot say that. You see, he helps people, sometimes. I don't know his chromosomes, but he ain't no congenital meanie. For a couple of beers he would help the working folks in the mill; he might do the jobs of twenty, overnight. It is when he gets mad, when he sees there is no percentage in being good, then it is just drowning, nothing but drowning. He would hang colored ribbons on the bushes along the pond and kids would try to get at them and whoops—another soul on the shelves in the jar collection."

"How about his sex life?" Peter asked, as I would have expected, knowing him for many years. "He seems to have the lifestyle of a couple of my bachelor friends. Except that drowning part, I think."

Ivan changed his diction to a professorial tone: "Sometimes, he kidnaps a shapely maiden—keeps her for years. Understandable. But he also has a wife, Hastrmanka!"

"And Hastrmanka, the wife?"

"She has three main characteristics. One, she is ugly. Two, she can't cook. Three, she is sneaky. Sound familiar?" he laughed, which, I thought, might have revealed something about his life experiences.

"Often, she changes into a frog or a toad and sneaks close to women working in the fields to listen to what they say. She must be a lonely creature." Ivan looked at his watch. "They are opening the restaurant. How about going?"

Walking toward Velkoprerovsky Mlyn, we met the lovers again. There had been no progress with her blouse buttons, so I turned my mind back to contemplating Vodnik, another of those Czech personalities whose behavior intrigued me with its ambiguity. I became determined to understand better why in Bohemian ponds and forests a peasant could not bear a fairy tale character who would be straightforwardly evil, like a cannibalistic grandmother, or one positively lovely and politically correct, like Snow White. Would I be able to find out, to understand these titillating Bohunks?

The Restaurant

The restaurant sat right on the bank of Certovka Creek and from the window, next to our table, we could observe the enormous wheel of Velkoprerovsky Mill, after which the restaurant was named. The wheel had been nicely restored for the tourists' sake; it even moved and creaked, driven by the India-ink stream. I ordered fried breaded carp and cucumber salad with sweetened vinegar. In having the carp I wanted to impress my friends and, indeed, they expressed surprise at my audacity. The second reward for me was its taste, which was delicate, non-fishy, and pleasantly adventurous.

The wine was a Moravian Muller-Thurgau white from Hodonin. It was a thin, slightly acidic, unremarkable fluid, but revered by natives (with raised eyebrows, puckered lips, and smacking sounds). Peter explained this lack of objectivity, with a dose of sarcasm, as due to the defeat of Czech nobles on Bila Hora in 1620—and the resulting three centuries of darkness, which had deprived the nation of the opportunity to learn of the Grand Cru wines of Bordeaux and the great white vintages of the Mosel region. Indeed, our first glass of wine was a mediocre experience, but it got clearly better with each subsequent glass and bottle we downed. I commented on this phenomenon with surprise, only to be informed that it had been observed by King Charles IV and a fellow by the name of Busek from Velhartice in the fourteenth century already.

"...And, also, its taste depends greatly on the drinker's company and their feelings of friendship toward each other. This, of course, defies the international criteria used in judging wines. Pity," said Ivan. We had achieved the spirit of special camaraderie after the third bottle, I think, drinking to Vodnik, just the same. But the restaurant was closing, and the waiters were leaning the chairs so that their backs would rest on the edges of the tables. I understood that this position for chairs signified a physical exclamation mark at the end of hours.

"Hauuuw How How, don't do it! " Ivan howled dismay that we had to leave; then he calmed down. "You have two options now." He turned to me. "The first option is to go home and have that healthy sleep. The second: to dive into a smoke-filled tavern to try another vintage of Moravian—and to hear me telling my personal story about Vodnik. A true one." Then he looked at Peter as if giving him permission to decide for me.

Peter did not hesitate: "Be it Vodnik! No question about that." Peter looked at my face for traces of rebellion.

"Sure thing," I said loudly, feeling native and proud of it. "Sure thing." Czechs don't separate when a story is imminent, regardless of the hour. I'd read that.

The Tavern

It seemed we actually dove in—the stairs were so steep into the underground hall, filled with blue smoke, as promised by Ivan. Storytellers saturated the space with vehement voices; wine flowed in the hive. We found a place at a table of darkened oak planks so heavy no drunk had ever even tilted it. It was pleasant to lean on it. My friends commented on the Rieslingoid acidity of the green Veltlin Moravian we ordered, and exchanged greetings, or insults(?), with strangers at the next table.

"I am warning you. There isn't much tender romance at the end of THIS Vodnik story." Then Ivan told us about his tender romance with Lida Zabranska.

✻

"She was the second most beautiful girl in our school. She was put together a little awkwardly, perhaps: everything was long about her. Her arms were a bit too slender, her legs like a gazelle's, even her face was Anglo-Saxon, and her breasts were long, too, with narrow bases—not a bright future for them, but in the good old times of tight sweaters it was something to get dizzy about." Ivan remedied the sudden dryness of his tongue with a gulp of green Veltlin.

"She was different. Never wore any makeup, not even lipstick and, I think, this was one of the reasons I can still remember her eyes, which radiated in that unpainted, alabaster face. Pure milk chocolate with pupils as wide as if atropine had done it. I can tell you I used to get lost in those eyes. Just lost, no way out.

"1 was seventeen, and she was one grade lower. At that age a woman can look like an angel still. But there were these rumors circulating in the hallways of the school that she was not one of the angels, which only enhanced my shyness, and it took me a year before I joined her on the way home from school. Then she let me pay for the movie. It was *Rhapsody in Blue*, and there I held her hand. *Vole!*

"On Sunday afternoons we went to the 'Tea', to the tea dance in the gym up in Hanspaulka. She would wear a pink dress of imitation silk, tight around her waist and high to the lace collar around that Modigliani neck. You wouldn't believe it, but I remember clearly, still today, how her waist felt against my sweaty palm, and when we slow-danced to 'Moonlight Serenade', how I bent myself forward so my hips wouldn't touch hers, and how she pulled me closer, and I felt her breasts, which made me all burning and confused, and then, how my schoolwork went straight to hell, and I almost flunked that year.

"I am not sure, now, if I was in love because she was so beautiful, or if she appeared so beautiful because I was in love. It bothers me now, but comes as no surprise, that I cannot resurrect that feeling, but I know it was an emotion of such power and purity that the gods allow it only in a single dose and only to a selected few innocents. It even prevented me from kissing her, which is always an irreparable mistake.

"And then, one day, she disappeared from school. Gone. Just like that. It took me lots of detective work to find out that her parents had put her in an all-female monastic boarding school of the Vorsilki Order. A fucking prison, if you ask me. Sorry," Ivan said, pouring himself some more.

The waiter brought another bottle and leaned over the table to hear more about a prison. Peter waved him away. I noticed that the Veltlin green was getting better, as expected, and that it had put a permanent smile on Peter's face. The still handsome, somewhat dark features of Ivan showed only the concentration required to revive the memories. He pushed his Minnesota Twins cap (a present from Peter) backwards.

"She was gone and unreachable, which must have been a blow to me. But, frankly, I don't remember it well. One of those mechanisms which the brain uses to suppress bad events from the memory, to keep us dreaming without nightmares, must have been triggered later. Anyway, about a year passed, and I still had this longing, like a pain here, in the heart, still not diminished, not even a little.

"Then one Sunday evening I found myself collecting fossils, alone and lonely, on the Barrandov Silurian cliffs on the outskirts of Prague (our Secret Paleontology Club had disintegrated). Despite finding an undamaged specimen of a trilobite and an orthoceras, I wandered back to the tram station without joy, thinking about Lida locked in the Vorsilky Monastery. I decided to take a detour by tram to see the place, the Monastery.

Should I scream her name at the windows? Or should I ring at the gate and tell the nun gatekeeper that I carried a message of great importance for Lida Zabranska? Or some other bullshit? Or simply beg to see her? Maybe?

"I got off the tram in front of the National Theatre and walked half a block to Vorsilky School. It was dark already, but the door of the Monastery's cathedral was open. I could see the lights inside; it was filled with people. So I crawled in, found a place near the aisle, wondering what might be happening at this late hour. I hoped she might be around somewhere; I would have even prayed for that, if I had known how.

"The organ music filling the space suddenly acquired more celebratory decibels. There was a commotion in the pews, and people turned their heads toward the side entrance; some half-raised from their seats. By twos, a procession of young women in white, floor-length robes was entering, slowly; their eyes turned down to the marble floor. In their right hands they held candles with flickering flames. They were like angels on hidden wheels, since one could not perceive their steps. Only an occasional glance to the side by some made them humanly alive. No smiles were offered.

"Then Lida appeared. She was taller than the others and attracted stares from the audience. She passed by me three, four feet away, and did not see me. She had managed to put on the face of an angel, a face so beautiful it stays with me still today, veiled only slightly. She put on a small, brittle smile, a suggestion of a smile enhancing that amazing beauty.

"Her eyes were turned down, but just before she approached me she looked up, and I could see clearly how those eyes were narrowed, telling all who watched her that she hated this show, that she didn't belong here. That is how I interpreted it. There was a little mist in those eyes, and that pained me then. I whispered something, but she did not hear me. She had no notion I was right by her. And that was the last time I saw her, gentlemen, the last time for years.

"Later I learned that she was dismissed from the Monastery School, that she tried to escape over the border to Germany with her parents. They were caught; her parents were put in prison, and she had to work at a forced labor assignment in a clothing factory in Northern Bohemia. I lost track of her fate."

The Stairs

"What a deal!" Peter said.

"Thank you, Ivan," I mumbled, moved a little, I admit. We sat in silence for a while. The acidity of the green wine had disappeared from its taste completely, by then. I tried to order open-faced sandwiches for everybody, in Czech, but the waiter gave me a blank stare.

"But Vodnik? Where has he been?" asked Peter, a little tipsy, spilling some of his wine, since while Ivan had been talking we had drunk his share.

"Well, don't worry about him," said Ivan. "He will come if you want to hear about him. Outside. Look around, and you'll see we are here alone." The waiters were tipping up the chairs on the edge of the tables again, and the place was empty. We paid (went Dutch), thanked them, and promised to come again soon.

The street was deserted. Not far from us we could see the sprawling stairs of St. Nicholas Church. I carried the unfinished bottle of liquid sun from Moravia. We spread out on the church steps, passed the bottle around, and Ivan and Peter shared their last cigarette. I took my shoes off and hyperventilated the fresh air.

"So, Ivan!" Peter motioned with his hand.

✳

"It was about five years ago. I met her, Lida, on Charles Square," Ivan started. "I was sitting on a bench watching the bronze orchid in the bronze hand of the statue of Rossler. Something obstructed my view, and there she stood in front of me, with a smile. I recognized her right away, after all those years, and called her name.

"'Ivan, Ivanku!'" she said.

"I will not describe her, since you know how unkindly time works on tissues. She had aged, of course." (We gave Ivan the last of the wine. I wished that I could get him a cigarette, or something good. It seemed he had difficulty in continuing, so we just waited.)

"We talked about nonsense while we found a table in an espresso place near Faust's house. We talked about high school—the usual. I could see she was not uneasy with me at all, which made me sad, a little. She had forgotten we'd had a date, once. And I did not tell her. Did not mention Vorsilky, either. So we followed the chronology of her life, the common milestones of marriage, two kids, jobs, hopes found and lost and found again.

"We ate open-faced sandwiches and drank espresso and ate 'rakvicky,' pastry coffins filled with cream. Then a strange thing happened. While we talked and time passed, I noticed that her face was changing, that she looked younger and younger and more familiar. The metamorphosis made me feel a little confused, and I decided I did not want this meeting to finish as plainly as was her story, so far. I wanted to hear the real stuff

153

about her. If there was any. About her insides, because she was going to disappear again, maybe forever.

"I found the courage to ask her: 'Have you ever been in love, Lida? Like, really in love?' She was surprised. She did not look at me, but twirled the coffee in her cup. Then she talked with her eyes on the cup, as if she were reading the past, not the future, from the coffee grounds.

"So, I tell you, Ivan.' She whispered it. 'It was a long time ago, it seems. He wrote for me:

> trees laugh at the thunder
> air scented after hope like you
> rain covers your face with a hundred happy tears
> narrows your eyes, wets your lips to be mine.

'I still remember it. For a poet he did everything right: long hair to his shoulders, a sad jacket, and his shirt buttoned all the way; no tie. Even his cheeks he kept hollow, and he coughed, too. I thought: of course, he is my eternal love, the first and the last one.'"

A few drops of rain rang on our heads. I looked up at the immense gilded cliffs of St. Nicholas Cathedral looming above us, at the sleeping palaces across the square, and wished the story would not end soon. I looked at Ivan's face. When the end of the story comes, let it be a happy end, please, I wished. The story continued, mercilessly.

The poet had written Lida letters full of metaphors so strange she could not understand most of them. But the yearning in the poems she understood, because when he recited them for her, he held her hands and looked at her with eyes so narrow she thought his verses must be beautiful and only for her. Sometimes, he seemed to be a child, laughing at silly things, a child with tantrums and little evil jokes. But his eyes were never the eyes of a child. The time came when the eyes did not look at her when he recited his poems. And then, one evening, she saw him looking into the eyes of another young woman, holding her in his arms, leaning on the railing of the quay across the Rudolphinum. She went to pieces, then somewhat pulled herself together and within a few months was married—to Rudi, engineer Rudi Skala.

The truth is, she had never recovered. She used to fall into a depression every year; something had always been pulling her down. She saw those eyes of the poet; she heard his verses and could not understand why the passing of time did not help her, as it should. It did not console her that Rudi was a solid man: he was liked by his many friends; he loved their two boys, and they loved him; he took good care of all of them, and he was kind to her and worried about her.

At last, she found a doctor whom she could trust and who would listen to her with compassion. The old medicine man prescribed long vacations, without kids, in South Bohemia, preferably in a village, far from the city, from the bullshit of her work and from being hounded by crowds. Only the two of them, Rudi and her.

They rented an old farmhouse at the edge of a village, with a creek running through the garden and a private spring-well in the cellar, where a pair of blue salamanders lurked. The neighbor's sheepdog became their faithful friend and would follow them on their excursions. Daily they woke up to the sun; the meadows were warm, and dizzied them with colors. They walked through them from the village to the town market. They picked boletus mushrooms in the pine forest up the hill and made picnics by the cross in the fields, from which Jesus watched them with a smirk, suspicious but kind. Rudi was also kind, as usual, but now he laughed with her, and often he held her hand. For the first time in years, she felt unshackled, as if freed from an exile in some icy, confusing world.

On the last day of their vacation, she prepared a special dinner of mushrooms they had collected in the pine forest, and Rudi made a tomato salad fragrant with herbs from the meadow. Pleasure-bearing endorphins flooded their brains. They entrusted to the salamanders in the spring-well in the cellar two bottles of wine to cool for later, in anticipation of a romantic night. After dinner they went for a walk in a breeze which carried the perfume of the fields and touched them as softly as velvet. At the edge of the forest they observed a pair of deer, motionless as theater props, as if enchanted by the scented wind, too.

They entered the forest, and on a narrow path they walked hand in hand to the pond she loved. They sat down on the shore by the clump of reeds. There were pond lilies at one end. There was a moss-covered shallows with tiny white flowers clumped in pillows, arrow arums blooming next to the cattails and a willow tree. A solitary willow.

She knew this pond well. In the evening one could spy a muskrat there. Sometimes, in the morning, a white heron would keep his vigil near the mossy shallows, a merciless killer of frogs disguised in a white shroud of innocence. She believed him innocent. The surface of the pond would change each time Lida visited here. She liked it most when it mirrored a summer cloud. That night, the last night of their vacation, the surface was dark with ripples, making it shiver as if alive. Rudi took her hand.

"Rudi," she whispered. "Look at the willow. Do you recognize it?"

"What do you mean?" he asked.

"This is the willow Vodnik will climb on." Her voice was barely audible; her face had a tiny smile of conspiracy. "I can almost see him. On that branch leaning over the pond. He might come out if we are really quiet."

Rudi nodded, looking at the willow. She put her arm around his waist. "When it gets a little darker he will emerge, mend his shoes—and maybe, play his flute." She whispered and cuddled with him. She felt, she knew, that he shared the happiness with her. The breeze died; the silence was complete. "It is our fairy tale, Rudi."

She looked at him. He wore a navy blue sweater with a turtleneck. His profile was so handsome, with a strong nose and the chin of a decisive man, and dark, unruly hair falling over his forehead, with a few white streaks in it now.

"Rudi?"

He turned to her and smiled. "Let's get out of here!" he said. "It smells like shit here. Somebody did it here, somewhere. Holy shit!"

✳

Ivan stretched his legs over the steps of St. Nicholas Cathedral. Peter and I, we looked at him, but he showed no emotion. Just turned his head from side to side as if wondering. He asked for a cigarette, but there were none left.

"It's getting late," Ivan said, after a while. "Or early. I've heard the first morning tram already. But, I have to tell you, drunks: you have listened well. Real well."

We got up. "What happened to her, Ivan?" I asked, taking care to sound casual.

"Yeah, right, you should know. After that Vodnik incident, she disintegrated, of course, totally. No sleep, no food, didn't talk. Finally, her husband, the master of sensitivity, had to commit her to the loony house.

"After a couple of months the shrinks got the better of her, and she went back to old Rudi and her two boys. There were no choices for her, simply no choices. She became a sort of regular homemaker, as you would say in America. She remained slightly zombied out, but that only helped her to exist. Then Rudi died on her, of a heart attack. The old sport." We were walking to the other side of St. Nicholas to the tram station.

"She got over his death pretty well; the empty space he left behind was quite small. That's how life goes, right?" He imitated a brief laugh. "And that is the 'revenge of Vodnik' for you."

"Have you seen her since she told you this?" I asked. Ivan's face widened in a big smile, a wide smile with no eyes. The first one in the last hour.

"Oh yeah. I have seen her, since," he said, his grin still on, only with the eyes, now. "Peter, here, he saw her too. And likes her cooking. Don't ya, Peter?"

Peter laughed. They both looked at me victoriously, and I was standing there like an idiot, not comprehending what was going on.

"But don't worry, you'll meet her, ma gal, my wife! Tomorrow for dinner, as we have arranged," said Ivan. "I bet you'll agree that Lida is the master of knedliky, roast pork and sauerkraut." Ivan was still grinning. "And fun, too."

The Bridge

We came to the Malostranske Square tram station. Both Peter and Ivan insisted I should take a shortcut over the bridge and not wait with them for the tram. You need to get to bed fast, they said, to dream a Czech dream about Vodnik in living color; and they pointed my way toward Charles Bridge.

I went down Mostecka Street, past the McDonald's set in a house three hundred years old near the Bridge Tower, six hundred years old. It was getting lighter. The pre-dawn light allowed me to read the clock in the tower. The clock told me it was true that friends in this city can sit down and talk for ten hours without interruption, and then feel sorry they have to part. I did.

From under the Tower I emerged, suddenly, on the Charles Bridge. The magic of the view glued my soles to the cobblestones. The bridge, veiled in fog rising from the river, seemed to lead to dreams. The statues of saints emerging from the fog walked slowly toward me. When I stepped forward to meet them, they stopped and looked away.

There was nobody on the bridge except me and the seagulls. They were landing on the statues of the saints, knitting snow-white caps for the stony heads with their excrement. The whitest seemed to be the one decorating the forehead of Saint Jan Nepomuk, who was crudely drowned here, centuries ago. And whose soul, saint or no saint, rests in one of the clay jars with a heavy lid in Vodnik's shelter, in the deep, under the bridge. I stopped near Saint Nepomuk and leaned over the side, stealthily, not to make any fast moves. I scanned the surface of the river like a spy. There was a sudden movement on the icebreaker, then a splash ... and suspicious circles spread on the surface of the ancient stream.

The Four Thorns of Kilimanjaro

We're foot—slog—slog—slog—sloggin' over Africa!
- Ruyard Kipling ("Boots")

The East African shade is made by an imperfect shadow, full of holes. The outlines of the holes are jagged like Rorschach inkblots, so it is difficult to see the acacia thorns fallen to the ground. But on the semi-desert plains of Tanzania, beasts and men can hide only under the umbrella trees, acacias, since the upside-down trees, baobabs, are leafless most of the year, their branches resembling roots. People of the plains seeking the shade step on the thorns and die. Ariana Bella explained this to me on the way up Mount Kilimanjaro.

Kilimanjaro must be the only mountain in the world with its own airport for jumbo-jet direct connections. On this hazy February morning the Kilimanjaro International Airport offered us its runway, in view of baobabs and acacias, with one lonely Thompson gazelle taking off in panic. The overnight flight ended in a roaring but smooth touchdown, the windows clouded instantly, precipitating moisture from the humid heat. Within hours, after sampling marinated herring in Amsterdam and having dinner with Chilean wine on the plane, I found myself in the belly-button of Africa.

I am fairly well off, money-wise. So, a rented Range Rover, the Indian driver Ramesh, and a mountain guide and porter named Kunde awaited me. It was only a couple hours' drive to the town, Moshi, where we stopped to buy provisions. Once there, I recognized Africa by smell and started to feel the magic which is so difficult to describe, the infatuation which is untreatable and chronic. Cracks of the packed laterite earth oozed the smell of roasted chestnuts, flowering bushes added their perfumes to the odors of early breakfasting by street people, and outdoor kitchens mixed in their indescribable succulent whiffs. I would have known where I was blindfolded. I inhaled deeply.

"There she is: Kilimanjaro! You can see both peaks, Kibo and Mawenzi." Kunde, the porter, pointed somewhere to the horizon.

"Oh, I see her. Must have snowed there last night." I nodded at the tall mountain with a small white cap, so improbable in this near-equatorial heat and humidity.

"No bwana, that is Mount Meru. There…" Kunde pointed more to the right.

I strained my eyes in some confusion, seeing only the dark horizon of dense woods which looked like the lichen architects use for trees on their models. I looked higher and there were only the disorganized February clouds, dark pewter stratocumuli, which bring the first "short rains" this time of the year to Kenya and Tanganyika.

"Am I blind?" I asked.

"You look higher, *bwana*," Kunde laughed, amused. "Higher!"

I tilted my head way back, and there she was, high above the clouds, two white peaks growing up from the cumuli, no bottom to her, floating in the stratosphere like a fata morgana, a mirage put there by the shrewd African gods, to make her unbelievable and unforgettable. For a long time I remained silent, playing a mind game: I tried to imbed this image of Kilimanjaro into my memory, permanently. There it was, indeed, *Old-oinyo Oibor*, "white mountain" of the Maasai, snow white near the equator.

Soon we left behind the sisal fields and, higher, the sugar cane plantations, and took up the steep dirt pike to the end of the road, a village called Marangu. The scattering of skeletal trees and sisals of the arid country changed into a rain forest abruptly, as if planted and watered by some celestial Gardener. There the Chagga people farm in tiny plots claimed from the jungle. It looks like subsistence agriculture, suggesting poverty. But the creek along the road roared with clear water, plenty of it, fed by many small tributaries, a sight un-African, an inspiring sight. And the people looked well fed. The baked, parched plains of thirst seemed very far away, not just a half-hour drive. We were on the lower slopes of Kilimanjaro.

In the Hotel Maranga, two pleasurable surprises awaited me: I had a memorable meal and I met Ariana Bella. She was sent to me by the god of the mountain, no doubt, and the memorable dinner was prepared by Mrs. Lany, the owner of the hotel.

In 1893, two years after Dr. Hans Mayer climbed the mountain for the first time, Mrs. Lany's father came to Kenya from Bohemia. She grew up near Lake Naiwasha into an adventurous and attractive young lady, an acquaintance of writer Beryl Markham, Lord Delameer and of other famous and infamous inhabitants of the colonial in-crowd. Early on, she married a young Brit, a smashing novice "white hunter" who was gored by a rhino on their honeymoon hunt, but recovered well, only to be trampled flat into the fertile soil near Tana river by a rogue elephant. She inherited his industrial properties in England, which she sold well, and with the money she built Hotel Maranga, in the correct anticipation of tourism. She could still, at her advanced age, create the national Czech dish: crusty roasted pork with a layer of translucent fat still on it, dump-lings which soaked up sauce like ambrosian sponges, and sauerkraut, steamed with sautéed onion, caraway seeds, bay leaf, coarsely ground pepper, and mellowed by a dash of white wine. How could she have known that my magician grandmother was a Bohemian culinary sorcerer, too?

And the memories of Ariana Bella! Her smooth hair the color of dried vanilla beans, and pale lips. The structure and hue of her irises I can't remember; I only I know her smile was sincere and I liked to look into those eyes when she talked. She was an Italian nurse stationed in Moshi for two years, running a clinic for women with perinatal prob-lems. She would start the trek up the mountain tomorrow, making a team with me and four Danish climbers. It was her time off, a mini-vaca-tion.

We talked after dinner, cautiously, as is the strange habit among Western travelers in Third and Fourth World countries. I liked her sensi-ble demeanor, her straight answers; I suspected she understood a lot about this part of Africa, so I wanted to hear her. As early as the first eve-ning, I wanted to be her friend. She exuded sensibility even in her attire. She did not wear any woolen things, only lightweight fleece; no "death cloth" (as mountaineers refer to cotton) but polypropylene with wick action, Gore-Tex which breathes but is waterproof. The girl knew about layering. Of course, I thought, Italians—Alpini!

At noon the next day we started the trek up a jungle path ascending from Maranga to the first "station," the Mandara Huts, at 9000 feet. It was an easy walk of three hours over six miles, covering an elevation of 4000 feet. Which is not so interesting as the story Ariana Bella told me on the rest stops, after I noticed her bruised arm.

"It is from an IV, intravenous drips, you know. No heroin!" She laughed at my suspicious grimace.

"Were you sick?"

"Yep, and almost dead, too."

"Africa is dangerous to your health, everybody knows," I said, hesi-tant to ask prying questions, knowing about death, that toothy wanderer so common here that it could be considered aboriginal, endemic to the continent, like diarrhea. But Ariana Bella volunteered her story, since she had that irrepressible Italian trait, the urge towards rhetoric.

We had emerged from the dense and high rain forest, adventurous territory for a botanist, cool, beautiful. The trees became sparser and some acquired a stunted look, covered with moss, gray, green, flowing in the breeze like the Spanish moss of American South. Many orchid-like saprophytic plants hung from the branches, and giant heather appeared. We took a break to stretch our legs. The small triangular cucumber sandwiches (the pitiful heritage of British colonial rule) which Kunde, my faithful porter, unpacked were washed down by water from a nearby spring.

"I stepped on an acacia thorn when going to pee behind the clinic. Our toilet had became unusable … but let's not discuss that. It went through my sneaker," Ariana Bella continued, "and when I pulled it out the puncture did not bleed, and hurt a lot. Right away I knew it might be a problem. Thorn accidents here are much more dangerous than lions, rhinos and snakes put together." Ariana Bella devoured the sandwiches as if she had been on Tanganyikan diet for two years. Which she had.

Her story was interrupted. On the blossoms of a giant lobelia in front of us, a bird arrived. It was the Malachite Sunbird, a beautiful, iridescent flying jewel that hovered like a hummingbird about the cluster of blossoms, around which small flies gathered.

"This must be the end of evolution for that bird. No further mutations can create greater beauty, don't you think?" She was fascinated, lost to her story. It took some time, and the departure of the sunbird, before she continued her narrative, between bites, when she closed her eyes.

"Being a nurse with some experience in tropical medicine, I instantly opened a new vial of powdered antibiotics, diluted it with sterile water and injected myself." At evening she got another injection—but the pain increased and a red, then bluish, halo appeared around the puncture wound. At night she felt fever and pain. Next day the symptoms of sepsis started to appear, and she recognized the danger. The mortal danger. She doubled the dose of antibiotic. She did not have the strength to go to her clinic, but lay on her bed soaked in sweat and worried, since she knew enough to worry; to know was her job.

On the third day her condition became critical. The wound was grossly swollen, her fever increased and she experienced her first hallucination: she saw the wound ballooning to the size of a head, bursting open and releasing hundreds of tiny snakes. When she realized she was slipping away, she called for help—and was carried to Moshi Hospital, semiconscious.

"You are bored with my story because you know the end already—I am alive. Right?"

"I am not, I swear, I wait for the next page, truly!" I said, a half-truth. "And, Ariana Bella, I am very happy I know the end; the happy end is the thrill!"

She gave me a sly look with a shifty smile. At that moment I felt … it is hard to describe, but … something more than sympathy toward her. As if we, two total strangers, in the very short time we knew each other, had developed a certain secret understanding.

She continued. "The Moshi Hospital is run by a Dutch physician. The good doctor started me on new antibiotics, a wide spectrum, fourth generation types. He incised the wound, did tests. I became better, as if by a miracle. In just a few days I could walk." But the doctor was puzzled, since the antibiotics Ariana Bella had administered to herself before she came to him were the good kind that should have worked, too. He sent the vial of it to Nairobi to be tested. The answer came soon: the vial contained just plain flour.

"I bet it was not even semolina, the good stuff for making pasta," Ariana Bella laughed. "How I miss the real good vermicelli, fusilli, farfallini or ziti, *penne rigati e capelli d' angelo*! Mama mia!"

"Just naming your favorites sounds like you are singing a Neapolitan ballad," I said.

"It is… a love song." She closed her eyes.

"But what a horror, to inject yourself with a flour. You could have died!"

"I checked into it and found out that people of the Third World cultures fake and forge medicines as sort of a custom."

I am an American, so I withheld any comment, so as not to appear adverse to multicultural harmony and to remain culturally sensitive to the Third World. This is my bad habit, which I have tried to suppress, so my international friends won't call me a "PC refusnik of truth."

But then I smelled it. "Look, we must be at Mandara Huts!"

She sniffed the air, too. "And I smell the dinner."

Yes, Kunde was at it, already, and soon we found out it was edible. We put our parkas on because it was getting cold. The A-frame hut I shared with two Danes and Ariana Bella had hard cots but warm blankets. After the dinner all four of us shared, and finished, the bourbon in my flat flask, which I'd intended for a celebration of successful ascent to the peak. It tasted good at this altitude. We drank it in a clearing in front of the hut, from which we could see all the way down to the foot of the mountain. It was dark already and far, far down on the plains there were fires, their orange glow shimmering in all directions, all the land fuming. I felt as if we had escaped the nightmare of Dante Alighieri and were looking from Paridiso back down to the landscape of Hell the Beautiful.

Ariana Bella explained that people burn the sugar-cane fields just before harvest, to get rid of snakes which congregate there, gorging on rats, because rats congregate there, feasting on sugar cane.

"They found a black mamba fifteen feet long, last year. Making an acquaintance with such a specimen would leave you just several minutes to say goodbye. Green mambas, tree-huggers, are smaller but deadly, too, and the flat fat Gabon viper will do you in almost as fast." With this thought we prepared to sleep, except Tage, one of the sympathetic Danes, who suffered from a high-altitude headache. I knew, with regret, he had a slim chance of making it to the summit, which is 10,000 feet higher.

"*Buona notte,*" she whispered, "*lala salama.*" Swahili sounded like a flow of honey in warm milk, so good for sleep.

✳

Next day, the ascent to the second station, the Horombo Huts at 12,334 feet, would take us almost six hours. The landscape had changed rapidly after we left Mandara Huts. Trees became dwarfed, enormous heather covered everything; it reached four feet high. Alpine flora appeared on the exposed sides of hills, and on sites screened from winds, terrestrial orchids bloomed, their exotic appearance thrilling even to the mind of a botanic ignoramus. Everybody photographed.

On one of the three stops, by a cold clear spring, I listened to the second story about thorns.

"The Maasai was carried to the Moshi Hospital in pretty miserable condition, all the way from Oldoinyo L'engai volcano," Ariana Bella began. "He was an old man, so he took his spear with him; he had a metal ring with little sharp blade on it. His earlobes hung to his shoulders, one perforated with a wooden plug, the other containing a Kodak film cartridge. His foot was wrapped in an old rag, and from it emanated the stench of a few-days-old kill."

Ariana Bella appeared to be in good rhetorical condition, getting into her second story, despite the high-altitude dilution of oxygen, which does not favor memory recall. We sat by a spring of ice-cold water with a wooden sign announcing this to be the last opportunity to fill our bottles. Clouds moved rapidly under us, then through us, like the breath of ghosts. The heather rustled, the spring water rang; it seemed that everything was alive. Only the Maasai of the story seemed in the danger of silent death, so the Dutch doctor in Moshi Hospital had taken care of his problem with urgency. The acacia thorn embedded in the heel of the patient had caused damage which would require massive antibiotics, removal of dead tissue, drainage of puss and cleaning and dressing the wound daily, since necrosis had already set in. The nurses would perform the daily care, nurses from Chagga tribe.

All nurses in Moshi Hospital were Chagga, the people who have been living on the slopes of Kilima Njaro, their Shining Mountain, for an unknown number of centuries. They have made a decent living from small gardens and miniature fields claimed from the dense rain forest of the mountain. They have been very lucky, and unlucky, too. As we saw on the way to Marangu, they had abundance of perfectly clean and cool water running in streams from the upper reaches of the mountain—a great luxury in Africa. Their bad luck was their neighbors down on the plains, the Maasai, who would raid their communities, rustle their cattle and often kill, too. To hate Maasai became an old, well preserved tradition for the Chagga people. This helped them to stick together, too, since having an enemy does wonders for friendships.

The first night the Chagga nurses came to deal with the old Maasai, one removed the dressing and the other squeezed the wound. She pushed a ball of gauze into the hollow of the inflamed wound and twisted; she poked the raw inflammation with her gloved finger, always looking at the old warrior's face. The face did not move. His eyes did not blink nor close; there was no sign of anguish. His pain must have been agonizing, but the tradition of his people does not allow for showing pain, regardless of any circumstance. That has been the way of the Maasai, always.

Next day in the morning, and in the evening, and the day after the next, and for two full weeks, the nurses came and giggled and tortured him but never saw pain in his unmovable features. On the second week the miraculous antibiotics and anti-inflammatory drugs improved the wound; as the inflammation receded the nurses had to try harder for their torments. The old man's face became gray, his drawn features more and more skeletal, until his face resembled a human skull. The Dutch doctor, puzzled, tested his patient's blood and urine, and checked his heart, finding all the enzymes and blood components "within normal limits." Then the Maasai died. In his record it was stated that the death was due to unknown causes.

"Have you seen the patient, yourself?" I asked.

"No. The Dutchman told me about him. The doc learned the truth much later, from an orderly, who was not Chagga but to whom the nurses bragged. I heard the same story from a climber, Rob Taylor, an American like you. He was in the hospital with broken bones."

"I'll be damned," was all I could say. We sat in silence and then hiked in silence up another hill and over other gullies.

The first amazing mutants of groundsel appeared without a warning. The giant groundsel, *Senecio johntsonii*, a relic from Jurassic times, an unreal plant reaching ten or fifteen feet, were scattered over the hill like lost old men, some leaning in dangerous angles over the creases of gullies, some twins, some double-headed monsters. We stopped and contemplated them in awe. Then we tracked further. My thoughts came back to the story.

"The old Maasai ... he sacrificed himself just for his pride and honor? Am I right?" I stopped to question my storyteller.

"Yes. You got it."

"Think of it. Homo is a strange beast. Sometimes I think that a great virtue ... or any grand principle ... could be the badge of a fool. I don't like those things," I pondered when we stopped again to inspect a gigantic specimen of giant groundsel.

"Add religion to it, and you got a deal," Ariana Bella smiled.

"Deal, then!" We bumped our fists together, now clad in fleece gloves.

A few yards more and we emerged in front of the Horombo Huts. The smoke announced dinner in the making. At 12,340 feet, after a six-hour climb and one story, it would taste good, whatever Kunde could concoct.

I measured the pulse of Ariana Bella and it was 136 per minute; after resting for 10 minutes it went down to 78. She said she felt great, no headache. I told her I would like to measure her pulse for hours—it felt good to push on her radial artery.

"It might increase my pulse beyond the normal," she joked, giving me some hope!

After dinner we joined Tage in front of the hut on a clearing from which we could see down to the plains. He smoked a pipe, and his headache was gone. I was happy I'd made a mistaken prediction down in the Mandara Hut, that he would not make it. At higher elevations his condition improved, paradoxically, so that the policeman from Copenhagen rejoiced, and offered me his pipe. Then all of a sudden a small mouse-like creature appeared a few feet in front of us. It was carrying a yellow blossom in its mouth, like an animated cartoon character in love. It sat down and ate it almost at the feet of Tage. That was all, but the unexpected performance of chomping down the golden petals had a magical charm.

"The Spirit of the Mountain came to greet us," I whispered.

"Or a small rat," Ariana Bella whispered.

Tage laughed, amused.

It became cold.

Night!

Oh.

❋

In the crisp air of early morning we started on the third leg of our excursion. Soon the landscape changed to become more severe. Miniaturized flora appeared on the exposed slopes, but no creeks bubbled in the gullies. The wind was constant, so everybody put on their warmest clothing. Glacial sunglasses covered our eyes as the sun burned with cold rays; stops were more frequent, as were our inhalations. Would there be a third story on this third day of ascent?

After about two hours we emerged on a stony expanse—the immense saddle between the two peaks of Kilimanjaro: Mawenzi to the right and Kibo, the highest, in front of us. It was like a stratum of moon-scape, save for the small tuffs of gray grass and two-inch-tall white blooming flowers with silver mini-leaves, hiding close to the ground, behind stones. Volcanic stones the size of a fist to boulders the size of a small house covered this parched and cold landscape. We stopped to admire "the snows of Kilimanjaro," the glacier on the top of Africa. Kunde found a good resting place on the lee side of an enormous rock, which screened the wind off completely. Sandwiches were served and, as I had hoped, Ariana Bella started.

"A sick Maasai was helped to the Moshi Hospital." She smiled, seeing my curiosity demonstrated by an open mouth.

"And, there was an acacia thorn in his foot. Right?" I volunteered a guess.

"Right you are! I heard the story from Dr. Kashogi. Often, he used to stop by my clinic for a chat, bringing a couple of beers ... beers and sto-ries he brought, always. *Bieru barindi*, cold beer, he used to holler instead of greetings, even from the street.

"Kashogi was Kalenjin, the same tribe as was Moi, the crooked pres-ident of Kenya. So it was easy for Dr. Kashogi to secure a position in KEMRI, Kenya Medical Research Institute in Nairobi. But he liked to see patients in the field, from time to time, and so he used to return across the border to Moshi Hospital for a month or a few weeks, every year. Moshi Hospital had been his posting for his internship, but Kashogi, a romantic, would return there mainly for two reasons: he loved the views of the great mountain and the fatness of the Chagga nurses."

Ariana Bella paused to catch her breath, then continued. "The sick man in the emergency room was a young warrior, *ilmurran*, by the name Olepesai Ole Ngiyaa, who spoke some kiswahili, 'kitchen swahili,' and English of sorts that he had learned in the Mission School." They knew each other, she went on, Kashogi and he. Olepesai used to help interpret for a research project on experimental treatment of leishmaniasis of Maa-sai children, and they'd downed many a Tusker beer together. They greeted each other with several obscenities since it is the Maasai way not to kowtow to any authority, be it white man, *mzungu* or *wazungu*, doctor or minister. But Dr.Kashogi could see that his pal's smile was forced with considerable effort. His suspicion was confirmed when he removed the dirty rag bandaging the foot. Part of the foot had already disintegrated and necrotic tissue filled part of the hole; inflammation ascended half-way up the calf. It was a critical case of long-neglected infection.

The doctor prepared an injection of anesthetic while a nurse spread a set of needed surgical instruments. Olepesai asked about the injection and was told that the anesthesia was necessary, that it would take some time to clean the wound of the decomposed tissue. It would be very, very painful.

"No injection, Doc," said the Maasai. "I am *ilmurran*. Pain no problem. No injection!"

The doctor knew the Maasai disdain for pain, so he did not waste his time objecting but started his labor, cutting, cleaning, scraping away the mush. The warrior did not move; Kashogi did not want to see his face. He knew that the Kalenjin, his people, did not like the Maasai, hated them as "savages," thieves and murderers, but hated the Maasai mostly because they were brave, always; they laughed at authority. The Kalenjin disliked themselves through the hate of Maasai, the Nilotic race of long features and proud bearing, their beautiful women so inaccessible to Kalenjin. But Dr.Kashogi was different, because he had studied and lived abroad, in a land of culture and science, so he knew better. He had Maasai friends, liked the Maasai, secretly, and now felt for Olepesai Ole Ngiyaa. When he found an inch-long thorn deep in the wound, he cleaned it with a gauze.

"Olepesai, man, this is the goddamned arrow from your foot. Here you are, the thorn for your amulet!" Now, he looked into the patient's face with some anxiety, since it was ashen-colored, dead, expressionless. The gift of the thorn did not induce any change in the Maasai's face. He took the thorn, slowly, inspected it for a few seconds, dispassionately.

"This is what caused me much, much trouble?" he asked in a raspy, whispering kiswahili. Then he lifted himself with some effort on one elbow, bent forward and plunged the thorn back into the wide-gaping wound. He stretched himself back again; his grayness acquired a lighter shade, the hue of aged silver lightly cleaned, perhaps; his facial muscles contracted, his mouth remaining in scorn. The nurse covered her mouth with her palm.

Dr. Kashogi threw a scalpel back at the tray with instruments, removed his gloves, slowly, and tossed them on the floor. He left, saying nothing.

"When did the Maasai die?" I asked.

"Two days later."

✳

We trudged and stumbled further, to the third station, Kibo Hut, which became visible in the distance, at the foot of the steep slope leading to the top of Kibo. Part of the Ratzel Glacier was seen on the southern rim, but the view caused no exaltations. Nobody was in a great mood—the result of the altitude. Two of the four Danes lagged behind, but Ariana Bella seemed to be increasing her tempo with the decreasing temperature and increasing difficulties of the terrain. Often, she stopped to wait for us, but always either tying her shoelaces or adjusting the backpack or shawl with the intention (obvious to me) not to demonstrate that she was faster, in better shape than the rest of us. I liked that and I tried my damnedest to keep up. Deep down I knew I would have liked it even better if she had been in trouble and I could be the one to help her.

We drank lots of tea in the hut, but ate only a few biscuits, the infamous British Navy brand, since everybody had lost their appetite—and two of the Danes lost hope of summiting, of ascending Kilimanjaro tomorrow. One started to cough and had difficulty with breathing. It could have been the first sign of HAPE, the dreaded high-altitude pulmonary edema. The other, Sig was his name, had a monstrous headache, helped only a little by the barbiturates I gave him. Could it be the beginning of HACE, the feared high-altitude cerebral edema? Both decided to return. I cried, saying goodbye. Maybe, the tears were a sign of my elevated age in an elevated altitude. While the parting was as sad as Ariana Bella's stories, it left me downhearted longer.

Spartan bunks, spartan biscuits, a spartan outhouse and a miserable few hours of half-sleep fully clothed in a freezing temperature of 27 F did not invigorate anybody.

At one o'clock in the morning, the four of us remaining were on our way. In the darkness, bent down, with hoods over our heads, we looked like medieval executioners of the Inquisition ambling to the venue of their horrible deeds. But I felt more like their victim. It was five steps … and stop … and breathing five long inhalations, five steps … and stop … and on and on. The only thought I had was to maintain balance. To keep my balance became the most important purpose of my life. To loose it would mean the end of the climb and visit to the hospital of the fables about thorns, Moshi Hospital. The slope was a steep scree, rubble, but not a technical climb, so there would be injuries but not death. We followed the route of the men who climbed here first, Germans, Dr. Hans Mayer and his friend Herr Peutscherel, in 1891.

After a couple of hours on the slope I decided I'd make it, that I would never give up even if I had to crawl on all fours, in pain, half frozen, for hours. This emotion is well known to climbers and it is considered one of the dangerous, and often deadly, states of mind to acquire since it manifests the loss of healthy judgment.

After four hours we reached Meyer's Notch and emerged on the rim of the crater at Guilman's Point. All of us four collapsed, breathing heavily, regaining full consciousness slowly, straining the lungs in the oxygen-depleted air. Then Kunde arrived; he was closing the ranks in case his help was needed on the climb. He smiled his widest Chagga grin at us, pulled out a box of Benson & Hedges, and lit the cigarette. He inhaled deeply, emanating satisfaction. It was a sight of great inspiration and awe to me, almost as memorable as the view from the top of Kilimanjaro.

"There is smoke again on the volcano," Ariana Bella kept her humor, as always.

Moonlight seeped up from below the thin shreds of clouds on the south. It was five in the morning, and already a pink, then purple line had appeared on the eastern horizon, an announcement of many colors to come. All aspects of life on the equator are slow, as if dragged through an oil slick—except dawns and dusks. One minute we had deep night on the West and bright morning on the East ... and in another minute ... sunny day was everywhere, while the sky was spilled India ink, as if seen from a spaceship—black Heaven above! Theater of Magic and Wonderment!

I was tired but vaguely proud of making it up here, without a headache. Everybody kept to themselves, with private thoughts, slow and labored, until the sun ordered us to put on the glacier goggles and move. Then we continued to the highest point, Kaiser Wilhelm Peak (called Uhuru Peak by the natives), around the rim of the mile-wide caldera, touching the improbable glacier in blues and white that formed frozen lakes under the sixty feet of iceberg, amazed by its changing colors and mass, lamenting its disappearance while crunching and licking a part of it. It will be gone in fifteen years. The great diamond on the royal crown of Africa will be removed; it will sublimate! The majestic crown will become just a tall headdress of a pauper, the Black Continent.

At the top we all hugged, ate some chocolate, then a few pictures, the usual for summiting mountaineers. We were at almost six thousand meters, 19,335.6 feet. Ariana Bella asked about my state of health, my head, legs and other parts, but did not talk about hers. Was it the nurse in her, or was she such a good sport? I was impressed by her beneficence, thought her a great mate, and tried to learn.

The descent was painful but nobody complained. All four of us were in good shape when we reached Kibo Hut and, later in the day, the Horombo Huts. We sank into the realm of oxygen only slightly diluted by the scent of sage. Each thousand feet descended increased our exhilaration by a rate immeasurable, which made me to wonder about the simplicity of the workings of the brain of the animal homo sapiens. How easily it was influenced by gasses and their relative pressure. It was a beautiful day.

At the Horombo Huts we went to sleep early; it might have been nine, or so. I huddled under the blanket, Mr. Sandman at the ready. Then Ariana Bella appeared at my bunk and knocked on the blanket.

"Knock, knock," she whispered. "I am cold."

Thus began the exhilarating affair which, at first, was more an emanation of the body than of the heart, but ending in trust, not speaking about the laughs we'd had.

In the morning all I was thinking was how to make her happy. When we reached Hotel Maranga to pick up our luggage, I first rewarded good Kunde for his help with shillings and for his friendliness with my watch. Then I invited Ariana Bella for double Kenyan espresso with goat milk and proposed that we had to have a recuperation period of a few days, plain lazy rest in a great hotel… Could she take another week off? Because she did not have enough money to go with my plan, she declined. Therefore I had to reveal to her that I am quite well off, and have absolutely everything except a friend like her. It took another espresso for her to understand and to agree to my masterful stratagem.

✳

Hotel Tanzanite is a well-preserved relic of the great old colonial times, on a hill between Moshi and Arusha. The Presidential Suite we occupied had a posh verandah facing the wilderness in the back, where a watering hole illuminated with floodlights allowed us to admire the night wildlife, while we imbibed the medicine prescribed by my personal Italian nurse and lover, the medicine for black water fever, falciparum malaria: gin and quinine water, sliver of citrus included. But the first night a black domestic cat came to the watering hole, which meant that no lion, leopard or cheetah would approach. This phenomenon is not understood by experts in animal science, the barman told us, later, mixing us the deadly sloe gin of colonial alcoholics.

The first night we heard a lion call, so close, the low-frequency roar reverberated in my chest when I inhaled. We lay silently in the darkness, holding hands as kids do, trying to be scared, trying to embed it into our memory.

In the swimming pool, where frogs mimicked the chirping of birds at night, we dove, frolicked and swam in the morning. On the backstroke laps we marveled at the over-flights of marabu storks, fish eagles, kites and a secretary bird. By the pool was the first time I saw her body fully illuminated. Smooth, wet like a leopard seal, she was a stunning centerfold, in my book. In an anthropologist's book she would be approaching the ideal modern Venus, the Olympic swimmer. When she dove into the pool she seemed to will herself to remain suspended in the air.

Up till noon, and after, we slept, then loved with abandon of those who know the best value in life, and ate with voracity of those recovering from cucumber sandwiches. I told her she made me very happy. She laughed a lot and touched my shoulder and hand, often.

Early next morning, when the sun rose above the silhouettes of the flat-toped thorn trees, acacias, and "the trees where man was born," baobabs, and cast their mile-long shadows on the brick-red ground, Ariana Bella got up and walked around; she wanted to be alone, I thought. It took some time before she reappeared.

"Got something for you," she said and handed me an inch-long acacia thorn. "It got through my sneaker, but sideways. Missed my flesh by millimeters."

"It looks like it's made of forged steel," I said, and checked its sharpness.

"It is for your amulet." She smiled the smile I liked dangerously, by now. "Talisman, you know."

"All your stories started with a thorn. Does this one have a story, too?" I asked. "Might it be a part of our story?" I dared.

She remained silent as if reading my mind, which asked the question differently: is this thorn the end of our story?

She just hugged me without a word or kiss.

I recovered. "Thank you, it is an important gift. It would mean much… But I'll take it only if you'll take my present to you." I wanted the thorn as badly as I wanted to find an occasion for giving her my remembrance.

She hesitated and than agreed. The white gold ring I gave her was topped with a tanzanite the size of a navy bean and the azure hue of diluted Caribbean. Then I received the one but last kiss of our sporting romance.

I still exchange letters with Ariana Bella, but only at Christmas. She married the Dutch doctor from Moshi Hospital, moved back to Rotterdam with him, and plans to start a family. And she said, her man and she, they both miss Tanganyika. Almost every other day. The nature of my affinity for her changed with passing time but still it makes me sad. I wish I could miss Africa side by side with her, that we could miss Africa together.

In Minnesota I keep the thorn, which passed by her foot by millimeters, and sometimes take it out and turn it around and around in my fingers. I step outside of myself, then, and enter a state of wonder. It happens often and causes me a slight pain in my chest.

Fausto's Afternoon

Summer is the time to wallow in the grass by a lake or river with friends, the time to hoist a few pilsners, hiding from a fast warm storm under the linden tree, with friends. The nighttime is for kissing a girl and hoping for more. It is not the time to die.

"We shouldn't have come here on a Sunday. There's a line for a mile by the beer stand," Speedy Venca Aschenbrenner complained as he handed a bottle to Fausto and canned Coke to Erika. "At least it's cold."

All the swimmers called Adam "Fausto" for his unrestrained admiration of one Fausto Copi, the Italian cycling phenomenon, winner of two Tours de France and two Giro d' Italia, the greenish, hollow-cheeked skeleton with two massive tree trunks of legs attached and the will of steel—in the words of Adam. Fausto was the college swimming champion. He knew about will; his own, supposedly of stainless steel, turned to water when Erika lent him a smile. It was months ago when he promised himself, and swore in front of the guys, that never ever again would he start anything with her. Ever.

But she was so killingly different, with her shyness, her quiet never-prattling voice, her strangely beautiful face without a trace of cosmetics, her forget-me-not blue eyes under that helmet of thick hair bleached harshly by the mixture of the pool's chlorine and sun, to a pure white gold. And her body, ladies and gentlemen, her body was sculpted to the perfect beauty of the human female by hundreds of miles of interval training for the junior record in the butterfly. Something to see! But in truth, and above all, Fausto had been keeled over in an obdurate love by her inability to play-act or pretend. Yes, that was the attribute of her character that prevented his reason from any control over his heart.

"Let me open it for you," Fausto reached for Erika's coke, looking away from her, to be on the safe side. She nodded and thanked him.

Speedy Aschenbrenner mixed the cards for another poker game. "We'll have a couple more rounds, hey cheaters? How about that?" Speedy was fast even with the cards, fast at losing today. The three swimmers played poker for matches, so sorry were their cash reserves. Nevertheless, their contentment with the sunny afternoon was on their faces, enhanced by the warm breeze perfumed with tanning oils and the scent of women in estrus, a few molecules of sweet tetra hydroxycanabinol, and the strange odor of the summer stream—a composite fragrance, the dizzying breath of vacations. It was a delight to spend an afternoon on the boards of the swimming platform, "the spa," doing nothing, nothing productive or useful. Just screwing around, if you will.

With each card Fausto dealt to Erika he laid his eyes on her breasts. Whenever he dealt a card to her, he wondered how the pointed acromammae had been so important for his life, and how unreachable they were now, godammit. When he got to looking higher, he marveled at those lips, of which the upper was as full and succulent as the lower, believe it or not. These were lips untouched by lipstick but surely touched by him. Oh, what a life it was before he ruined it. He couldn't live with this constant tension, seeing her every day in the Club. He must decide, right on this day, either to ask her out again, to apologize for being a jerk, or just decide, today, right this afternoon, that he would never date her again, period.

Distracted, he bet and lost twenty matches. Erika took it all, with a full house. She smiled at Fausto apologetically, which melted him like exposed ice cream on this subtropical, hopeful day. Erika flipped off a spider which paraded on her ankle. Tiny shrimp-like creatures wandered on the blanket.

"Damn bugs. All over the place!" Speedy complained.

"Only primitives say 'bugs,' mon. They are insects, insects," Fausto educated him. And indeed, immature forms of aquatic beetles, larvae of dragonflies and damselflies, wolf spiders of several species and many hymen-less hymenoptera seemed to descend on everything. Or rather, ascended—from under the boards of the bathing platform, which had become overcrowded and sank so that the boards touched the water's surface, driving the insects to the spa, then onto the bathers, into their hairy parts and under their bikinis, from whence they were fished out by eager partners, accompanied by hysterical screams.

✳

The close-up view of Erika's prominences created fantasies, which increased Fausto's metabolic rate. "It's hotter than Hell. Gonna go for a swim," he said and got up. Speedy joined him by the platform's edge, and they stayed there looking down at the interesting flotsam passing by on the murky stream. The opalescent, peaceful condoms were as much a part of the surface of this river as ducklings or the dorsal fins of carp. "I watch you Fausto, with Erika, I see you, man," Speedy shook his head from side to side looking for words, which was always a labor for him.

"With her you're asking for grief, again. You know that."

"Well, I'll swim for a while," Fausto said.

"Yeah, just think, man. Think with your head, not your pecker. Or better … drown!" Speedy Aschenbrenner laughed and pushed Fausto into the river. Fausto half-somersaulted and disappeared under the surface.

I'll scare you, smart ass, he thought, and started to swim under water in the direction of the middle of the river. He was a champion collegian, his heartbeat that of a whale, his lung capacity almost double that of an age-matched male. He held his breath for three minutes and he could swim one hundred yards under water. The visibility was just inches, so he swam with eyes closed, since his vision would be as useless as that of a cave-dwelling salamander. He used the breaststroke, his arms pulled from their forward reach all the way down to his hips. Powerful but deliberately slow, efficient strokes moved him forward at the right speed with the least exertion of energy. The swimmer felt every cell of his motor system swelling with confidence. He would emerge far in the middle of the river, somewhere between the rowboats of the Sunday fishermen anchored there. Speedy would wait for him to emerge, for minutes, and then he'd start panicking. Fun! Just keep at the right depth! There… He felt the cold water caressing his skin and was aware of the might in his shoulders and the power of his breast muscles, the feeling that is pleasant and so addictive to swimmers. As each stroke finished, his arms laid along his body, palms touching hips, he glided, smoothly streamlined, creating turbulence and maelstroms only in his wake. He moved and looked like a torpedo with a smile painted on its warhead. He brushed past a dead hen. It might have been two minutes underwater when his body started to call for oxygen. First, a tension in the upper chest and pressure in the belly. Fausto grinned. He knew his limits well. He knew he could swim farther till he reached such a level of distress, the pressure of the fist pushing into his belly and the pain by the claw squeezing his chest would become too much for just a joke. Then he would emerge. When the true hurt and spasm arrived he continued for three more powerful strokes in the murky deep, and then charged up to the surface. There, his head smashed into a hard object. His closed eyes saw a flash of bright blue light—which instantly went out, into a darkness. His body went limp as a freshly drowned man. Then he recovered, opened his eyes and looked up. He recognized the lines of light, the spars between the boards. He was trapped under the swimming platform. He pushed his lips under the planks, hoping for air. But today the planks, weighted by the crowd, were touching the water. There was no air for Fausto.

✳

For Fausto, in his second decade of life, death had been a horrifying but mostly remote proposition. Submerged in the coldness of the dark brown fluid, his mind acquired a sudden lucidity without the terror he had always imagined. *Now, I will die!* It was a calm thought—followed by a realization that he might survive if he chose the right of the two possible directions to continue his swim. One led to the river—and life. The other, opposite way, led to the shore, where the drums supporting the platform touched bottom. Taking that bearing would result in death by drowning. Both directions were 90° perpendicular to the lay of the boards. It was a gamble with even odds—Russian roulette was child's play in comparison.

Fausto started to swim. Still, there was no dread choking him, just a feeling of regret, of sadness, which was not overwhelming. He realized, with amazement, that the pangs of pain and spasms with which his body demanded air were gone. He had no need to breathe! He was impressed by his strokes being still efficient but after a while (the perception of time acquired an unknown, novel character) he felt that his legs were decreasing their performance and beginning to drag; he was slowing down, involuntarily. He continued to concentrate solely on the efficiency of his strokes, as if it was the most important thing in his life. Still no need for air! And then the top of his head thumped into a hard obstacle with a blow that reverberated through his body. With a mournful timber the boom of a hollow drum, it announced the end of the swimmer's journey. Fausto knew only that the drum was either one of supporting floats along the shore—or one of those along the open river. The exact number of strokes at the swimmer's disposal is finite, a secret known only to the gods. If forced to turn around after hitting the shore drum, quite soon Fausto's very last stroke would be performed—but by his body only. By then, the brain would be devoid of consciousness, which some call the soul, so the young man Fausto would have ceased to exist; the last stroke would be the dead man's stroke.

At the moment of impact, all these thoughts escaped with the stream of bubbles from his nose. More instinct than conscious thought directed him to dive deeper, under the drum, despite the disobedient protest from his muscles. He emerged from the river, into an atmosphere syrup-thick with sweet oxygen, under a sun spanning the whole wide dome of the sky. He did not gasp for air, but had to force himself to inhale and exhale with the right rhythm. He held, with one hand, onto the edge of the platform, hanging there, not thinking. Fausto spotted a ladder, crawled up on the boards, and sat down, his feet dangling in the water which had released a swimmer a minute ago as a reward for his conditioned physique of a leopard seal and for his sane, secular presence of mind. When he managed to stand up Erika was in front of him, watching him with curiosity written on her face. Fausto saw her hair was violet, her eyes salmon pink, her cleavage a rosy tint. He looked at the sky to confirm his vision's alteration (from overreaction to bright light by his red receptors, a hypoxic retina) and saw it emblazoned red as if by reflected fire, the boulders of summer cumuli colored aubergine. He lowered his eyes to his nails. Their beautiful sheen and reddish-gold tinge was identical to that of the antique ivory rubbed for years on the wrists of Africans.

"Speedy said he lost you. He'll pick you up, tonight, for the training, he said. You look strange, Fausto."

"I'm okay. It is nice you have waited for me."

"Where were you?" Erika asked.

"Oh, nowhere. I was … I almost … was nowhere. I'll tell you sometime, later," Fausto said, turning his sight away from her carmine eyes. He took a deep breath, leaned on the railing of the plateau and marveled at the crimson heaven. He pondered, maybe, his future in the wonderful rosy world of sporting life and lovers' sighs. His smile grew wide and wider as he reached for her waiting hand, the hue of a dusty rose.

The Banana

Tonight, after serving Malayan coconut chicken with ginger, peppers, and curry, I presented a culturally compatible desert, which is also the cheapest desert in the world. I bake bananas till their blackened skin tells me they are done, then peel and split them in half, right on the serving plates. Then I sprinkle some rum on them, and vanilla sugar, and make two lines of honey, and cover them with whipped cream. We licked our eager lips for about twenty five cents per serving, labor and transport from the original "Banana Republic," Honduras, included. Bananas. How plebeian!

But exactly sixty years ago, in Prague in the fall of 1945, the banana was the highbrow star performer in a different and more interesting dramatic spectacle.

The five-years-long war had just ended, but the battle in the kitchen to feed the family continued still, with undiminished ferocity. There were no victories—just draws, with boiled potatoes overlaid with cottage cheese and parsley, mashed potatoes with egg fried on lard, potatoes mashed with boiled barley and garlic, fried mashed potato balls, potato soups...

I was an eight-year-old girl with a growling stomach, as skinny and pale as all the girls in Prague, but with a brain succulent in information storage capacity, and endowed with curiosity and an eagerness to sponge up all data about the world around me, more like a black hole sucking in the Universe than the common sponge. I had known only life in war and thought the war was the normal way of existence, but in secret I suspected there was a different life elsewhere, certainly in the tropics. I reread *Orchid Hunter* from my father's library, the illustrated tome about Borneo, the island abounding with amazing orchids with names like spectabile, nobile, formosa and grandiflora. There were palms with thorns there, violin birds, jewel beetles, enormous insect-eating plants; the jungles were inhabited by cannibalistic Dayaks and the orang-utan, the "man of the woods," whom Dayaks thought to be a true man, but one who did not speak to avoid working. I did not understand some of the writing but I liked this incomprehension—for me it was a promise of future discoveries.

Such as the uncovering of the banana.

When Mrs. Benesova, our art teacher, entered the classroom we suspected an unusual event. She marched to her desk with the determination of someone on a mission, her steps high, her gaze into the distance. The class calmed down without the habitual teacher's insistence.

"Children," she said, and that was all. We thought it odd. She looked at us intently, for a while, then opened her purse and withdrew a strange object. She held the thing between her forefinger and thumb by its stem and lifted it up above her head as if to make it unreachable.

"Children … a banana!" All of us gazed at the slightly curved yellow object above her head with open mouth and in silence. Even Franta Kacidl.

"This famous tropical fruit, *Musa paradisiaca*, grows on gigantic herbs with tree-like stems. These stems die and disintegrate—after flowering and delivering this fruit…" she swung the banana with a loose wrist as one would ring a bell, "…this fruit with aromatic, edible flesh." Kacidl said "ding-dong-ding-dong," but nobody laughed.

Mrs. Benesova continued undeterred, after she laid the fruit on the desk. She lowered her voice: "A bisexual plant: male flowers are always on the top of the flowering stem and those of the female sex are on the bottom." Sykorova, who was the oldest of the class because she was delayed in the first grade and then flunked, burst out in a short giggle. Stupid Vokurka said "whoa." *Musa paradisiaca*—it sounded beautiful to me, like a secret sacred mantra. And I found it fascinating to hear about sex, delivery and death, all happening in paradise, and all in just two sentences.

The teacher instructed us to form a queue, starting the line from the first bench on the left. Then she spread a clean handkerchief on her desk, peeled the banana, and opened her Rybka pen knife. She motioned for the first pupil in the queue to approach. Sasha Shultzova looked daunted but stepped up to the desk. Mrs. Benesova cut a slice of the off-white flesh of the fruit and pointed at it as it lay on the kerchief, glistening with wetness. She had to prod Sasha again to take it and put it in her mouth. Sasha did not bite or swallow it—she closed her lips tight like a child refusing a dentist, and sleepwalked away with a smile, as if blessed. Everybody watched her intently with unrevealed thoughts, and since thoughts are silent there was a silence in the classroom. After this Communion Sasha's eyes were almost closed and her beam unfading.

The teacher dissected the banana into thirty-two quarter-inch-thick pieces, one for each pupil of the second grade Class B, each of the segments a slice of indelible memory for a child, who approached the desk in discipline, to receive.

I remember well how it melted slowly on my tongue as I refused to swallow the dissolved matter, to prolong the unprecedented delight! And I imagined this tropical ambrosia was just like potatoes for my favorite Dayaks, and orang-utans, too, and I felt I understood my Borneo of fables better. The promised paradise of *musa*!

The unholy Host I had just received was a promise of glorious times to come, now that the war of adults was over.

The Delta

"They still keep slaves down there. I know it for sure, massa." He raised his shoulders as if in apology.

"I bet you drank that three-day-old palm wine again, Chukwu. Who can believe you, then?" I asked. I wanted him to say more, since I had heard the stories, too. The slavery downriver in the delta was the talk of the town whenever nothing newsworthy happened here, as was the case in the season of short rains, the long rains and the dry season. The delta of the Niger River is a vast space known only to satellite cameras and native eyes; it is a secret territory in which strange things are fabled to happen.

Chukwu was very street-smart in the ways of communication. He just beamed a wide smile, knowing my system of extracting information. His round eyes on his globular head narrowed a few millimeters, his teeth flashed whiteness of near perfection and his fleshy earlobes flapped. I took pleasure in watching his glossy, black face talking beyond and above the words, despite the effusiveness too often lavished on me.

He was a master in justifying the old American cliché that it doesn't matter what you know, but whom you know—a real Washington man, Chukwu. As far as I knew, he never held a physical job, like being carrier at the market, or a hauler of logs from rafts. His calling and livelihood was as a carrier of news and messages, and a hauler of gossip. That is how we became acquainted and developed a saprophytic relationship resembling the binding between a tree and an orchid. We called it friendship—no problem with semantics.

"Here in Onitcha, many people will tell you the same, massa. The fishermen, they see the boats going down the river at night. In them kids, massa, and young women, tied down. The fishers, who spread their nets at night, they see them, is true." He nodded and shook his head to confirm his sadness about the situation. I liked him and trusted almost half of his pronouncements since, as I mentioned, he was my friend, besides being my "assistant"—we had both decided that. I paid him on time with pretty American dollars, just to affirm our mutual trust, and he reciprocated, offering me his handsome girlfriend with the pretty name Nenne

Chinello and the physique of J-Lo.

I had been in this town on the Niger for four months, my task of surveying the possibilities for widening the bridge across the river almost done. I am a bridge-man, true, but I have been much more interested in the life around me. Onitcha boasts the largest open-air market in Nigeria, but I found the life on the river even more interesting. So I longed to explore at least part of the Niger River's delta of mysteries.

Here I have to state that the Niger delta, one of the least explored places in Africa, is certified as the unhealthiest real estate in the whole world. Its thousands of square miles of lowlands are a maze of mangrove islands, innumerable creeks and rivulets connected to the river under the canopy of jungle—a river without a main stream, which divides, spreads, and opens into the Bight of Benin like a caput Medusae, with amputated tentacles bearing names such as Kwo'ra, Tsadda, and Bi'nne. It is sparsely populated by people and by larger tropical wildlife, but richly inhabited by miniature carriers of sleeping sickness, vectors of river blindness (all villages have their blind), black water fever (fatal falciparum malaria), amoebic dysentery (liver transformed into a bag of yellow mash), black vomit, tick fever, rinderpest, and, of course, by agents causing leprosy, schistosomiasis (all organs and skin infested with parasites), filariasis of the type where long pale worms thread through the body, and the other type, where the heart changes into a mass of tiny worms, elephantiasis, made famous by pictures of victims with scrotums reaching the ground, and kala-azar (liver and spleen fill with leishmaniasis and burst). While most are locally untreatable and some ultimately fatal, these afflictions still pale in comparison with deadly Ebola fever, Lassa fever, Mokola and Marburg disease, which even the inquisitor Savanarola describing the horrors of Hell couldn't imagine: organs disintegrate within days and blood pours from the body openings and eyes of the still-living victims. And there are more of the deadly bizarreries yet to be discovered. To exist on the losing end of germ warfare has been the normal way of life in the delta.

During the old colonial times the life span of a British officer in Onitcha was about a year—but in the delta only few short months. The delta—"the white man's grave!" I checked the literature, regarding myself a seasoned globetrotter (globetrotters check the literature): in 1805, during Mungo Park's expedition to the Niger River, 39 of his 44 companions died. Death within a year for a European was virtually guaranteed on the West African coast in the early nineteenth century—still a luxury in comparison with the delta.

I wanted to go anyway, though, because it would be interesting. Would I be able to actually see the slavery in its original environment, to touch this element from which the fabric of the social life of Sub-Saharan

Africa had been woven—in its not too distant history? In the present?

✻

One important contribution Chukwe made to my well-being was his introduction of Dr. Chiny Kaine. Not only did she treat my fulminant diarrhea, but she became my mentor in all things Nigerian. In this place, where one needs friends absolutely, I valued highly the amity of Chiny Kaine, M.D., an Igbo-British physician and good cook. She was well into her sixties when we met. Never married, always available—but too intelligent, I heard. Never in a bad mood or brooding, but always cheerfully complaining about her circumstance, she was an enigma which I did not try to resolve, and thus endanger the possibilities of having a good time with her. Her complaints were always directed at specific names, and contained the precise amount of bribes that went to government men, described as "Big Man's loot." She was an encyclopedia that I loved to leaf through, and which stayed always up to date.

She had attended medical school in Ibadan and received her residency and fellowship in London and Birmingham. Then followed many years of service in England, the period of which little of her was known—nobody asked. Why she returned to practice in Onitcha was a mystery to me, but obvious and understandable to her patriotic compatriots. She built a "clinic" and a large house in her ancestral village of Zidogu, down the river. I learned it is an obligation of all Igbo expatriates who "made it" to erect a big house in their ancestral home village, even if it is not to be ever used.

Physically, she was an example of a well-to-do African woman—there was no lack of adipose tissue on Dr. Kaine's ample behind or in the promontories of her opulent bust. But her face above the chins expressed intelligence, and her smile invited smiles. Her coconut chicken with red rice with chilies was a delightful experience—flames coming from the mouth had to be doused by several cold bottles of Star, the Nigerian equivalent of Budweiser, which Dr. Kaine always had on hand. And talking about the old times in Biafra, with ersatz tea afterwards, was for me the highlight of the evening because she spoke the truth, lacking all symptoms of racial or ethnic complexes, a trait as rare as the proverbial black pearl. One night after coconut chicken we planned an excursion to her native village, which she described with her usual mix of skepticism and empathy.

Dr. Kaine picked me up in her new Peugeot with Ojibi, her driver, at the wheel. I knew him to communicate in short exclamations and keep the car spotless. True, he had never constructed a full sentence, but in contrast to all other Nigerian drivers he slowed down driving through villages instead of accelerating in the usual display of power. That oddity was the main reason he kept his employ, I learned. Dr. Kaine was dressed African, colorful as a bouquet of wildflowers. It surprised me since it was the first time I had seen her not wearing Western fashion, but I figured it was appropriate for visiting Zidogu, the village of her roots. She smelled non-African, of lily of the valley, and seemed to be in a cheerful disposition, taking the sacrificial front seat.

Onitcha faded into the countryside; the township disappeared gradually, the distance between the huts and houses increasing, and the odor of motor oil mixed with garbage changed into the perfume of earth after rain. The crowds of idle young men, the exclamation mark of a steadily increasing overpopulation, became smaller, diminishing into groups of threes and twos, like a game of vanishing chairs. Eventually only fields of cassava, yams, cocoyams, dwarfed maize and scant remnants of nature were visible. A few bushes and bamboo clumps grew along the creeks, which snaked through the transformed landscape of hungry men.

Before this excursion, I had prepared a question for Dr. Kaine. I anticipated that she wouldn't be able to avoid some sort of an answer, because she couldn't escape my proximity being together in a car, and only two of us alone, the mute driver Ojibi disregarded.

"Why do you think Africa is still in such a trouble, Chiny? Would you mind thinking aloud?" I asked after we made it across a ford in a creek, not killing any of the crowd of kids who ambushed us like pack of laughing wild dogs, insisting to wash the car with creek water. "Some say it is even getting worse."

Dr. Kaine emitted her characteristic laugh out of the window, the bubbling wulla-wulla-wulla, falling in pitch, ending in a harsh, frenzied chuckle. Then she turned and looked me in the eye. "Ha!" she said. "You waited to be with me in this vehicle so I couldn't escape. So you got me." She leaned back in her seat looking sideways at the thick neck of Ojibi. "I'll tell you the summary of the truth. Behind all the troubles and hopelessness are our old African traditions, our culture, meeting and colliding with progress and individual freedoms… and then throw in the cruel climate and the unforgiving land." She paused. "So simple is the answer, my friend—and so complex it would be to explain. We would need not a short trip to my Zidogu but the overland to Cape Town, at least." She turned half back to me with raised eyebrows, as if surprised by herself.

"I imagine," was all I said, preparing, in my mind, the follow-up inquiry about details. But I found myself unprepared after such a clean and clear statement by the good doctor.

"And do you know what is the main problem? The real catastrophe waiting to happen?"

"The mixture of AIDS and corruption?" I volunteered.

"Oh no. Corruption, AIDS, malaria, droughts, famines … these are disasters. But overpopulation it is which will result in a true calamity of unimaginable dimensions. Mark my words!"

"I read about the doubling of population in less than a generation," I remarked, wanting to sound informed.

"True, and worse. And I am responsible, too. I learned in England to save children's lives, so few die, nowadays."

"But that is beautiful, Chiny."

"Yes, but our women learned from their mothers to be pregnant all the time, all their reproductive life, having one kid after another… would you say it is smart? Is it beautiful?"

I did not weigh my words. "It's stupid, I say." Lengthy silence followed and I worried a little about my rash candidness.

"Yes, my friend, yes… and I think none of your countrymen would ever say what you said. And Europeans wouldn't even think it! But, you see, I like your candor and openness, I do." Kaine turned to me with a wide grin. "Especially when you are right!"

Ojibi swerved the car violently, without warning—we almost rolled over. He had tried to hit a ten-foot-long, living whip of shiny black spitting cobra—and missed the impressive animal, to my great delight.

The car continued to travel the speed of a sherpa's yak, climbing up and down—also like a yak—over the enormous potholes, some filled with a red solution of liquid mud, others extending laterally into ravines. Still, we were faster than pedestrians (all Africans are born and die as pedestrians, save the obese "Big Men," *wabenzi*, in their Mercedes-Benzes, and the "Big Woman" in her Peugeot) and caught up with four women who marched steadily in line, colorful as a photo from National Geographic, each one with a basket on her head. In an instant I forgot the fate of Africa, the global concerns, even the overpopulation—that's how shallow I am. I played my usual mind game to identify from behind which one was the grandmother and which one the granddaughter. Passing them their faces will tell. But only the faces, because from the behind, their athletic legs of a middle-distance runner, their posture and pace were always identical, regardless of their age. So far I have been right only half the time, which in the language of statistics means success only by random chance. This time I failed, again.

"These women go to Zidogu too, to the market," remarked Dr. Kaine, noticing my interest.

"I admire their physique, their build," I said.

"Me too. It's from the hard life, you know. Good life kills the body and, sometimes, the mind, too. This has been well known, since ancient times. It is market day, today; you might find the people there interesting. Some things here have not changed in centuries."

"Well, the men wear jeans." I pointed to a barefooted fellow with a *panga* (machete) in his hand and stone-washed jeans. "That's a change. Levi's."

"True, in some ways things have changed, but only in the last decades—these women we met, they would have been all naked when I was a girl, with only *jigida*, beads, around their waist. But just before coming to the market, they would put a cloth or a strip of underbark around their hips." Dr. Kaine laughed quietly to herself as one would remembering a joyous event. She added: "When one would forget to take off the rag coming back home to their village, her husband would beat her."

Before long we arrived at the market on the outskirts of the village, and Ojibi slowed down to a crawl. Dr. Kaine rolled down the window and spoke in Igbo to some women; she was greeted with such reverence, as if the Savior had arrived. And I believed she just might have been the Savior here, in the place where she built her clinic. I wondered how many of these women, who curtsied and smiled at her, owed her their life and the lives of their kids. Their smiles seemed to offer their heart, their only valuable possession. A few older men bowed as they had learned from the Brits. A goliath beetle, the size of a baseball, crashed into the windshield, and Ojibi uttered two Igbo words: *mara mma*. We arrived.

The clinic was built of cinder blocks, its cracks hosting a few ferns. Molds and fungi, in subdued hues, abounded on the walls, but it was a functional structure. It consisted of three rooms: the "ambulance," where patients were seen and small surgery performed, "preparatory," where supplies, files, and junk were stored, and the back room, where the nurse-health officer lived. She was outright beautiful. Her name I forget, but I learned she came from the delta years ago and was saved by Dr. Kaine from a certain grim future. Chiny had provided shelter and money for schooling, and so she had remained eternally grateful. She was of the Bantu race, but with a few features of the East African desert tribes like Pokots and Samburu: high cheek bones, a slight oriental slant to her eyes, and a narrow, aquiline nose. Her smile had a killing effect on me and I decided I must find time to talk to her—who knows? Only later, on the walk to her house, did Dr. Kaine tell me that the nurse looked so "healthy" because she was a carrier of the gene for the sickle cell anemia trait, which protects her from all types of malaria. She explained it as a result of "intelligent evolution" within the black race of Africa.

"And, by the way, you might know that she was raped, a few times, during the Biafra War, and so she ain't no friends of male-kind. You could understand that? Could you?" Kaine looked at me as if I'd done something wrong.

I nodded in the affirmative, being shocked by the casualness of her statement into silence and a few minutes of intense thinking. Thus ended, sadly, my dreams surrounding the nurse.

She cooked for herself in the open air kitchen while patients waited outside, sheltered from the rain by a corrugated metal roof. There were about twenty patients there, already. Most were women, in different stages of pregnancy or disease, or both. Again, they greeted Dr. Kaine with gestures of great reverence and an expression of happiness. At me they looked sideways, as if afraid of the pale-face, *onya-acha*. They would be seen in the afternoon—we had to tour the village, first. I suggested we walk instead of driving and Dr. Kaine, hesitantly, agreed.

"There is the house of my family; here I grew up." She pointed to the biggest dwelling of the village, surrounded by a mud wall. When we entered through the carved gate of iroko wood, I realized it was a compound with several smaller huts, some with roofs of corrugated sheet metal and one with a thatched roof. By the wall there was the ubiquitous family shrine, with revered wooden statues of secret symbolism (ju-ju things one does not talk about) and sacrificial objects in one large and several smaller clay pots. There was a bicycle leaning against the largest, scary-looking carved figure—an old rusty, English machine.

"These huts were for my dad's wives. He was a 'Big Man' but had only four wives. He thought more wives would be more trouble than the prestige was worth. Do you understand?" Dr. Kaine greeted a few old men and an ancient grandmother who shuffled to welcome us. The old woman's face was the face of a Caucasian granny—the creases, wrinkles and sags masking her race. I noticed how the clay courtyard was spotlessly swept as if hand polished to resemble the surface of lightly glazed terra-cotta pottery. With a smile I shook the hands of all who welcomed us, feebly, limply, as is the custom here. Then we helped the grandmother to the bench under the enormous dogon-yaru tree, which shaded everything.

A young fellow in Nike jogging shorts and a ski cap with a Norwegian caribou pattern brought us two bottles of Fanta on a tray. He was an albino, anyale, with squinting eyes, personifying the aesthetic incompatibility of Negroid features without pigmentation—and the unfortunate result of lack of pigment when living near the equator: scabs on his nose and forehead suggested the incipient stages of skin cancer, already. I felt relieved to sit down in the shade, next to silent Grandma, who leaned closer to me, and half whispered something in Igbo in my ear. Dr. Kaine translated with laughter: "Grandma told you, you must stay here, with them. She insists—or she will kidnap you, she said!"

I nodded in agreement. I felt vividly alive, all of a sudden, with people both exotic and familiar at the same time, who fit their space so well, who enjoyed our company without demonstrative exuberance, just simple hugging and three alternating kisses. I luxuriated in the shade and warm yellow Fanta bubbly. I wanted more heat and sweat … yes, to physically feel even more I was in my Africa, in the secret corner of Africa, where nobody from my old world would find me—and I would not find them … I felt so ready for action.

Then tall man of regal carriage approached. He carried a black umbrella and a necklace of agates, and his black patent shoes—without socks—shined. He was an important *ozo*, an associate chief of sorts (the title of veneration could be bought for 20,000 niara). He sported a pith helmet, now a very rare symbolic relic of colonialism. It surprised me because I had been aware that colonials in their pith topees were hated by *ozos*, chiefs, and almost all educated Igbos, although the masses, the plain folk, still remember the Brits and their rule with nostalgia. We broke cola nuts with him in a welcoming custom. Smearing the cola nuts with the red-hot red pepper paste was a new experience for me. Soon I learned the associate chief used to be a constable in Liverpool, and seeing his face maimed by the tribal ID scars I could easily imagine him striking terror in the lowlife of the old neighborhoods that produced the Beatles. His British-accented English was excellent, his physique impressive—he was an interesting specimen. But he looked disappointed when he learned I hailed from the land of American "football," not the real football, because he was eager to talk more about his favorite Liverpool Reds annihilating Manchester United with two flick-on headers and curling a free kick seconds before the end of the championship game.

"This tree changes the climate of the compound. The luxury of shade!" I broke the silence after the *ozo* marched away with his regal bearing, as if inspecting his imperial guard.

Chiny Kaine leaned to me and said: "I hate this tree, I always did." She shook her head, looking at me as if waiting for my reaction.

"You hate a tree? Is it because the dogon-yaru leaves are still used to treat malaria?" She had told me before that the tree's bitter leaves have absolutely no medicinal effect.

"No, no," she shook her head. "I'll tell you why. The tree has been here since I was a little girl. We played under it. Then, when I grew up my father bought a slave for his new wife, Ese. He was just a boy—and he soon took a liking to me. I started to look like a woman, my breasts exploding, my buttocks rising. Once, father saw him watching me. He beat the boy. Then, some time later, he saw the boy following and looking at me again." Kaine waved her hand as if shooing away an annoying insect or a bothersome memory and became silent. We sipped warm Fanta and I remained silent, too, expecting a bad ending to the story.

"Father had the slave tied to this stupid tree." Dr. Kaine got up, then; there were people approaching her wanting to talk to her. She turned and leaned closer to me. "It took the boy whole week to die. Eaten alive by ants and insects, then rats at night. The screams…" She looked at me with eyes which might have been washed by tears. I cudgeled my brain for words, but I just managed to make a sound—similar to the one I made when Al Hadji Okoronwa, the owner of a gas station in Onitcha, told me about the killing of one of his father's wives; that time it was she who had looked with desire at the young slave. I calculated: both events must have happened as recently as in the late Thirties.

Dr. Kaine held audience with relatives of different degrees and ages; everybody spoke in low voices to show respect. They arrived at the compound to greet her, summoned not by talking drums but some mysterious telepathy people have when blessed by the absence of phones. I think she distributed some money, too.

A young man with a camera (a student visiting home, I learned) gathered people around us to form two rows for a group picture. He sent a teenager, with baby at her breast, to the rear row: "You are too black, you'd spoil the picture. Go back!" She just smiled at him. An older fellow, who brought a bottle of schnapps for Dr. Kaine as a present, raised it high, and I put my arm around the narrow shoulders of Grandma. One exposure was made. Nobody smiled—it was a serious occasion.

Then we left, accompanied by a small crowd. We sauntered to the gate of iroko wood, past the shrine to souls of ancestors and its bicycle, and out of the compound, followed by the ubiquitous pack of naked children with umbilical hernias.

As we neared the house Dr. Kaine built in the village, a young fellow in a ski cap with a pattern of snowflakes approached Dr. Kaine with a deep bow and spoke to her in excited Igbo. She gave him a five-naira bill, asked him a few questions, and thanked him: *dalo, dalo.*

"The guy tells me that there is an American woman here in Zidogu. She just arrived and will be leaving tomorrow. How about that?"

I had not seen a white face for a couple of months, and I certainly did not expect to meet one here, in the boondocks of the Niger, the last place one can reach by car, before the delta. And a real American?

"That is not possible!" I exclaimed.

"Yes, it is possible—she came to get a boat to take her to the delta, that is what the fellow told me. To the delta—to the place I told you you would never leave alive!" Dr. Kaine snickered. "And a woman is going there, my friend. A woman!"

A meeting with the mysterious American had been arranged; she would be escorted to Dr. Kaine's house for the dinner. The house stood at the edge of the village—it was a two-storey, semi-European, untropical, out-of-place dwelling in no particular style, with a neglected garden and heavy iron bars on all windows. I got a room upstairs with a view of the jungle.

The equatorial rain forest—it reminded me of an absinthe-induced painting of a passionate tropical wilderness: clumps of bamboo, tall buttressed trees connected with luxuriant philodendrons, some decorated with stag horn ferns and bromeliads. Each single tree—a unique botanical garden joined to the next by flowering creepers. The view was the dream-vision for a dreamer made even dreamier by the mist, which was actually microscopic dust brought all the way from the Sahara and sahel by the harmattan wind. The mosquito net over my bed looked new, which was good news. The warm, rotten smell of must I found tropically enchanting, almost romantic. I felt a lucky man—for whom total happiness could be reached, at this moment, by having a cigarette and stiff drink. I needed the impossible: sloe gin!

While Chiny went to see her patients I took my un-American nap, the siesta.

✳

"I'm Nancy Lepardeau, Philadelphia." She smiled at us. "With the Peace Corps."

I couldn't imagine a lovelier apparition more out of place in this location. She affected my ability to breathe! Imagine: Shirley Temple curls tightened by the humidity, chestnut hair bleached at the tips by the near-equatorial sun, which made a halo around her angelic face, which was, unlike the anemic faces of angels, beautiful. She moved unhurriedly, as if she did not want to impose on others' space, and shook hands with us firmly, which I found odd, used to limp handshakes by now. She was in an oversized T-shirt featuring Bruce Springsteen, a crumpled skirt of African design, and the ubiquitous sandals. To say I was in love would be a far too hasty a judgment, but I was stunned.

I had met Peace Corps volunteers in Africa before. Often on their faces was an expression of determination to better the world, a do-gooders' zeal. There might have been a pretense of toughness or worldliness in their attitude but, sometimes, they wore just a sagging face of frustration and fatigue, not unlike the sad face of a bloodhound. But Ms. Lepardeau, at first sight, had only a look of slight confusion, as if things were developing too quickly. After a short while she seemed to regain the appearance of refusal to get unsettled. I contributed a few easy and conventional lines from my abundant fund of small talk, and she became at ease, relaxed; I could recognize the demeanor of a young woman leaving a flower shop in the sunny Philadelphia morning. Here, in Zidogu! Ms. Lepardeau. Her name suggested a leopard—most unfittingly, I thought.

After I recovered and introduced Chiny Kaine and myself, I asked what brought her to the backwoods. We had some palm wine tapped earlier that morning, which the tapper did not dilute with water, I was assured (it would induce diarrhea). The beverage was mild and cool, and it was consumed while we heard a brief synopsis of Nancy Lepardeau's curriculum vitae.

She did not know the origin of her name, but she was sure the tips of her roots were Sephardic Jewish, despite the fact that she did not look like an Arab's cousin at all. Her father's ancestors came to America from North Africa by way of Spain and then Cuba. Her ma was of Bohemian heritage. Nancy graduated from the University of Pennsylvania, one of the Ivies, double-majoring in Spanish and history. We had a pleasant discussion about almost nothing. She made a long face I couldn't read when saying that she considered herself a hard-core liberal, but a realist, too. She did not care much about religion and supernatural gods, she said, but I saw her look at the kitchen door—she cared much about dinner. This was an African trait she acquired, no doubt, since on the Dark Continent food is of prime concern for individual survival, sex being only second on the scale, for survival of the family or clan. Looking at our lovely guest, sex was rated a step above the food and survival of the species, in my book. We were served mashed yam with the choice of obono soup of melon seeds or the slimy ebosi soup that had the viscosity of used motor oil, and, as another course, very good poached dried catfish with my favorite red rice. Regardless of her gentle, shy smile, golden curls and all, Nancy devoured it like a lumberjack. I saw sympathy forming on Dr. Kaine's face.

As a surprise our host ordered Nestlé Swiss instant coffee with sweetened Dutch Peak condensed milk to be served in dainty little china cups. I had to remind myself we were only a hundred feet from the impenetrable jungle.

Nancy told us about her first year in the Peace Corps in the Santa Marta Mountains of Colombia, where she investigated vectors of malaria. She recorded species of mosquito carriers in the region, the prevalence of malaria and, also, the types of affliction. She used her microscope, insect dissecting tools and her specimen microscopic slides. She perfected her Spanish, learned to live on simple diets and to enjoy simple pleasures, not unlike the people there, the indigenous Indians with basic values she learned to like very much. She fell in love with a not so simple Indian Affairs Officer from Cartagena. It ended badly, as she predicted it would, and she asked for a transfer from Colombia. Thus for the second part of her service as a Peace Corps volunteer she arrived to Lagos to learn that her assignment would take her to the delta of the Niger River. I thought that the Peace Corps coordinator in the Lagos office was either a moron who did not know about the delta, or a sonofabitch who did not give a damn about killing Nancy Lepardeau. I wanted to say so, but held back. It sounded incredible to me that she would disappear down the river tomorrow. I looked at Dr. Kaine, who listened intently, but I could only guess her thoughts through her eyes. In a voice muted with kindness she asked Nancy if she had all the necessary vaccinations, and what kind of medicines she carried with her, in the event of … just in case.

"You are aware of the health problems in the lowland, down the Niger, aren't you?" Dr. Kaine asked, keeping the sympathetic face.

"Yes, Doctor, I have been through the Peace Corps preparatory course in Lagos. I learned how to boil and filter the water, and, of course, the importance of repellent-impregnated mosquito nets."

It was obvious to me that Nancy didn't have a clue about the place where she was supposed to spend more than half a year. I interceded: "How about in case of an emergency, if something happens? There is no doctor or clinic down there."

"I know the settlement where I will be working is not more than three days by boat from here—and Onitcha, I think." Everything she said had a wry humorous twist, definitely not pertinent to the situation as I saw it.

I did not mention my plans to go to the delta—and Dr. Kaine joined me in my conspiracy of silence. It felt ridiculous to me to talk about my plans, which were so vague and uncertain, to somebody who was going the next day and considered it no problem! I decided to change the topic, because discussion with somebody uninitiated in all the dangers was hopeless, and also because I saw Dr. Kaine getting disturbed: she played piano on the table with her fingers and her leg twitched on and off. It seemed obvious she had come to the same conclusion about the impending demise of our new friend. She excused herself—going to sleep, she'd had a tiring day, she said, and wished Nancy all the best, and any help she might need... She was an old pro, Kaine; she knew her country, the river. The way she nodded her head saying "good night," I knew she was actually saying "the last goodbye" to innocent Nancy Lepardeau.

As if on command, the lights went off. Nancy rejected Dr. Kaine's offer to bring a hurricane lamp—she had to leave, too. Our host disappeared and we stumbled outside. In this land, doused or extinguished lights are not considered a potentially romantic event but a failure of the system, so most Africans have learned to move in the darkness like nocturnal felines, out of necessity.

The man who had brought Nancy here for the dinner was sleeping, leaning against the gate. He woke up in a panic but calmed down when he regained full consciousness. I promised Nancy I'd be at the river bank at dawn, at six o'clock in the morning, to see her on her way.

"I want to witness the launching of the expedition which will enter the annals of exploration of the Dark Continent, Dr. Nancy Livingston," I dared to joke, because my blushing could not be noticed in the darkness.

"Well, dear Stanley, I'll be there, pith helmet, bottle of gin and all." She smiled, perhaps. I felt it in the tone of her voice but couldn't see. She added, disappearing: "*Buenas noches, catedrático.*"

"Hasta luego, letrado. Sleep well." I felt vacant, rejected, as I shouldn't have. Why did I resist my natural urge to follow her to her shelter?

❋

I climbed up to the cave of my room, where an oil lamp was already lit, illuminating the dome of the mosquito net above my bed, which looked beautiful, like a conical iceberg in the mist. After splashing some water from a washbasin onto my face, I extinguished the lamp and climbed naked inside the iceberg, to bathe in sweat.

This night belonged to the creatures of jungle. Different insect species, miniature musicians with instruments of unimaginable construction, played fortissimo, each one of them. Director be damned. The roar from the forest was so exotic and adventurous that I realized no story of African exploration could be related, half convincingly, without an audiotape. I tried to cast this equatorial Nacht Musik into my memory, knowing that I would long for it in my sub-arctic home in the future.

Sleep did not come—Nancy Lepardeau did not allow it. I recalled her face, her hands holding the petite cups of coffee with two fingers, her eating like there was no tomorrow, her shy smile and soft voice. Again I asked myself the question: was she brave—or innocently uninformed? She appeared from nowhere—and would disappear to nowhere. What could I bring her the next day for the trip? A book? I did not even take a book with me for this Zidogu excursion. A knife! I had the Kershaw pocketknife, US-made, a heavy, solid instrument which would stay sharp forever like a samurai sword. The thought smoothed out my mind, uncoiled my tension. I could imagine her, tomorrow, at the landing, when I would give it to her. It's nothing, I'd tell her, just something from the old country. All I would say.

❋

Rain came down in buckets, creating a reverberation in stereo, much unlike the susurrous rustling of a civilized mizzle. The yellow river was boiling; it looked as if the stream wanted to lift itself up heavenward and fuse with the sky. There was not much air between the raindrops—it was just like a waterfall, and the visibility was no more then few yards. She was standing motionless by the edge of the water when I arrived and when I approached her she barely moved to acknowledge me. She wore a yellow waterproof oilskin raincoat, and from the edge of the hood water fell as from an overflowing gutter. Behind this water screen I saw only her eyes, glittering inside the grotto of the hood: two stationary fireflies. I attempted to laugh into the rain, to lighten the situation, but in truth I suspected that this downpour was a last warning from the ju-jus of the evil forest.

The hired dugout with its Mercury outboard was tied to a tree. One box in the bow and another one in the midships were wrapped in plastic tarps and tied down. One seat, an upside down bucket, squatted at the stern by the motor—for the skipper, I assumed. There were a couple of hardwood paddles, and a bamboo fishing rod at the bottom of the vessel.

"Here, I got a little something for you. It might come in handy." I gave her the Kershaw knife, trying to sound nonchalant, and I showed her how to open it, which was not necessary, but it replaced an uneasy exchange.

"Thank you so very much. How wonderful. You shouldn't have…" The Philadelphia clichés rolled off her tongue, and only later I realized these were the last words I had heard from Nancy Lepardeau.

"Just a small thing from the old country," I mumbled.

Then two men emerged from the rain and approached the boat. They appeared to be in their twenties or thirties, half naked, both tall, with the supple muscularity of those whose livelihood depends on it. These, I estimated, were the elite "defensive backs" of the Zidogu fishing crowd. Their hides were as black as the letters on this page and glistened under the water cascading down their shoulders. They did not defy the rain—they disregarded it.

The men passed close to us without giving us a look, without paying the slightest attention to their passenger, or me. One carried a gas container and the other a plastic bag, which he tossed into the bow of the boat. They seemed to exchange a joke because they laughed. The one with the gas tank had a shaved head, which sparkled with bouncing raindrops, and a strangely handsome face with a self-confident expression. The facial cast of his companion was formed of prominent bones and bulging meat about vacuous eyes. His block-shaped head sat on a neck as broad as the head itself. The men moved fast, their strong cords of muscles pulsating like pistons of a well-oiled machine. The handsome one sat by the motor and motioned Nancy to board by jerking his hand as if to fan himself. I observed, with irritation, that it was a casual gesture, meant to appear as an afterthought.

Nancy waded into the river, climbed into the boat and sat down, leaning with her back on the box in the midships. She was so small, she looked like a child in a hand-me-down oversized raincoat. Within seconds the boat was off shore, taken away by the current. The last I saw of Nancy Lepardeau was her hand waving once or twice from behind of the box. The dugout disappeared into the thickness of the rain.

I turned around and walked to Dr. Kaine's house, forcibly paying attention to the oil palms, to a fisherman carrying his net, to the staghorn ferns hanging from the trees, to everything around me. By this mental manipulation I was able to expel from my brain images of the terrible fate of little Nancy in the jungle, the first night alone with her two boatmen.

The little creek I had crossed earlier at dusk over a few flat stones was a muddy stream, now, with waves, debris and a roar. I was forced to idle for some time, waiting for the current to subside. I crouched down, squatted to form a small, cozy tent with my umbrella, with resignation and time to think. In that umbrella tent by the rushing brook, I decided to drop the idea of sailing to the delta of the Niger river. The coward reasoned loudly, because nobody was around to hear and snicker. Everybody likes a winner, but I think that everybody likes even better the winner later defeated. I knew for certain Dr. Kaine would approve of my decision, since she would not lose me, her faithful listener. And Chukwu would be delighted to retain an *onya-acha*, a paying employer and, possibly, the first person who (partially) trusted him.

✳

So, in a couple of weeks I returned to my Minnesota from Southeastern Nigeria, healthy. I felt like I had returned from war. I had won the battle, in a way, suffering no chills, fevers or ulcerations, only the faint prodromes of "mal d'Afrique."

This rather epic narration has its culmination in the hygienic and uber-sentient civilization of Minneapolis.com, the cultured twin of St. Paul. One day a short message on my answering machine announced that … she would be passing through Minneapolis, could she stop by to see me? Nancy Lepardeau! Then the habitual crackling of electrons in the machine assured me it was not a call from the afterword.

She arrived in a small Chevy pickup, in jeans, Nikes, a polar-fleece pullover, and the same Shirley Temple curls shimmering around her face—which seemed older but no less lovelier than I remembered. In the driveway I hugged the woman I had barely known as an otherworldly apparition for one short evening in a far-away world; I couldn't contain myself. However, at first, my happiness was tempered with a guilty feeling, which bordered on just a faint sense of betrayal. In Africa, I wrote her off, I buried her six feet deep. Unquestionably, she would perish in the delta. How could it have been otherwise?

"How did you do, down there? Half a year?" I spread my arms and closed my eyes to let her know I know I was asking a question requiring an epic discourse, and I felt I might be hurrying it. We drank Shiraz from Southeastern Australia and cut into cheddar from Northern Wisconsin. She talked and talked willingly, no metaphors, no "show—don't tell." She told me the synopsis of her story.

In her village she had to learn a lot from the first day, to make it. The larger part of every day was spent on obtaining and preparing food—as was the task of the villagers, too. She learned to fish for catfish, soak cassava of its cyanide and grind it into garry. She pounded coconut copra, dried fish, ate roasted caterpillars, collected water and filtered it after boiling, gathered wood for fire, peed standing, brushed teeth with a chew-stick, and more. She learned how to coexist, in daily minutiae, with the tribe of which only a few elders had ever seen a white man and none had seen a white woman. It required some mental effort to get used to having her hair, breasts, and skin touched by everyone. Her skin was admired for the light pigmentation but ridiculed for its efflorescent reaction to insect bites, which she painted with iodine or mercury tincture. She learned never to show curiosity about ju-ju of the jungle and never to mention the human sacrifice, an "evil forest" custom, or the killing of twins. Except for the local sorcerer (a separate, long story about the proven uselessness of native medicines) people showed her only kindness, and there were many times they made her feel happiness, almost overwhelming her with their empathy. She despised their tendency to hysteria, and, what colonialists called "childish reactions," and the many ways of abuse of women by the men, which most of the women believed was the only and right way. But their toughness, and sometimes, almost peaceful resignation in the face of death and adversity, she had to admire. And the adversity in everyday life of "her" jungle settlement was multifaceted, unexpected and at times and often fatal. Disease was the greatest danger; half of the children died and all villagers were sick most of the time, or at least once a month, it seemed. But regardless of the conditions of their existence, they laughed often, and showed short bursts of elation, which must have been infectious and life saving.

Nancy succeeded in staying healthy by having some tropical experience from Colombia, by using mosquito nets religiously, but mainly, by the power of her intellect: you don't use water into which your neighbor and their goats pee; you don't drink palm wine diluted by the water from the creek; you don't go out when the night-biting mosquitoes start their feast...

I asked about the slavery. She hesitated with the answer. "All I'll say is that in the village there were a few adopted youngsters, mostly girls. That's what I had been told: adopted from other tribes." I dropped more questions, knowing that adoption from alien tribes does not exist in West Africa.

"I never got malaria," she changed the topic, "just a little diarrhea, as usual, and one parasite, which I brought home with me in my gut." She seemed to enjoy seeing concern on my face. "Which of the parasitic worms would you like to discuss? Round, flat, thread, tape, loa-loa or hook?" She happily displayed her teeth.

"Hook," I said, understanding her play, but queasy, still.

"Worry none," she continued smiling, "it has been fully treated. And you know where? In one of the crown jewels of your Minnesota—the Mayo Clinic, the second best hospital in the world." She nodded. "How about that!" Then she modified her speech into the more formal tone to express an uncomfortable thought, perhaps. "When I returned from my stint in Nigeria to Philadelphia my friends there were forewarned—and organized a welcoming party. Everybody was very nice, politely inducing my culture shock. I haven't recovered since." She peered sadly into the wine glass. Sadly beautiful, I thought; the tenderness I remembered returned. I asked her to explain and she related to me the Philadelphia story.

She liked the faces of her friends, unchanged after two years, with optimistic grins, wide smiles, even exuberance; how they thanked her for the occasion, since without her arrival they wouldn't have met, so very very busy they all were. But everything was great, wonderful, fantastic, they "got life," they'd "got a grip on things." They talked about buying a new SUV, VCR, PC, DVD, about the results in the NBA, PGA, NASCAR, how important it was. Some worried about Democrats, Republicans, Neocons, Christian coalitions of nuts, of interest rates and remortgaging, Dow Jones, S&P and that goddamned NASDAQ volatility. Nancy talked fast, and her eyes got bigger; she shook her curls when she said how lost she had felt, such good pals they used to be and now she didn't understand them, and that what she could comprehend seemed to be so silly, like a babble of alien children who descended from some distant planet. It made her sad when she realized that she, not they, might be the child from a distant planet—how could it be otherwise? She was alone.

"I felt like Jane who lost her Tarzan, in a jungle—which she forgot existed. You understand?" Nancy tried a laugh, the pressure of her eyes on me.

"Nancy, this is not unusual. I feel just like you describe when I come back from Africa. Every time," I said. "But then it goes away. Slowly." It was a form of politeness to say this, since I have been actually feeling permanently—and pleasantly, I must say—alienated all the time. It never left me.

"It hasn't gone away for me, that disappointment. After a few months I just had enough," Nancy said. So she got a job as a teacher in North

Dakota on a Sioux Indian reservation, the place to where she would continue to drive, tomorrow.

"Well, I think you might find folks different from your Philadelphia crowd on the reservation. Maybe that's what you need for a while—different folks," I proposed, feeling I had descended into insincere talk. "Let's drink to that, to Sioux Indians." I opened another bottle of Shiraz.

"I hope so," she said, looking at me through her wine glass.

Then I answered about myself, my bridge jobs, as if in a job interview; I reported about my other interests as in a college application. I told her about my interest in the "cultures" of people of the Third and Fourth World, in art, in photography, and good music, and good wine, just the usual… I lied about my age. Because my physique has been an integral component of my soul, I apologized for the deposit of fat, in the form of a bicycle tire, across my belly. The adiposity had remained in position, perforated by the belly button, pale, trembling, even when I lost all other fatty tissues in the land of the Igbos (who could have used some). I felt she was not satisfied with my answers, because she narrowed her eyes and thinned her lips. I suspected she wanted to know who I was, really. But how could I explain who I was, in a short evening, when it took me thirty years to find out for myself? After all, it took over fifty thousand words to paint the picture of Dorian Grey.

"I know, I offered you my portrait only as a simple sketch … in charcoal," I added, thinking it a clever remark. She dismissed the topic by wave of her hand.

"Your girlfriends?" She insisted.

"All in the exotic lands. And your boyfriends?" I shot back.

"Two years ago. Colombia."

We did not venture into this dangerous theme further, but remained on the safe shore of logorrhea, of the flowage of words. Then I laid my hand on her hand, which she did not withdraw. When she went to pee she touched my shoulder, lightly, with a quizzical smile. At that moment I felt molecules of sympathy released into the air; they induced in me a sudden surge of happiness of dimensions I have not remembered for a very long time. The happiness arose from a hope. Viewing her from the profile I observed that her breasts displayed an opulence I hadn't remembered either. I knew so little of her.

When she returned I offered advice, which I have learned to do only rarely: "And… I am thinking that if, by chance, you wouldn't be able to speak with them Indians as you'd like, to communicate … with some meaning, you know … then talk to yourself … write! Nancy, write! You know more interesting stories about homo sapiens as a species than Updike and Roth combined."

She looked at her watch. "I should go. I made a reservation at a Super

8 nearby. On the map it looks like the motel is just a couple of miles away."

The Australian wine had induced a velvet evolution of my mind, which became mellow, though the reduced inhibitions did not prevent daring. And so I decided to say it, without angst: "Why don't you stay over here, Nancy? I have a spare bedroom." It was not predictable she would nod in an agreement—and she did not. She just raised her eyes and we looked at each other for a long time, silently, without a readable expression. *Alea iacta est*, I thought, trying the best not to betray my tension, which was increasing in size like a disturbed puffer fish.

"Okay," she said, and raised her eyes up to the ceiling in a mock resignation. That was all. She raised her shoulders, too. However, on the ticker tape of her mind I could read: "I am pleased."

Just before we made love, she denied me her kiss. "We don't know each other well enough," she whispered. We were both hesitant at first, but then we laughed. We laughed holding each other. Then we drank some more and talked about Africa, with my hand on her breast, which had the consistency of cartilage.

"It was so hard, there. Sometimes," she said.

"I know. And you would like to go back." We reached an unsurprising agreement that we both are captives of Africa, held hostage by her, without much hope for the freedom of forgetting.

In the morning, before she left, she promised to come down from North Dakota for my New Years Eve party. It has become a famous tradition, where only a few of my best friends come, the best wines are consumed, and the felicity of true friendship rules for twelve hours.

She honked, turned out of the driveway, and waved out of her pickup's window. I felt sure this was not the last goodbye; not like the waving hand from the dugout boat in the downpour on the Niger River, leaving for the delta. The pickup disappeared in the bend of the street and I stood in the driveway alone, with only my longing for a grim companion. When she returns I will not mention that I had to wipe a tear from my lower eyelid when she left. When she'll return I'll say it. I'll tell her.

After Night Comes Morning

Everybody dreaded being summoned to Bartolomejska Street or commanded to Konviktska Street in Prague 1. The names of these streets had been whispered by the majority—the timid ones. But the "refuse-niks" and other losers of unbending character called the names loudly, then spit on the ground or flexed their forearms at the elbow in the Czech analogy of the "up yours" pantomime. Still, the knees of all who received the summons in the bureaucratic idiom, with precise indication of the time in minutes, but without an indication of purpose, would slightly tremble.

An accidental foreign visitor lost on these streets would see only gray apartment houses of undistinguished architecture, and too many cars with strange license plates parked in both directions. A Czech wanderer would make the passage at an increased speed with head bent and eyes on the pavement. The Second District Headquarters of Contra Intelligence was located on Bartolomejska and the State Security Directorate was on Konviktska. These two streets were only a block apart and were connected with an underground tunnel which served for secret transfers of suspects and detainees from Bartolomejska to Konviktska, where a few cells for "preliminary detention" were maintained. And for Jirka "Poncho" P. it was Konviktska tonight.

It was drizzling from a low cloud and the sewers reeked like aged Limburger, as could be expected for such an occasion. Poncho had forgotten his umbrella, left home without either his wristwatch or his perennial composure. He felt worse than when he was rolled in for his gallbladder operation. In his summons no reason was stated; he was requested for the late evening hour, which added to his puzzlement and apprehension. Poncho knew it would be an interrogation about the play—and the poster.

Jirka "Poncho" P. was a well known somebody in the cultural circles of Prague. Not an artist, singer, or musician himself, he was recognized as an expert on jazz history, a genius in organization, and the owner of a nose for talent. But apart from these traits of some substance, his lighter personality charms made him celebrated. People noticed the smile on his

Slavic face, always at the ready with the revelation of many teeth, his lower jaw non-threatening by its recession, his unzipped lips forming the letter "u". His eyes, which seemed to narrow at any opportunity, made him likable at first sight. He could hurl jokes at grim circumstance, and he delighted in switching diction from exaggerated sophistication to truck drivers' lingo, and back. In the crowd he was noticed: he sported the ascot of degenerates and a checkered Esterhazy jacket—both so out of place in that regimented, totalitarian graveyard of fashion. But his ownership of the US Army surplus Jeep topped all and attracted the unwelcome attention of the "authorities."

The file on Jirka "Poncho" P. in the Secret Service Registry grew in thickness when he became the director of an experimental theater, Traffic Lights, which he founded together with suspicious characters like Ivanov-English, the sailor and master of seven crafts and seven languages, the unforgettable entertainers Jiri Vyschly and Jiri Silter, and the sensational singing symbols of sexual benevolence, the dizygotic twins Jaana & Marja.

It must be highlighted that the all-important financial backing of the theater was secretly provided by the perennial medical student "Doc" Hanak. He had to remain a hidden maecenas since in the gloom of the socialist peoples' republic all citizens were supposed to be happily poor. Only the communist bosses could show off their cigarette lighters from the West, their hookers from the Hotel Alcron, their mistresses from the School of Applied Arts, and their jeans made by Mr. Levi Strauss himself. Doc's money came from the sale of art objects he inherited from his father. The old man had been a true capitalist, an enemy of the working class, and an admirer and collector of post-impressionists. He only narrowly escaped communist persecution by means of lethal heart ventricular fibrillation.

In Prague "Doc" Hanak was known as a lover of young women and a self-described "friend to damsels in distress" who, he hoped, would also be members of the actors' guild. He loved to rub shoulders with theater people. In underground circles he was noticed as a "sympatak," a sympathetic, a handsome boy with both the means and the goodwill to contribute to a good cause. Only a few people knew that "Doc" lived on the infamous Konviktska Street, in a posh apartment across the State Security Directorate.

Jirka "Poncho" P. was certain the secret service goons would grill him about that play, *The Peddler's Triangle*. Great tunes, the best cast, perfect script—but everybody knew from the beginning it would be trouble. Never mind the plot—it was the peddler himself who was the bad news. He was a bureaucratic, faceless type, with a mediocre income, two kids, a handsome wife, and a succulent mistress, Rosalinda, with many demands. To support her whims the peddler designed a scheme which was the main plot of the play. He buys cheap desk lamps and on their paper shades he paints a simplified image of Lenin. He peddles the lamps for many times the original price to CEOs and Directors of the big state firms, all confirmed members of the Party. With an ingenious sales pitch he cautions his victims not to reject his wares, not to reject the opportunity to have their desks illuminated by the image of the Great Leader and Philosopher, Comrade Lenin. The audience in the theater roared with laughter when the peddler switched to Russian to impress and depress his victims: "…*fonar iz abzurom iz izobrazeniem bolshovo tovarishcha Lenina!*" The proceeds of the sales of lamps went to mistress Rosalinda, who spent part of it on her secret lesbian lover—the wife of the peddler, himself.

So, the play was a major hit, people stood in queues two blocks long for the tickets, and the theater Traffic Light was closed after the second performance by direct order of the Ministry of Culture. And who would get screwed for this? Jirka "Poncho" P., the director of the theater.

He entered the building on Konviktska with a feeling of angst and resignation, more than in the grip of true fear. The uniformed guard, with Breznev's eyebrows, looked at Poncho's summons and sent him to the last, fifth floor, Room 10. "Good night," he snickered, amused by his irony and wit. Poncho knocked on door number 10 and, hearing nothing, he entered. A bored-looking secretary with a beehive hairdo pointed at another door with a little brush she used for painting her nails. Poncho shuffled in after a timid knock.

"So, Comrade P., you wanted to make a theater. You wanted badly to make it go, to be a success. Right?" The interrogator was in civilian clothes—a light brown cardigan, and an open neck shirt. On his nose-bridge he pushed conservative steel-rimmed glasses. His flint face wore only a rudimentary expression of sympathy which changed to an acetylene torch of a gaze.

"We knew about your love of the arts; we thought we understood you. Such promise to enrich the cultural lives of the masses, Comrade—and such a failure! Do you follow me?" He looked at Poncho over the simple formica table. A coffee mug sat on it next to the two inch thick folder with Jirka "Poncho" P. in big letters on a label. Poncho noticed the thickness of his file with a sinking feeling. The interrogator chewed on his nail and with the other hand arranged and rearranged two pens and a pencil in perfect parallel next to the folder. He did not resemble the vulture-like interrogators from spy movies. Anal-retentive weirdo, not some creepy tough of the feared Konviktska reputation, Poncho thought, with some relief. There was a silence.

"Yes … no … yes," Poncho cleared his throat.

"You knew about the play… everything, of course. Right? You knew the script, you saw it rehearsed. Did anything disturb you?"

"Yeah, yes … but, actually, I did not see the rehearsal, I swear."

The interrogator let the silence fall, he smiled a strange grin, then emitted a hard little laugh.

"*Pivo*, Bozenka!" He called the secretary for a beer. The door opened and a bottle of Smichov Staropramen Lager arrived. The Smichov Brewery was just across the river, so close to here—but the brew on the desk was so far from the desiccated throat of the interrogated suspect. Poncho emitted a rasping gurgle while the interrogator took a swig of the cold fluid from the bottle.

"Well, well, let's say I believe you … but still I'd like to enter your mind, to understand your thinking process, you see … to learn how you could collaborate on the production of a play, which…" the interrogator paused and shook his head "…which ridicules one of the greatest philosophers of all times, Vladimir Iljich Lenin!" With an exaggerated sadness on his face he turned his head from side to side in disbelief, like an anhinga with its monocular bird vision fishing mangrove flats. Then he played the recovery:

"Bozenka!" Again he called the door, which opened after a while; the beehive peeked in. "Could you get me some coffee, too, pumpkin?" He looked back at Poncho and scratched his cheek with its clearly delineated five-o'clock shadow.

"But, you see, I am not a total simpleton. I know you wouldn't reveal those thoughts which you think might do you harm, so—I'll ask you only that question which you must answer, clearly and truthfully, and—now! This is the question, Comrade P., you were summoned here to answer." All of a sudden his hard-bitten face induced an atmosphere of affronted hostility. He stared at Poncho with sclerotic stillness.

"Who paid for the poster?" He leaned forward and then back in his chair. Bozenka entered without knocking and put on the desk a mug with steaming coffee. "Here." She took away the empty one. Despite the critical moment of the interrogation, Poncho noticed the heavy, generous contents of the secretary's push-up bra. He answered with the pretense of total ignorance of the Good Soldier Sveik that he didn't have a clue, sorry that he was about his innocence. He felt the rivulets of sweat descending downwards from his armpits. He would give a kingdom for a cup of coffee and a cigarette, which he'd denounced a week ago.

"I'll ask you once more: who got you the dough for that disgusting poster of the play?"

It all came to the sale of one oil painting by Kamil Lhotak, of a hot air balloon, striped wind sock, and a motorcycle in the forefront, Doc Hanak's inheritance. It was enough to pay for the costume designer, one cutter, and two stitchers. He had enough left to have the poster made the samizdat way (he wouldn't reveal where) and even to buy "volunteers" who would paste the poster all over Prague in one night. Only Poncho, the director of the theater, and Ivanov-English knew. And in Poncho's mind that would be the way it would remain. Nothing about Doc could be revealed because he loved theater truly and hated Bolsheviks. And because not to squeal would be normal. Poncho decided this for Doc and for himself, too: how cool it would be to look at himself in the mirror!

"Truly, I swear, I have no notion who paid for the poster or who made it. If I knew I would like to help you, I cross my heart."

"Well, if that's the way you want it … but you are making a big mistake!" The interrogator got up. He left the room showing no anger or related emotions; he had fulfilled his socialist monthly plan of fifteen interrogations a month. Poncho half rose from his chair to look into the coffee mug. It was empty, not a drop left. He looked at the wall clock: it was one in the morning.

"So, I heard you refused to say who was the rich prick, you shmuck." The new interrogator arrived and collapsed on the chair behind the desk and thrust his neck forward. He was a bullnecked lard-face with a double chin and feeble lips. His round pig eyes darted like a damselfly before they settled on the pale face of Poncho.

"Well…" Poncho just lifted his shoulders.

"Do you know, you little sunovabich, what our brothers, *nashia druzia*, in the Soviet Union would do with a fucker like you? Do you?" Lard-face paused as if expecting an answer. "No, you don't. But do you know what I'm gonna do now?" He burst into a short boisterous laugh, which made Poncho's knees quiver and new sweat rivulets join in creeks on his back and temples.

The lard-face got up and sat on the corner of the desk, his short stumpy legs swinging in the air.

"I'm gonna take a leak, that's what I'm gonna do. And by the time I'm back you'll decide if you want to be treated like an enemy of people, as a subversive element, a saboteur of our socialist system, or, even as the supporter of the capitalist enemy. So, think, now. Get a grip, fucker!" He waded away. Poncho heard him laughing with Bozenka the Beehive. Poncho recognized by now that the "good cop - bad cop" technique was being used on him, combined with the first step from the textbook of torture—sleep deprivation. He was scared, but also he was overcome with admiration for himself, for his resistance by acting stupid and confused, for his congenital wit. He would never tell them about Doc Hanak. Never! His physical misery, overheating, and thirst caused his hands to shake, but not his determination.

Then came more questions by lard-face, screaming, a raised fist which never fell, threats, and more threats. It was eight in the morning when the interrogator gave up, slamming the door behind him. Poncho closed his eyes. "Fuck 'em," he whispered and tried to spit on the floor unsuccessfully. Was it over? If not—he felt he might faint of fatigue. Sweat dried on him in a thin layer which felt as if he was painted by with glue. His throat was the Gobi desert.

Bozenka came. "Wait a few minutes, Mister, I'll bring a form you have to sign." She barely looked at him—she hurried. Her night shift was over, too. "Then you can go," she said, and pigeon-toed to the window and raised the shutters.

It was a hopeful bright morning outside; the early sun illuminated the roof of the apartment building across the street where pigeons, totally free birds, soaked in the warming rays before their flight to Old Town Square. The top floor of the building was edged by a long balcony, half of which was domed by a glass greenhouse with tropical greenery. In the middle of the open half of the balcony a tall man leaned over the railing and then straightened up.

He was dressed in a black shiny robe with gold embroidery, which Poncho thought might have been in the likeness of a dragon. Poncho looked at the apparition with amazement, his all-night vigil forgotten, his eyes' hurt gone, his deep funk dismissed. He recognized the man and became engulfed in the feeling of a fine, pure moment of his life.

The robe of the man, of Doc Hanak, opened, revealing his bare chest. He took a drag from a cigarette and a sip from a tiny cup held in the other hand. He turned back for a moment and talked briefly to somebody in the apartment. He spread his arms, smiled widely at the sun as a man would without a worry in the world, after an amorous night. Doc flipped the cigarette butt down onto the street; it fell trailing a blue gossamer ribbon. Then he vanished, as if made of just a dream. Maybe he disappeared into the Fourth Dimension, where, Poncho was certain, there was a life of nightly pleasures and daily feasts, right on the stage of his own beautiful theater,
with friends,
all gentle people
with flowers in their hair.......

Vagrant

The walker just smiled at the clump of delicious-looking boletus mushrooms. Resisting their temptation, he stepped around the deadly amanita, nodding in acknowledgment of its deceptive beauty. He was a bit sluggish, the old man, but he knew his way. When he emerged from the spruce thicket on a path he turned one way without hesitation, not changing the slowness of his gait.

Even a superficial glimpse at his face would detect his seniority: a short, white and stubbly beard covered his cheeks like an albino hedgehog's coat, covered his chin and descended down over the Adam's apple into the depths of his shirt. Obviously, his was not a cultivated hirsutism, but simply the result of neglecting a razor blade.

His nose was strong, beaked and cleaved at the tip, a little. His eyes shined kindly between the skin-bags above and below, with brightness which would be difficult to describe in precise anatomic terms. Above it all ruled a mane of disheveled hair the hue of white foam on the lake shore, with its yellowish tint. Altogether, his face could be judged as an "intelligent face."

On the smooth sandy path the walker did not need to pay attention to obstacles or inedible mushrooms, so he allowed himself to become immersed in thoughts, navigating on autopilot at a relaxed pace. He emerged out of the forest between the fields. All of a sudden he stopped. Stunned, his hands came up with palms forward, as if he wanted to protect himself. But he retook the composure instantly, shook his white mane, and parted his lips.

"Goddamn it, you scared me! Old men can drop dead … like that, you know?"

The policeman in front of him repositioned his cap into a more official forward slant with one hand; the other hand buried itself in his bulging waist. He attempted to push his chest up, but the pectus failed to compete with his beer belly. He cleared his throat, twice.

"So, where are we heading, my man?"

There was no answer.

"Do we know, mister, where are we going, I said!" The constable insisted.

The walker nodded, his expression indecipherable. "I do, constable, I do. And … I now I want to … wish you a very good day." The old man thought it an interesting situation—a Turgenev moment, perhaps—and he smiled. He started to move, taking just two steps. The obstacle in the form of the village policeman did not yield.

"No hurry! No hurry, I have a few questions!" The constable smoothed down the jacket of his uniform and straightened up. The object of policeman's inspection was, obviously, a vagabond, some homeless character with the tendency to poach a rabbit by a clever snare, with the knack for snatching a chicken on the outskirts of a village, or stealing a shirt hung out to dry. The constable had known vagrants like this one. You can never say where they come from—some might even have a record! Just look at him!

The walker sighed loudly; he waited patiently for the next development. There he stood on the path, every second button missing on his tunic of nondescript design, his trousers recalling the ravages of the First World War. These rough peasant's breeches, off-white with just a slight yellowing around the fly, were held in place by a Juta rope. And the man was—barefoot! The barefootedness suggested insanity, more than just homelessness—states which were closely related, at least in the opinion of the village constable Ladislav Ruzicka of Jindricha Hradek.

Ruzicka took the air into his nostrils—but he failed to detect the expected musty and sour odor of old sweat, the pungency of cold tobacco smoke conjugated with alcoholic vapors. Just the fragrance of pine needles in the sun, the perfume of sunny wheat, the evening breath of mustard fields. It was the optimistic end of a day of light warm breeze, with the sky still blue like forget-me-nots but the sun almost touching the jagged line of the horizon, ready to retire. The constable was in an amiable mood, his thoughts halfway home, imagining the half-liter of cool Regent beer from Trebon in his tight fist. Then he saw it.

"I'll be damned! Where did you get that?" He pointed at the hand of the walker. The golden wristwatch on a snake skin band reflected the falling sun's rays. "Where the hell … now how … where did you steal this?" It seemed the uniformed man searched for better words to express his surprise. In vain.

'My watch? Do you like it?" The walker raised his arm to display the expensive gold Schaffhausens, the pride of Swiss precision.

"All right … you thief … no fooling around, I warn you. Now get goin'! And no foolishness, as I said!"

"Where are we going, officer, may I ask?"

"To the station, that's where. To Hradek. And hurry up!"

"Oh, good, that's the direction I'm headed anyway." The walker composed himself and started without hesitation in a determined gait, a smile on his face. "We should be there exactly in thirty-five minutes, if we take the shortcut around Blahuv pond." He sounded upbeat, as if pleased with his new companion. "Voilà, here we march, two comrades with common destination, to the marching band of evening crickets!"

"I ain't no comrade of yours, weirdo."

"You should not reject friendly companionship on the edge of the wilderness. You know, it is the loneliness of the traveler which causes sadness. This has been proven." The walker lifted his hand with the index finger erect.

"No fancy bullshit will help you. You'll see."

"Officer, I do not look for help—I am looking forward to the resolution of the stolen Schaffhausens."

"Just shut up, weirdo, and don't drag your sorry ass!" The law raised his voice when the steeples of Jindricha Hradek appeared.

"Why do you suspect me of a criminal act, officer? Is it my worn-out sporting attire, lack of shoes perhaps, or my facial hair?"

"Oh, just shut up!"

"It should not be the watch, since I told you it is my property, didn't I?"

"Just shut the mouth!"

"You contribute to our conversation with such brevity, officer," the walker shook his head. "I'll resign," he added to himself.

"You'll shut up behind bars, you'll see." The constable wiped his nose—his official, full bodied globular proboscis—adjusted his belt and pointed at the entrance of the police station. They arrived. He wanted to push the vagrant forward, to give him a good push, but changed his mind at the last moment, not knowing why. There was something different about this strange bird, this vagrant; the constable had a funny feeling. But the chief would straighten him out. There were very few citizens in the county who looked forward to meeting the chief, for he did not have a reputation for excessive compassion or kindness, or a love of the human race. Constable Ruzicka preferred to stay away from him, too, but this time he was sure he'd get a pat on the shoulder. To notice this expensive watch on the vagabond's hand was an excellent piece of police work.

✳

The police chief welcomed them with a smile so wide it made his face triangular. Ruzicka had never seen the chief smile at him so happily—and in truth it was not he who was smiled at this time, either.

"Doctor Schultz! What a surprise, sir!" The dictator of the station stepped forward; he even bowed and extended his hand for a handshake with the speed of a handball player. "We are honored by your presence, sir, we are!" The chief hurried to pull a chair. "Please, take a seat. It looks like you were on one of your excursions … and it was a hot day … tiring, perhaps. Have a seat, doctor, please." The chief smiled spastically. "How about a shot of *slivovice*? My cousin sent it from Moravia, homemade stuff, quite good I should say, at least seventy percent!"

"Oh, no chief, thank you, I'll be on my way. My sister is waiting for me with the dinner, I am sure." The walker, Doctor Karel Schultz, shook the hand of the police chief vigorously, combing his white hair with the other hand. "I was passing by, so I just stopped to check on you and inquire about my little patient."

The chief turned to Constable Ruzicka: "Ruzicka, what do you want? You don't look so good."

The constable's face had acquired a light gray complexion, and his thick lips narrowed—both unusual phenomena caused by the loss of blood from constricted capillaries. He answered by shaking his head from side to side and backing away sideways in a crab-like fashion.

"I have to tell you, Doctor," the chief continued, "that our Sashenka, after you gave her those pills and Priessnitz patch, and talked to her so nicely, she is just back to her usual rowdiness … no fever, she's even started to eat. We are so grateful to you!"

The constable was reaching for the door, when he heard the Chief.

"Ruzicka, take a good look. This gentleman is the most renowned pediatrician in all of Prague. Even professors there seek his advice. And all Hradek … we are happy he returns here every summer. Don't you know his summer house near Nevratka stream?"

Constable Ruzicka emitted a croaking sound, but the chief was no longer paying any attention to him. With an awkward formality he addressed Doctor Schultz: "And happy we are that our good doctor finds our town and countryside the best place in the world to relax and … how did you say it, sir? To dress, undress, shave, unshave, to do exactly what you want. Right?" The chief pointed at the chair, again.

"Thanks, but I must go now. I'm happy your little girl is okay."

"Certainly." The chief saluted briskly. "I am going to drive you home, of course, sir. I insist. And … Ruzicka, bring the car to the front. In an instant!"

The doctor and police chief walked out of the entrance of the station, both smiling, as if happy with each other. Perhaps they were.

"My wife is fattening a goose for you, sir. She'll be all lard and filled with liver … she'll have two kilos of liver, at least. I mean the goose." Chief lowered his voice in conspiracy and raised his eyebrows: "And the wife got for you some *rhabarbermarmelade*, too."

The police car arrived and the mute Ruzicka held the door for Doctor Schultz, who gave him a good smile but remained silent also. The chief whispered to Ruzicka to drive around the main square slowly, so people could see who his passenger was. After they crossed the bridge over Nevratka stream the summer house appeared at the edge of a spruce forest. The western facade still held the rays of the falling sun. Both men were silent.

Then they heard the sound of the steam choo-choo—its two hoot-hoot whistles. (The engineer always greeted the Schultz's summer house when passing by.) Doctor Schultz looked at his golden Schaffhausens and nodded in an appreciative manner. The local to Jarosov was one minute early. It meant that engineer Pepa Benesu had not had his five beers yet and was paying attention to the timetable.

Schultz got out of the car, smiling. How nice it would be to smell the beef with mushroom sauce and to make the easy choice between the Muller-Thurgau white from Moravia or the spatlese from Mosel. And then ... how wonderful it would be to read in bed in the complete silence, windows agape ... and at night, to hear the hooting of an owl.

Doctor sighed "thank you" to the police chief and the still-astonished constable Ruzika. His bare feet were getting wet with the evening dew as he sauntered across the little meadow homeward; he sniffed the air like a hunting dog, in the direction of the kitchen. Oh, warm summer vacations! And cool evening dew.

Hurricane

The dead volcano's
chilly surface—and also
wild strawberries.

Having a fatal disease,
how beautiful my fingernails
over the coals of charcoal!
- Dakotsu Iida

The power went off right after the announcement of the hurricane's eye at 24°6′ latitude and 81°4′ longitude. That was still a few miles offshore, just about on the reef. The voice of the weatherman was controlled, business-like, too cool, perhaps. After all, his radio station was at Key West and they had already had gusts of over seventy miles per hour. US-1 was barricaded by fallen trees on Stock Island. Planes were piled up at the airport.

All of Pelican Key was under water, except for a small elevated section next to the sinkhole by the westernmost point. That area was thought to be an ancient Indian mound, Calusa Indian.

Erik's house was on lower ground and did not fare well. It was constructed almost three decades back, before county building codes and federal safety rules required building on stilts at least ten feet above high water level. Erik had it set on wooden pillars massive enough, but only shoulder high. They served as an imaginary protection working more against the crawling critters of the tropics than against the hurricane surge that now flooded the house.

The house resisted the wind force at the beginning of the cyclone, since all the structural wood was oversized and tied, by skilled imported craftsmen, to the enormous forty-foot-long central beam that supported the cathedral roof. Erik had had the beam, solid Douglas-fir, shipped all the way from Oregon. It was carried from the road to the construction site by thirty slender Cuban refugees hired in Miami, all in identical tennis shoes donated by Centro Cubano. Heavy machinery was avoided to prevent the trampling of even a single botanical specimen of the "hardwood hammock." That is what the native mini jungles are called in the Florida Keys.

A few minutes after noon Erik Lance Bauer stood by the bookshelves observing the lowest row of his collection of first printings, half-submerged. The house itself trembled, creating ripples on the water reaching to the knees of the old man. Waves were peeling off the gray back of the binding of *The Cantos* by Ezra Pound. *The Cantos*—that was ages ago, years before Emily, even *The New Cantos* was before her. He pronounced her name aloud, but not loud enough to be heard over the howls of the hurricane. *Emily.* He had not known any other prayer for several decades and it was time to pray now. *Emily*, he whispered again.

A crushing sound reverberated from the bedroom, then a heavy thing, a tree branch perhaps, ripped into the shutters of the library. Erik decided to move to the inner bathroom, which seemed to be the safest bet for survival. He gave one last look at his books, and then at the south wall, with its series of Picasso engravings and the one Chagall he owned. If the house goes, he pondered, that one will be lost, its existence unknown to the history of art. It was a rare painting from the master's Vitebsk period. Never mind that Chagall's daughter refused to authenticate it—he bought it from the painter himself.

On the opposite wall, he kept only one painting in a simple pine frame. A dot of a fishing boat nearing the horizon, leaving a Norwegian fjord, a dreamy sort of watercolor by Emily Ruzicka. His eyes lingered on the painting for a long while. Then he waded away, holding on to the shelves.

He had built the home away from his family. The farthest away he could determine from studying a map of the continental United States. As far away as possible to escape his family's constraints, to get outside the conventions of those gregarious folk. He himself built his own solitude. He was well aware of it. His independence, and more, had been taken care of by a generous trust fund and, later, by the inheritance. *I have never worked a day for money*, he used to proclaim with conscious arrogance in his younger days, and with a tone of regret, perhaps, in the lassitude of the last stages of his life.

On the day of the hurricane, Erik L. Bauer seemed much aged for his seventy years. He had felt the decline with more confusion during the past year. His steps had become uncertain. And lately his mind had become increasingly forgetful.

More and more the past had become a refuge to him, sheltering him from the present, a cheerful sanctuary. More often his thoughts had been going round in circles, with himself at the center. He had been finding that tropical solitude harder to bear—finding the infinity of the emerald Caribbean sea and the azure sky *ad perpetuum* being just dreams, nothing more.

He found only a few alternatives to the solitude of his shelter. There were excursions to the raw oyster bar near the park of trailer houses. There were affluent neighbors, kind people in his and hers Bermuda shorts and individual small hats, who often referred to the Florida Keys as Paradise or "a little slice of heaven." They revered Erik. His appearance had been a valued asset to any party—long white hair, features suggesting intelligence and learning, and wrinkles that could have had their origin in a decadent past or simply in exposure to the Caribbean sun endured for decades. They admired their neighbor for his oddities. His use of English puzzled them pleasantly, and sometimes his sarcasm or irony awed them. They were intrigued, too, by his total dismissal of the importance of finance, since they had all worked long and hard for their millions (no old money on the island). They secretly rooted for their old man when Erik would answer a newcomer about his line of business. "My line has been retirement. Since the age of one."

It was rumored that women sometimes arrived from the airport to stay with the bachelor for days. Where they came from remained a mystery discussed often and in hushed voices. Were the acquaintances of Erik's from his yearly trips abroad? What did they come for? To the old man who had to stop in the middle of a staircase to recover his breath, while faking interest in the view of the garden or a carving on the banister? Those lucky neighbors who stole glimpses of his visitors all agreed that the women looked "foreign" and were of different ages. The hair of the last one had been cut to one inch. The one before that had had a single braid—she must have been no more than twenty years old and looked "different," an observer reported. All the neighbors knew that Erik would not evacuate for a hurricane. He was "different," too.

Before hiding in the inner bathroom Erik surveyed the situation. On the lee side of the house he tried the door knob. The door was sucked open in an instant, creating a whirl of water that almost took his legs from under him. Holding onto the casing, he peered out. A red polystyrene buoy, torn from a lobster trap, flew by horizontally in a spray of foam and mangrove leaves. A casuarina tree, which he had been planning to have trimmed for a long time, split in front of his eyes with a cannon sound and half of it crashed into the palm grove. Palms were bent as if made of rubber. The driveway was deep under water. Surreally, waves with white caps rolled on the driveway toward the road. His garden of orchids and bromeliads no longer existed. He recognized some of his rare vines plastered on the wall of the garage as a tangle of leafless ropes. He retreated, leaving the door agape and vibrating in the wind.

Erik made it to the bathroom on trembling legs. He climbed on the tank of the toilet, put his legs on the seat, and balanced precariously above the muddy water. Some seaweed squeezed in under the door. He was cold and fatigue kept him motionless. The train of the apocalypse roared with steady vigor outside. Thumps of branches crashing into the house sounded like blasts of shotguns in a successful hunt. Suddenly, the clean note of a trumpet penetrated his ears, then drums, and a French horn sounded a wind-powered symphony never recorded before. The beautiful sound of a flute slowly climbed the scale. The wind instruments prevailed in the music of the hurricane. Erik listened and a smile appeared on his face.

He leaned back on the wall behind him. His eyes closed, freeing him for the voyage back in time.

*

It had happened about four decades ago. He had met Emily on the shore north of Trondheim, on one of those crisp sunny days which startle Norway in the fall. It would have been surprising to encounter anybody on the coast near the fishing village of Hopen, since the tourists mostly flock to the established fjord circuit near Bergen or to the mountain treks past Lillehammer. The shore near Hopen was out of the way of any traffic, except for the rare local settler looking for stray sheep, or as a destination for a forbidden rendezvous of fisherfolk from the village. That day Erik had decided to find a deserted place to make a picnic for himself. After two days of Trondheim he wanted to own the North Sea privately, determined to let himself be enchanted by the sound of the swells washing the shore.

After parking his rental car near the village pier, he looked in vain for a pub or a store to buy a bottle of beer to go with his sandwich. But this was not Europe proper. His disappointment faded soon after he found a path out of the village and disappeared behind boulders the size of nearby houses. Between granite outcroppings he crossed a springy bog fed by a spring gurgling from under the stone in the shape of a sheep. He waded through a growth of dwarf willow and foot-high birch, slid down the smooth rocky wall, and then——the view of the sea.

She was standing against the sky on a flat rock above him and facing the fjord. Her straw-colored braid, hanging long to her waist, flowed over her windbreaker. She was concentrating on her painting and could not hear his steps hushed by the moss.

Afraid to startle her by his sudden appearance, he cleared his throat. Her paintbrush froze for a moment, then she turned to him slowly. The features of her face muted him. It took him a long time to recall the Norwegian greeting.

"God Dag," she answered, paintbrush motionless in her hand. Erik felt at a loss. He had exhausted his Norwegian vocabulary in his greeting. "Do you speak English?" he asked finally.

That was the moment he saw the first of her smiles, and he remained speechless. He did not realize what the gods knew already about the love at first sight of Erik Lance Bauer and Emily Ruzicka.

She was an American on vacation, staying in the village for a week, painting the sea every day, lonely sometimes and now happy to meet somebody who spoke her own language, she said. Soon they shared the sandwich, drank from the nearby spring, talked about her watercolors, and about the paintability of the fjord and the impossibility of painting the sunset. The orange discus, inclining toward the western horizon, amazed them by the speed of its disappearance. Then they parted, promising to meet on the same flat rock above the fjord Erik had come to view alone.

On his return to Trondheim, Erik lost his way to the ferry in Rorvik twice, and was already worried about losing her, too. He realized his foolishness but he could not calm his mind. In his hotel, after only a few wistful hours of sleep, he awakened in the darkness, dressed, and waited for the sunrise by the window. Staring at the harbor he saw only her smiling face. When she smiled, one corner of her lips was slightly higher—he remembered that clearly. It was strange that her brittle smile did not match the expression of her eyes. They did not narrow into a smile, they expressed openness, candor or sincerity, he thought, which was not altered by amusement. He could not remember exactly their color, which bothered him, but he was certain he had never seen a face like hers, beautiful like hers. Emily.

They met again above the fjord on the flat stone near the spring. She painted the fjord undisturbed by his attention. The sea was marked by a silvery ribbon drawn by a fishing trawler, which caused her difficulty. He watched her clean forehead creased by concentration and became sure he must be the favorite of Destiny. They walked to the shore after she finished. He helped her over the rock and their hands remained together. They did not release this hold until they came back to his car.

The road took them around the baldheaded mountain with a waterfall falling silently into its own rainbow. Driving through pine and spruce forests she pointed out mushrooms of gigantic dimensions. "My ma would never leave this place till all were safely in a basket. Boletus, *hribek*." She wondered why nobody picked this rare delicacy. They tried to pass a herd of well-fed cows sauntering down the middle of the road, their teats full. But the animals panicked and ran alongside their car, splashing milk all the way up to the windows. Emily was much amused—Erik was embarrassed. They surprised a moose by a small lake. The waterweeds hanging from its snout did not diminish the majesty of that motionless advertisement for pristine nature. It is possible they both thought about embracing one another at that moment. Erik almost reached for her.

Then the unpaintable setting sun ordered them to separate. He had to leave for Oslo. She would stay a few days longer to finish the painting of a red fishing boat leaving the fjord for the open sea. He did not kiss her—she was too beautiful—he just put his hand on her braid and slid his palm along its length, looking into her eyes. He would remember those eyes now, the blue-green irises—like the fjord farther from the shore when the sun is in the noon position. Pretty color on the pure white of the eyes.

Alone in Oslo, Erik woke up every day long before sunrise, surprised by the intensity of his confusion and longing. During those nervous days, he revisited the Edvard Munch Museum, imagining her next to him and talking to her in front of each distressing painting. Walking the streets, he whispered to her about characters passing by, made up strange stories about them, as if they were trolls of a bizarre fairyland. He thought about her every waking minute and dreamt about her every night in dreams which loitered in his mind all day.

At the predetermined day and hour, they met on the stairs of the Palace. When she saw him across the street she waved, then ran to him. She looked stunning with the city in the background. Gracefully long-waisted in creamy pleated slacks, the fashion of the time, her tan sweater tight on her slender chest, her endless neck in harmony with the single braid descending to her waist and reflecting the Northern sun in golden hues. She gave him a kiss, a fleeting kiss which surprised them both and prevented the conversation for what seemed an eternity to Erik. They held hands as they walked through the village-like capital of Norway, by now his favorite city.

In Cafe Ethiopia she told him about her stay up north, about her Chicago family, her Slavic origins, her Midwestern college.

He told her that he came to Norway to visit the family of his father's new wife, a woman who, before the death of Erik's mother, had been one of their maids in Oregon and his father's lover. And whom Erik liked the best of his relatives, by far. He did not tell Emily that he had never worked for money but he did tell her he was a student of English literature. Instantly he felt stunned by his lie and confessed it, with sweat erupting on his forehead. It was an awkward moment. She withdrew her hand from his and it took an hour for their communication to improve. Then she accepted his invitation for dinner at his hotel. "The only place in town with an edible menu," he assured her. Leaving the cafe he noticed, with pride, that she attracted the admiration of all the guests, ladies and gentlemen alike. They parted with some hesitation.

For dinner Erik dressed carefully, rejecting several alternatives from his wardrobe, including a carnation in the lapel. Finally he left his suite in a dark woolen blazer, white linen shirt and a silk ascot of conservative pattern. He parted his chestnut hair precisely and ruffled it on the temples. The mirror satisfied him that his handsome face hardly gave away his age—he was fifteen years senior to the dazzling young woman.

She arrived on time, radiant in a blouse of dusty rose color with a spray of pink pearls around her neck. He told her they were otherworldly. Touching them, he realized they were artificial, and then he became unsettled by the fact that he even paid attention to his find. He was determined to admire everything about her and to reward her beautiful existence by the dinner-perfect night.

The dinner was made easier by Erik's acquaintance, the head waiter. He was the oldest employee of the hotel and he attracted Erik's attention by his unusual expertise in all culinary matters, by his eel-like fluidity between the tables, and by his peculiar habit of whistling thinly an unrecognizable melody, so faintly that one could hear it only in closest proximity to him. His brilliantined jet-black dyed hair was parted in the middle, and his complexion was so white it appeared blue. He and Erik took great pleasure in communicating with each other.

"Sir," the whistling waiter whispered and bent down to Erik's ear, "just a few hours ago, Japanese Matsushima oysters were delivered to the Hotel Grant. The greatest oysters in the world, as you certainly know, sir." He nodded slightly to Emily. "They came on a fast ship from Stockholm, having been flown directly from the tanks of Sendai, the nearest city to the archipelago of Matsushima."

"Oh, really, my friend," Erik responded with an expression of surprise. "From Matsushima? The pine islands, where they have been artificially raised to achieve the length of eight inches at least—twenty centimeters, you would say." They both took delight in this way of speaking. Emily observed the room.

"Pleasure to serve you, sir, madame, indeed." The waiter bowed slightly with approval on his blue face.

"One dozen. Lemon only. Please," Erik ordered.

For the main course Erik and the waiter conspired on langostas in dry vermouth sauce, but Erik requested the replacement of vermouth by sake to honor the Japanese provenance of the oysters. For desert: whole unripe walnuts aged for a year in brown sugar and cognac.

"No lefse or lutefisk, Emily," he pronounced with self-satisfaction as he adjusted his ascot. With the langostas, against the rules, the wine he ordered was red—Hotel Grant stocked only one of the Premier Grand Crux, by chance the one that Erik admired the most. The Chateau Latour would surprise her, he was certain. Not exactly the smooth perfection of the Rothschild Lafite—but a rowdy complexity which changed with astonishing speed when decanted.

"Get ready for this, please," he gestured with excitement. He held up his wine glass. "The world of science, Emily, has not the slightest notion about the chemistry of this phenomenon." She nodded and pointed out the arriving guests she was sure were the U.S. ambassador and his wife. "How ambassadorial-looking, isn't he, and look at her blouse. Wow!"

Emily refused the oysters but liked the langostas, dessert, and the famed wine which she judged as "really good, if a little strange." Seeing Erik's expression, she said that he was so much preoccupied with food that he might get fat. Then she laughed and leaned her calf against his leg and put her hand on his and smiled at him. The warmth of her hand disturbed him. She laughed often that evening.

Most of the guests had left. She asked him to lend her a book to read and suggested going with him to his room to pick it up. She admired his bedroom while he selected a few titles for her.

Then he called a taxi and accompanied her to her bed and breakfast place. The city lights gave off a cold blue light. Almost nobody walked the streets. They watched the passing houses without words. She thanked him for the dinner, shook his hand, and disappeared into the house. Back in his hotel he lay on the bed repeating one word, many times: idiot, idiot. At three in the morning he woke up from a restless sleep and sat by the window, waiting for the sun to rise. Then he ran.

He lost his way and in a state of panic found her house by mere luck. She opened the door and without a word let him in. She was just wrapped in a towel and her wet hair was flowing in streams smelling of lavender soap. She emanated the warmth of her shower. She embraced him and looked at him for a long time. Then they kissed with passion true lovers know. He carried her to the bed, lay her down gently, and looked at her face again, trying to absorb her. "I love you." He said these three words for the first time ever, since his sense of honesty had prevented him from making this promise to any of the women in his past.

He had to force himself to close his eyes to make love to her. So beautiful she was.

Then they lay still, holding each other. A feeling of happiness filled him with such an unexpected intensity he started to laugh. He became aware of only her and himself with her, nothing of the past and nothing of the future. Laughing, he looked through the ceiling into his heaven.

His laughing alarmed her, and she sat up in uneasy surprise. He assured her, first, that he was a simpleton and an idiot, then, that he was the happiest man in all the world.

"Emily," he explained, "in Inuit, the Eskimo language, to make love is translated as 'to laugh with the woman.'" He sat up with her and cupped her breast with his hand. "Can't you see the depth of the meaning? Only the happiest love will fit the Eskimo term, the loving of only true conspirators in friendship." He did not wait for a response. "I think it must beat, hands down, any passionate passion, any torturous torture of love—to laugh with each other, to…"

She put a finger on his lips. "You use so many words, Erik. You do, and I like it, Erik. But right at this moment you know what I want to do with my Inuit?" She pulled him down to her. She did not laugh saying it, but broke into a smile, with her eyes partly closed in an expression of intrigue and conspiracy. A streak of hair lay over her chin. From her body it seemed as if "…sudden rosy smoke was rising"—a verse by Yusuke Keida flashed into his mind. He wrapped her body in his, tightly.

They showered together for a long time in a bathroom with warm pinewood walls and ceiling on which the vapor condensed into drops fragrant with resin. He licked the drops from the wall and the dew from her body. He assured her of his thirst and hunger, and proposed making her breakfast.

"The greatest meal Frenchmen ever invented!" He dressed in a hurry and jogged out onto the street like a kid, bursting with energy and barely controlling the urge to sing. Back in her room he saw with satisfaction that she had already put a clean towel over the table and washed two glasses from the bathroom. She confessed to her curiosity about the best food Frenchmen ever invented. Erik pulled a morning-fresh baguette out of the bag he was carrying. He cut it along its length into two halves and with his Swiss Army knife spread unsalted butter on each. On it he layered malosol caviar a quarter of an inch thick, the best from the Caspian Sea. The glasses he filled with cool, inexpensive Riesling, tinted lightly yellow.

"Genius of simplicity, Emily, my love!"

She liked it, he saw with delight. With caviar on the tip of her nose and on his chin, they ate hungrily and drank. They talked silly—what a discovery for Erik. Then Emily told him she loved him, too.

They kissed with mouths full of those sturgeon eggs salted and smoked to perfection. They sipped the wine with slurps, spilling it on their naked chests and without showering curled together in sleep.

They slept at any hour those days and nights, and made love simply and in complex gymnastic exercises. She proudly called it their loving orgy. He insisted on a term from the Inuit language. That was their only argument. He believed he had climbed clear out of the hold of reality and fallen—in love.

"To make love to you, Emily, is like breaking fresh village bread, with its heavy crust and heavenly smell and its soft insides. A taste so delicious that one cannot describe it," he told her, and soon was on his way to the nearby liquor store.

"Grappa! Here you are. The simplest distillate of the Italian peasant. Drunk with the breaking of village bread!" They drank and made love with enthusiasm and altruism, and often.

She also praised the grappa and drank it straight. And she laughed at the idea of bread and loving. He embraced her behind and kissed it since it was pleasingly out of proportion to her slenderness. "Come up here Erik," she called. "Up here, close to my soul. And kiss me." She believed that the soul rests in the brain and could be easily shared by the kiss of lovers. Grappa made it easy for him to accept her belief.

They danced to his whistling, watched in disbelief the people on the street hurrying about instead of making love. They handfed and groomed one another, compared the darkness of their nipples and the luster of their nails. Erik told her many things, and she listened—most of the time.

He became sad only in the moments he realized, with increasing clarity, that it would be impossible to attain the emotion of these extraterrestrial days again. She was never sad. "I love her," he assured himself. "I love her." Time acquired a peculiar quality: the hours and days and nights became progressively shorter and shorter.

When the date arrived, Emily decided that they should say goodbye on the street. There he stood steady, his lips in a contortion of a smile. She held his hands. He had to be the one to walk away not looking back. He managed that on the street in Oslo. But he had looked back ever since. He wanted to believe that it was with true love that he loved her. He knew he worshiped his love for her and the small watercolor of the fjord he carried home with him.

✳

Erik Lance Bauer was awakened from his past by the complete absence of sound. From his toilet tank throne he stepped down into the water and walked away on uncertain legs, holding on to the walls. He could not pry open the main entrance door. Above, the main structural beam, the one carried in by thirty slender Cuban refugees, was sloping down at one end.

He could barely get through the kitchen. The water there was covered with floating garbage. He managed to push out the kitchen door leading to the back deck and instantly became blinded by the light. The sky was ultramarine blue, without a blemish. In the cypress door a large splinter of black ironwood was embedded as a warning arrow. A collapsed lobster trap was wrapped around the only standing post of the deck's railing. The railing of the "widow's walk," blown off the roof, was leaning on the stump of the pigeon plum, like a ladder. The sad remains of a pelican, his favorite pterodactyl of the islands, floated near his knee, half-submerged, stripped of most of its plumage, the pouch under its beak flopping in the water like a rag.

For decades Erik had been living surrounded by greenery. Trees, ground cover, even the sea was green when the northwestern wind blew. Now there was not a spot of green anywhere. Not a single leaf in the forest of splinters and skeletons of trees.

Erik understood the situation. He was in the silent center, the eye of the hurricane.

"The eye is looking at you, kid." He forced a grimace and looked up to relieve his eyes of the desolation—only to see an event which filled him with emotion. Hundreds of birds, voiceless dark silhouettes, soared against the blue. There were several species, all together in a large circle with different rhythms to their wings. Some were gliding motionless. All were hiding in the eye of the hurricane. When the eye disintegrated they would all be destined to smash into the waves or on the land. They would all perish violently, he knew. But now, in the eye of the hurricane, the birds were one big community, with hope in each of them.

Erik tilted his head backward, stretched his arms apart, and flapped them slowly, up and down. Again and faster. He felt as if he were lifting up. Just a few inches. But would they want him to join them in their last gala flying performance, these magnificent frigatebirds, these Royal Terns and kingfishers? They would laugh at this crow, this scarecrow, this fragile, spindly marabou. He longed to go with them, even to share their fate, just not to stay here alone, as always. He tried lifting his wings again, feebly, but tired soon. Streams of tears mixed with the salty wetness of his face. His hands rested on his heart.

The rising breeze made him shiver, and then a sudden puff of wind. The hurricane's eye was moving away. He could see the black wall of clouds on its fringe moving in. It would be just a few minutes before the sheets of rain and the wind would return, their force increasing rapidly to a hundred and fifty miles per hour or more. This time the wind would come from the opposite direction to complete the destruction.

Erik waded back to the shelter of his bathroom where he managed to close the door behind him. The screams of the hurricane increased rapidly. The gunshots of breaking wood announced the beginning of the symphony of wind instruments, deafening the old man who again held on to the tank of the toilet.

He observed his legs, hairless on the shins and around his ankles, pigmented spots, skin loose and shriveled where muscles used to bulge. His bony hands were spotted, too, and his fingers were bent and knobby. But his nails were still beautiful—pale, milky, opaline, fluorescent in the darkness of his cave.

Erik found two new companions in his shelter. A pair of gecko lizards was attached to the ceiling. He had always felt a kinship with these ghosts of his house. In the evenings they amused him by wiggling across the bedroom ceiling, moving their hips like Caribbean whores at the beginning of the night. Geckos also worked the night shift, catching a stray mosquito with a sudden surge of speed, or dining on a confused moth attracted to the lamp, licking their lips with pink tongues afterwards, "*Tres faciunt colegium*—we will make a hurricane party of it," he forced a cheer.

Suddenly, with one powerful gust, part of the ceiling tore away and was sucked up violently. With it went the two pale geckos. At that moment, for the first time in his vigil, Erik was overwhelmed by a feeling of indifference to his survival. To hope seemed fanciful, the inevitable became irresistible.

But it was the last of the great screams of the hurricane. The apocalyptic train outside departed to the Gulf, the forte of the symphony unrecorded before changing into moderato. The water level subsided, and more light came in through the missing roof. It was all over.

Erik slumped slowly to the floor, into the corner. He bent down his head and embraced his legs. He rested his forehead on his bony knees in a peaceful, fetal position. His breathing was slow, in the rhythm of a sleeping man. He closed his eyes, opened them in wonder, and closed them again. His eyelids were the only moving object on all of Pelican Key.

He drifted away. There were shadows all around him, moving shadows he had to avoid. He flew through them into the clouds of brilliant dust, like millions of stars in all directions. The speed of his flight increased until all the stars fused in a bright-lit space. He recognized it as an ocean stretching to the horizon.

Then he saw her. On the bog flat boulder above the fjord, waiting. She was smiling, her face unchanged. After four decades, not a single crease, not one wrinkle on her pale complexion. Her lips were full, the upper a little fuller than the lower, as he remembered. Erik could not make a sound but felt his tongue and lips form the words he had often dreamt he owed her. He wanted to ask many questions and say pleasing words to her.

"I have been waiting, Erik," she whispered. "And you came. It is time to be with me now, my love." She stretched one hand to him, palm upwards. That was her way—when reaching to him she always held her palm up.

He shivered when she locked her fingers with his. She led him carefully between the great boulders down to the sea, on which the waves were motionless as if frozen. They walked so lightly they seemed not to touch the ground. Silence ruled the space around them. The only sound came from somewhere in the wreckage. It was the high-pitched buzz of the seven year cicada calling to all who might have survived the hurricane on Pelican Key. The white head of the old man lifted slowly and turned, his ear searching for the direction of the insect's mating call.

Mal D'Afrique

Harmattan, the northern wind of the dry season, was blowing steadily, covering all of West Africa with fine red powder brought from the lands of *sahel*. It entered everywhere: into houses, inside cupboards, into pots, into ears, caking faces when mixed with sweat, making a ring of solid clay around one's collar. It swirled invisibly around the oven-like cabin of our van. Opening the windows did not help at all, but we did that anyway, hoping to relieve the heat.

The road cut through secondary forest, mostly bushes, palmettos, small twisted trees entangled with vines, in some places forming green walls, impenetrable without a *panga*. Firewood was scarce in this country, and all the hardwood had been burned a long time ago. Now, even dried ferns were used for cooking fuel.

I liked to travel this part of the road, passing the colorful markets, the children carrying water in pails on their heads, water splashing on their faces then being licked by pink tongues. Old men had a fishing pole or an old hunting rifle, always with a *panga* machete in their hands. And there were sellers. A boy sold a small python, for roasting no doubt. A "man of the woods," with his bare-breasted woman, held a baby alligator. Strange pangolins were offered for sale, covered with fish-like scales, resembling the fossil stegosaurus. Or hunters sold duikers, the smallest antelopes, the size of a small dog. They dive into the bushes, hence their name.

Today, so far, a naturalist might have taken delight in seeing a six-foot black cobra crossing the road. We almost rolled the car over when my driver, Chukwu, swerved at full speed to hit it, and missed. (I had to smoke two cigarettes, lighting the second one from the butt of the first, to calm myself.) It was very hot, and after the first rain of the coming rainy season the humidity increased my misery.

After we crossed the small Ubue River, we passed by the freshly burned wreck of a minibus, still smoldering. As always, when passing the scene of an accident, I remembered meeting a white student on the campus of a West African university, the only European around. That happened on one of the first days of my stay here. Somehow he assumed that I must be a novice in West Africa, and he soon volunteered a series of instructions. The one I recalled now was about caution.

"You have to be really cautious, sir," he said. He was an eager fellow, young, with hollow cheeks and a yellowish complexion. I was sure he had gone through his malaria and amoebic dysentery already. "The number one rule is to slow down when the minibuses crash in front of you." Minibuses, like *matatus* in East Africa, are made to take about ten or fifteen passengers. To double the number is the custom in this country, and half of the passengers carry living hens and canisters with gasoline.

"When the minibuses crash," he continued, "bodies lie all over the road, and if you don't slow down, I mean really slow down driving through, you are as good as dead yourself." There must have been some questioning expression on my face that compelled him to explain: "You know, if you go over them too fast, the bodies tend to wrap around the axle and wheel and all. And you'll go flying right—boom—into that iroko tree." I was not unhappy never to meet this nervous fellow again, but his bizarre instruction often came to my mind, driving the most dangerous roads in the world, African roads.

We were easily going eighty kilometers an hour on a bad surface, and still the driver enjoyed accelerating through the villages, where most of the business and socializing seemed to take place right on the road. Almost all of the minibuses we met played the old African roulette with us: the driver with the best nerves avoids a head-on collision at the very last second. After months of traveling these roads, I had to devise a strategy to keep my mental state sound and intact. It was not true stoicism or even fatalism; I called it "observatism." I had trained myself to ease back and simply observe myself driving, or sitting next to the driver, from a distance, from a safe distance—outside the car. And that was the state of mind I successfully put myself into, on our drive to the capital city, to the town with an international airport from which I hoped to journey home in an air-conditioned airplane, with a toilet, running water, and electric lights.

Would I ever again journey on this road in the opposite direction? Would I return? I knew the road so well, taking it to the hospital when sick, or to buy a can of Campbell's soup in town, or to attempt to use the telephone, or to have a couple of sloe gins in The Green Virgin, the infamous bar by the market. A few turns after the place we called Dead Man's Curve (there had been a dead man lying there for two days last month), we pulled up in a ditch for a break in our "flight" and to stretch. We got out right next to a simple roadside sacrificial place, with remnants of a chicken and dried blood in a clay pot with a few coins in it and a couple of cola nuts.

I used to be interested in these strange altars to ju-ju spirits, and I have always felt a little adventurous, seeing something unexplored, rarely talked about, and somewhat dark and secret. But now I did not have a good feeling, being around it. It was no longer a cultural curiosity to me; there was nothing romantic about it anymore. It was too real. There were too many stories, too many newspaper reports. And most were confirmed by silence and resentment, understandable resentment, from anybody, even friends, that one would ask.

Not everybody was silent. The university students went on a strike with loud demonstrations for several days, when their colleague from engineering was found dead, his heart and head missing. The heart was thought to have been used for a sacrificial ritual, the head probably sold to a ju-ju priest. Around that time the newspapers reported the arrests of those who had sold human skulls at two for forty-two dollars each and one for thirty-five dollars—the cheaper one had been offered at a discount, as a remnant of an albino. All included the lower jaw. I also remembered now the embarrassed silence when, in the Aronzi village near my house, the meeting of neighbors was joined by a woman in a black mourning dress, the mother of a boy whose body parts were sacrificed near the river where the lowland begins, by a big tree.

"Prof, we should go. To make the city before dark." My reminiscing was interrupted by Chukwu, the driver. He did not feel comfortable around the sacrificial shrine either, walking around the van, faking inspection, kicking the tires.

"Why hurry, Chukwu?" I asked, knowing about his uneasiness and also knowing that there would be a curfew at night in the capital city, because of robberies and murders.

"No lights on the streets, Prof. Many people walking when it gets cooler at evening."

Slowly the landscape changed from woods to fields, and more eucalyptus and euphorbias appeared along the road, not green but reddish or gray. Approaching the city, the road became pockmarked with more and more pot holes, its curbs eroded more deeply. With the decreasing distance to our destination, the spaces between wrecks in the ditches diminished until there was an almost continuous row of junked cars and vans and lorries, smashed into bizarre shapes, squashed to convoluted tangles of burned metal by the losers and the winners at African roulette.

The number of people walking along and on the road increased, too. I never tire of watching the lanky men in African tunics, worn dinner jackets, and an assortment of pants (from swimming trunks to bellbottoms), dragging sandals made of tires in their peculiar way—some picking their noses and chewing on a chew-stick at the same time. Often two men would stroll by holding hands, smiling and laughing in incomprehensible optimism. And the women—so perfectly straight, with colorful headdresses made of yards of cloth—carrying everything on their heads, from a postage stamp weighted by a stone to a tree trunk that two men could hardly have lifted. There went one, with a door perfectly balanced on her head and carried at a speedy pace. Her exquisitely sculptured face was decorated with a pleasing smile, to tell every passerby that her burden was balanced easily, of course. It never ceased to surprise me, how most of the people were clean, in the midst of garbage and dust. Even the children, those ever-present benign vultures of medina and village, who screamed at me "*Bekee, Oibo anya acha! anya acha!*" ("Blue eyes! blue eyes!"), and followed and followed me everywhere.

We had entered the city. "Chukwu, did we lose the way? *Ebeki needje, wako?*" I wanted to know. It had gotten dark with a speed usual for the near-equator, and we had turned off the main road to travel between the squalor of makeshift shelters of canvas, sticks, and flattened aluminum containers. The surface of the "road" now resembled the waves of a confused sea. "*Odjo ato nage;* no worry, we go by river," the driver replied, and turned to me with an apologetic smile while letting the van go by itself for yards without smashing anything or anybody.

He was a pleasant man, easy to be with, and I already felt some sadness that I would leave him soon, having never had a chance to really understand the incredible abandon of his driving, his resistance to thirst, his constantly level mood, and so many other mysteries of his existence. He rarely tired visibly, could fall asleep in a second anywhere, any time of day, and never put headlights on at dusk until the complete, blackest darkness. His movements always seemed measured and sparse: only when he shifted up to fifth gear did he let his hand slip off the gear-stick, lifting it high before he brought it down on the steering wheel, so proud of his act of driving. The only thing we seemed to have in common was that we both sweated, and, perhaps, smelled, equally as bad. And I liked that bond.

We had been passing a gathering of Hausa in long white robes and white caps, and scattered groups of Fulani women with their elaborate hairdos, dragging or carrying their children with angelic hamitic faces. "Chukwu, why are there so many people from the north here?"

"I pray that God would send the Saviour," answered Chukwu, turning his eyes up. The occasional surrealism of his answers was enjoyable but not easy to understand. His "acting" was easier on me than were his Kafka-like discourses. He "acted" his driver's tasks and his concern for pedestrians; he "acted" his rare anger and maybe even delight. I don't know if he ever distinguished his acting from reality——I have rarely been able to understand that.

Chukwu did not seem to act worried when our van was stopped by a gathering of agitated people, some screaming and running in different directions in front of us. The confusion increased every moment. We were surrounded. Chukwu stopped the van, rolled up the window, and motioned to me to do the same—while invoking the names of several saints.

First a fist hit the windshield, then one hit the body of the van, then more and more, reverberating in a tremendous noise like a hundred drums. This was no ebullience, nor a prank. There was anger and frenzy on the dark faces behind the windows. I did not understand the reason for this, but very soon I saw the seriousness of the situation, feeling the fear spreading like catatonia through my legs, inside my belly. Chukwu's face became gray, a color I have known before—from the morgue. The van started to rock.

Then he—or it—appeared in front of the van. A tall figure was slowly approaching us, surrounded by a group of young men with sticks and clubs in their hands. At first sight the creature seemed enormous. Covered with a tunic of straw, he had a chain of bones around his neck, bells around his feet and wrists, a club in his hand, and his face was concealed under a wooden mask. He moved unhesitatingly toward us, spreading his legs wide with jerky movements, turning his head slowly from side to side, as praying mantises do. His guards kept the road opened in front of him, gesturing wildly, lashing with sticks at anybody in their way. When he approached the van, the beating on the windows stopped. The crowd separated, all watching the mask—and us.

An agitated crowd in Africa loses control easily, and often with disastrous results. I knew that great danger; Africans know it, too. Sweat was soaking my shirt. I tried to think. There must be an initiative from us; it was our turn for action now, even an action involving a risk. I rolled down the window and gestured briskly to the mask to come. With effort, I tried to look calm and, I hoped, to appear self-confident. After a pause (which seemed very long to me) the mask, with a few deliberate steps, approached, his hand with the club extended to the side.

Up close now I could see the crudely carved features of the mask, painted white, with black lips and black eyebrows, a black ridge for the nose and red circles around the hollows of the eye-holes. One foot from our open window, he stopped and remained motionless. A voice, muted by the mask but understandable, came out in the sudden silence of the crowd.

"Happy Easter, Sir."

"*Dalo*," I said, thanking him. "*Kedu*."

I had not seen his eyes behind the wooden face. It was too dark. Only cooking fires flickered along the road, their smoke mixing with the dust, the heat, the smell of urine and rotted fruit—the smell of a town at night, unmistakably West Africa, for which I felt affection at this moment.

We stumbled further into the city, over holes filled with water, where frogs gathered, roaring their mating sounds that resemble the grunting of pigs rather than the booming or croaking we know. I was very tired, holding onto the vision of a hotel room with a bath and a real bed. The hope of a cold beer seemed too good to be possible. We looked for anything resembling a hotel for another hour or so, sometimes retracing our way when a street was blocked by a pile of refuse. On one of these barricades, a dead body lay distorted in the beam of our headlights. In the next street we found a "hotel", a two-story structure owned by an older man in suspicious off-white underwear.

It was time to say goodbye to Chukwu. We shook hands, the Igbo way, softly, letting our limp fingers slip apart. We looked into each other's eyes, saying something meaningless. I felt some sadness but did not want to put it into words. It is not done here. Chukwu solved the parting by a sudden smile, a sad or tired grin. *"Kimesja,* Prof, *kachifo."* Goodbye. Good night, without much cheer in his voice. He would travel through the whole dangerous night to get back home.

There seemed to be nobody around. Only the buzz of insects disturbed the silence.

My room had air conditioning that worked. Full blast. When I collapsed naked on the bed, totally bushed, the electricity went off and with it the stream of cool air. In an instant, of course, sweat covered me and soon was soaking the pillow. After failing attempts to fall asleep, after turning the wet pillow over a few times to find a dry place, I gave up, put on shorts, and walked out. I soon discovered a veranda. There, around a table, two men were holding bottles of Star.

"Have a beer. Have one of these, friend." I poured it down my throat in one swallow: bitter, warm, but wonderful. But the two Canadians were quite subdued. The young one, in his twenties, smoked a local brand of cigarette, one after another.

"You ask how it was, down there? I say it was not good—like hell. No food, no water to drink, no soap, no shit. I was sick every goddamned day there, and I'm still sick," the young one said as he opened another bottle for his friend, using the inside of a lock on the door to the veranda as an opener.

The other man was much older, retirement age. His skin did not take the sun well: his face was covered with blotches, nose peeling, lips cracked. He still had lots of hair, reddish, with gray, now stuck together with sweat. He had a kind face, one with sleepy eyes and wrinkles everywhere, and when he smiled you saw only the upper teeth.

The two men were cartographers on their way home from several months of mapping the delta of the Niger River. The young man seemed eager to talk about the Niger. The delta was still unexplored, he said.

Nobody dared to go much further downstream than Onitcha.

People live in the old ways there, he said, some still practicing slavery. The majority of people had never seen a white man nor traveled beyond their village. Some are hospitable; some look for strangers to be used for rituals or simply robbed and disposed of. And more. With more beer, more. Some of it I knew to be true; most of the rest of it I believed and found it interesting. My fatigue slowly went away. I brought from my room a bottle of palm wine.

The older man rarely talked, until the last bottle of their beer and the last drop of my palm wine (which I had bought from the village palm-tapper to bring home as a present). When I asked him why he was not happy—"Tomorrow an airplane, and home!"—it took him a while to answer. "Well, my pal died a week ago. You see? We were sitting under a big mango, near the village where we stayed. Black mamba hit him in the hand. Big snake." He nodded his head, looking away.

"We had worked together for 14 years—for Shell, the first ten. There was nothing we could have done for him, nothing. He was gone in twenty minutes, André. It hurt him bad, too." He drained the last of the palm wine. "I'll have one of those—what the hell." He asked for a cigarette. "Just made the arrangements today with the airline to take him home, to Quebec."

We did not talk for a while after he said the word "home." Then the older man smiled, and it was his first smile of the evening. He leaned back in his chair and took a long drag from his cigarette. "I'll tell you what going home means to me," the old man continued.

The mosquitoes were biting now. I feared the night-biting sons of bitches, having seen so many deadly diseases they transmit, but I forced myself to concentrate. I wanted to know everything about going home.

"Tomorrow evening, when I get to Quebec, my wife will be waiting for me at the airport with the station wagon, and we'll take off straight north. That's how we arranged it. We'll bypass the city; it will be late, not much traffic."

His face looked different now, a smile on it all the time he talked. "And you should see the country up there. We'll drive two hours through the forest: just spruce, tamarack, some white pine—real tall ones—and clumps of birches, white like the snow under them. And nothing and nobody there, just forests, and snow, and lakes, and it goes for a thousand miles, all the way to the tree line by Hudson Bay." His companion sat motionless, mouth agape, his cigarette burning forgotten in the ashtray.

"The path to our cabin from the road is not too long, and the neighbor plows the snow off it for us. You should see the piles of white stuff along the path. The last of it melts in May. Sometimes we already swim in the lake by then!" He looked much younger now. He paused, and his expression asked us if we could believe such a wonderful thing.

"It is still on the ground when the crocuses and the snowdrops have come and gone. In the cabin," he continued, "in the cabin I'll change, first thing—put on a thick Irish sweater and fur-lined moccasins. We'll make a fire in the fireplace—and woodstove, too. The fire will light up the place, and that looks real pretty, and smells great, too—the light on the knotty pine walls!"

This all sounded so strange now, like nothing less than paradise. The young man and me, we sat transfixed, trying to imagine the snow, the pines, while slapping mosquitoes, wiping off sweat, in the humid heat of the night. "Then my girl will pull out something to warm me up, here," and he pointed at his belly covered with sweat. "I am sure there is a old bottle of Armagnac there. We'll warm it up a bit with a candle, and sip it by the fireplace.

"I tell you what I like to do before hitting the sack. I'll put on an old fur parka and light a pipe," he said, looking at his cigarette. "Then go out on the shore, just a few yards from the door, and stay there for a while. The lake under the moon, ice covered with fresh snow, so white that you could see like in daylight; tracks of deer running along the shore, and tracks of otter sometimes. You know, the otter likes to run a few steps and then slide on her belly and run again and slide. It makes tracks like no other." He paused and continued: "There are spruces all around, with caps of snow on them, tall, reaching all the way to the stars—stars, like I have never, ever, seen anywhere."

He stopped talking for a long time, just smoking. "Ya, I like to stand there in the silence. So cold and so quiet—until the snow owl cries. So quiet."

I don't remember anything much after that. The next morning on the way to the airport, I didn't look around. My mind was far ahead of me, in the plane, somewhere above the predatory kites in low flight along the road, above the vultures soaring above the hospital. My mind was already in the plane that would take me home. Coming home I felt like coming from a war.

✳

That year, in the fall, we bought a cabin on a sandy river not far from the Canadian border. In the winter I see the tracks of deer and coyotes dotting the frozen river, and the strange tracks of a playful otter sliding on her belly over the snow. At night, under the moon, it's as bright as in daylight. Then I walk to the river's shore and under the northern lights, sometimes, wait for the call of a snowy owl. My heart starts to ache a little, my mind fills with memories, of Africa. I dream of the Igbo girl singing her whole song with eyes turned down. I long to go to Africa again.

Africa.

I know my malady is incurable, its origin poorly understood. The French call it *Mal d'Afrique*.

Pearls of Lady Seraphim

I still hear her saying clearly, "It was a beautiful time; everything." This simple sentence has been returning to my mind for many days. She was 91 years old when I met her in Prague, in a small bookstore, Publishers of Paradise, where she was allowed to earn some money to supplement her joke-of-a-pension selling good books.

Her appearance was interesting; my first thought was that even a very old woman might look handsome. Mrs. Blanka Paulova dyed her hair with vinegar and a few drops of picric acid the hue of a Florida tangelo, denying them whiteness, as if her name was whiteness enough—Blanka. It was the curls that first attracted my attention. These thin twists cascaded down along her powdered cheeks, shimmering when she moved. With some oversized Dali-like sense of fantasy one could resurrect Shirley Temple—a strange reincarnation.

Mrs. Blanka mostly smiled while talking, her dentures reflecting the rays of fluorescent lights in the store like a regiment of oversized porcelain incisors, which they were. Their slightly yellowish tint, resembling that of uranium glass, could be seen only at certain angle. Out of loyalty to her, I will not describe her face in any great detail, except confessing that her teary eyes under their hoods still sparkled, her smile warmed an observer, and all the wrinkles, grooves and sags conspired together into an expression of kindness, not unlike those of Galapagos turtles. I was very curious to hear the story of the old lady. I did not know anything about her prefrontal cortex, her frontal cingulate, amygdala and hypocampus, which make up the character of a human and are his or her soul. But I liked what I saw, and what I heard stopped me in my contemplative tracks.

She buried the first of her husbands many decades ago. He was run down by a truck. This loss carved a few permanent scars into Blanka's heart because she liked the man, and the scars were still there, she told me. The second husband disappeared while on a diplomatic mission in Mexico. She was convinced the communist government had arranged it, as she was told in certain terms that he might have been disloyal to the masses, possibly engaged in collaboration with the capitalist enemy. The disappearance of her husband also made her an enemy of the socialist state; enemy of masses, of the peoples.

The interrogations in Ruzyne prison were long. Nonsensical questions were hollered in screams and then in conspiratorial whispers. The classical technique of bad cop/good cop was used repeatedly and primitive methods, such as light in the eyes, no drinks, and hours of waiting while standing were applied. All of this failed to extract information on conspiracy or sabotage from Mrs. Blanka because there was none in her grayish matter.

A female judge with gray face and hair, who did not pay much attention, being often amused by some whispered remarks of her assistant, pronounced the sentence of three years behind bars. Wooden mallet down—bang. That was it. They did not put chains on her legs while leading her away.

Nowadays, Mrs. Blanka has only seventy dollars worth of crowns left per month after paying rent and utilities. Because she owns a hand-held calculator to plan her life, she manages to have food every day and drip coffee twice a week. She mends her wardrobe carefully and keeps it clean in the way of old ladies with a history of elevated social standing. Her makeup is improvised by applying the juice of red beets to her cheeks and just a touch of beet slice to her white lips to make them, as she believed, seductive. She stopped using shoe polish for her eyelashes, since the cilia fell off some time ago. She consults her antique mirror during the morning hours, and at that time pleasantly distorted memories are often recalled from another mirror—the warped mirror of her past, her private Dreamtime.

Eskimo grandmothers, just before they walk out of the igloo into the deadly arctic snowstorm to disappear, instruct young women to enjoy life. They tell them that a woman at her senility doesn't look forward to pleasures of life. That an old woman looks backward at the pleasures of life, such as the happy times of loving their little ones and adventures copulatory (*nagligpungo koayok*, as they say). For Mrs. Blanka this wisdom of Inuit elders would be understood very well.

Her acquaintances have been dying all around her and her only true friend, Josephina, died recently. She dried up, the doctor said. Her internal organs were all shriveled, desiccated, and her uterus was calicified into just a whitish pebble. In her attic they found baskets of dried bread crusts. Josephina could not chew them because her dentures were made by a dentist-criminal, and she could not throw them away because her God claimed bread to be the gift from Heaven.

Blanka Paulova's work in the bookstore is the highlight of her life now. There she meets people, talks to tourists in German, French and rudimentary English. She considers books her foster children, she told me, and loves them whether they are nerdy, rowdy or outright geniuses. When she mentioned Shakespeare's sonnets as her great companion in prison, I was compelled to inquire more into that period of her life. She talked about it with a smile, not a salad of words but lively, abbreviated memories.

"Well, after being drilled in Ruzyne lock-up they took me to that gigantic Sing-Sing in Pankrác. Soon I was in a working detail cleaning offices. It was not so good because there was the 'capo' woman who hated me since I was always singing, a song from the operetta 'Pearls of Lady Seraphim'… it was like:… my princess arise, the moon dove to the glade … la la trala … I forgot the words. Do you know the song? It was by Piskacek."

I confessed I'd never heard of it and I asked how the "capo" beast made her life miserable.

"I don't want to talk about that, but it was not so bad. I just cried a lot. We were four cleaners, we could talk, tell stories—you would not believe some stories, you wouldn't. Sometimes we found food left by officers, and we celebrated. Then they transferred me to the prison in Pardubice, an all women prison."

"There was a prison there?" I asked. "I know they make Semtex in Pardubice, the explosive, world infamous stuff."

"Ma boy," she nodded, "we did not know about anything behind the walls, we were sort of slave laborers, had to work, eat a little, and sleep. That's all. We made 'spiderwebs,' that is what we called it, a mesh of colored wires, part of a television set. I'll show you."

She made a rough sketch of interwoven lines, which had an artistic look, kind of dada; the lines were rippled, choppy, because of the essential tremor of her fingers. She looked at the finished picture in disbelief, her mind not in the present, I thought.

I changed the topic: "Did you make friends there? Like real friends…?"

"Oh yes, in those years I made a few friends of a certain kind. It was very important, essential for life to have a friend, you know. Maybe, it was the most important thing for me. Different than having friends when living outside the wall. Yeah, the walls were very high, very high. We knew there were trees behind the walls … and children … sometimes music. Music—that was hard. I was pretty close to the girl who killed an old woman, for money, they said. She did the woman in with an iron… Not the electrical one we use today, but with the old-fashioned iron that has to be filled with hot charcoals. A very heavy iron. But I do not judge people, I don't."

Mrs. Blanka's face seemed to flush a little; her breathing became heavier.

"You might ask about men? Ha—we met them only in stories, so it was safe." Her upper denture dislodged and she clicked it back.

"I had sonnets by Shakespeare," she changed the topic, "and you know, that was my great treasure. The sonnets kept me the same, the same Blanka Paulova, the same to the end. When they took my treasure away from me, I had only a few months left. I laughed at them—because I'd memorized most of the poems, I laughed at them. And I had another good friend for the last year. Her name was Milena, she was a village girl, big girl she was, and she gave me a spoon."

Blanka paused and looked at me as if she expected amazement. I listened intently.

"She threw her mother-in-law into a well. And when the woman climbed out she cut off her hands with an ax. I did not ask her why. You did not ask many questions in Pardubice, you just told your stories. And I did not judge people, I still don't. Milena gave me a nice aluminum spoon."

I looked at the shelves of books and Blanka looked at her sketch of a "spider web." We stood quietly in that kind of silence you worry about.

"It was a beautiful time. Everything," she said, nodding. "Beautiful time."

Her gaze told me she was not with me. So I left her to wherever her angel wings took her and kissed the veins on the dorsum of her hand, in the old way. I wanted to say something nice but managed only an onomatopoetic syllable. Like eh? As a somnambulist I sleepwalked onto the street where a truck almost ran me down because I was too deep in a thought: how Ivan Denisovich of Solzhenitsyn marveled with a happy heart at the beauty of crystals of frost on the barbed wires surrounding his Siberian gulag.

The truck missed my thoughts only by a few inches. So I could return.

How I Came to the Feast

The cause of my distraction is prosperity. It is everywhere around me. At some times it tranquilizes me to the extent of sleepwalking. It slows my movements as if they were filmed by a slow-motion camera.

The abundance, the affluence.

My employer, Universitat Giessen, has been endowed well, almost famously, even through recent times of leaner budgets, and therefore my lab lacks nothing. I can look forward to working, when I get up in the morning, in air conditioning set to a balmy 21° centigrade, opening the refrigerator and removing low-fat milk and orange juice at 5° centigrade, and pouring the milk over American cereal supplemented with enough fiber, vitamins, and trace minerals to "satisfy the recommended daily dosages." Every day I sin with a cup of freshly ground coffee, and off I go on my perfect machine, a titanium 21-speed mountain bicycle, on the paved bike path leading safely to the University. I pedal between the alleys of chestnut trees and through a park past the Goethe statue surrounded by flower beds, uphill between villas with rock gardens in bloom and a show of geraniums under each window. Everywhere I look, there is a tranquility and well-being. Some people I meet smile at me; some greet me with a waving hand—civility prevails. It is enjoyed, but without exuberance.

In a way one could be proud, being from Giessen in Bavaria, and most of the inhabitants are. I hasten to say that I appreciate it too. I do, indeed! But—my problem could be diagnosed as a recurring restlessness, as the urge to disappear to some malarian hole at the edge of a jungle, with sauna-like heat and humidity, about as healthy as a hospital sewer, under a leaden sky that pours five meters of water per year on the palm-fronded roofs of some sorry shacks sticking out of a permanent mudpie. Always, when I have managed to land in a defeated territory like that, I have felt such exhilaration and happiness that a conventional judge would assume I was wallowing on a topless beach in a Club Med with a Viper Key cocktail in my left hand and an incarnation of Brigitte Bardot supported by my right. And that, exactly, was the state of mind I attained trotting down the jungle path from the hills of the Golden Triangle on the Thailand side.

The forest was like a botanical garden, enchanted by singing and shrieking birds, butterflies the size of swallows, and beautiful beetles of bizarre shapes, the colors of gems. I stopped often, rested, and observed this curious world, the sweat and thirst only enhancing my feeling of adventure and, therefore, my exaltation. It was later in the day when I began tripping over the exposed roots because I'd lost concentration. My eyes were still watching the wet laterite clay of the trail, but my brain had started to turn over the kaleidoscope of images recorded during the past few days I'd spent up in the hills.

(The Lisu people grow the poppies and harvest them for the Karen people. They live in utter misery: diseased, scrambling for meager grub to survive. The opium dough is prepared by Karen tribesmen, who own the fields, tilled by the Lisu for almost nothing. The opium is bought then from the Karen by a solitary Hmong, who is ripping off the Karen expertly. The Hmong transfers the opium to a Chinese, down in Chiang Mai, who roars with laughter at the profit he's made from ripping off the Hmong. The stuff goes to a Thai military man who, of course, rips off the Chinese. And the Thai officer has further connections to the villains who make heroin from the raw opium. And the further way of heroin—that is a story too dangerous to know.)

I woke up from my ruminations to a strange noise coming from everywhere around me. It was an uniformly susurrant *shshshsh*. I stopped. I was not in the botanical riot of the jungle anymore but surrounded by a forest of slender trees of equal size, standing in neat rows about ten feet apart, obviously planted by man. The sound was coming from the tops of the trees, which looked like skeletons, almost devoid of leaves. Puzzled, I resumed walking and turned a bend in the path.

I almost ran into him, a white man standing there motionless, looking at me. He did not seem to be surprised; he'd probably heard me coming. My first impression of him was his tallness, and the visor on his head. He must have been six foot six, in a bleached-out shirt with a Hawaiian design, shorts, and sandals. He had a leather visor on his head with a narrow shield as long as I have ever seen. It was a well-worn thing; sweat had made patterns on the shield resembling a horizon of mountain ridges. The wearer did not allow any frivolous tilt to it—the shield was pointing straight ahead, like a raven's beak, at me.

"Hi." I used the American greeting and smiled.

"Hi."

I stopped, took my eyes off him, and pointed at the tops of the trees. "What a strange noise!" I said in English.

"Yeah, caterpillars." By his accent, he was an American.

"Caterpillars?"

"Yes. The destiny of monocultures in the tropics," he said. I must have looked puzzled. "Yeah, they are eating the leaves of those teaks. They're almost finished. That is what you hear."

"Hah!"

"When millions of those microscopic jaws gnaw—one can hear it. I wonder how many millions we hear?" he said. "Very interesting."

I extended my hand: "Lothar Burgdorf. How do you do?"

"1 am Rick Gorlinski." He grasped my hand firmly. Rick was built quite impressively, sturdily; lanky tall, his spare movements gave the impression of power and speed, that his sinews held everything together tightly. His skin was sallow but darkened evenly, as goes with long stays in the tropics. He had not been suntanned on a beach. His unruly hair, of no particular color, was bleached rusty at the ends. One could see he was not in the custom of smiling readily; a suggestion of scorn was carved around his lips. His poked-in cheeks added to his stern look, quite in contrast to the pleasant, bright blue eyes flanking the beaked nose of impressive dimensions.

We walked together down to town, because he also was staying in Chiang Mai. Somehow, at first, his appearance made me cautious, and so I avoided small talk (to which I have an unfortunate affinity), at the expense of long silences. Slowly, our exchanges took the form of conversation. I learned that we were visiting the same mountain tribes of the Golden Triangle, but we did not go deeper into it. *Maybe later, if we could trust each other a little more*, I thought.

His home was San Francisco, which he had left almost two years ago. He had traveled through India to China, through the Philippines to Malaysia, before he arrived here in Thailand—for how long, he did not know. It was his rule to globe trot without rules, with one exception. Every morning, before he would set out on his excursions, he studied the local language. Later, it impressed me to hear him ordering our food in Thai and being understood. Thai sounds to a Western ear like gurgling, with lots of *krch-chrch*, and it pours out like an uninterrupted stream over sharp rocks.

From the first village, we were lucky to catch a bus to Chiang Mai. Darkness came with a near-equatorial rapidity at the time we arrived, and we entered the first lighted eatery at the outskirts of town. I ordered just a salad, since my German palate was sick of the spice that flavored everything here. Was it cilantro? Lemon grass? Fish sauce? It seemed to be in every dish I had eaten during the three weeks of my stay. And I did not want any more. Lately, I had become preoccupied with dreams about fresh rye bread with a crust, just butter spread on it, a glass of cold milk, potatoes sprinkled with chopped parsley—plain potatoes, the simplest. Rick seemed to enjoy the thick chicken soup with some leafy vegetable that emanated the smell of *that* thing. He seemed more relaxed after the soup, and we talked about his travels.

Then I told him about my interest in liver cancer and about my research in the university hospital here. I was collecting biopsies of tumors and setting them up in tissue cultures, forcing the cancerous cells to grow in flasks. Rick seemed interested in my project and asked many questions that revealed a surprising knowledge of the malignant process. Surprising, because he was a computer specialist by trade. We talked about remissions and prospects for treatment of cancer in the future, about mortality. Mortality?

"Sometimes death is okay, I think. Sometimes it isn't," he declared.

"Why do you say it is okay?"

"Not long ago, a good friend of mine died, you see. He fell asleep during some meeting. They pulled the chair out from under him, for fun. But he was already dead when he slumped to the floor. The 'falling asleep' was a massive heart attack," Rick told me, his gaze blank, seeing his friend perhaps. "That is an 'okay' death, I think. You see, for himself he did not die. Only for others: for friends, family. Not for himself."

"But he died. That is the sad fact!"

"Yes, but the last thing on his consciousness, the very last, was perhaps a vision of a shapely female, a pile of great food, or the smile of his kid. Isn't that what people visualize during meetings? So death, dying, did not enter his mind, even in the last second of his life—and then there were no thoughts any more."

"I understand—death without dying, simply an end of existence. Comfortable, great stuff! And it should be like that for people of any age—but the hitch is that for those who remain, for family, friends, the age of the dead one means much. That is the bad part," I said.

"I was thinking about that. One can draw a 'curve of ruin,' so to speak, a curve of the degree of devastation for those who remain. It might be relatively low at birth, rising and rising, then descending down again in old age. Would it make sense, you think?" He asked himself more than me, and continued: "I am Jewish, Lothar, so I checked in some old books from a rabbi, once. But I couldn't find anything explicit, blunt enough about this curve."

"Jewish or Catholic, no matter; ethicists, they would struggle with such a curve, I imagine. I think it would almost imply that over the age of, say, a hundred and under the age of one day, or before birth even, the curve would approach, or reach, zero. On both ends of your curve, death would mean nothing, no grief. How about that, then?"

"The sanctity of life! A sacrosanct concept—or a folly of Western man?" Rick raised his hand. He had a pleasant smile, a little sad though. I forced a laugh, thinking that we were deviating too far from anything resembling a pleasant discourse over dinner.

"By the way," I said, "did you notice that girl who just came in?"

"I noticed her," Rick said dismissively, still in thought. "You know that the Eskimos, Inuit, have solved all this, in old times. They had it all figured out, what different values life has at which ages."

I ordered another Tsing Tao, Chinese beer, which tastes as bad as Miller Lite—doesn't even vaguely resemble the brew at home in Bavaria. "Why the hell do we have to talk about death, Rick, with waitresses around like the one serving the back tables. Why? Have a beer," I said.

"Because. You know why?" He sighed and did not look very happy, at that moment. "I have been bumming around Asia for two years, I told you. That's why." I did not understand the connection. He topped our glasses, leaned back, and started to unbutton his shirt, from the top. I looked around, but nobody seemed to be paying much attention to us.

He undid the last button and opened the shirt so that his chest and belly showed. He had the suntan distribution of a peasant: the darkness of his neck descended in a V-like triangle pointing to his chest bone. The rest of his body was white. An enormous scar ran down from the edge of his rib cage, turned sharply across his belly, and disappeared sideways under the flap of his shirt, at least a half a foot long, down, and maybe a foot across.

"What happened?"

"Melanoma, my friend. My brother, he's a surgeon in Tucson, he took it out two years ago." Rick watched my reaction. "My dad is a doctor too. They couldn't guarantee anything—no way to know about metastases, about the risk that it will come back; nothing. Just the usual: let us hope." He paused, looked at the scar and then at me. "That was not good enough for me, so I sold everything and went to India and decided to travel till I'd either spent all the dough or had a relapse—and that would be it." His mouth smiled, but his eyes did not.

"But you look great; you are in great shape," I said.

"Well, I don't know. Can't sleep well for over a week now—I worry. Look here." He pointed at the scar. "See it? You are a cancer man, aren't you?"

Right in the middle of the scar there was an elevated lesion covered with a scab, a little wet with lymph. It was surrounded by a pink halo. It was not too big, just about a couple of centimeters or smaller. "They told me in Tucson to watch for something like this." He started to button up the shirt. "It doesn't heal; seeps a little lymph, doesn't hurt, and it crusts. It ain't pigmented, though. But they said it need not be."

"How long have you had it?"

"It's been about ten days since I noticed that."

"Let's have another beer, what do you say?" I suggested, and Rick called the waitress over, the uglier one. "I think I can help you, Rick. You are in luck. At least I hope you are in luck."

I told him that, by coincidence, my friend in the hospital, a Thai surgeon, had spent five years in Germany studying and operating on skin cancers, and melanomas were his special interest. He might be the number one melanoma expert in all of Thailand. Great experience; nice guy, too. I knew he would be in the outpatient clinic tomorrow. So we would meet at the hospital in the morning, and I would arrange for Rick to be seen by my friend. First thing tomorrow.

✳

I arrived at the hospital half an hour before my rendezvous with Rick, to set up his exam with the surgeon. Rick was already pacing in front of the entrance. He looked different without his visor, his hair combed, his clean khaki shirt crumpled a little, and in fancy cotton pants. He was tense but tried his smile on me; the effort to behave casually showed. I made the arrangements at the clinic (there would be no charge), came out, and told Rick to go straight in. I'd come back to meet him in front of the gate in an hour. I had to attend to some business in the lab, I told him, which was not true.

"It will be all right, man," I said, doubting it, of course; melanoma is a killer because of its rapid metastases. Everybody knows that. I went to the open-air hospital cafeteria, drank two cups, and fought the thought of starting to smoke again. I watched passing girls and the morning acrobatics of butterflies over the clusia bushes. I did not identify the butterflies and did not register the proportions of the girls, paying true attention only to the arms of my watch which moved like an injured snail.

Even before the hour had passed, I went to the entrance of the hospital. Rick was just coming out. When he saw me, he walked to meet me slowly. In that instant I knew—his face was changed so much that he only vaguely resembled the person I'd left an hour ago; only his nose was the same. "So, how was it?" I asked, to break the silence.

But he just took my hand and shook it as if we were old friends who were meeting each other for the first time after years. He nodded his head and held my hand. Then his face erupted into an enormous smile.

"Okay, let's go and get a morning Tsing Tao. I know a place near the market where they keep it pretty cold," I said. We took a short cut, trudging through a construction site, alongside a Buddhist wat in ruins, crossed the canal, and he told me.

"Lothar, it was an insect bite. An infected insect bite! The doctor took a scraping, checked it under the microscope right there."

"I'll be damned," I said.

"Great guy, your friend. It is absolutely certain; no need for a biopsy, even. Sonovabitch, he laughed at me. I am going to buy him a bottle of the best stuff I can find here. The best!"

We got our beers in the shade of a sprawling bougainvillea vine that covered all of the terrace of the Happy Dragon, and Rick talked about his plans. When he went back home to California, he would look for a teaching job, some private college out in a small town in the hills. Artificial Intelligence, that's what he would get into; there is a future in it. And being an old computer hacker would help him too. And hell, he might even get married. We paid.

"Lothar, how about at seven, tonight? Do you know the Austrian place?"

"Austrian? Like—Austria?"

"Good, you don't know it. Then I have a surprise for you, mi amigo. Good," he said, beaming. He still could not get the grin off his face. Neither could I.

✳

At seven-zero-zero, on the nose, Rick appeared in the lobby of my hotel. (I love when people come on time. It must be the German in me.) In olive slacks, a black shirt, and an off-white cotton parka over it, he looked twice the size of the people around him. I had my white jacket and shirt with an ascot—almost too colonial, too Graham Greene, I thought. But we were terrific, fabulously handsome, intelligent faces, in tremendous *esprit de corps*. We kept our posture straight and paced with military deliberation, as if awarded medals.

I thought about some of my culinary adventures of the past. There was the breakfast of pelagic palolo worms in Western Samoa, the sweet and sour pig's Fallopian tubes with stir-fried ovaries in Taipei, the marinated sea cucumber-holothuria in the Penghu Islands of the South China Sea. I recalled the fish, cooked for twenty-four hours, in Chinatown in Yokohama. But tonight it would be different—it would be the good old times, the old Viennese times!

The last droves of fruit bats were passing low over our heads on their way to night-feeding haunts, shitting happily, and I worried about my jacket. But only for a moment, since my single-minded desire for food had overtaken my imagination. I could not believe that nobody had told me about Grinzing, the Austrian restaurant, which was only a few blocks from my hotel. Surrounded by a bamboo-fringed tropical garden, it stood on stilts at least three meters tall. The structure was designed in the traditional Thai style, with a broad verandah encircling the house on all sides. Teak railings, teak paneling and pillars, teak ceilings—all were bathed in the balmy stream of air coming down from the hills for the night. The only obvious Austrian feature was a snowy damask tablecloth over each table, and the vase on it. Blossoms of hibiscus, *rosa sinensis*, elevated the class of the arrangement.

Before we'd even found a table, Rick announced, with mock formality, that he considered this evening a celebration and that everything was to be on him. How could I have objected? The menu read like a fairy tale I knew would come true. And it did—on imitation Meissen porcelain plates, sprawling over the rim, the *wiener schnitzel* of my youth. The thinly pounded breaded veal was fried to perfect consistency by a Thai hand, undoubtedly guided by the frowning ghost of my grandmother (let the gods endow her with eternal glory). It came with steaming golden potatoes sprinkled with melted butter and finely chopped parsley.

The cold cucumber salad, *gurkensalat*, was of the optimal acidity and salinity, as I have known it from home. Yes, G. B. Shaw understood: "There is no love sincerer than the love of food." I loved it so sincerely when the dessert arrived. It was the world famous Sachertorte, indistinguishable from the original pride of Karntner Strasse in Vienna. I had arrived in heaven, finally.

The majordomo, Herr Karl Prochaska himself, came to discuss the wine. He apologized for the limited selection from his wine cellar, but there was no agony in deciding about the vintage of an Austrian riesling, since all are delicious with food, be it in the tropics or an alpine chalet. He was a balding, short fellow of about fifty, with a swift smile, blotches on his forehead attesting to the might of the equatorial sun, with a Burgundy-tinted bulb of a nose, suggesting expertise in wines. Rick told me that Prochaska had married the Beauty Queen of Chiang Mai and stayed here, so she could be close to her relatives and would not fade. It was a festive evening, and before it was over even Rick had noticed the angelic waitresses who fluttered around in gossamer Thai silks as if suspended in the evening breeze, jasmine blossoms in their hair and smiles reserved only for us, we were certain.

So, that is how I came to a feast—and how I made a friend for years to come.

Kamikaze Dream of the Butterfly Collector

It has been well known that people want everything, and in an instant, but he had only two great wishes, which he nourished and cradled in total secrecy. Tetsuo Kubota lacked the usual ambitions of high school seniors because his twin desires overwhelmed him in his dreams and daydreams, too. As a collector of butterflies he yearned for *Ornithoptera alexandrae* from the family *Papilionidae*, the largest butterfly in the whole wide world, so immense that the natives in Papua New Guinea had to shoot it down from the jungle's canopy by bow and arrow.

His other object of desire (and of his post-pubertal fantasies) was lovely Kumiko Ishihara, of the family of Ishiharas who own the Harley-Davidson franchise by the river. She dazzled him with her unusual comeliness. Her cheeks—those bony structures beloved by sculptors—were so high that viewed from the profile her nose became invisible. He thought her black lacquered helmet of hair shined like a black leopard in the rain. He loved her eyes, which were just narrow slits as if in a permanent beautiful smile. As could be sadly expected, there was no escape from fantasy to reality—and so, Tetsuo's daydreams about Kumiko's Eskimoid pulchritude interfered mightily with his sleep, and with his academics, too.

But *Ornithoptera alexandrae* was unobtainable since there was a war in the South Pacific, a losing war, where desires of lepidopterists are not to be considered.

And Kumiko Ishihara was not available to Tetsuo because he was slightly pudgy and of short stature, at a mere fifteenth percentile of his age group, and also, because his forehead was marked by burrowing acne like a volcanic landscape covered with livid eruptions. He was shy above the high school average, too.

✳

It was on the last day of school when Tetsuo Kubota went home, taking Gakko-cho-dori lane where the ancient Ishiki-san had his stand with charcoal barbeque for squid—*ika*. On a split bamboo stick, Tetsuo got his specimen cooked to perfection—and for a discount, since he always had a good chat with the retired seaman, Ishiki-san, who liked to tell stories about the sea to a schoolboy. That day, again, they had such a pleasant discourse that Tetsuo did not want to leave. As he went home, chewing on the squid, it occurred to him that the old man he knew just by his last name might be the only, single, person friendly to him, in all the world. At home he locked himself in his cubicle, took off (for the last time) his school uniform designed for ugliness, kicked it into the corner, and sat on his bed motionless for as long a time as it took to arrive at a fateful decision.

Rehearsing the speech he used a muted voice but with harsh guttural tones, the way he heard the generals sermonize on the radio in speeches to encourage nationalistic frenzies:

"Yeah, I will become Kamikaze, The Divine Wind!

"I'll learn to fly Zero fighter planes in a squadron of young heroes, they will become my great friends, we will sacrifice everything for the homeland.

"I'll tie the white *hachimaki* headband with the rising sun on my forehead. I'll write Kumiko Ishihara on the back.

"When the happy time comes, as the Divine Wind I shall dive at the enemy battleship loaded with explosives in a bansai charge, following the Bushido code of the samurai, causing destruction. Victory."

Tetsuo changed his voice to its usual thinness, its normal intonation.

"My family will be congratulated for the heroic deed of their son, my sacrifice will be reported in the newspaper, my father will march on the street with his head high!

"In my school there will be a memorial service, school mates from my class will be proud they knew me, and will pretend they were my friends; teachers will be amazed.

"Kumiko Ishihara will cry!"

✳

There was not enough food during the war, so it was a special event when mother prepared sukiyaki for dinner. As if she suspected an important event to happen, as if she foresaw the momentous announcement of her son, Tetsuo. He waited for tea time—then approached his father. He repeated the speech of his intentions he had rehearsed.

"Father, I want to become Kamikaze, the Divine Wind…" He continued uninterrupted and ended "…your son will be honored to be part of the special Tokkotai attack units. I will do it for Teno, our Emperor Hirohito, father."

Old Kubata-san listened with his face expressionless as in sclerosis, without a word. Then he got up and ambled to the garden, leaving the paper screen door open behind him. In the garden he started to dig a hole for planting new *akamatsu*, red pine. He dug the hole deeper and deeper, feverishly, as if running out of time, staring only into the hole, the spade stabbing the earth fast and faster.

The next evening the father called his son into their eight-tatami room and sat him in front of the small *kamidana*—the family Shinto shrine in the corner. In a low voice, with sentences short—as if disinterested—his eyes on the shrine, he talked.

"Son, I was thinking about your plan. I decided you will not become Kamikaze, the Divine Wind." He lifted his gaze and looked into his only son's eyes, his face unreadable, still without perceptible expression.

"It was decided," he said, "that you will become a dentist. Preferably in the orthodontics subspecialty."

Kubota-san got up, slowly, with an effort of an old man, and walked to the garden where for a long time he sat and observed the newly planted *akamatsu* grow.

✳

The big war ended and was followed by peace, as it usually happens. Things in the country changed beyond anybody's expectation. While some people's relations remained unchanged from the times of the Tokugawa shogunate, many things in life became modern like in America. There was more protein and vitamins and so the children grew one foot taller than their parents; bullet trains arrived on time measured in seconds; the country became the technological leader of Asia; universities sprouted from Kyushu to Hokkaido; even Nobel prizes were awarded. Nothing prevented young Doctor Tetsuo Kubota from becoming a man of means, from becoming rich straightening incisors and canines into winning grins.

Soon he acquired both male and female specimens of *Ornithoptera alexandrae* for his growing collection. Then he acquired Kumiko Ishihara, still lovely and, possibly, virginal. Then he acquired a membership in the Niigata Sailing Club, by invitation!

The date was the 31st of August, the last day of Summer, as ordered by the Emperor, but the sky was Caribbean blue, the air balmy and tasting of sea salt; conditions optimal for a sail. Tetsuo steered single-handed his shoal draft sloop windward on the long swells of Nihon-kai, the Sea of Japan.

He shook his head in wonder. The western wind from China increased to twelve knots and remained perfectly steady for a while before rising in speed again, filling Tetsuo's cruising spinnaker. A school of bottlenose dolphins frolicked about the bow and their teenagers surfed the wake. Arms stretched wide, head bent backward, the skipper hollered into the wind: "*Kami-kaze! Ne! Kami-no kaze desu!*" You are the true Wind Divine!

Tetsuo Kubota laughed like a madman deranged by the gust of the incipient gale. Some dolphins smiled at the strange navigator.

248